a chorus
of innocents

a chorus
of innocents

a sir robert carey mystery

P. F. Chisholm

Poisoned Pen Press

Copyright © 2015 by P. F. Chisholm

First Edition 2015

10 9 8 7 6 5 4 3 2 1

Library of Congress Catalog Card Number: 2015931963

ISBN: 9781464204609   Hardcover
         9781464204623   Trade Paperback

Poisoned Pen Press
6962 E. First Ave., Ste. 103
Scottsdale, AZ 85251
www.poisonedpenpress.com
info@poisonedpenpress.com

Printed in the United States of America

To Jane Conway-Gordon, with many thanks

List of Characters

Tim	barman at Wendron
Simon Anricks	barber surgeon who might be a Jesuit
Clem	alehouse boy
Lady Elizabeth Widdrington	Carey's love
Mr Tully	horse trader
Blackie (a grey)	murderers' horse
Pinkie (a chestnut)	ditto
Milky (black)	Tully's horse
Mouse (dark chestnut)	Elizabeth's horse
Mary Trevannion	Elizabeth's cousin, learning huswifery
Mr Heron	Widdrington reeve
Poppy (Proserpina) Burn	Minister Jamie Burn's wife
Minister Jamie Burn	the dead churchman
Dandelion	cow with good milk
Mrs Stirling	midwife
Young Henry Widdrington	Sir Henry's eldest son
Jane, Kat	Elizabeth's dairymaids
Prince	Jamie Burn's horse (hobby)
Rat	Elizabeth's horse (half-hobby)
Sir Robert Carey	Elizabeth's love
Johnny Forster	eldest son of Sir John, Marshall of Bamburgh
John Carey	Sir Robert's elder brother, Marshall of Berwick
Lady Agnes Hume	dowager lady

Jock Burn	Jamie's uncle
Ralph o' the Coates Burn	headman of the Burns, Jamie's father
Laird Hughie Hume	heir to cadet Hume estate
Maitland of Lethington	Scottish Chancellor
Maria	village girl
Jemmy Burn	Ralph o' the Coates' younger brother
Archie Burn	his son
Humphrey Fenwick	Widdrington cousin
Sergeant Henry Dodd	Land-Sergeant of Gilsland
Patch	Dodd's horse (hobby)
Sorrel	Carey's horse (hobby)
Twice, Blackie	other horses (hobbies)
Young Hutchin	young scoundrel
Andy Nixon	member of Carlisle castle guard
Sim's Will Croser	ditto
Bessie's Andrew Storey	ditto
Red Sandy	Dodd's younger brother
Bangtail Graham	member of Carlisle castle guard
Janet Dodd (nee Armstrong)	Dodd's wife
Kat Ridley	Lady Hume's tiring woman
Jack Crosby, Sim Routledge	Wendron villagers
Cousin William	Hume byblow
Jimmy	Hume groom
Hector (Ekie) Widdrington	Widdrington cousin
Sim Widdrington	ditto
Daniel Widdrington	ditto
Piers Dixon	schoolboy
Andy Hume	schoolboy
Cuddy Trotter	schoolboy
Jimmy Tait	schoolboy
Jock Tait	Jimmy Tait's father
Goodwife Tait	Jimmy Tait's mother
Goodwife Trotter	Cuddy's mother
Clemmie Pringle	Wendron baker
Sandy, Eric	dogboys at Carlisle
Butter	Ekie's horse (hobby)

Geordie Burn	Ralph o' the Coate's eldest son, Jamie's eldest brother
Young Geordie	Geordie Burn's son
Nick Smithson	leader of Essex's soldiers
Denham	leader of one of the Carlisle trained bands
Blennerhasset	ditto
Beverly	ditto
Jack	young lymer dog
Teazle	older lymer dog
Lady Philadelphia Scrope	Carey's younger sister
Lord Scrope	Warden of the English West March
John Tovey	Carey's secretary
Brother Aurelius	Austin friar at Jedburgh abbey
Brother Constantine	ditto
Brother Justinian	ditto
Brother Ignatius	ditto
Lord Abbot Ninian	Lord Abbot of Jedburgh
Lord Spynie	Royal favourite
James VI	King of Scotland

Prologue

It was a small chapel, stone built and once dedicated to some Papist saint. Since then it had been whitewashed, had its superstitious coloured windows broken with stones and the head knocked off the saint, although her cow was left in peace. The old altar had been broken up as the reign of the King's scandalous mother came to its riotous end, the relics hidden in it levered out and thrown on a bonfire to burn as superstitious trash. By the early 1570s there was a respectably plain altar table, well away from the eastern end so as not to be idolatrous and a very well-made plain and solid high pulpit for preaching. Mostly by visiting preachers, though, because who would choose to live in the village so close to the Border with England and the bastard English raiders?

Once upon a time, memorably, the Reverend Gilpin had come there after the mermaid Queen was safely locked up in England. This was very unusual. The reverend's summer journeys kept him on the southern side of the Faery Wall, among the God-cursed English, but a laird had heard him there and invited him to come and preach and paid his expenses forebye, and everyone for miles about had gone to listen. They still tutted about it.

They had heard some very strange things from the pulpit that day. For a start, Gilpin didn't read the Bible texts they knew and liked, the good ones about smiting the Philistines or the book of Joshua or an eye for an eye and a tooth for a tooth, which was good sense they wholeheartedly agreed with. Nor did he talk about the wickedness of starched ruffs, or vestments, even.

He read them some unfamiliar parts of the Gospels: nothing useful about Jesus bringing a sword, no. Strange unaccustomed things he read them about making peace with your brother before you laid your sacrifice on the altar and some outrageous stuff about loving your enemy.

The men and women shifted their feet where they stood and looked at each other sidelong. Did Christ really say that? Really? Loving your enemy? Was the English reverend sure? It sounded…well, it sounded Papistical.

Love everybody? What? The English, too? Jesus never said that, did he?

And the Reverend had smiled with a twinkle in his small grey eyes and closed the Bible with a snap, then leaned his arms familiarly on the rail of the pulpit as if he was leaning on a fence.

"Did you ever in all your lives hear anything so mad?" he asked in reasonable Scotch and they all laughed with relief.

He must have been reading one of those wicked Papistical Bibles the Jesuits spread about, that must be it. Jesus couldn't have said that about enemies. What you did with enemies was you hunted them down and killed them and all their kin, which made far better sense. Honestly, the idea!

But as the Reverend had spoken on, they felt uneasy again. It seemed Jesus had said those mad things. He had actually said, right out, that they must love each other, not just their own sur-names—which was just about doable, mostly—but everybody. Even the English.

It seemed Jesus had said the thing about enemies too; he really had. There it was, in the Bible, which was as true and good as gold, golden words from God, incorruptible, like blasts of the trumpet against the ungodly. The foolish Papists had hidden the glorious words of Jesus in Latin black as pitch so only priests could know them; now the words were Englished and turned to Scotch as well, so anybody could read them, yes, even women.

So what were they to think? What should they think—that Jesus was mad? Crazy?

Everyone had goggled at such…surely it was blasphemy?

A stout woman spoke up from the back of the church where she was standing with the other women. "That's blasphemy!" she shouted. "You can't say Our Lord was mad…"

The English Reverend's long finger stabbed the air as he pointed at her.

"That's right, goodwife!" he bellowed. "You are the truest Christian here! It's blasphemy to say or even to think that Jesus Christ was mad because he was the Son of God!"

He was standing up straight now, leaning over the rail. "And if he was the Son of God, then how dare we listen to his words in the Bible and not follow his orders? How dare we hate our enemies? How dare we feud and kill and raid and burn? For if we do, shall we not burn in Hell?"

And from there the sermon had turned both familiar and frightening. Familiar in the loud words and gestures, but frightening in the meaning. For the Reverend was not inveighing against the Papists nor the French nor the courtiers. He was preaching against themselves. Against any of them who went up against an enemy to fight him, steal his cows and sheep and burn his steadings—which meant pretty much every man there of fighting age. He bellowed against those who cooked and brewed ale for the fighting men or quilted their jacks in the old surname patterns—which meant every woman and girl there.

He told them that they were wrong and damned, that keeping a boychild's right hand covered with a cloth at baptism so it was unblessed and could kill without sin was a wicked Papist superstition. That the whole of them, body and soul, was blessed in baptism, so that they could rise up, soul and body both, at the Judgement Day—which might be very soon.

Yet because they had not obeyed their true headman, Jesus Christ, then they would be damned just as infallibly as the Papists or the wicked Anabaptists.

Many of the men were scowling and putting their hands on their knives or swords. The women were gasping with outrage while the children stared in astonishment at the small man's daring. What was an Anabaptist? Did it have a tail?

He quieted for a while, playing them like a violin. It was all right. Jesus was a just and kindly headman, unlike many of the lairds hereabouts (that got a small titter). They could make things right anytime they wanted: All they had to do was love their enemies, make peace with those they were at feud with, and...

"Die?" sneered the laird at the front, who had his arms folded across his barrel chest and his henchmen in a tight knot around him. As he was the one who had paid for the Reverend to preach he was understandably angry. "That's what will happen if we make peace with the bastard English. We'll die and our families with us!"

"You will not die," said the Reverend Gilpin, pointing at the laird. "You will receive eternal life."

The headman spat on the stones. "I didna pay your expenses for ye to preach this shite," said the headman. "Get on wi' yer job and curse the ungodly, man!"

"I am," said Gilpin, seeming blithely unaware that every man there was on the point of drawing steel. Or perhaps he believed God would protect him. Or perhaps he didn't care. "If you fail to do what our Lord Jesus ordered—love God and love each other—*you* are the ungodly! You and the English both. All of you, both sides of the Border, are the ungodly."

The laird drew his sword and shouldered to the front. "I paid ye!" he bellowed. "Now do whit I paid ye to do!"

A purse full of money flew through the air and bounced off the headman's doublet with a thump.

"I don't need yer money," said Gilpin. "Thanks to God and mine own weakness, I am a wealthy man. Ye've got a free sermon here. Now will ye listen to the Word of God, or not?"

There was a moment of total silence. Then the woman who had spoken before (against all scripture) started laughing.

"Och," she shouted, "he's a brave man at least, not an arselicker like the last one. You let him preach, Jock o' the Coates."

"So," said Gilpin after a pause, with a friendly smile to all of them as some hands relaxed from the hilts of their weapons, "we have a problem. If the Lord Jesus wisnae a madman, then ye all are mad for ignoring his orders."

There was a growl from some of the men and more laughter from the women, sniggers from the children. You had to say this: It was a more exciting sermon than the last preacher who had had a lot to say about the wickedness of vestments, whatever they were.

Over the next hour the Reverend Gilpin proved that Jesus had actually said they should love their enemies and that He had actually done that very thing when the Romans had nailed Him to a cross, which must have hurt. And then, to show them all what they were dealing with, hadn't He risen from the dead, come back to life, not like a ghost or the curs'd knight in the ballad, but as a living, breathing man who ate grilled fish and drank with his friends?

There was no possible question that He had said it and meant it and done it.

Now they had to forgive their enemies, too, and live in peace with them. That was all there was to it. And once they set their minds to it, they would find it easier than they expected; for wouldn't the Lord Jesus be right there at their side, helping them all the way?

By the end of the sermon some of the more impressionable had been weeping. One of the Burn grandsons was staring transfixed into space, as if he could see something marvellous there instead of just a smashed Papist window.

Gilpin left them all with the blessing, the full blessing from the evening service: "The Lord bless you and keep you. The Lord make His face to shine upon you and be gracious unto you. The Lord lift up his countenance upon you and give you peace."

Then he went calmly to his horse that was tethered outside and, with his servant behind him, mounted up and trotted slowly away so the laird could catch him if he wanted.

It was so memorable a sermon that the laird sent a message to an Edinburgh minister, in case Jesus really had said that about enemies.

He had, apparently. He really had, though according to the Edinburgh minister, that didn't count for Papists and a number of other people—including, of course, the English.

So that was all right then.

Strangely, the laird invited Reverend Gilpin again and, even more strangely, he came, riding a solid ordinary hobby with his silent deacon behind him on a long-legged mare.

However as he came to unlock the wooden chapel door, he found a gauntlet nailed to it with a badly penned paper that said whoever took it down would be the Burns' blood-enemy for life.

Gilpin looked at it for a moment and then ripped it down. He carried the gauntlet into the church with him where he explained to the assembled people why feud was wrong, challenges to single combat were wrong, and the headman who had challenged him was not only wrong but stupid. He was risking not only a lightning bolt, not only the wrath of God, but also an eternity in Hell, which was no laughing matter.

Foolishly, the headman wouldn't leave it be. He sent to Gilpin to ask where he proposed to meet and what his weapon would be. Gilpin replied that it would be at the tower of his Lord with the sword and shield of God.

The headman arrived at the chapel the next day with his sword and buckler and a crowd of his surname who came to see him beat up the preacher who had defied him, or to laugh at him when he didn't arrive.

They found Gilpin standing there in his plain cassock, holding a large Bible.

"Och," Jock o' the Coates said disgustedly. That wasn't fair. The book looked heavy enough to do some damage if he threw it, but what if he made a lightning bolt come out of it?

"Well?" said Gilpin, coming forward with the Bible open and his thumb set in one of the end chapters. "Will you draw and strike, Jock Burn?"

"Ye're not…ye're not armed," growled Jock, horribly suspecting some of his grandsons and nephews were laughing at him inside, which indeed they were.

"I am armed," said the mad preacher. "I am armed with the sword of God's Truth and the shield of God's Word. Will ye not strike? Perhaps yer sword will not wither like a twig in the fire nor your whole surname go to dust and ashes with you left alone until your enemies catch ye. For those who live by the sword shall die by it."

Jock Burn backed off, paling. No more was ever said about the challenge and the gauntlet.

That was the Reverend Gilpin. He helped broker the deal between the Dodds and the Elliots in the late 1570s, which calmed upper Tynedale no end, and saw to it that the worst offenders left the area. He kept coming every summer, at first with his quiet young manservant and then, after the man died of a fever, he came on his own, sadder, gentler now. He preached at several Warden Days, on the invitation of Sir John Forster, the English Middle March Warden. He carried no more than an eating knife and a Bible, he slept wherever he could find shelter, and he ate whatever the poor people he lodged with could give him. He preached from his Bible whenever anyone asked him to and always on Sundays.

Nobody had ever seen or heard of such a strong minister, such a mad churchman, who had said publicly that he gave not a feather for vestments and as for the Papists—well, hadn't he been a Papist himself once, before he read the Bible and understood God's Word better? And surely most of them were good men misguided, with only a few actively serving the Evil One.

What was more he never laid a hand on girl or boy, though he had no wife either. Many were the snares and traps set for him by cunning mothers with girls who would have liked to be mistress of his rumoured large and comfortable living in the south. When a gentlewoman twitted him on his wifeless state across her dinner table, with her daughters on either side of him, he smiled and toasted her and her daughters.

"You see," he told her, "I swore before the altar of God to keep chastity and although I was certainly a sinner when I was young and hot-blooded, now I am old and tired and no use whatever to a woman." He smiled and bowed to both the girls who blushed. The mother found herself wondering about his deacon who had died of the fever but she said nothing and nor did he. All the girls who had hopes of his rumoured magnificent house at Houghton le Spring were sadly disappointed.

He only came to the Borders in summer. For the rest of the year he kept a school at Houghton le Spring, boarded likely boys at his own expense, and paid for some of them to go to Oxford where he himself had studied Divinity and sung the Masses with the rest of the young men before Henry VIII's divorce.

Slowly, little by little, some of the men of the surnames came to like him, the women too, despite his obstinate refusal to wed any of them. The children had loved him from the start and the lads ran to meet him when they saw his solitary silhouette with his soft flat churchman's cap and warm cloak over a ridge along the road from Berwick.

Then in 1583 sad word came. He had been trampled by an escaped ox in Houghton market, lay wounded for a month and died of lungfever on the fourth of March. Both sides of the Border were stricken at the news and Jock o' the Coates Burn and some of the headmen from south of the Border as well went to pay their respects in the south at Houghton le Spring, and with them they brought some of the boys Gilpin had taught, the bigger ones, to sing for him at his funeral. Jock died a few months later, leaving his grown son Ralph as headman and the grandsons grown as well—a lucky life Jock never admitted he attributed to not cutting Gilpin's head off when they had met at the chapel in the early 1570s.

And the seeds that Gilpin had sown, dangerous and revolutionary seeds that they were, lay in the soil of the people's minds, and here and there they set down their roots.

thursday afternoon 12th october 1592

The men had been riding for two days, and were now into the broad fat lands of the East March of Scotland where the Humes held sway. They had instructions but those had been vague on the important point of position.

"Och, we'll never find him," complained the younger one. "A' the villages look the same."

The older one shook his head. "We ainly need his kirk," he said.

"Ay, one kirk in hundreds."

It was surprising and the older one thought a little shocking that there were so many kirks, and not all of them burnt or in ruins like in the Low Countries. Some old Catholic churches had been torn down and a new one put up, but more often they were just altered with the heads of the saints knocked off and the paintings whitewashed. Not every village had a kirk, by a long way, but a lot did.

They came over the top of a shallow hill and saw another little scatter of cottages and the kirk on the next hill, with a nice tower on it to keep an eye out for raids. It was October, so only a few women were out in the gardens, mostly tidying up for winter or planting winter cabbages. The surviving cattle and sheep were scattered over the infield and most of the pigs had gone to make sausages now so there wasn't a lot of noise. There was ploughing going on nearby, with the village plow and its oxen struggling through some new Earth that might grow some wheat next year, while the children followed it gathering up the stones. The harvest had been poor thanks to the bad weather in July, and no doubt the people were hoping to grow a bit more on the new field next year.

The two of them didn't need to talk much. They knew what they were about, had done it before, and so they decided to make for the church alehouse. That was a small thatched building next to the church in the old way and the church was one of those that had been altered, not demolished.

It was cold and damp and the men were out of their own country. They rode into the village, tethered their horses by the duck pond and walked up to the alehouse. They weren't very many miles north of Berwick itself and hoped to get to the city that night and find lodgings there. They didn't expect to find any in this village, any more than they had in the last two or three.

The village alehouse was no longer run by the church. A young man stood behind the bar and the usual people were there, despite it being afternoon. Two men sat in the corner playing dice, a third was hunched over his quart by the fire, a fourth was asleep. The fifth and sixth were standing by the bar, arguing over whether a billy goat could beat a ram in a fight, if you could get them to fight and how would you do that anyway. The seventh was a travelling barber surgeon, obvious from his pack, sitting in the corner, reading a book. As they came in, he stood up and stretched his back, put his book carefully in his large pack, and said in a London voice, "I'll pay you now, shall I, Tim?"

"Nae need, Mr Anricks, ye paid for more than your tab when ye drew my tooth for me."

"Are you sure? You paid me for it at the time."

"Ay, but I never lost a tooth before so nice and easy. I'll be telling ma dad about ye, that's sure, he's got a bad tooth too."

"Well thank you, I appreciate it. I'm for Edinburgh now and after I think I'll head west and see if there are any bad teeth in Dumfriesshire or even Carlisle."

"Bound to be, Mr Anricks. Me dad'll be waiting for when ye come back."

"Now mind what I tell you, the invisible worms that eat your teeth, they love sugar and honey and so if you scrub your teeth with a cloth and salt, that'll keep them away."

"Ay, and I'll keep the charm ye sold me too, that's even better."

"Hm. Good day to you."

"Clem!" bellowed Tim. "Bring Mr Anricks' pony round for him."

A boy leapt out from under the counter and pelted out the door and the tooth-drawer followed him out, moving a little stiffly, as if his back hurt.

"Ehm…" said the older traveller, "good day to you." Everybody turned and looked. "That'll be two quarts, please."

This was an event. Two strangers coming into the alehouse. A smaller boy was staring from where he'd been whittling under the counter. The older man hated the feeling of being conspicuous, but you couldn't help it.

The quarts were drawn from the only barrel and the younger man paid, twice as much as usual on account of them being foreigners of course. That was all right, they had plenty of money.

After both had taken a drink, the older one said, "What's the name of this village?"

Several people answered and it seemed you could choose between Lesser Wendron or Minor or the old one of Wendron St Cuthberts.

"Ah. St Cuthberts," said the older man wisely, "would the minister here be a Mr Burn? A Mr James Burn?"

"Why?" asked the man at the bar, with narrow suspicious eyes.

"Well," said the older one, not looking at the younger one, "we're from a printer in Edinburgh to see about the printing of his sermons and selling them too."

This was what he had been told to say by his principal and he was happy to see it worked like a charm. The man might well have been suspicious, after all, and it would be so much easier if they could get him alone.

"Yes," said the barman, "that'd be the pastor." He wasn't at the alehouse which was a little odd for a pastor. What was more, he was at the manse and teaching the children.

The younger man choked on his beer. "Teaching?" he asked. "Why?"

This touched off a dispute. The dice players looked around and said it was all this new-fangled religion, the arguers agreed and sniggered about it, the barman said it was all very well learning your letters but then what could you do with it, the sleeper said nothing because he stayed asleep, and the man who was hunched over his quart straightened up and told them all that they were fools because the truth was in the Bible and the children would be able to read it for themselves, whereas they couldn't. One of the dice players snorted and said that was all very well and the truth might be in the Bible at that, but what was the use of it?

The older man cut through the talk and asked where the manse might be, and learned it was right behind the alehouse from the days when the alehouse was the church's and ran church ales.

Both men finished their ales, parried a couple of questions about where they came from. No need to send the boy with them, they could find the manse themselves from the sound of it.

They went out the door and round the back of the place and there, sure enough, was the manse, a handsome building of stone like the church, though perhaps older. It looked like part of it had once been something else, maybe a little house for monks or something.

The door flung open and twelve boys came pouring out, shouting and pummeling each other, two of them fell wrestling at the feet of the men. They stepped around the boys and spoke to the man standing at the door, smiling at them.

He bowed slightly and led them inside. The boys all scattered to their homes except for three who had planned a fishing expedition at the stream. A woman arrived in a hurry, and went in smiling. There was a quiet sound of talking, a woman's voice, a man's voice.

A pause. Then a sudden grunt, like a pig being stuck with a lance, a thump, then a sound like a cabbage being cut. Then the sound of a stifled scream, thumping and bumping and some muffled groans, going on for a while.

The two men walked out of the house, grinning and rearranging their hose and round the duck pond to where their horses were tethered. Unhurriedly they untied them, mounted and trotted away to the little copse nearby where they had some remounts and a boy guarding them.

Then they changed horses and went to a canter out of the copse and round by the little lanes that threaded across the countryside, although they could have crossed the ploughed fields in a straight line. As it happened they went north first on an errand and to throw anyone off the trail, and then they went south and west. The boy took the West March-branded horses straight south to a horse-trader.

fRIÔAY MORNING 13th OCTOBER 1592

Lady Widdrington looked at the farmer in front of her and waited for him to stop lying. The horses in question were nice beasts and she knew they were not local. The question was, where had they come from and had they been reived.

"Mr Tully," she said, "I've never seen the brands before. Where are they from?"

"They're Middle March horses, your ladyship," he said promptly. "Bought from my brother-in-law in Jedburgh."

She sighed. "Those aren't Jedburgh brands."

His face flinched a little and she read it easily. She was a woman; she wasn't supposed to know about brands. It had taken Elizabeth two years to know all the main brands and variations hereabouts, but she knew them now. In fact she wasn't completely sure she didn't know these particular brands, only she couldn't bring to mind which surname they belonged to, which was odd. They niggled her. Probably they came from the West March, Armstrong, Nixon, Graham? But they certainly weren't from Jedburgh and they were good horses. Not as good as Robin Carey's beautiful tournament charger Thunder, which he had sort of sold to the King of Scots that summer, but…

She sighed and pressed her lips together. That familiar ache in her chest had started up again. It had been three and a half months since she saw him riding Thunder, tipping his hat to her seriously as he rode past. Less time since she saw him at the Scottish Court where…

Mr Tully saw her face lengthen and become stern. It was a handsome face, rather than pretty, the long nose and chin would probably draw together eventually but hadn't yet. He drew a couple of wrong conclusions and decided she must be a witch.

"A' right," he said sadly, "they're no' from Jedburgh,"

"I know that," agreed Elizabeth.

"Fact is, I dinna ken where they're from. So now…"

Elizabeth folded her gloved hands on the reins and leaned back slightly. Her horse tipped a hoof and gave a resigned snort.

"They were running loose in the woods."

She looked around her at the plump farms and copses. There weren't a lot of woods anywhere near.

"Which woods?"

"Aah…in Scotland."

She could have asked what he was doing north of the Border, but she didn't. She nodded invitingly.

"Ay, I'd been north of Berwick getting…ah…getting supplies and up to Edinburgh forebye for I couldna find what I was looking for and I got lost in the wood meself and so I found 'em."

She waited patiently for him to start telling the truth. "They had nae tack on them or nae ither signs and they were sad and sorry for themselves, so they were, and when I found them they were hungry too…"

Likely since these weren't tough little hobbies who could live on a couple of blades of grass a day, but taller bigger horses who would need more food.

"And one of them had thrown a shoe and the other was lame too, and so I brung them south with me to help and comfort them and that one's called Blackie…"

"That's the grey?"

"Ay and that one's called Pinky."

"The chestnut?"

"Ay," Tully looked at her cautiously. "It's a joke, ye ken, missus. Ah niver name my animals for their right colours."

Elizabeth nodded. Why else would the man be riding a beast as black as pitch and known to all as Milky?

One of the Widdrington cousins who was riding with her and waiting a little way off, chuckled softly.

Elizabeth moved her own horse, a very dull dark chestnut called Mouse for good and sufficient reasons, to a nearby stone wall. She unhooked her knee from the sidesaddle and stepped down to the wall, then picked up her skirts and climbed down the other side to go into the paddock with the horses. There were other animals dotted around the pasture, which was looking bare and brown. Among them were two billy kids, nearly grown and making themselves useful by calming the horses while awaiting their inevitable fate.

She went among the horses and patted them, felt their legs, lifted their feet—yes, they had been shod a while ago, though Tully hadn't re-shod them yet because that was expensive. She checked their teeth as well. Blackie, the grey, snickered with his lips and pushed his nose into her chest, looking for carrots, no doubt. She patted his neck and found Pinky on her other side also wanting attention.

"These are quite young and good horses," she said.

"Ay, ladyship," said Tully, looking at her sadly. "But I didna reive 'em."

"No," she agreed to his great surprise, "I don't think you did but you'll have to wait until I write to the Scotch Warden and ask about them." Tully sighed. "I'll try and get you a finder's fee for them if I can," she added since he had told her some of the truth eventually. and what he had been doing in Scotland was probably just smuggling and nothing worse.

"Or," she said thoughtfully, "I could take them off your hands now and give you something for them and then keep the fee if we find the owner."

Tully scratched the back of his head and looked at the sky scattered with clouds, though it was not raining yet. He was not a wealthy man and although there was horse feed available now, it would get short before spring because the harvest had been bad. The horses were geldings and she could put them to use, whereas he couldn't. On the other hand, the Borderers all loved horses, which she did herself, of course, and were ridiculously sentimental about them, too, when they could be.

Slowly Tully nodded. If the horses did turn out to have been reived in some way, the Widdrington surname would be better able to deal with that than Tully, who had come to the area from further south and only had two sons and a daughter.

"Ay," he said. "Ay, that's fair, my lady. I dinna need them, only they was there, ye ken."

"Of course." She smiled at him. "I can give you twenty shillings each or take it off your rent."

Tully nodded. It was less than the beasts were worth but not much less. It more or less split the difference between that and the risk that they would be trouble.

She came back across the field and climbed the stile, drew off her glove and spat in her palm to clap her hand to Tully's and shake on it.

"There's ma hand, there's ma heart," he said. "Ye can take 'em now if ye like. I trust ye."

"Do you want money or credit?"

"Oh money, missus."

She checked her purse which only had a couple of shillings in it.

"I'll send the reeve to you tomorrow."

Half an hour later she was riding back to Widdrington with the horses on rope halters and feeling quite pleased with the deal. They were nice horses with nothing obviously wrong with them, and she always needed horses for the eternal problem of dispatches. Sir Henry would probably tell her she should have paid less and he would probably find something else to complain about, but he knew they needed horses.

She took the horses up to a gallop along a little ridge of the road, feeling happy as she always did when she was riding. Sir Henry was in Berwick on Tweed doing his duty as a Deputy Warden. He would turn up to harass her at some stage but probably not yet because October was peak raiding season and he would be dealing with raiders from the Middle March or, indeed, doing a bit of raiding himself.

She came onto the Great North Road which actually passed through the village of Widdrington and cantered until she came to the stone tower and barnekin of her castle. Some of the women tidying gardens, or sitting on their doorsteps knitting or spinning, waved to her as she went by with her colour high and her hat pinned firmly to her cap so it didn't come off. She found Mr Heron, the reeve, up to his knees in a collapsed drainage ditch and asked if he would take forty shillings to Tully the next day. Heron smiled at her, came and examined the two new horses and said he thought they were worth forty shillings each, unless they had some kind of horse disease, of course. "I think they're healthy enough," Elizabeth said, "but we'll see."

The boy on the gate opened to her and came to take her horses as she clattered into the yard. Two more boys were hard at work on the dung heap in the corner but they stopped to come and stare at the new horses.

"They're nice," said one of them, "not hobbies, though."

She dismounted to the stone by herself and passed Mouse to the biggest boy to whisp down and feed. One of the empty stalls had a very tired hobby in it, snoozing on his feet. She knew him but couldn't remember his name so she assumed it was a messenger's. "Yes," she said, "that's Blackie and that's Pinky."

The youngest lad snickered and the middle boy elbowed him and told him whose they were. She let their curiosity fester and was about to go and check the new horse in the stable when a girl came running out of the manor house by the tower.

"Missus," she shouted. "Ladyship, you've got to come quick."

It was a Trevannion cousin, sent to her to learn huswifery, a scatterbrained good-hearted creature with brown hair and eyes, who was being assiduously stalked by several unsuitable men.

"What is it, Mary?" she asked, expecting some tale about a spider.

"It's Mrs Burn, missus, she's been crying and crying and I can't get her to stop…" Mary's eyes were full of tears. "I don't know why either and I'm frightened for the babby…"

Elizabeth had already changed course and headed for the manor, the back way through the stableyard, into the kitchen-yard, through the kitchen—where she saw that the last pig carcass for winter had been delivered and was awaiting her attention in the wet larder—into the hall and through into the parlour, which had been built by Sir Henry's father soon after he had taken over the little chantry down the road. The chantry had provided the handsome stones and was now almost gone.

There sat Poppy Burn, otherwise Proserpina, one of the few women with whom Elizabeth could have a good conversation, and she was in a terrible state. Eight months pregnant, in a blue velvet English gown that had some mysterious dark stains on it, hunched over like a little old woman and tears dripping steadily out of her eyes into a sodden wad of linen. She lifted her head slightly, saw Elizabeth, and tried to rise to curtsey to her but couldn't get up.

Elizabeth went to her and put her arms around her as tight as she could and said things like "there there" and "now now" and signalled Mary closer with her eyes. There was a distinct metallic smell around Poppy.

"Fetch in some wine, mull it, and put in a tot of aqua vitae from the barrel in my still room," she instructed Mary. "Where's Young Henry?"

"He's out checking drainage ditches."

Probably findable then, but he wouldn't want to be bothered. "Fine. Go and get the wine."

Mary came clattering back grasping a tankard full of hot wine and Elizabeth put it in Poppy's cold white fingers.

"You're freezing, and wet through," she said as she felt the heavy velvet of the gown. "What happened, Poppy? What happened?"

"It…it…" The woman started hiccupping and stared into space, as if seeing something terrible, her fingers gripping the hanky and the tankard until Elizabeth wondered if the handle would come off.

"Has something bad happened to James?" Elizabeth asked carefully, it was the only thing she could think of that could cause this. Poppy was not an hysterical person, though she was young and perhaps idealistic for the Borders.

Poppy nodded once and tears started to flow again.

"My dear, we must get you out of your wet clothes and into bed. I'm worried about your baby."

She looked down in surprise at the mound of her stomach and then crossed her arms over it and started to wail. It was a terrifying sound that made Elizabeth's hair stand on end.

Right, she said to herself, this is obviously worse than just James being dead. She sent Mary upstairs to get the smallest bedroom cleared of her sewing things and the bed made, and sent a boy out to find Young Henry and bid him come in at once with some men. Then she untangled herself from Poppy and went to the dairy to tell Jane and Fiona to come and help. When the two girls came with her, she told them to keep their mouths shut.

Jane and Fiona formed a bridge with their strong white arms smelling of cheese and milk. Elizabeth sat Poppy on their arms and they carried her up to bed that way, with Poppy still hunched and still weeping.

"Milk Dandelion—she still has good milk—and bring the milk straight to me," said Elizabeth to Fiona. "And, Jane, bring me up a bowl of hot water and some clean cloths." She settled Poppy on the bed and unbuttoned the doublet front of the English gown and the let-out petticoat and shift under it. The petticoat, too, had brown stains on it which Elizabeth sniffed and confirmed her suspicions.

"Poppy, my dear, are you miscarrying?" Elizabeth asked. Poppy shook her head and hunched over tighter. "Then is the blood someone else's? James'?"

No answer and no sense. What in God's name had happened to the woman to cause this? Elizabeth had to check to see if she was in fact miscarrying, because in that case she needed to call Mrs Stirling immediately. Luckily she lived in the village, though she might be out with a patient anywhere around the country from here to Alnwick.

When Jane came hurrying back with a big bowl of hot water, cloths, and—praise God— one of Elizabeth's shifts under her arm, Elizabeth thanked her and sent her out. Then she stripped off the rest of Poppy's clothes and found what had turned her from a bright-faced happy person into sobbing human wreckage.

She could see bruises and grazes all round the tops of Poppy's legs and lower down as well, grazes and blood on Poppy's privates, too. She stopped for a moment to take a breath and calm herself because Poppy had clearly been raped. She put her ear to the big belly and thought she heard a heartbeat, thought she felt movement but she wasn't a midwife and she wasn't sure. She put her head round the door and told the waiting Jane to run for Mrs Stirling at once. The dairymaid's eyes met hers with understanding and then Jane turned and fairly sprinted down the stairs. Jane didn't say much, and wasn't pretty with her square young face and broad figure, but there was something steady about her that Elizabeth liked.

She looked out the window and saw Jane running at a good clip out of the gate and into the village with her skirts bundled up into her belt and her boots occasionally striking sparks from the cobbles. Elizabeth's hat was still on her head and she had her velvet gown on, but Poppy needed to get warm as quickly as possible, so she turned back to her and started washing her gently with the hot water and cloths. Poppy let her do it, passively, only tears leaked out from under her shut eyelids. When that was done Elizabeth put her own smock over the woman's head, chafed her freezing hands and feet, and went and got some socks from the linen cupboard. She had to pause again as she did it: What kind of man did that to a pregnant woman? And what had happened to James? It was clear he was dead, probably killed. Had there been a raid?

Poppy was still sitting on the side of the bed and so Elizabeth gently lifted up her legs, put the socks on her feet, and got her under the coverlets at last. She got the brandywine into her, which was the best thing to stop a miscarriage and seemed to relax Poppy a little.

Just as the last of the wine went down, Fiona came back with a bowl of Dandelion's best creamy milk, still hot from the cow. Elizabeth left her with Poppy, went to her stillroom, and found the precious bottle of laudanum and put a few drops in the milk, then spooned it into Poppy while Fiona stared unselfconsciously at her. Elizabeth sent Fiona to finish up in the dairy, and in particular, wash and salt the butter. It was aggravating that the time of year when cows gave the most milk was in summer when it was too warm to keep butter very long, whereas in autumn and winter, the milk was much less in quantity and creaminess. The butter made now was paler than summer butter, but if the weather didn't get warm it might keep to be used for Christmas.

The pig wouldn't wait forever, either, but it could wait a while. Elizabeth went and got her work from her bedroom and took off her hat and gown while she was at it, put on an apron at last, and went back to Poppy.

Poppy was sitting bolt upright again, twisting her hands together and making little moaning sounds. It would take awhile for the laudanum to work.

"Well, I think this gown is wet through," Elizabeth burbled at random as she picked up the heavy weight. "I'll hang it up and brush it once it's dry. The colour's good, though, it didn't… er…get on your clothes so we'll see if we can rescue it."

She put a broomhandle through the arms and hung the gown up on the wall to dry, bundled Poppy's shift and petticoats for the laundrywoman to have when they next did a wash, and put them in the bag. Then she sat down and started stitching a new shirt for Young Henry, who got through them faster than anyone she had ever heard of. She continued burbling about the cows and how she would keep Dandelion's calf even though it was male because Dandelion's milk was so good, and the old bull was getting on a bit, and Dandelion's son might make a good replacement.

By that time, the sound of boots on the stairs told her that Jane had found and brought Mrs Stirling. There was a knock on the door and Elizabeth answered it to find a flushed and triumphant Jane and the small grey-haired midwife.

"I woke her up, missus," said Jane, not breathing too hard.

"I'm very sorry, Mrs Stirling," said Elizabeth politely, "but I think this is an emergency."

"Ay," said the midwife. "Ah heard fra Jane."

"Jane, will you wait in the house? Fiona's finishing up for you. And thank you for running so fast."

"I like running," Jane said. "Is Mrs Burn better?"

"I hope she will be."

Jane nodded and plumped herself down on a bench in the corridor.

The midwife had already gone to Poppy and held her hand to feel the pulses. "Now, hinny, ye're to be a brave big girl. Is there pains?" Poppy shook her head. "Did ye feel a great movement or turn at any time?" Poppy started leaking tears again.

"When he…when he…"

"Ay, when he was on ye, the filthy bastard. Were there pains after, coming in waves, like this? Like ghost-pains but stronger?" Mrs Stirling held up a fist and clenched and unclenched it. Poppy shook her head. "Now my dear, I need to have a feel of ye, inside, ye follow? Will ye let me?"

Poppy nodded. "I thought…the babe was killed for sure." She was whispering but at least making sense.

"Well, mebbe not."

Mrs Stirling was gentle as she slipped her strong wiry hands under the covers and felt Poppy. She smiled. "Well, ye're still closed up tight there and the babe isna head down yet, so that's a mercy. How did ye get here?"

"I…I rode. I got on Prince and rode to the Great North Road and rode south and…"

"Did you find lodgings in Berwick?"

Poppy shook her head. "I just rode round the walls because it was night and kept on because…because…I wanted to find you."

Mrs Stirling and Elizabeth exchanged looks. "Wis there naebody nearer ye could ha' gone to?" asked the midwife.

"I wanted Lady Widdrington," said Poppy, as if this was obvious. "They killed Jamie and they…and they…"

Mrs Stirling held her hands for her.

"…and I want them hanged for it."

"Them?"

"Two men, not from round here, strangers. They came when I was at the river with the laundry and I came back because I thought they were the men from the Edinburgh printers about James' book of sermons, and they were talking awhile. I went to get some wafers and wine and while I was away…they killed Jamie. They stabbed him and he tried to fight so they cut half his head off."

"God above," said Mrs Stirling, shaking her head. "God a'mighty."

"Then they…did this. Then they went. And then I thought, if I can find Lady Widdrington right away, she'll help me find them again and hang them. So I tacked up Jamie's hobby, Prince, and I rode."

"When was this?"

"Yesterday. I don't know when."

Mrs Stirling had brought out her ear trumpet and put the large end on Poppy's belly, moving it around with her ear pressed to the other end. She paused and a large smile briefly lit her face.

"Well now, that's a lovely heartbeat," she said. "Would ye like to listen?"

Elizabeth would, very much but hadn't liked to ask. She put her ear to the narrow part of the ear trumpet and heard Poppy's own heartbeat and then the lighter quicker beat from the babe. Her face lit up too. "Oh yes," she said, "That's a good strong beat."

"It didn't get killed by the…by them?" asked Poppy.

Mrs Stirling took her hands and sat down next to her on the bed. "Listen, child," she said, "it's a terrible thing that happened and ye'll want yer vengeance, I understand that. But you must try not to mither over it nor yer man's death. Ye must be calm as ye can until the babe is born and then while it's a little babby too. Take your vengeance late and cold."

Poppy nodded. "The Good Book says, 'Vengeance is mine, saith the Lord, I will repay.'"

"It does," allowed Mrs Stirling, "though sometimes the Lord needs a little bit o' prodding. Now go to sleep and think of the babby."

Poppy lay down obediently and closed her eyes. Elizabeth led Mrs Stirling out of the room and took her downstairs to the parlour for wafers and wine and advice.

"She should be no worse for it than bruises and a sore quim for a few days, if she hasnae bin poxed," said Mrs Stirling consideringly. "As to her body, with luck. As to her mind, who can say? There was a girl raped in a raid that never spoke again nor made any sense. Another girl who was treated the same in another raid by the same man, as it happens, was well enough in a month, though a mite jumpy and couldna abide the tolling of a bell."

"Does it happen often?"

"Not often. But it happens. Especially when the raiders are far out of their ain country and they've caught a girl who's not from a riding surname and think they willna be known."

"I've never heard of it...."

"Ay, well, they dinna tell anyone but the midwife when they come to me for tansy tea and if they're a married woman, especially, for they'll be afeared their husbands will think they were willing, especially if they kindle."

Mrs Stirling polished off her wine and Elizabeth paid her.

"Don't leave her alone," advised the midwife as Elizabeth saw her out the door. "She was alone when it happened, keep her company. I'll call back in a day or two."

Elizabeth nodded at this and went into the dairy first to see that the place was clean and tidy to keep the faeries happy. It was, so she told Fiona and Jane they could go home. She found young Mary sitting eating hazelnuts in the hall and told her to come with her and went back upstairs to Poppy who was lying rigid with her eyes open. She relaxed as they came in.

Mary she sent to get her crewelwork and sat down by Poppy.

"Will you be able to sleep with Mary here?" she asked. "I must make a start on salting the pig for winter."

Poppy was weeping again and her poor eyes were already red and swollen.

"Read to me," she whispered. "Please."

"What shall I read?"

"Anything."

Elizabeth went back to the bedroom and looked at her precious store of books, kept in a box under the bed where Sir Henry couldn't see them. He didn't see the point of women reading and had burned some of her books once. She chose a couple—one a book of sermons of staggering dullness that she used to get herself to sleep sometimes and the other a Tyndale Bible.

She read the Gospel of Matthew about the Nativity and a couple of Psalms and then decided that beautiful though the language was, what Poppy needed was dullness. She chose the dullest sermon in a very dull book and started reading about how one should never wear velvet or any colour other than black, brown, grey, or white because of worldliness and the sins of the flesh.

Poppy shut her eyes and seemed to doze off at last and Elizabeth left Mary to sit in the same chair and read the same book if necessary.

She went downstairs, ready to make a start on the pig and found Young Henry and four other Widdringtons tramping their boots into the hall.

"What's happened?" asked Young Henry, looming over her as he always did now. When first she had known him, he was a boy and much shorter than her. She hardly noticed his spots anymore but there was a particularly fine one on the end of his nose—a beacon of red and white. She found it mesmerising.

She told him to come with her into the wet larder where she took her sleeves off and put on her wet larder apron to make a start on the pig—opening it up and taking out the innards.

She called the boys in from the stables and set them to fetching buckets of water from the well and then to the really unpleasant job of cleaning the intestines, to ready them to make sausages, while she dealt with the pluck and got it ready to make a haggis. It was a nice pig, quite fat and had come from the post inn where they got a lot of leftovers. She believed the pig had been called Bucket, like its predecessors, for obvious reasons.

Young Henry stood in her wet larder in his third best suit and his buff jerkin, which he was wearing because it was a bit proof against water and didn't get as heavy as a jack when it was wet. His boots were in a terrible state because inspecting drainage ditches often meant you had to get muddy. The four Widdrington cousins were no better and had wisely decided to come in no further than the kitchen where they were getting some ale from the cook.

"Just like that?" asked Henry. "They just rode in, found out his name and killed him?"

"And raped his wife."

Young Henry shook his head. "Have you told Father?"

"I've told you," she said. "You can decide whether to tell him or not when you go through Berwick, though I don't think he'll care because it's Scotch East March business, not his."

Young Henry nodded at that and Elizabeth finished putting bits of pig in various bowls and cleaned her knives carefully before giving them to the smallest boy for further cleaning and sharpening. The first stage was over and the carcass clean inside, with a bit of washing by the middle-sized boy, and the next stage of cutting up and salting could wait several days, unlike the innards. The liver was nice and big; she thought she might make a liversausage out of it. The other two were gasping and complaining in the kitchenyard at the disgusting job she had put them to.

What she really wanted to do was go north to Wendron and take a look at the house where it had happened and see the corpse if it was still there. Had anyone found it yet, done anything about it? What had happened afterwards, after Poppy left? She particularly wanted to know if Tully's two found horses had anything to do with it.

The problem was Sir Henry. He thought women should stay at home and do as they were told, not ride about the countryside. Ever since she had been to Carlisle and back in the summer and with what had happened there and in Dumfries, he was even worse than before.

On the other hand, he was in Berwick at the moment, concerned with governing the East March with Robert Carey's pompous elder brother, John. He'd find out about it, of course, but if she could find a good enough excuse…

She shrugged as she washed her hands in the bucket of cold water and took off her wet canvas larder apron, hung it up on its hook, and put on another clean linen one. He would probably beat her again, and if she didn't go to Wendron, he would find another reason to beat her. There was no point trying to please him because he could not be pleased with her.

Young Henry was still there, looking shrewdly at her. "It's only about forty miles across country," he said, "but I don't think you should go."

She said nothing to this. He was right, of course, but she had a terrible itch to see for herself.

She went upstairs to check on Poppy and found her awake again but not crying. The rest of the milk with laudanum in it was cold now and Poppy wouldn't take it.

"I've been thinking," she said. "I shouldn't have come here, should I?"

"No," agreed Elizabeth, "with the babe and all, it would have been better if you'd sent for me. Not ridden for a day and a night on Prince."

"I couldn't think," Poppy said. "All I could think of was getting to you and telling you."

Poppy had her fists clenched but was at least making sense now. She had no family nearer than Carlisle and her mother and father were dead; there was only an uninterested uncle who had something to do with mines in the lakes and not of a riding surname. Nobody could actually say Poppy's maiden name either, it was so foreign, though she herself had been born in Keswick.

James Burn came of the Burns, all right, but had shocked the family by going to university as a servitor and gaining a degree in Divinity and then coming back to the East March to be a minister of the kirk. Elizabeth had made the match at Christmas two years ago and had been there when they had married the following March. She had also prodded a powerful friend of hers into preferring Jamie to St Cuthberts with some sweeteners to the Elders to ensure his election.

"Well," said Poppy, "I've come here and I'll not leave for a while."

"I don't think you should ride anywhere until after you're churched, at the earliest," Elizabeth agreed with her. "In fact, you should be sleeping now." She picked up the milk and prepared to spoon it into Poppy.

Poppy shook her head. "Ye have to go to Wendron for me," she said. "Ye have to. Please? Who's the living going to go to now that Jamie's dead? There's things I need like my other kirtle, there's his will, and who else can I trust? And make sure he's buried right. Make sure…" She stopped, clenched her fists and took a deep breath. "Otherwise he'll walk for sure."

Elizabeth wanted to get away from that kind of thinking. "Ah," she said. "What did the men talk about with the minister before they killed him?"

"I don't know. They were talking quietly, Jamie sent me out to get the wine and the wafers and when I came back he was… he was…"

"Can you remember anything, anything at all about what they said?"

"It was just talk. Oh, the older one said something about scripture. He was quoting some scripture."

"Which verse?" Poppy just shrugged. "No threats, nothing?"

Poppy looked proud. "My man wis a man of peace, he was a man that turned away from war and reiving and toward the

Gospels. But he knew how to fight, so if they'd given him any warning at all, or a threat, it wouldn't have been so easy for them. And he knew them. He recognised the younger one as I went out. He shook their hands and he was asking them about the Low Countries and were they back for good now?"

"All right, Poppy, I'll go to Wendron for you. It'll take a few days and I want you to stay right here and not go anywhere. You can borrow my English gown if you want to walk about, but I wouldn't even go out the door. Give the babby a chance to rest. He's had a couple of shocks."

"You don't mind all that riding?"

"Not in the least."

Elizabeth starting feeding Poppy the milk and halfway through she suddenly bent over and cried again.

"Och Jamie," she sobbed. "You'll never have curds and whey to your breakfast again."

fRidAy AfteRnoon 13th octobeR 1592

Two hours later Elizabeth was in her green riding habit with her best black velvet gown trimmed with coney in honour of the funeral, a cloak over her shoulders and her low-crowned hat on her head, in a style that had been fashionable in London four years before. She was cantering north along the Great North Road that passed through Widdrington and had done for hundreds of years, the second-to-last post inn before Berwick. Young Henry rode beside her and the Widdrington cousins were two in front and two behind, very happy to have escaped from the eternal autumn job of clearing ditches and checking waterways. Young Henry was happy as well because he liked his stepmother and it always made him feel better about his father when he saw her like this, cheeks flushed, eyes sparkling, swinging along with the rhythm of the horse. She was riding a half-hobby called Rat, because he looked like one with his pointed nose, and had her jennet, Mouse, behind her for a remount.

They would break their journey at Bamburgh on the coast, and from there it was only fifteen miles to Berwick. They would take fresh horses from the stables in Berwick that Young Henry's father maintained, go into Scotland there in daylight, and into the Merse, and so to the quiet village full of raspberry canes that Jamie Burn had been living in.

They wouldn't be visiting the Burns in East Teviotdale, which was his family and a dangerous riding surname, with a Jock Burn in every generation. Jamie was the second son of Ralph o' the Coate.

The management of Sir Henry had taken half an hour to think about. In the end, Elizabeth had prayed about it to God and left it to Him. If God wanted her to go to Wendron, Sir Henry would agree and if He didn't want her to go to Wendron, she'd catch the Berwick market because she needed more salt, since the salt in the wet larder was poor stuff, and go home again.

As usual she was thinking about Sir Robert Carey while she rode because Sir Robert was always where her thoughts went when they weren't occupied by something else. His behaviour in Scotland in the summer had been disgraceful and then he had been ordered south by his father at the end of August. Since then she hadn't heard a word about him; she wouldn't hear from him because Sir Henry had forced her to write that letter to him, ending their friendship. She didn't know for certain if her verbal message had got through but she thought it had.

Sir Henry had overreached himself at Court in his attempt to kill Carey. The Scottish king liked Carey and had said some things privately to Sir Henry that he hadn't seen fit to tell his wife but which seemed to give him pause sometimes. There had only been one really bad beating since then. He always kept away from her face because he didn't want the rumours to start going round as they had with his first wife, but now he didn't use his belt so much. It was something.

Carey would love to have an excuse to kill him but wouldn't get it. Sir Henry was not a young man to be inveigled into a duel; if Sir Robert challenged him, he'd use a champion. And probably cheat. Nobody stayed headman of an English riding surname like the Widdringtons without being canny and clever and hard to kill. However Sir Henry had gout which didn't usually kill you but was very painful when he had an attack. She tried to think of him charitably as a creature in pain who wanted to lash out, rather than a man who enjoyed hurting her and humiliating her, but it was hard.

They clattered through the gate at Bamburgh just before it shut at dusk and up to the keep where Sir John Forster's unfortunate son, also called John, held sway. He was drunk as he usually was and explained the rotten state of the rushes and the filth of the solar as the consequence of there being no woman there. Elizabeth had seen worse, though not much worse, and accepted Johnny Forster's offer of the main bedroom which at least had a four-poster, though no clean sheets. Or blankets. In the end she rolled out the truckle bed and slept fully clothed on that because it seemed to have fewer fleas and much less dog hair. Johnny Forster was no threat to her virtue, not as drunk as he was, and with Young Henry endearingly sleeping on a pallet across the doorway with his knife in his hand.

She was up before dawn and saw no reason to awaken the marshal of the castle who had passed out in the hall while explaining how heavy his responsibilities were to his two lovely hunting dogs, both of whom listened carefully and were as sympathetic as they could be. From the state of the blankets in the four-poster they normally slept there with him when he went to bed. Not one of the servants in the place had changed the bedclothes since last Christmas at the latest.

She shook her head at it. Men were very strange creatures. Surely even if you were drunk it was uncomfortable to sleep in a dirty bed full of dog hair and an old bit of mince pie turned to rock?

SATURDAY 14th OCTOBER 1592

They were out of a postern gate, opened by a heavy-eyed Forster cousin, and back on the Great North Road before the gate usually opened. The fifteen miles to Berwick were gone in a flash because the road was very good here, where the town council of Berwick maintained it, with hardly any potholes.

At the Widdrington house in Berwick they found that Sir Henry wasn't there. The steward explained to Elizabeth that Sir Henry had gone north of the Border two days before and was suppposed to be meeting the opposite Warden and somebody from the Scottish Court, in a secret matter. Yes, John Carey was in town and they could see him tomorrow but not today because he was busy, which she suspected meant he was hungover. That suited her perfectly and meant she got out of hearing John's perennial complaints about the town council and mayor of Berwick, as well as not having to deal with her husband. She, Young Henry, and the four Widdringtons stayed only long enough for breakfast, with Sir Henry's steward tutting because she expected bread and ale for six.

They were out the northward gate against the flow of people, crossing the Tweed on the narrow rickety Scotch bridge into the Merse, with Elizabeth now on Mouse with Rat behind. Everyone else had got hobbies from the stables. The hobbies needed a lot of persuasion to set foot on the bridge which was in a bad condition. This was one of the major connections between Scotland and England; couriers passed both ways across it every week—it was like Bamburgh. What was the point of not keeping it in good condition?

She shook her head again as her horse stepped off the end of the bridge and both of them breathed easier. No doubt the King of Scotland thought it was better to have a bridge that would not stand an army crossing it.

Wendron wasn't very far from the road to Edinburgh, the continuation of the Great North Road which was well-used by travellers and merchants, not to mention the ceaseless hurry of post messengers riding to and from London and Edinburgh. There was at least one bag of dispatches a week and sometimes one a day if Scottish politics suddenly got interesting. The raid on Falkland in the summer had produced staggering quantities of paperwork.

As they rode into the village they found two boys sitting in a tree by the side of the road and one ran off purposefully as they passed. Young Henry nodded approvingly. The church alehouse was full and the manse had a man standing by the door with a reasonably good jack on his back and a billhook in his fist. Young Henry dismounted and went forward to speak to the man who pointed at the alehouse.

Eyes watched as they left their horses tethered near the alehouse, leaving two of the lads outside to keep an eye on them, and went into the smoky commonroom. The laird of the area had died of a flux a year before, and his wife had died in childbirth ten years before, so the land was in wardship to the Crown and theoretically being administered by Lord Spynie on behalf of the ten-year-old boy who was the only heir and now his ward.

His grandmother sat in the best chair in the house, the Dowager Lady Hume of Norland, a tall hat on her head and a ruff at her neck, her fine dark grey wool kirtle under a magnificent gown lined with sable from Muscovy.

Elizabeth hadn't met her before. She thought she had been a great beauty fifty years before and her face still had the bones of it, but the flesh was gone the way flesh goes and she had two grim lines on either side of her mouth.

Young Henry did a tolerable bow and Elizabeth swept a curtsey to her. She felt dowdy in her small hat and old green riding habit, but on the other hand, perhaps that was all to the good. At least she had her furred velvet gown.

Grey eyes narrowed as the lady took in the whole of them.

"Whit's the interest of the Widdringtons in this outrage?" she demanded. "Our minister's been foully murthered and his wife is aye missing. Well?"

"My lady," said Elizabeth, "Mrs Burn is at Widdrington and as far as we can tell both she and the baby are well."

The creased face relaxed a tiny bit. "How did she get sae far south?"

"She rode, ma'am. She was in a terrible state and all she could think of was to get to me. I have no idea why. She rode Mr Burn's hobby south all night and came to us yesterday afternoon."

"Is she hurt?"

How could you answer that? "She is getting better and I've had the midwife to her and she says the babe is well."

The eyes narrowed again. "Why did ye come all this way?"

"I wanted to fetch clothes for Mrs Burn as I feel she'll be better to stay at Widdrington until she's churched and I wanted to find out the truth of what happened to Mr Burn if I could. And of course, Mrs Burn asked me to see to it that her husband is properly buried."

It was an honest answer and there came a single proud nod. She didn't mean to, but her eyes locked on Lady Hume's. Lady Hume could choose to send her away once she had the clothes, but she hoped…She really hoped she wouldn't. She had liked Jamie Burn; he was a good man, perhaps a little hot-tempered, perhaps a little intolerant, but he had started a school for the children of the village and his sermons were only an hour long. She had come to Wendron to stay several times when Young Henry was in Berwick, and it had touched her heart to see how he smiled and let his wife speak and would find excuses to touch her hand or her shoulder and how Poppy would find excuses to do the same.

Touched her heart with envy, true, but it was good to see that a marriage could be...kindly.

"Ay, the truth," said Lady Hume, the two lines by the corners of her mouth lengthening and deepening. "The truth is, we dinna ken. He was stabbed and had his brainpan laid open in his ain parlour, we dinna ken who by, except there were two strangers in the village. D'ye know aught of them?"

"Nothing except that two horses with West March brands were found by a man called Tully. He says they were wandering in the forest not ten miles south."

"Hm," said Lady Hume, tilting her head on its long neck. "Come with me."

The manse was a scene of frantic activity as women scrubbed the walls by the plate cupboard and swept the rushes into the yard.

"Where's the corpse?"

"In his church, in the crypt."

"May I see it, to pay my respects? I'm sorry for his death for he was a good man."

"Ay," said Lady Hume, "he was."

She led the way to the church, where there were black candles lit, and down the narrow steps into the ancient vaulted crypt. Among the Papist statues lying as if it was a strange stone dormitory, was the bier with James Burn's body.

His head was actually in two bits, sliced through his face, held together awkwardly by a linen bandage. There wasn't much blood. The corpse lay as it had fallen, twisted to the right, though he had been laid out and cleaned and wrapped in his shroud ready for burial.

"Ye canna see the stab wound. It's in his back, the cowards. Stabbed in the back first, then that done by a good sword."

Elizabeth took a look at the hands. They were big hands and the knuckles of his right were grazed.

"He tried to fight, I think."

"Ay," sniffed the Dowager Lady, "of course."

"When is the funeral?"

"Tomorrow or the day after. Nae reason to wait about, some of the Burns are here already. His wife willna be coming, I think?"

"No," said Elizabeth. "It's a miracle she didn't miscarry the wean as it is. I can be her proxy if you like, ma'am."

"Yes, that would be fitting, Lady Widdrington."

Young Henry had come down the steps behind them and was standing, head bowed by the body.

"Ye willna be praying for his soul," said Lady Hume flintily.

Young Henry lifted his head in surprise. "No," he said, "for his family and his wife. He's already gone to Judgement."

Lady Hume nodded once. Elizabeth felt sad that you couldn't pray for souls the way you could in the old days that her nurse had told her about. What harm did it do? But only Papists did that nowadays and she wasn't a Papist so she kept quiet about it. Silently she asked God to have mercy on Jamie and keep him safe until Judgement Day.

"God rest him and keep him," she said. "He was a good man and a good husband."

Lady Hume sniffed eloquently. "A pity his wife betrayed him, then."

"What?"

"Ay well, why else would she ride all that way? You mark my words, Lady Widdrington, the girl brought in the strangers to kill him and then rode off wi' them and she's told ye a fine tale to draw your sympathies but."

Elizabeth felt her colour and temper rise at the idea that Poppy could have betrayed her husband like that, but she said nothing for a while. Lady Hume was a powerful woman and no doubt would be even more convinced of Poppy's guilt if she knew of the rape.

"I doubt it," she said finally with a glint of humour. "I really doubt it, Lady Hume." She shook her head at the idea.

"Well then, explain the death of Mr Burn."

"I can't. He was a good pastor."

"Ay, he was, a good pastor and a good dominie but a fire-eater he was not. His sermons were respectable and his life exemplary.

He may have come from a riding surname but he himself was no reiver."

Elizabeth nodded. "You're right, Lady Hume. He never showed any signs of being a reiver." Lady Hume gave Elizabeth a long and considering look which Elizabeth returned blandly and then curtseyed low to her again.

They went in silence up the steps from the crypt and straight into the alehouse which was full. Elizabeth went into a corner, called for double beer for Young Henry and his cousins and mild for herself and settled down on the bench to watch what happened. The presence of Lady Hume made the church alehouse respectable. She wondered whether the lady had simply taken up residence in the manse for the duration. Elizabeth also wondered where she herself would sleep. At least she had an official position here for the funeral, so she supposed Lady Hume might do something about it eventually.

Jamie Burn had come from a riding surname of the Middle March and was a son of the headman. The Burns were coming in all day to the funeral, feeling the need to make a point of it, and she hoped that Lady Hume had brought supplies with her to help with that. She watched the man she thought was Jamie's father by the bar as he drank and stared into space and stared into space and drank. She wasn't sure what had happened between him and his son when Jamie decided to go to university. Had that been with his father's consent or had there been a quarrel?

After a moment she got up, left her pewter mug of mild ale on the table next to Young Henry, and went over to the man.

"Mr Burn?" she asked.

"Ay. Ay missus."

"Are you Minister Burn's father?"

"Nay missus, his uncle, Jock. His dad's Ralph o' the Coate."

"May I speak with you?"

"Ay, why not?"

"I was very, very sorry to hear of Jamie Burn's death, Mr Burn," she began inadequately.

"Ye were. Why?"

"He was a good man and a good pastor. There aren't enough of those about that we can afford to waste them."

Strangely there was a brief moment when the man in front of her seemed about to laugh, but she thought she had mistaken it. "Ay," came the answer, "I backed him agin his father when he wanted to dae it."

"You did?"

"I backed him, ay. His big brother Geordie thought it was hilarious, him studying Divinity at St Andrews as a servitor, and his dad wanted him to stay with the family. There was a lot of argufying."

"I wondered if his father was against it."

"Ay. Agin it. Ye could say that."

"Will he be coming to the funeral?"

Jock Burn's face shut tight. "Ay well. I dinna ken. He might."

"The rest of the surname seem to be coming in."

"Ay," said Jock Burn, "we need to make a bit of a show."

"Why?"

He paused, thinking. "Somebody came up to a Burn, stabbed him, and part took his heid off wi' an axe. We're coming in so no one thinks we're afeared."

"Good Lord, Mr Burn, I don't think anyone could possibly think that."

"Hm. And I think kindly on ye, that the Widdringtons are showing support."

"I liked the minister, Mr Burn. He was a good man."

"Ay."

She went back to Young Henry who was looking wistfully at a game of shove ha'penny that was starting up in the corner.

"What do you think about it?" she asked as she sat down with him again and finished her mild ale. Young Henry flushed and hid his nose in his beer.

"About Jamie?"

"Yes."

"Well, I liked him too. I wish he wisnae dead. That's about the size of it."

"Hm. What do you think about how he was killed with an axe?"

"It wisnae an axe; it was a broadsword."

"How do you know?"

"Well an axe mashes up more of the flesh and that was a sharp edge that took him, right down through his skull at an angle, left to right. That's not an easy blow forbye, it was an expert with a good sword."

"And stabbed from behind. Before or after?"

Young Henry didn't need to think. "Before. If ye get his kidneys or his heart, it's all over. He probably didn't even shout."

She thought about this and nodded.

"Ay," Young Henry said judiciously. "So one man kept him talking and the other went round, drew his poignard, and struck from behind."

"They didn't want him to know."

"No, well, he's a Burn. They're a' good fighters."

"Even the one who got away and into the church."

A fractional pause. "Ay."

Elizabeth smiled brightly at Young Henry and left it. He went off to join the shouting crowd round the shove ha'penny board and started betting on it. Even without the murder, she was beginning to feel very interested in Jamie Burn and his history. What had he done before he went to St Andrews, and why had he decided to become a minister in the first place?

It was a nuisance that Poppy Burn was at Widdrington and not here, thought Elizabeth. Blast the woman for taking it into her head to ride away. It gave a perfect opportunity for all the clacking nasty tongues to work.

Looking at the problem from a man's point of view, Elizabeth had to admit that the killers would have had an easy job of it if they had had Poppy's help—and it was very difficult to show she hadn't helped them. Elizabeth was sure she hadn't, but who could be certain of anything like that? The bruises and the state of her showed it had been rape, but a man might say she was willing to start with, and then changed her mind and it wasn't his fault if he couldn't stop.

Elizabeth shook her head and frowned. Lady Hume had been welcoming the headmen of the surnames coming in to the funeral, who certainly were an impressive bunch of killers and robbers. Now she was gathering herself up to go, and so Elizabeth went over to her and asked where she would advise Elizabeth to find lodging?

"Are ye afeared of ghosts?" asked Lady Hume.

"I've never seen one," Elizabeth answered steadily.

"Well I'm staying at the manse since it's a ten-mile ride back to my Lord Hughie. You're welcome to join me, Lady Widdrington, and your stepson as well, though your men will have to find space in the alehouse."

"Thank you, Lady Hume." Elizabeth was relieved at solving the problem so easily. She went back to Young Henry with the news and discovered that he'd rather find a space at the alehouse than the manse. Not that he was afeared of ghosts, oh no, but he felt he should stay with his cousins since there were a number of reivers come into the village and while none of his men had feuds with anyone likely to come that he knew of, it would be well if no feuds started up, especially with the Burns, who were dangerous that way.

With the village full of reivers, she decided to bring the hobbies and Mouse and Rat into the manse with her. Lady Hume was agreeable and so Elizabeth went back to Young Henry who thought it was an excellent idea and sent the youngest Widdrington cousin with her to lead the horses.

They went round the back to the stableyard where the hobbies shared two loose-boxes and Mouse and Rat shared another since they were friends. There wasn't much horse feed there but all the horses got enough to tide them over.

The manse was a small stone-built house, the chantry of St Cuthbert's somewhat altered by the previous incumbent. Poppy had been proud of that—living in a stone house with a slate roof was better than one of wattle and daub and thatch, though she

admitted that it was a lot colder and harder to heat. There was a
large handsome entrance hall, decorated with Papistical carvings
nobody understood anymore—who was the woman with a towel
in her hand and why did a stag have a cross between its antlers?

The small parlour was still damp and had no rushes on the
tiled floor. Lady Hume led Elizabeth to it and opened the door.

"Ye may as well satisfy yer curiosity," she said.

"Thank you, Lady Hume," said Elizabeth and went in to
look. That the plate cupboard was open and bare of plate was
the first thing she saw, gone were the three silver goblets and a
handsome bowl with dancing cherubs on it that she had seen
when she stayed with Poppy. The benches along the wall were a
little at angles, probably moved by the village women when they
cleaned out the rushes. There must have been a lot of brains to
clean up, very unpleasant and fatty.

The gore was gone but she could trace where it had been from
the scrubbing and wet walls. It was mainly around the plate
cupboard, though not on the cupboard itself. She shut her eyes
and tried to imagine James going to get the plate, probably the
three goblets, and then one man coming up behind him with a
knife, the other man sweeping his sword out and finishing the
job when it went a little wrong.

Who had held Poppy still? Or no, she had been fetching
wafers and wine. And who had taken the plate which belonged
to Poppy?

"Hm," she said aloud, "where are Poppy's silver goblets and
bowl?"

Lady Hume shrugged. "Nae doubt but they took them.
Why not?"

Reivers would know someone who could melt it down for the
silver, probably Richie Graham of Brackenhill who made a very
good thing out of buying plates off reivers for not very much
and then minting it up himself into the debauched Scottish
shillings to trade over the Border. The plate had been taken by
way of a bonus; it was far too little to be worth the raid by itself.

Still, the fact Jamie had opened the plate cupboard was very interesting, since it showed that the men were indeed known to Jamie, were in fact honoured guests. You wouldn't give them wine in silver goblets if they were just messengers or strangers unless there was something else about them that made them important.

"Hm," she said, pleased with herself for thinking that one out, and looked around for more interesting details. Robin Carey had told her something about that once, that truth was like gold and essentially indestructible although you could bury it. But there would be traces.

What would he do, faced with such a puzzle? Well for a start he would be in the saddle looking for the tracks and prints that would show which way the killers had gone, probably with Sergeant Dodd alongside. She couldn't do that, and in any case, any hoofprints would be indistinguishable from all the people coming into the village. Robin would also be charming the Dowager Lady Hume like a bird out of a tree.

Before she could get lost in thinking about him, she turned and came out of the parlour, shutting the door firmly behind her.

"I suppose Mrs Burn's larder has been pillaged?" she said to the lady who sniffed.

"Since she no longer has any claim to it, I have taken it over." She gave Elizabeth a bold look. Elizabeth knew well that the living was not in her gift but in fact in the gift of the man who held the Lord Hughie's wardship, which alas, currently was Lord Spynie, the King's minion. Elizabeth also knew that it could be hard to make ends meet even if you were a lady, here in the north where the living was difficult, certainly if you were trying to hold the lands together for a son and heir aged ten.

It had taken a great deal of conniving and letter-writing for her to get the living for Jamie a couple of years ago when Chancellor Maitland held the wardship, and it was annoying that the effort had all gone to waste. How inconsiderate of Jamie to die like that! she caught herself thinking.

"Ah," said Elizabeth with a smile, "I wondered if there's anything there I could make a supper out of."

"I'm afraid I don't know," was the withering response, from someone who had probably always had a cook and was therefore helpless.

Elizabeth forayed into the kitchen, where the fire hadn't been lit and where there were no servants at all, and found a hacked loaf of bread and the end of a ham hock and some crumbs of cheese. In a crock in the wet larder behind she found some soused herring, and in a bag in the scullery she found some carrots and parsnips, a little withered but perfectly edible. She took a look at the modern brick range and found it was stone cold, which was a pity because her stomach was aching with hunger.

She peered out of the wet larder door into the little stableyard and found two boys there, arguing over whether they should knock and ask for some pennies for a job or two, and pounced. One, she sent to the alehouse to fetch some hot coals. The other she sent to the woodshed for kindling and logs, and then to the well to fetch water.

Half an hour later she was boiling the parsnips in a saucepan on a sharp fire at the small end of the range and heating the soused herring in the warmer.

She found the plates for the Burn's dinner sitting in cold scummy water and gone mouldy, so she trimmed some bread trenchers from the stale loaf and even found a wooden platter and two serving spoons. The pantry had a crock of butter, which was wonderful news, and even a big crock of oatmeal for the morrow, which she immediately mixed up with some water, butter, and salt ready to go in the warmer overnight when the herrings came out.

Best of all, in a carefully hidden crock amongst the dirty pans, she found Poppy's little honey oatcakes which weren't even stale.

Lady Hume seemed astonished when Elizabeth called her to a late dinner at the table in the parlour, but she took the place at the head of the table when Elizabeth invited her. Over the food she folded her hands and said grace.

"Lord and father, we thank thee for this food which thou hast vouchsafed to us here in this house of sorrow…" There was quite a lot more of that until Elizabeth's stomach gave a heroic growl at which Lady Hume said amen halfway through a sentence. They didn't speak for a while after that except to say things like "pass the salt" and "would you help me to some more neeps?"

The soused herrings were very good, well soaked to clear them of salt and then cooked in a mixture of stock and vinegar until they melted like butter in the mouth. Elizabeth's neeps were less good, as they could have done with a little more time in the water, but the butter made up for that.

Lady Hume had a good stomach to her meat despite her frail looks and her eyes lit up when she saw Poppy's honey oatcakes.

"Ay," she said, a little strictly, "I'll have just the one of those."

Elizabeth felt pleasantly full if a little guilty at eating Poppy's food. Only it wasn't her food, anymore, was it? Surely Lord Spynie would give her a month or two to get her bearings after the will was read? It wasn't a rich living, nor yet a multiple, surely nobody would want it too quickly.

Of course, if they did, that could be a motive for murder by itself.

Lady Hume ate four of the oatcakes and then declared herself full. Elizabeth gave the bread trenchers to the boys who had done errands for her and an oatcake each, plus a penny each from her private funds. The lads ran off with the news, very happy to be gulping down the soaked bread, and Elizabeth suspected that every boy in the village would turn up in the morning. That suited her because she suspected there would be things she could find for them to do.

"I can fetch the coals from the kitchen range and get a fire going here in the parlour," she said as it finally got too dark for her to see. "Or perhaps we could move to the kitchen where it's already quite warm." It was going to be extremely cold in the bedroom.

After only a moment's hesitation, Lady Hume approved the move to the kitchen where Elizabeth sat her in the only chair there and brought a stool in from the pantry for herself. She had also found some aqua vitae in a small bottle, or uisgebeath as the Scots called it, and Lady Hume accepted a small cupful.

Like many elderly people, Lady Hume didn't know when she was cold and hungry. Now she was fed and warm she began slowly to thaw.

"Yes, I was married for twenty years until my lord died of gout," she told Elizabeth. "And my son died of a quartan fever a few years ago. I never thought he would, which was my black sin and God's just judgement upon me. I thought he might die in a raid, never of sickness."

Elizabeth made a sympathetic noise. She learned many things about the son but the main one was that he had left her a grandson called Hughie who was the light of Lady Hume's life and the apple of her eye. And she would sooner die than let him go to the household of the Lord Spynie to learn knighthood.

"Ah," said Elizabeth, "is he a good-looking child?"

"Ay," said Lady Hume, sourly, "fair as the month of May and blue eyes and blond hair. Lord Spynie saw him last year and since then has been badgering me to let him come to Court, saying it will be the making of him and I'll have a dower house and a better jointure and such things." The firm jaw clenched. "But I willna." The eyes narrowed. "He's wasting the land, too. He's already cut down two woods and sold the timber and nobody's seen to the drainage ditches since my son died."

"Does Chancellor Maitland know this?"

Lady Hume shrugged. "Disnae know, disnae care."

"How did the wardship change hands? Was it when my Lord Maitland was in trouble with the King a couple of years ago?"

"Ay. That's when. How d'ye know?"

"I took in Maitland's son for a year when he was frightened for the boy. He's an old friend of mine."

"Ay?"

That had been an odd year. Carey had been in France and she had been praying for his safety every night. Maitland's son had been running about the place, full of delight at getting away from his tutor and riding for England in the middle of the night with his father. The political weather had changed again in Scotland a year later and he'd left her without a backward look, feeling even sadder that she had no children and wasn't likely to have any.

Sir Henry, surprisingly, had been very pleased to take in Maitland's son and had taught him to use a longbow. She had seen a glimpse of her husband then that had made her confused: He had been a little bit kind to the boy, why couldn't he be kind to her?

Kindness. It was such an important thing, she thought, once more seeing Robin with his horse Thunder and how he had gentled the animal, how he had even dealt gently with Young Hutchin Graham, despite the fact that the boy betrayed him. You could say that the entirety of the Gospels was a plea for kindness. Not the Epistles, though, nor yet the Apocalypse.

Lady Hume had been speaking. "I'm sorry, my Lady?"

"I asked, would ye be willing to try and get the wardship shifted to the Chancellor again? I'd make it worth your while."

Elizabeth paused, thought about this. "I'm not sure, my Lady. I could tell you all sorts of lies about how I'm certain I could, but you wouldn't believe me." There was a tiny grunt and a little flash of a smile. "I'll think about it. Chancellor Maitland is quite old now and doesn't want to deal with wardships anymore." Also Chancellor Maitland had made enough money out of wardships and other perks to build a large and handsome fortress for himself at Thirlstane. Quite good for a man who had been arraigned for treason on account of fighting for Mary Queen of Scots many years before.

"I can hold out for a while but no' for long," said the Lady. "Spynie's already sent Hughie a lovely chestnut horse and a boy's back and breast for martial exercises."

The sarcasm in the Lady's voice could have withered a stand of pine trees.

"Can I ask you if you knew the Burns?"

"The riding surname?" Her voice was wary.

"No, just the minister and Mrs Burn."

"Ay, I'd come to dinner a few times and fed them as well. Minister Burn was a good sound man as to religion but his wife was a silly little fool."

"Really?" Elizabeth said, trying not to sound offended on Poppy's behalf.

"I'll say nothing against her kitchen skills, she understood them. In fact, she didn't have a cook. The last one had left and she was doing his job."

"Oh?"

"Only temporarily of course."

"Of course."

"And it kept her away from the books which was all to the good. What business does a woman have with reading, answer me that?"

"Er…she can read the Gospels for herself."

"Well the Gospels…yes. But not wicked books full of lies and phantasies like that shocking thing the Morte d'Arthur."

"Hmm." Elizabeth enjoyed chivalrous romance, though she always found it very funny that there were only three possible women: the young and beautiful maiden, the lady of the house, the wicked crone. "I'm wondering did anyone else see the strangers before they did the murder?"

"Och, aye," said Lady Hume. "They had quarts of beer at the alehouse and asked the way to the manse."

"And how was the murder discovered? With Poppy ridden off in a panic?"

"Hmf. In a panic. Ay. He wisnae found until yesterday morning, when the boys came to the school and found him on the floor and blood and brain all over the place."

"What about the servants? Surely they saw the body?"

"Ay. well, they were trying to save money. They only had a woman coming in to help Poppy and the rest of the men were working on the estate."

"How about the tithes. Were they paid?" Elizabeth knew how bitterly arguments over tithes could work in a village.

"Ay they were, though usually in kind, ye follow, naebody has much money here."

"So Poppy and Jamie Burn would be alone in the evening?"

"Ay. They invited me to dinner a few times and ithers of their friends but they were allus pawing at each other, kissing and cuddling and the like. Disgusting, it was."

"And James Burn's body lay where it fell until the next morning?"

"Ay. Shocking."

"Could I talk to the schoolboys who made the discovery?"

Lady Hume shrugged. "If ye want, though they'll likely tell ye a pack of lies."

Elizabeth smiled at that. According to Robin, lies were often more informative than the truth.

"What did the boys do?"

"They ran for the nearest dad and told him and he ran in from the field and saw and sent one of them off on a pony to tell me."

"So they didn't hit anyone else for his plate cupboard?"

Lady Hume shook her head. It was now getting too dark to see, despite the glow from the brick range with its door open. "I came out as soon as I could. I saw the body with half the head nearby and the blood and I tried to find Mrs Burn but I couldna and so I went and found Jock Crosby, who was there cutting back the hazels, and Sim Routledge to take the corpse into the crypt of the church. Then I turned out the women to clear the blood from everywhere. There was something not quite right about that."

Elizabeth could imagine it and how the women must have disliked being called from their own work to deal with such horror. "I was still looking for Mrs Burn but then I saw that Prince was missing from the stable and that was when I knew she betrayed her husband."

Elizabeth got up to light a taper which made the wrinkled planes of Lady Hume's face even stronger. "That's what you learn from that kind of nonsense in books, you mark my words," she added.

"Goodness," said Elizabeth, working hard not to sound sarcastic. "And why did she do it? After all she now has nothing since the living was settled on the minister and she doesn't have much for a jointure and the babe on the way. I'm not certain she has anything at jointure. At least I have five hundred pounds a year when Sir Henry dies." When I'm old and grey at forty and Robin will have gone off and married money by then as he ought to do and as every one of his friends, including me, has advised him to do.

"She was in love with one of the strangers," said Lady Hume with a straight face.

"Really? How do you know?"

Lady Hume's face tilted up slightly. "It's the only explanation for why she did it, is it no'?"

"Lady Hume, this is fascinating. If you know she was in love with one of the strangers, then you know his name and where he might be found."

"I do not."

"I think you do," said Elizabeth, thoroughly annoyed with the old lady now. "I think you know a great deal more about this killing than you say. Either that or you are allowing romantic phantasy to run away with you."

"I?"

"Yes, Lady Hume. If you have a reason for thinking that Mrs Burn knew the strangers, then say what it is—it may help us to find them. If your only reason is that you dislike Mrs Burn, then, with respect ma'am, that is not enough." Though it might be enough for a Scottish jury of men.

Lady Hume glared at Elizabeth and then rose with final dignity. "Good night, Lady Widdrington, I am going tae my bed. Thank ye for the supper."

Elizabeth rose and curtseyed to her and watched her as she went out and to the hall where the smart stair used each of the walls in turn as support. So much for charming her like a bird out of a tree, Elizabeth thought, that's put her against me and Poppy as well.

Although it was cold in the rest of the house and still quite warm in the kitchen, Elizabeth felt too restless to sit there and too wide awake to go to bed yet. She slid the crock of mixed porridge into the warmer, ready for the morning, and put the curfew over the coals. She picked up the taper and went back to

the parlour with its odd-looking tiles bare of rushes. It was still
damp in places. She tried again to imagine what had happened....

The strangers come to the manse and Jamie invites them
in. He goes to unlock the plate cupboard and while his back
is turned, they kill him. Poppy says she was out of the room
because she went to fetch the wine and wafers, so she might
have come in later, perhaps after she heard the body slump to
the floor. She is raped. Then the two of them leave, mount up
and ride away. Later two good horses turn up south in Tully's
keeping with West March brands on them, so the men must
have come from the Debateable Land or possibly Carlisle. If
the horses are theirs.

And then nothing happens. Poppy is riding desperately south
on Prince; they have no live-in servants, no children, no relatives.
A very peculiar household, in fact. Poppy had told Elizabeth
how lonely she sometimes was in the evenings when Jamie was
riding around his large parish, and Elizabeth had advised that
she should certainly bring in a woman to keep her company.
She said she did, one of the boys' mothers usually.

Had she perhaps found a friend, someone who could comfort
her? It wouldn't be easy in a place where everyone knew everyone
else and their business, but Elizabeth supposed it could be done.
She had never tried it but it was possible.

So her lover comes with a friend of his and cuts off Jamie's
head. One of them rapes her, they leave, and Poppy rides about
forty miles to her friend Elizabeth in England, without even a
cloak against the wet. Why?

She had made soused herring for their supper and taken
trouble over it. Why would you do that if your husband was
about to be killed and you knew it?

There was another room downstairs—James' large study—
which Elizabeth hadn't looked in yet. She went to it, carrying
the taper, and found the door locked. She checked for a key but
there wasn't one. Infuriated, she pushed it hard and then put the
taper on the table and went out the kitchen door and round the
house to see if there was another way in. That part of the manse

joined onto the church alehouse in the higgledy-piggledy way of old church architecture. If there was another door into the study, it was through the alehouse and at nearly midnight, it was locked and there was no one in the place to let her in. The village was as quiet and dead as a doornail.

She went back into the house through the kitchen and as she passed into the hall and went toward the stairs to go to bed, someone hit her with a piece of wood.

It cracked across the side of her skull and made stars cartwheel round the place, she went sideways and almost down and glimpsed white linen, thought briefly about ghosts, then grappled the very solid though small attacker. She was used to being hit; she wasn't as shocked by it as someone who wasn't. She twisted the arm up the back and managed to take the bit of wood away, although it had broken when it connected with her. The taper was still alight on the table and then she realised that it was an old face and white straggly hair plaited for sleep.

"Lady Hume?" she asked in astonishment.

"Ye'll no' get me again, ye wilna, ye bastard…Lady Widdrington?"

"Jesu, ma'am, why did you hit me?"

"I didna."

"What?"

"I hit a reiver that was sneaking in the house. What are ye doing here?"

"You hit me with a piece of firewood and…" She felt her ear which had taken some of the blow though her cap had protected it a little."…crushed my ear." She shook her head to try and clear it. "What were you thinking, ma'am?"

"It was a reiver."

"No," said Elizabeth, "it was me. I was coming upstairs to go to bed. Are you quite well, ma'am?"

"Oh." Lady Hume's eyes had cleared. "Perhaps I was dreaming."

"Yes." She let go of the old woman's arm and picked up the bit of firewood that had broken. "If I come to bed upstairs, will you knife me?"

"I don't know what you're talking about."

Elizabeth rubbed her ear and blinked at Lady Hume. "Do you remember me?" she asked, "Lady Widdrington? Mrs Burn's friend?"

"Of course I do. Now the reiver's gone, will ye come ben to bed?"

Elizabeth was too tired and still muzzy from the blow to work out what was going on. She picked up the taper, gestured for Lady Hume to go in front of her and followed, feeling a headache on its way.

There were four bedrooms upstairs and Lady Hume gestured to one where there were rushes on the floor and hangings on the wall to try to do something about the perennial chill from the stone. Really, thought Elizabeth abstractedly, you needed to put in paneling to get it to warm up a little. Sir Henry had required careful manoevring to get paneling installed in the main bedroom at Widdrington castle, but it had been worth it.

There was a four-poster bed and a truckle under it as well, a jordan, and a couple of clothes chests and a table covered with clutter that Elizabeth couldn't identify in the darkness. Lady Hume went and used the jordan and then sat on the bed and watched her every move like a little bird while Elizabeth got ready for bed.

Despite the freezing cold, she took her gown and riding habit off because she wasn't prepared to go to bed fully clothed for a second night running. She draped them on a clothes chest because Lady Hume's clothes were on all the available hooks, dropped her petticoats, bumroll, and stays and left her stockings on because they were warm knitted ones. She shivered in her shift and started to pull the truckle bed out.

"Get in wi' me," ordered Lady Hume. "There's a hole in the truckle's mattress and it's aye cold."

There was indeed a hole in the truckle's mattress, and it was indeed cold. But Elizabeth hesitated. She didn't mind sharing a bed, what she minded was being hit on the head with firewood by an old lady.

"Get in," said Lady Hume. "That reiver's gone and he's hurt my wrist forebye." She held out her wrist and Elizabeth saw that she had grabbed it tighter than she thought and there would be bruises in the morning. Well, she'd been stunned. "I'll see to him if he comes back, hinny. Ye're safe wi' me."

Jesu, thought Elizabeth, I'm too tired and muzzy-headed for this. So she smiled and climbed in next to Lady Hume, who immediately curled onto her side.

"Now curl into mah back to keep me warm there," said the old lady. "Dinna kick, dinna wriggle, dinna talk, and we'll hae a story to help ye sleep. Would ye like a story?"

"Ah…"

"Ay, I'll tell ye of when I wis a girl and it wis all different, eh?"

Lying curled into the old lady's back with her ear throbbing and her headache setting in properly, Elizabeth thought that the last thing she needed was a story. She got one anyway.

Once upon a time, and a very good time it was, there was a little girl called Agnes, which means lamb in the Latin, and she had three brothers called Ralph and Jock and Hughie, ay, Hughie like you, and they played nicely though sometimes Jock and Hughie were rough. Jock and Hughie were boys so they would practise with swords and spears and Agnes had to learn to be a wife so she had to learn huswifery and a little cooking, which she didn't like, and needlework, which she loved. She had a beautiful piece of silk that she was embroidering for an altar front, for it was before the change and churches were pretty places, all fu' wi' pictures ye could make up stories wi'. And they were as happy as could be in their tower and farm with all their surname around them and so they were as happy as birds in a tree, as happy as conies in a meadow. Then Agnes went away to her aunt at the big castle to learn huswifery better and that was sad for then they weren't together anymore and the boys were riders like their father and uncles before them.

And then war came and Agnes rode away with her aunt from Bad King Henry's men, she rode and rode, all day and night she rode for there was no telling which way to go, and all you could see was the smoke by day and the fire by night and she didna know what had happened to Ralph and Jock and Hughie nor any of her family, for Bad King Henry's men were burning and killing all the way up the Merse to Edinburgh, the Rough Wooing they called it, for it was to get the little Queen to marry the little Prince Edward.

And one day Agnes was in a wood and she had been riding and riding with her aunt's people and the men around her frightened, and she fell asleep for she was very tired and when she woke up she was all alone. That was frightening for she didna ken which way to go, didna ken even which way was north nor she had no horse neither for her palfrey had wandered off. She wandered for a while and so she came on a pavilion and in the pavilion was a sleeping knight wearing white samite and gold. She went away from there and found a man shooting arrows at a target in a red coat. She went away from there to a cave and the King of Elfland came to her. He was in disguise, of course, as an English archer and he treated her gently enough and he was kind to her and he gave her a beautiful collar of gold with emeralds and sapphires in it and showed her the way back to her aunt and…

At that point Lady Hume started snoring, leaving Elizabeth wondering just how gently the King of Elfland in disguise as an English archer had treated her in fact. It took her a while to go to sleep, with not being accustomed to sleeping with anyone else since she usually took the truckle bed when Sir Henry was home so she wouldn't accidentally bump him in the night and hurt his gouty leg.

sunday morning 15th october 1592

Elizabeth woke before dawn as she usually did, lay for a while listening to Lady Hume's snores and wondering why she had no woman with her. You'd expect at least one to help her with dressing and undressing and to do necessary things like emptying the jordan. It seemed the Lady Hume had come from whatever she was doing, straight to Wendron without even stopping to change her clothes. That was odd as well.

She got up into the freezing dawn, used the pot and wiped her face with a napkin from the cupboard, then she dressed herself in her old riding habit again and put on her riding boots before kneeling to pray as she always did.

It always took a lot of effort now to bring her mind to God. It was as if her mind was a tent and outside it was Sir Robert Carey, in a sportive mood, poking his head between the tent's walls and smiling at her with that wonderful smile of his, that curled up on either side and had a little bit of danger in it for salt.

She sighed and brought her mind back to the Lord's Prayer again. Forgive us our trespasses as we forgive those who trespass against us. She always tried to forgive Sir Henry for the way he treated her since he had a right to do it as he'd told her many times.…But he did it without justice, that's what made her angry. She tried to smooth out the anger, pat it down, but there it was living inside her and making her feel contempt for her husband. She knew that was wrong. She may not love him, and indeed she didn't, but she should respect him as her lord. She could respect

Robin, despite his love of finery, which kept beggaring him, and despite his tendency to come up with crazy dangerous schemes that could get him killed in dozens of different ways.…The way he kept finding excuses to come north to see her, for instance, despite the fact that Sir Henry hated his guts even before he had any idea that Elizabeth had lost her heart to the man. That crazy wager of his a few years ago, when Carey had seemingly bet everyone at Court that he could walk to Berwick from London in ten days and had done it with a day to spare by running some of the way where the road was good—he did that so he could come upon her unexpectedly while she was dealing with the very stinkiest part of the flax harvest and…For a moment she thought about how near an escape that had been for her virtue. The lord he had riding behind him to make sure he didn't get on a horse had kept tactfully back at a distance. And she had been so surprised and pleased and flattered at how Robin had come to her, she had let him kiss her and been utterly overwhelmed by the…the happiness of being kissed. The utter pure joy of it.

She sighed again. And lead us not into temptation but deliver us from evil. That was the line from the Lord's Prayer she always had trouble with, and for good reason. Robin Carey was temptation personified. Robin Carey was every married old man's fear. She wanted to be tempted by him.

She finished her prayers while Lady Hume still snored and went out into the dawn to see what needed doing. It was Sunday but there was no minister to give the church service so she supposed that would go by the board. For instance, would the Burns want some kind of funeral feast? If they did she had no idea how she could provide it without a trip to Berwick to get supplies and more money than she'd brought for the journey.

Jock Burn was there, practising a veney with a young lad who was enthusiastic but rotten at swordplay. He stopped and had a drink when he saw her and pulled his cap off a bit.

"Good day, Mr Burn," she said, as always promoting him above his proper rank which was goodman. Robin had taught her that as a quick and cheap way of flattering people.

"Ay missus," he said, "m'lady."

"I was wondering about the funeral meats," she said without preamble. "Would your family be wanting to go to Berwick…?"

"Ay," he said, with a broad smile, "we thocht of that last night and my little brother Jemmy and his son Archie and some of our cousins went out the night to…ah…to find some sheep."

She glared at him in annoyance. "From our ain herds," added Jock, "our ain herds and…And our friends' herds…"

"I hope," she said freezingly, "that you weren't planning a raid into the East March of England."

"Nay, nay," he said hurriedly, "ainly the Middle March…ah. Where our friends live, ye follow?"

"Well, I hope, if your friends miss any beasts, that you'll pay for them."

"Och aye, we will, missus. Sir John Forster'll see us right."

"Hmf." She didn't doubt that the deeply corrupt and ancient Middle March Warden would want paying; she was thinking of the families that owned the herds.

She thought about that and although it was probably too late, she went over to the alehouse and found Young Henry out in the front on the village green with the targets, practising archery.

"We should send a message to John Carey and Sir John Forster, the Burns are out looking for funeral meats."

Henry looked annoyed. "I should have thought of that," he said. "I haven't got a man to send but I'll find a boy."

"So should I," Elizabeth agreed. "I think Forster in the Middle March is more urgent."

Young Henry nodded, handed his bow to a cousin and went into the alehouse. Elizabeth went to enquire among the women about beer and found they only brewed for themselves and their families and none of them could supply anything like enough for a funeral. She went back to the manse and up the stairs and found Lady Hume sitting on the bed, ordering a village girl around.

"Child, I want ye to fetch me water in that bowl and while ye're at it, take the jordan and swill it out and come back quick for to bring me my breakfast,"

"I'll bring that," said Elizabeth pleasantly. "I need to talk to you, my lady."

"Och aye, and who're ye?"

"Lady Elizabeth Widdrington, ma'am. We met yesterday and shared a bed last night."

"Oh."

"I'm not sure about beer but there's some hot porridge in the warmer."

"Ay," said the old lady with dignity, "that's a' I ever have is porridge or toast if the bread's old."

Porridge it was, with the last heel of the loaf, and the crock of butter and some mild ale that Elizabeth had begged from the girl's mother who was cleaning downstairs. The hot coals in the brick range had been hot enough to bring the fire back and there was quite a sharp fire in there now, enough to fry bacon if there had been bacon to fry.

By the time Lady Hume had eaten her breakfast with Elizabeth keeping her company, they had agreed that the funeral could not be held without baked meats nor beer and that Elizabeth would take one of the cousins and go to Berwick in search of beer—which was plentiful there, thank the Lord. That meant the funeral would be tomorrow. Lady Hume recommended a brewer called Atchison in Berwick, whom Elizabeth had never heard of. As for money, she went to Jock Burn who was now playing a veney with another black-haired, grey-eyed man who looked remarkably like himself and doing rather better, while a nice-looking young man watched carefully.

"Ay," said Jock. "Ah wis wondering about beer and I'd think kindly of ye if ye'd see to it, my lady." He reached in his purse and brought out two English pounds and some Scotch shillings which made Elizabeth frown because she knew so much money could only have come from blackrent.

There were still some Burns coming in and Robsons and Pringles as well, so she estimated she'd need a cartload of beer at least. She found a Widdrington cousin by the name of Humphrey

Fenwick and he agreed to come with her to Berwick. She saddled and bridled Rat herself and mounted up.

"Will ye fetch marchpane fra Berwick too?" said Lady Hume, coming out into the stableyard. "And I've found her store of raisins o'the sun and dried plums fra last year and I'll make a cake wi' them but I've nae marchpane for a cover."

Elizabeth nodded. "I'll try, ma'am," she said. "I'll go to Sixsmith and see if he's got some."

"Ay, he's good. Or Johnstone?"

Elizabeth said nothing. There was no confectioner in Berwick called Johnstone, although she thought there had been one long ago. She walked her horse out of the yard and joined up with Humphrey, waved to Jock who waved back, and put her heels in.

saturday 14th to sunday 15th october 1592

The bell had rung at two in the morning and they had gone out half an hour later with the trod. Dodd carried the lance with the burning turf on it and Red Sandy behind him with the other men, including three of the Southerners who could ride well enough. It wasn't raining for a wonder and they had caught up with the running herds on the edge of the Bewcastle waste and had a running fight of it all the way to Kershopefoot where the Elliots and English Armstrongs had broken for Liddesdale, leaving most of their booty.

So all in all it was quite a successful night with some nice kine and sheep to choose Warden fees from and nobody had taken any hurt except for Bangtail who had managed to twist his ankle somehow and the Courtier was getting much better at letting his hobby choose his own pace and just going with it. The Earl of Essex' men were still stiff-backed, though, and seemed to get very tired as the night went on. Carey was happy as they sorted out the herd on the hills and took them back to their owners—for a wonder, most of the beasts were branded and identifiable—but as they came back toward Carlisle he seemed to lose his bounce again and become morose. Now Dodd wouldn't have been surprised at, say, Ill-Willit Daniel Nixon being in a bad temper, but, really, the Courtier should have been happy at the way the night had gone.

He had bags under his eyes as well and now he thought about it, Carey had been in a bad mood for over a week. Was he missing

London and the South? Was he missing his lady-love Elizabeth Widdrington? Was he missing pretty doublets and hose? What the devil was wrong with him?

As they returned the last of the sheep to some Carletons and took their fees on to Carlisle, Dodd dropped the last bits of turf off his lance and hurried his horse up to Carey's. The man was swinging along and didn't look sick. He had the loose-backed look of a proper reiver. If it wasn't for the plain anonymous stitching on his jack and his fancy chased and half-gilded morion helmet, you couldn't tell the difference, really, especially as his goatee beard was getting a bit overgrown.

Being late in the year, the Sun was only just up, and in fact it was a nice day. You couldn't complain at the weather; the Moon had been at half but the skies had been clear and they'd had plenty of light…

Maybe it was Carey's creditors again? He'd managed to pay the men for September with what he'd brought with them from the South, and as far as Dodd knew, his tab wasn't too heroic at Bessie's. Had he been gambling at cards? But Carey was the best player in Carlisle; if he had, he'd likely be happy. Was he bored?

Was it some problem with his ugly Scottish servant Hughie Tyndale or that skinny boy John Tovey he had acquired as a clerk? Or with Philadelphia, his sister, who was tired of the north and talking about going south again to serve the Queen at Court once more. The Queen had sent her a letter, what had been in it?

So when they clattered through the town and up to the castle yard, Dodd stuck by Carey. They penned their fees in the enclosure for the purpose and then there was what looked like a great confusion of men dismounting and leading horses into their stalls and untacking them and rubbing them down. It wasn't, it was highly organised because Carey had ended the habit the men had of leaving their horses to the care of the boys. Each man took care of his own horse and there were nosebags and buckets of water there in the yard ready, on Carey's insistence that your hobby was in fact more important than you were, and harder to replace, and you had better see him or her fed, watered, untacked, wiped down and comfortable before you went to breakfast, or he would want to know why. The southerners had moaned about it for a bit but they got no sympathy and Dodd had given one of them a kicking to make the point. The habit had spread to all the men of the Castle guard because the hobbies went better and didn't go lame so often.

Oddly enough, Carey did exactly the same as the men though of course he could have used one of the boys running about with feedbuckets. Dodd stood in the next stall with a whisp of hay, rubbing down his horse, a big lad called Patch while Carey did the same thing with his usual hobby whom he had named Sorrel.

The movements were the same, but there was something still very wrong with Carey. Dodd realised what it was when he found himself whistling "The Three Witches" between his teeth and realised that Carey wasn't singing, humming, or whistling anything, not even one of those irritating Court tunes he liked so well.

Dodd was shocked enough to stop rubbing Patch's big black and white whithers and peer over his horse at the Courtier. Carey had given Sorrel a swift wipe-down while he munched, was just now checking the hooves as he always did and after a stern look around the stall, picked his helmet off the manger and walked out into the yard again. Dodd finished up quickly and followed him.

Carey stood for a while, watching what was going on in the stableyard. Young Hutchin Graham was now in charge of the boys, by dint of fighting and beating the boy who had been doing it before, and his soprano yell rang out at once when a hobby took a bite at the one next to him.

"Ye're soft, ye are," sneered Hutchin to the small lad there. "D'ye no' ken Twice and Blackie are at feud, eh? Go on, take Twice down th'ither end o' the yard."

Andy Nixon looked abashed as well and went with his horse.

Carey nodded once and continued across the yard and down the passageway to Bessie's, where the breakfasts would be hot and waiting—bacon, sausage, black pudding, onions, sippets, eggs. Bessie could hear the bell as well as anyone in Carlisle and knew to get ready for when they came back.

Dodd followed him, trying to look as if he was just going the same way into Bessie's very loud commonroom, which was already full of men filling their stomachs. Dodd got himself a trencher, served himself from the dishes laid out on the tables, and sat opposite Carey where he could keep an eye on him without being too obvious about it.

Now that was odd. Carey had taken black pudding, onions, and eggs, but no sausages and no bacon. And it was Bessie's bacon, which was more in the nature of fried collops and smoked in the large chimney. There were half a dozen flanks and haunches hanging there now, getting ready for Christmas.

Dodd put his head down and started to eat into his pile of food because his belly was cleaving to his backbone and he was starved. Once he'd taken the edge off his hunger with a few sausages—not so good these, from the butcher and not of Bessie's making; she probably hadn't done her sausages yet—and three large slices of bacon and the fried sippets of bread he liked so well, he took a glance at Carey's trencher and saw that the eggs and onions had gone but the black pudding was still there. Why? What was wrong with it? He tried some and it was fine. And no lovely golden crispy chunks of stale bread fried in the bacon fat for sippets either; what was wrong with the Courtier? The three Southerners were sitting at the next table with the other ones that couldn't ride properly yet and Dodd could hear them boasting about what they had done while they powered through their breakfasts.

However Carey was on his second quart of beer and sitting back. While Dodd watched, he beckoned one of the potboys, said something quiet to him. The boy came back with a small horn cup of something Dodd would swear was aqua vitae and Carey knocked it back with an odd swilling motion then drank more beer.

Dodd cleared his plate and leaned back himself to drink beer and keep an eye on Carey. Everybody else was in a good mood, shouting at each other, paying bets they had made on how many sheep there would be or similar, twitting Bangtail for twisting his ankle when he was running after a calf that had gone up the side of a hill. Not Carey. Carey was staring into space and pulling a sour expression with his mouth sideways.

Dodd was on the point of asking the man what was wrong, when he scowled and stood up, stalked out of Bessie's and away up through the orchard to the castle. Dodd thought of going after him, but then decided to finish up Carey's black pudding for him.

"What's up wi' the Courtier?" asked his brother, Red Sandy, who had taken seconds of the sausages since no one else was finishing them. "He's gey grumpy."

"Ay," said Sim's Will Croser, who usually said very little. "He damned my eyes when we was fighting the Armstrongs and I knocked him accidentally and then he said nathing all the way home."

"He's been like it for a week," said Bessie's Andrew Storey, "like me mam sometimes, says nothing and then shouts at ye for nothing."

"Ten days," put in Bangtail, "after ye came back from the Southland, Sergeant."

Dodd nodded. "Ah dinna ken but ye're right," he said. "He wisnae so quiet on the road back fra London and Oxford town. He was in a good mood."

Dodd had been in a good mood himself. Carey, Dodd, and the two new servants had arrived in the late afternoon, down the road from Newcastle with a couple of extra lads on horseback with the dispatches to help out if someone thought it worthwhile to take the Grahams up on their offer of ten pounds for Carey's head. It wasn't worth taking more, despite the Borders being in a tickle state, what with the Earl of Bothwell still hanging around and the Maxwells and Johnstones at each other's throats again. If you needed more, what you needed was an army and it was better to be inconspicuous. Carey kept his flashy morion in his saddle bag, wrapped up and just wore an old-fashioned velvet hat.

The Earl of Essex' quondam soldiers were on the way but they were walking and would take longer. Eight had already gone to John Carey in Berwick and the remaining eight could shape up or die in Carlisle. And little Kat Leman had been left with Lord Hunsdon's household after Dodd had had a serious word with her to explain what it was like in the North and how hard it was for small maids. She had looked at him grimly, with her little face set.

"I want to stay with you," she insisted. "Could I come and be your maidservant in your tower in Gilling?"

"Gilsland," Dodd had corrected her automatically, and he'd thought about it. There were a few girls around the place, relatives of Janet's, so it wasn't half as impossible as Carlisle castle.

"Mebbe," he'd admitted, "that's possible. But ye're still too young for huswifery and my wife can be rough with the girls." Kat had nodded. "In a year or two, perhaps, when ye've grown a bit. All right, Kat? Stay wi' my Lord Hunsdon's household, he'll see ye right and then in a few years when ye're grown a bit, ye can write tae me."

Her face had screwed up at that. "I don't know how," she said. "That's priest's work."

"Ye can learn," Dodd told her. "And be a good girl for the Steward's wife."

Kat nodded, her face very serious. "I like my Lord Hunsdon," she said decidedly, "even though he shouts. He told Mrs Leigham to get me some new duds and these are wool and nice and warm." She looked proudly at her cut down old blue kirtle and the different coloured sleeves. "I'll do what you say, Sergeant Dodd, and I'll see you in a few years."

He had left her with a slight feeling of uneasiness. Why was she so determined to come to Carlisle with him? Perhaps a few years in Hunsdon's enormous household would convince her to stay in the South. He hoped so. By the time they got to Newcastle he had put her to the back of his mind.

The Courtier seemed to be in funds again, which was all to the good. He had apparently played primero with the merchants of Oxford on their last night, and begged all of them, although Dodd knew better than to think that the money would last. He had already spent a horrible amount on secondhand doublets for Essex' deserters to replace their tattered and impractical tangerine and white.

Carey hadn't sent anyone ahead and so the first the garrison knew about their arrival was when they clopped through the gate of the city and two of Lowther's bad bargains had called out to them. A boy was sent running up to the castle to tell Lady Scrope and they had carried on up English street and past Bessie's, up the covered passage, and into the castleyard itself. Dodd had felt very self-conscious in his fancy wool suit, which wasn't as fancy as the previous wool suit he had lost, but fancy enough since it wasn't homespun like everybody else's. Hardly anyone in Carlisle had anything like it. Thomas the Merchant Hetherington wore black brocade and the headmen of the big surnames would have their finery from Edinburgh, maybe a few of the merchants or the mayor would have something like it.

"Where's ma brother, and whit have ye done wi' him?" demanded Red Sandy with a fake scowl. He'd come hurrying into the yard almost before Dodd had dismounted and there was the usual commotion and fuss with the horses.

"Ah killt him and left him in a ditch," said Dodd dryly, because he did feel a completely different man from the one who had ridden South some weeks before.

"I know that's a lie, ye musta poisoned him," said Sandy and clapped Dodd on the back. "Who did ye kill for the clothes, brother? Ye look like the mayor."

"I'm no' as broad as him, and the man give me the clothes nice as ye like and I didna even ask him," Dodd said, which was true because his fine new duds had been Hunsdon's under-steward's and the man had been perfectly willing to give them up in exchange for a new suit from Hunsdon. That made the other men laugh, though, as they crowded round him and they were all asking the usual questions about London such as: Was it as big as they said? And did Londoners have tails like Frenchmen?

Dodd allowed as how London was far bigger than it had any business to be and no, as far as he could tell, Londoners didn't have tails like Frenchmen, though their hose were so fat they might. Certainly the women didn't.

"Ay, I told you," said Bangtail knowingly.

Carey's sister had come running from the sausage-making and he'd embraced her and swung her round as he always did. Scrope wasn't there; he'd gone hunting and Philadelphia was furious with him for some reason, possibly connected to Madam Hetherington's bawdy house.

Bessie's Andrew was the one who told Dodd about the mysterious package that had arrived by way of the carter from York a few days before. They went in a body to Dodd's cubbyhole next to the door of the barracks and found it sitting on the bed—which someone, probably Janet, had seen to having the sheets changed. There it sat with the label on it in Dodd's handwriting which only Sim's Will had been able to read. Red Sandy had been too young to go to the Reverend Gilpin and then there had been the feud with the Elliots so he never got the chance to learn to read.

Dodd looked at the package and remembered sending it and felt utterly estranged from the man who had done that, and he almost couldn't think what was in it—his homespun doublet and breeches, to be sure, dyed dark red with madder by Janet, the breeches made of wool from a black sheep so they didn't need dying and wouldn't run in the wet either. And the hat.

He batted the men back from the package and started undoing the painstaking hessian wrappings and lifted the wicker lid to find his doublet there. He unpacked his clothes from round the hat and then unwrapped the linen folds from around it and held it up.

"This is for Janet," he said, thinking how Barnabus had told him she'd forgive him anything when she had a hat like that and wondering if it was true. Not that he planned to tell her some of the things that had happened in London, but still.

There was a silence from the men. They may never have been south of Carlisle in their lives but you could see the London fashion almost glowing in that hat: dark green, high crowned, and with a long pheasant's feather in it. It looked as out of place there as Carey; more so because at his roots, Carey was in fact a Berwick man. That hat was all London.

"Och," said Bangtail, "what did ye pay for it?"

"Ye ken the infield at Gilsland?"

"Ay."

"More than ye'd pay for that."

"Twenty shillings?"

"Twenty-five shillings."

More silence. Come to think of it, he wasn't quite sure why he had done it now, especially as he had lost the rest of the bribe shortly after. But the Queen had made that up to him and more. He wasn't going to mention that, though, until he had talked to Janet about it.

"Er...where did ye rob sae much cash from?" Red Sandy asked tactfully.

"I didna," said Dodd. "It was a bribe, fair and square."

The men looked at each other. "A bribe?" squeaked Bessie's Andrew. "Who did ye have to kill for it?"

"I didna. It was what they call a sweetener. There's sae much money in London, it just flows around. The serving maids have velvet ribbons to their sleeves and golden pins to their hair. The serving men wear brocade some of them, secondhand, but rich as Thomas the Merchant's. Ye have no idea...There's a street called Cheapside where they have shops with great plates and goblets and bowls of gold and siller in the windows and nought but a couple of bullyboys and some bars to keep them."

The men were exchanging looks again.

"The Bridge...the Bridge has got shops full of silks and velvets....The armourers, oh, the armourers..." Dodd felt overwhelmed at the task of telling them what he had seen in the South. "They have armourers that sell nought but swords and some that sell guns and ay, they cost a lot but..."

"Where's London exactly?" asked Bangtail, with the slitty-eyed look of a Graham with a plan.

"Hundreds of miles south. Three hundred at least." Dodd smiled at him. "D'ye think I didna think what you're thinking now, how could I raid it?"

Bangtail nodded and so did Red Sandy. "It's a long way," said Bessie's Andrew, "and wi' the cattle to drive…"

"Cattle, sheep, all out in the fields with naebody bar a boy to keep them," Dodd amplified. "Ah've thought and thought and I canna think how to bring the loot back. Go there, ay, get it—ay, though they've Trained Bands in London. But bring it back—that's yer problem."

More silence as seven highly honed reivers' brains considered the problem of bringing your loot all the way from London with the hot trod after you.

"Anyway, I bought it and I'm fer Gilsland tomorrow to give it to Janet…"

"Nae need, brother, she's in town."

Dodd had waited right there by the hat while someone went to fetch Janet, his heart suddenly beating hard and fast. He heard her voice in the doorway.

"What are ye doing, Bangtail? I've no need to check the bed, I changed it last week and I'll thank ye…"

Red Sandy ceremonially opened the little door and Dodd stood up and there she was, in her second-best homespun kirtle, coloured dark green with moss and nothing like the London fashions, and her shift open at the top and her cap and old hat over her blazing red Armstrong hair. She paused as if she didn't know him.

"Henry Dodd, is that you?" she asked, looking him up and down as if they were at a harvest dinner and he was asking would she like to dance.

"Ay, wife, it's me."

"Well, look at ye," she said with a slow smile. "Look at ye," and she gave him a nice curtsey. Not to be outdone he did a bow which was getting better, he knew, and then he stepped one step across the narrow floor and grabbed her and held her.

"Och Janet," he heard himself say. "Ah missed ye," which was true, he had, worse than he would ever have believed he could miss his woman. She had been there in his imagination but now that he was holding her tight, he knew the difference.

"Well, Henry…" she started and he stopped her mouth with his and Bangtail ceremoniously shut the door on them and Red Sandy sat down next to it to make sure nobody barged in on them.

They were lying in a breathless heap on the bed when Janet said, "What's that?" and pointed at the linen-wrapped item they had somehow moved to the floor and then somebody had put a pair of breeches over the top of. Dodd retrieved his breeches and put them on again, while Janet had less to do, she only needed to do her stays up at the top again and rearrange her petticoats.

Suddenly Dodd felt worried and embarrassed at his extravagance. Surely she would prefer the money to the hat, to buy a field with, but then he remembered he had got most of his bribe back, less the forged coins, and it was still a substantial sum as you reckoned things in the North. But still. Would she like it? Maybe he could sell it to Lady Scrope if she didn't, though the colour was wrong for my lady.

Janet was up off the bed and picking it up. She looked narrow-eyed at Dodd and when he nodded gravely, she started unwinding the linen. Before she'd finished unwrapping it he had decided she wouldn't like it and would call him a fool and his mouth turned down.

The glory of London fashion glowed in the tiny room, smaller in fact than the inside of the four-poster bed Dodd had slept in down in London. In silence Janet put it carefully on the bed and folded up the linen wrapping, then she lifted it up and held it out at arm's length.

"For me?" she asked, in a thunderstruck voice. "From… you, Henry?"

"Ay, Ah'm sorry, it cost a lot but I looked at it down in London and I thought, that'll look fine on Janet to go to church, that green on your red hair, that'll look finer than all the fine ladies down in London and their powders and paints and their gowns, and so I bought it." That wasn't exactly what had happened, but it was indeed how he had thought. "Barnabus helped," he added, lamely, though the man was dead and couldn't call him out, "I didn't want to at first because of the cost of it and then…"

He couldn't speak anymore and he saw something glittering in her eyes before they reeled backwards onto the bed again and the hat was nearly crushed.

Outside Red Sandy tipped his head at the closed door. "Is Sergeant Dodd no' finished yet?" Bessie's Andrew was saying. "Ah wanted tae ask him about Blackie…"

"Ye've no style at all," said Red Sandy, "Get oot of it, the man's back fra London and discussing matters wi' his wife and ye want tae bother him about a hobby?"

Bessie's Andrew looked bewildered for a moment and then looked sly. "Och," he said, "Is he no' finished yet?"

Both of them listened. "No," said Red Sandy, raising his voice slightly. "Ah think he's still busy."

Bessie's Andrew was standing there like a lummock with his mouth slightly open.

"Oot!" said Red Sandy and he went, while Red Sandy went back to his whittling on a bit of firewood.

After the hat had been rescued and dusted off, Dodd watched while Janet tried it on in front of the piece of mirror she had found. She wasn't a woman who liked fripperies and yet there she was, tilting it one way and then the other to see which looked better.

"Ye like it?" Dodd was surprised. What Barnabus had said looked like it was true. "Even though it cost twenty-five shillings?"

She shook her head and grinned. "Well," she said, "I'd like it more if ye'd reived it o' course, but I like it fine as it is. What else did ye get down South? A pot o' gold?"

Was now the time to tell her or should he keep it quiet still? It was a serious business and changed everything and nothing.

"Ay, I did. In a way."

She sat down next to him on the bed. "Och, what?"

He thought he should tell her the story of how he came by it and then he thought it would be simpler to tell her after, and so he reached in his smart wool doublet front and pulled out a leather packet, opened it, and took out the legal document. Gilsland had come to him from her after Will the Tod, her father, had acquired the leasehold in a mysterious way from the Carletons. Come to him—but he was a tenant-at-will, who owed rent. Or he had been.

"What's this?" Janet asked. "I can read the letters but not the words."

She was an amazing woman, he thought, learning to read and all. "Nay, nor can I. It's in Latin. See that word there, it's "dedo" which means "I give.""

"And who gives what?" she was frowning now.

"Gilsland. That paper there is the deed to Gilsland. I...we own it now, freehold. There's ma name in Latin, see, Henricius Doddus."

It suddenly struck him that he could even vote in an election for parliament now, or better still sell his vote to the highest bidder. Janet was staring at him, open-mouthed.

"We already own Gilsland..."

"Ay, but no' legally. We're tenants, we should pay rent." She paused and then nodded slowly. "Tae the Earl of Cumberland, ay?"

"Ay. I think ma dad paid him something in the seventies."

"Now we don't owe rent. We own it. We could sell it, we could...mortgage it, we can pass it to our children. The Courtier tellt me it doesnae matter so much now but when the old Queen dies and James of Scotland comes in, it could matter a lot that we own it."

She looked down at it and spotted the signatures. The Earl of Cumberland's scrawl was there and next to it the graceful sweeping tropes of the Queen's signature.

"The Queen gave you this, Henry?"

"Ay," he said, thinking of the Queen's red hair and snapping black eyes and how he hadn't known who she was. "I met her twice and the second time she give me that."

"But why, Henry? Why would she do that? You haven't got the money…"

"Och no, I saved her life…" he explained. "It's a wee bit complicated but there was a petard under her coach and I pit the fuse out."

She took a sudden breath. "You put the fuse out?"

"Ay, it was lit and a' and I cut the coal off the match with ma iron cap and emptied the chamber o' powder and so it was all right."

Suddenly her arms were round him so tight he could hardly breathe. "Jesu, Henry!"

"Ay, what of it, Janet?"

"You could have been blown to pieces."

"Ay, but I wasn't. And she gi' me that."

He didn't understand why she had tears in her eyes for something in the past that hadn't happened anyway, but he liked it when she held him too tight so he let her.

"Och dinna fret Janet, it coulda happened any time, oot on the Border or in a tower or something, and me nae better for it after than a bit of a Warden's fee."

She laughed then and folded the paper up again and put it in the leather pouch and gave it back to him with her colour high in her cheeks.

"We'll keep that safe and tell nae one."

"Ay, I think so too. Though the Courtier says it has to be entered in the rolls and he'll see tae it."

They looked at each other for a while. "Ye went down South my ain Henry Dodd, Land Sergeant of Gilsland, but what have ye come back as," said Janet slowly, "Is it a lord, mebbe, wi' all the fancy foreign people ye know."

"Sir Henry Dodd," said Dodd and laughed at the sound of it. Janet didn't laugh, though.

"Could be ye'll end as that, ay."

"Och come on, Janet, the sea will a' run dry and the land turn tae haggis before that'll come aboot."

She was doing something to him that he liked while she was busy with her other hand, unlacing her bodice. Now her kirtle came off with a heave and she had to leave off while she undid the strings of her petticoats and then again with her stays and her shift under that and there she was in all her pale, freckled glory with her cap off and the London hat perched sideways again on her red curls. Dodd took in a deep breath at the sight. He'd imagined it often enough down in London but this was much better because he could smell that smell of warm woman and he could cup her breasts and take a taste and listen to the fast beating of her heart and start counting her freckles again. He never counted more than twenty of them because he always got distracted. Dodd was tired but not too tired and for a miracle the hat survived the next ten minutes as well, making it a three-times lucky hat, only slightly dented from the pillow.

Outside Red Sandy shook his head and grinned and wished he'd had a bet about it with Bangtail. That was a wonder and all, the way miserable Henry was still as smitten with Janet as he had been as a young man and she was working for her dowry in the castle. It was hard to know why there wasn't a whole string of sons and daughters considering they'd been married nearly ten years.

sunday 15th october 1592

Elizabeth drove a hard bargain with the brewsters of Berwick and with Mr Sixsmith the confectioner as well, and came back to Wendron with not one but two wagons of beer, albeit the second wagon was mainly mild, and a couple of pounds of marchpane.

She came back as the dusk came down on the Merse and found Lady Hume tired but triumphant with two large cakes cast in barrel hoops and proving in the kitchen of the manse, waiting to be baked. The village baker had agreed to fire his oven twice that night so long as someone else paid for the wood, which the Robsons had agreed to do after some discussion with Jock Burn and so the faggots were being fed into the oven and the flames leaping high.

The two beer wagons were greeted with cheers and cheeky orders for gallons of the double beer, and so Elizabeth instructed the drivers to bring them both into the stableyard of the manse where they only just fitted. She set all four of the Widdrington cousins to guard the beer in watches during the night.

There was one fine bullock already butchered and being colloped by the cooking fires of the Burns and several sheep on the way to the same fate. She glowered at Jock Burn who told her they had been bought and paid for from some Routledges, which was obviously a lie. Nobody ever paid the Routledges.

She found another elderly woman in the house with Lady Hume who turned out to be her tiring woman, a stout person called Kat Ridley, who beamed at Elizabeth as she came into the kitchen of the manse.

"Will ye like to see the funeral cakes go in, my lady?" she asked and Elizabeth, tired from the ride back from Berwick and from the long arguments she'd had with the four main brewsters of Berwick, suppressed a sigh and agreed she would.

They smelled good with the winey smell of dough and she helped Kat carry them over on their slates to the baker who opened his oven ceremoniously and slid them in on his long spade, to sit side by side.

"She ay had a good time wi' the kneading and the pulling," said Kat confidentially to Elizabeth as Lady Hume watched the cakes going in with an odd expression on her face.

"Good," said Elizabeth, wondering why Lady Hume was being spoken of as if she was a child. Lady Hume didn't seem to notice.

"She'll sleep well the night. Did ye have any trouble wi' her last night? She tellt me ye shared."

"Ah…well she hit me with a piece of firewood."

"Ay, she does that. She's very afeared o' reivers, poor soul."

"And she told me a story about the King of Elfland in disguise as an English archer."

"Ay. Ye ken, she's well enough i' the day, but nights trouble her sorely. I was afeared maself when I found she'd gone from Norwood yesterday morning and not told a soul where."

"I see."

"I thocht she'd gone over to Hume castle and sent a boy over there and then when he came back wi'out news of her, well, I was mithered all day, I dinna mind telling you."

"Of course."

"But then I heard that the minister was killt and o' course I knew where she was then and come over as fast as I could this morning. I dinna ken how she knew the minister was dead…"

"Didn't a boy come out to her?"

"Nay, I dinna think so. But o' course when she knew, she had tae come."

"Why?"

"She's a Burn herself, Ralph o' the Coates' auntie, I think. It's family."

"Ah. Is that why she doesn't like Poppy Burn?"

There was a kind of twitch of Kat's broad face there. "Ay, in a way," she allowed and then closed her mouth firmly.

Shaking her head, Elizabeth saw the oven door closed up properly with bits of dough which would fall off when the cakes were likely to be baked and agreed that the baking of the funeral cakes was thirsty work and worthy of some of the beer. She brought a firkin of the mild over herself rather than allowing anybody near the beer and causing a riot.

She tried some and found it was well enough but would be sour in a couple of days, which explained the excellent price she had got it for. Never mind. If there was anything left of the beer by evening tomorrow, she would be extremely surprised.

They sat in silence for a while around the kitchen range with the door part open, the three of them, Lady Hume who was nodding off, Kat Ridley who was knitting a sock on four needles, and Elizabeth who was tired herself but couldn't go to sleep. In all the hurry and business of getting the funeral beer, she had forgotten the oddity of the killing and now it had come back to her redoubled. Also she was in no haste to go to bed since she would no doubt be sharing with Kat as well as Lady Hume.

"I'm puzzled," she said slowly at last, on the grounds that asking was probably the simplest way of going about it, "how did Lady Hume know that the minister was dead before anyone else did?"

"Ay," said Kat Ridley, "it's a wonder. Ah wisna there; I was taking the linen down to Goody Robson before dawn and there was a big load of it. Last time we can dry anything outside this year, I shouldn't wonder…"

Elizabeth nodded. She'd taken a cartload of linen to her washerwoman two days before Poppy arrived, shirts and shifts and caps and underbreeks, quite apart from all the sheets to the good beds and pillowcases and cloths for the dairy and the wet larder. She thought of Poppy's bloodstained shift and petticoat in the linen bag and wondered when they'd be able to launder it. She'd put it in some cold water as soon as she got home to start taking the set stains out of it.

"I left her at the needlework in the solar with a candle till the Sun rose and she was happy enough for she allus is when she's making something with her needle. Ye should see what she makes, all bright colours and strange figures, and she never uses a pattern. It's some hangings for Young Hughie's bed and she only has one more curtain to make. She has stories on them, she's a wonder for the stories."

"Yes, she told me a story last night after she hit me with the firewood."

"Yes. She gets confused at night. Not in daylight, but when the light goes she often thinks she's a girl again and lost in the woods with the English army after her."

"How old is young Lord Hughie?"

"He's ten. He's a quiet boy, very well-looking. He likes reading ye ken and the minister was tutoring him twice a week for Latin too. He's clever. He said he wishes he wasn't a lord and it was the old days so he could go to university at St Andrews like the minister."

Lord, how did that happen with Hume blood? Elizabeth wondered. "And his parents are dead?"

"Ay, poor wean. He never knew his mother, for she died to give him light, and his dad died of a quartan ague about three years ago so that was hard for him. There's an uncle at Court, but the land goes to Hughie first. The wardship is with Lord Spynie now, who thinks the world of him, he says, but her ladyship willna let the boy go to Court, not even to his uncle."

Elizabeth nodded tactfully at this. "He's far too young," she said. "I wouldn't send him myself."

"The minister liked the boy and the boy liked him. I think he may come to the funeral tomorrow if Cousin William allows it."

"Cousin William?"

"A byblow of Lord Hume of Wendron, he acts as steward and he's good at it."

"So you left her at her needlework in the early morning to take the washing down to the washerwomen...?"

"Ay and I left it wi' them and came back after they'd started in on boiling it, down by the river, ye ken, where the water's clear, and there she was, gone. Naebody had seen her go for they were all busy except she'd taken the boy's horse."

"What did the groom say?"

Kat looked a little uncomfortable. "Well he's no' too strong i'the head is Jimmy and he just said her ladyship had come tae him before the Sun was up, must have been as soon as I went, and he'd saddled the horse as she bade him and helped her to the saddle and then she was off. She's a good rider. She still goes hunting sometimes with Lord Hughie and Cousin William."

"Without a woman to see to her?"

Kat shrugged. "Well there's only young Fran and Cissy and the girls in the dairy, and none o' them can ride better than a sack o'meal so I see why she didna take one, and she allus forgets what happens at night."

For a moment Elizabeth had a strange thought of Lady Hume being the murderer and then dismissed it. How could she have handled a sword like that, to cut the man's head in two? It would explain the plate cupboard, though.

Elizabeth shook her head. Lady Hume could not have wielded a sword like that; Elizabeth couldn't herself. She was strong enough, perhaps, but it was a matter of skill that took years to grow.

Robin Carey of course, could have... She thought of him once, in the garden at Court in the Armada year, in his fine black-worked shirt and breeches and boots, showing off to her his skills with a sword, playing a veney with George Clifford, the Earl of Cumberland, and then playing tricks with his rapier like lunging through a thrown apple and slicing a hanging bread roll. Putting his head back and laughing with delight at her admiration and...

"When did she ride off to Wendron?" she asked, automatically crushing the memory because the pleasure it gave her hurt so much.

"The morning after the minister died." said Kat.

The man's body was lying unburied in his own parlour and his wife had fled. Who had come to Lady Hume to tell her?

"Was there anyone new at the castle, anyone you didn't know?"

Kat shook her head. "Only of course I dinna ken who may have come after I left with the wagon."

A piece of wood in the fire broke and settled with a shower of sparks and Lady Hume suddenly woke up. "Oh," she said, looking hard at Elizabeth, "who are ye?"

"Lady Elizabeth Widdrington, ma'am. Would you like to get to bed now?"

"I'll get yer spiced wine, m'lady, will ye go up wi' her ladyship?"

"Oh Kat, there you are, I wis having the dream again."

"Ay, but it's only a dream. Only a dream, my lady."

"Ay but…" The old lady looked about the kitchen at the shadows. "Who's outed the light, then?"

"Ay, the Sun's gone down a while now. We'll get ye to bed…"

"I'll make the spiced wine," said Elizabeth quietly. "You take her ladyship to bed. I don't want to get hit on the head again."

"I've brung it in ma work bag down there, in a flask, it's a syrop wine water, all ye need to do is mix it wi' the red wine and the aqua vitae, half and half."

"I'll manage. Do you have any?"

"I'll share with her ladyship."

Lady Hume went upstairs to bed with Kat, holding her arm and asking querulously where the light had gone, while Elizabeth bustled about the kitchen, cleaned a goblet she found on the table. and used a chafing dish to warm the spice syrup on the hottest part of the range.

There was a man standing by the entrance, looking at her oddly. For just a second she wondered about ghosts and then she realised it was only one of the Burn cousins. She hadn't seen him before.

"Good evening," she said to him forbiddingly, "can I help you?"

"Jock tellt me to come and see if ye needed anything. He's right happy about the beer."

"So am I. Please thank Mr Burn and tell him I think we're well enough now."

"I'll be guarding the door in case anyone thinks of trying it on, missus. And the beer of course."

"Hm, yes. I already have two cousins of mine supposed to be guarding that."

For a second he looked nonplussed. Elizabeth took the spice syrup off the heat, wiped her hands in her apron, and walked out the door ahead of the man.

"Who are you?"

"I'm Archie Burn," he said, with a knowing grin, pulling his cap off, "yer servant, ma'am."

"Come with me, Archie." She walked round to the back of the stableyard where there was a gate, and found nobody there. Nearby round a corner, however, she saw a little campfire and a couple of figures who seemed to be drunk. At least one of them was singing tunelessly.

She shut her eyes and struggled for a second. She was tired, her ear was sore from last night, she had spent the entire day going to and coming from Berwick to get the beer, and now, in a village full of reivers who were no doubt at that moment advancing from all sides on the beer, the men she had asked to guard the gate were drunk and blatantly not guarding it.

Her temper snapped. She could almost hear it. She marched over to the campfire where one man was lying down and the other man was sitting giggling over some incomprehensible drunken story and she kicked him in the bollocks as hard as she could. She then turned on the other one who was trying to get to his feet and kicked him in the face so he went over again.

She lit a torch at the fire and then she went to the two precious wagons and found that the barrel she had tapped for herself and the other women had mysteriously gone missing and she thought she heard a suspicious noise as if someone was scurrying away as fast as they could from the other wagon. "Young Henry Widdrington," she bellowed, "get out here."

She checked all the others and found none tapped and none of the ropes loose, went back to the other wagon to find at least one other barrel loose and a third with the ropes cut.

The one she'd kicked in the face was on his feet, wambling toward her with a knife in his fist while the other one was still lying on his side nursing his cods. Which only went to prove, she thought, where men kept their brains.

Archie Burn was grinning by the gate and drew his sword as she was looking at him and the firelight went up and down the blade and made the waterings in the metal beautiful. However she was too annoyed to let him deal with Hector Widdrington, who was coming toward her with blood going down his face and a knife.

She unknotted her apron and flapped it in the air in front of him so he flinched and paused and swayed. Then she put it over his head and punched him several times somewhere so he went down again tangled up in her apron and dropped the knife since he was drunk. She picked it up and waited for him to fight free of the apron and let him see she had it. He paused and then looked around at Archie Burn and Jock Burn and Daniel Widdrington and Young Henry Widdrington, who had all come to the sound of fighting. Jock was laughing so much he had to hold onto the gate of a stall with tears of laughter rolling down his face.

"Get them out of here," she snarled. "I never want to see either one of the useless lunks again, that means you, Hector, and you, Sim, as well."

Sim still had hold of his cods but was on his feet. Then he was sick down his jerkin, which made Jock hoot even more and even Young Henry crack a smile.

"Out!" she shrieked and pulled her now dirty apron off Hector as he struggled to his feet and kicked him in the arse so he landed on his face in some manure from the carthorses. Sim broke into an unsteady run out of the gate, followed a moment later by Hector. She went after them at a fast walk and closed it with a loud slam and barred it.

Archie and Young Henry put their swords away and tried to stop grinning. Jock was starting to calm down again with "ahoo" noises. There was the ugly sound of him blowing his nose onto the ground for want of any such thing as a handkerchief.

"I did not spend the whole day getting beer for the funeral to have it drunk by Hector and Sim Widdrington," she said icily to Young Henry. He looked contrite, as well he should since it was his fault he had put the two of them on to guard.

"Ay, my lady," said Young Henry, "I'll see it's safe."

She turned on Jock Burn. "And you can find the barrel that's gone missing," she said to him.

"Och, we haven't got it…" he started.

"It's yer ain beer," she shouted at him. "I bought it with your money for your nephew's funeral, who's lying in the crypt with half his head off. He's no kin of mine, I don't care if his funeral has nathing to drink but I thought that at least ye might."

She folded her arms and stared him down. "Ay, missus," he said, "ay. We'll find it, though it'll likely be empty."

They agreed on three watches of four men each, mixed Burns and Widdringtons so they could keep an eye on each other as well as the beer. Elizabeth waited until the watches were set and the barrels tied down again and then stalked back into the house where she found Kat just finishing with the spiced wine. She was carefully filling three silver goblets with the mixture.

"The men were at the booze, nae doot," said Kat. "Is there any left?"

"Ay there is," said Elizabeth, "we only lost a barrel."

"That's a mercy," said Kat. She emptied the chafing dish of coals into the main part of the range and piled them up and put the curfew on. Then she took the stems of the two goblets while Elizabeth took the stem of the third goblet and followed her upstairs into the main bedroom where Lady Hume was tucked up in bed in her shift already and her clothes hung on one of the hooks on the wall. She looked fragile and little as she sat up and took the goblet, warming her knotted hands on it and sipping the hot wine-water. Kat sat beside her and took several sips before putting down the goblet.

"So the King of Elfland came to ye, did he?" she said encouragingly.

The little bird nodded and took a bigger sip. "Ay, he did. He was disguised as an English archer, so first I was affeared of him for they were bad men, all of them. He was disguised with brown hair and blue eyes and he was a big strong man with a big chest and big strong arms and he said, 'Dinna be afraid, I'll not hurt you.'"

And he showed her his big bow, as big as himself it was, and she had a try at pulling it but she couldna budge it o' course, for it was a magic bow and the King of Elfland was the only man i'the world that could string it. Then he strung it and he said to her, "Will ye come to my kingdom with me?" And she was all dirty with running through the woods so she said, "I'm ashamed to come to your kingdom," and he took out his pack and gave her a beautiful collar, a necklace of gold with emeralds and sapphires, fit for the Queen of Elfland herself and so she put that on and didna feel so bad. And then he pit her on his horse and he rode behind her through the terrible dark woods where terrible dark deeds were being done and he took her to Elfland where there are great round houses with pillars of gold and garnets and lapis lazuli and tourmaline and cat's-eye, like in the story of Tam Lin. And there he took out his other stringed instrument for he was a harper as well, and he played to her all night long, beautiful music he played to her…

The little bird had snuggled down under the covers with her head on the pillow and her hand under her cheek and she slept. Elizabeth and Kat's eyes met and then Kat stood up and started undoing her kirtle.

They peacefully helped each other to undress, which speeded the process considerably.

"I'll drink my wine now," said Kat."It's got a spot of laudanum in it to help her rest but she willna drink it if I dinna keep her company." And she drank down the lukewarm spiced wine, got into bed next to Lady Hume and went to sleep.

Elizabeth left hers on the table and went downstairs again with the taper. She didn't have keys to the place, but she pushed the kitchen table against the back door and barred the main door from the inside. Then she went wearily upstairs again, thought about taking off and washing her stockings which were beginning to smell but didn't have the energy for heating the water to start with and picked up the goblet of spiced wine-water to drink.

And stopped dead. She lifted the goblet up and looked at it carefully. Yes. It was Poppy's. So were the other two.

She lifted the quilt and checked in the bed, then looked under it and saw a nicely washed and scoured jordan, blessings upon you, Kat, and next to it the beautiful silver bowl that Poppy had from her mother and was most of her dowry.

So the plate cupboard hadn't been raided by the murderers. On the other hand, that meant it should have been closed and locked and if anyone wanted the contents they would have had to break it open. So the plate cupboard had been opened by Jamie and then even after he was killed, the murderers hadn't bothered with the plate.

She looked at the goblets again—they were nicely made with roses and lilies chased around them, probably from an Edinburgh silversmith. Perhaps Lady Hume had found them in the plate cupboard and put them upstairs for safekeeping and then forgotten about it. She drank only half of the wine-water because she didn't like the thick-headedness you got from laudanum, climbed into bed on the other side of Lady Hume and fell asleep with Hector and Sim Widdrington and the goblets whirling round her head.

monday 16th october 1592

Around eight in the morning the tooth-drawer came back into the village on his little pony from Edinburgh where he was starting to get a good reputation although he had only been there a day this time. He tethered his pony in the yard and went into the commonroom of the alehouse, finding it a great deal more full with people than he had ever known.

"So it's true," he said to Tim, "Minister Burn was killed. I came back when I heard."

"Mr Anricks, I'm glad to see ye. Were there no teeth to be drawn in Edinburgh?"

"Hundreds, possibly thousands, but there are also barber surgeons there who don't like competition. What happened here?"

"Well, ye wouldna credit it, but the minister was killt stone dead wi' his head chopped off not an hour after ye left…"

Mr Anricks was a good listener and sat seriously while everyone vied to give him the story which everyone else had heard. There had been two strangers in the village, that was certain, or perhaps there were three, oh no, that included him and you're no stranger, Mr Anricks. The minister had his brainpan sliced for him probably in the afternoon but no one was sure because his wife had disappeared, though the word was she had ridden all the way to Widdrington and was there now. He had been found in the morning by Lady Hume who had come avisiting and been taken into the crypt and wrapped in his shroud and the house cleaned up a bit by some of the village women and then

Lady Widdrington had arrived too. And the Burns were coming in, so they knew, and some of the Pringles and Routledges...

He listened, he nodded and he agreed with the storyteller. Whatever the story, no matter how wild the story—there were several who were convinced it was his wife that did the job or helped in it somehow—he agreed with the storyteller.

The strangers were the favourites, though, especially as there were two horses apparently found in the South with West March brands on them, just left to take their own way home.

"My lady, could we sing for the minister's funeral?"

Lady Widdrington looked around and down and found a boy standing there, twisting his cap in his hands, with two others behind him. The boy talking to her had red hair and freckles. All three of them had red-rimmed eyes and blotchy faces.

"What?"

"Only we're the boys from his school," said the boy. "He was teachin' us oor letters and numbers, like the Reverend Gilpin did him, and now he's deid and we willna learn them at a' nor be ministers like him and...and..."

"We wantae sing for him," said another boy. "We wantae make a song tae the Lord..."

"And warn 'em in heaven, there's a Burn on his way..."

"...ay, and so everyone can see what we wis learnin' and that we learnt it gude."

"Will ye let us, yer ladyship?"

The red-haired lad had tears rolling down his face and the brown-haired boy behind him had his face screwed up. The black-haired boy was gripping his fists together until the knuckles showed white.

"How many of you are there?" she asked.

"There's twelve on us, ladyship, like the Apostles," said the black-haired boy.

"But we're the eldest so we came to ye."

"What are your names?"

The red-headed lad ducked his head. "I'm Cuddy Trotter, he's Andy Hume, and that's Piers Dixon."

"Come with me."

She led the way into the parlour of the manse and the boys looked sideways at each other and the black-haired boy who was a Hume said, "Can we no' go intae his study, ma'am? That's where he taught us."

"I'm sorry, boys, the study is locked and I haven't the key."

They looked at each other, looked down. Piers Dixon started to speak, "Ay, but…"

"Och," said Cuddy Trotter.

"Where's his lady, ma'am?" asked Andy Hume.

"Mrs Burn is at Widdrington in the English East March and I hope she's staying in bed and resting so she doesn't have her babe too soon."

All three of them nodded solemnly. "Ay," said Cuddy, "the minister was right proud o' that…"

"Do you have a key, or know where the key is? For otherwise I shall have to ask some of the men to break the door because I need to know if the minister left a will."

"Ay, he did, ma'am," said Piers. "He made it last month and he got Cousin William and Tim at the alehouse to witness it forebye, so it's as legal as can be."

"Oh, did he?"

There was a certain amount of elbowing and looks exchanged.

"Do you know of a key?"

"In a manner of speaking," said Cuddy. "Here, I'll show ye."

He went across the hall to the door of the study and he took his knife out. Then he jiggled it in the lock until the old-fashioned levers moved and the door opened.

Lady Widdrington went first into the study and found it neatly arranged as a schoolroom with three benches and a teacher's lectern pushed to one side, a clerk's desk at the other side, a chair with arms, and a whole wall of books. There was a pile of papers on the clerk's desk, an inkpot, and several pens. The window was locked shut. She sat at the clerk's desk, opened the drawer and there was Jamie Burn's last will and testament staring up at her. She picked it up, folded it in three and put it in the inner pocket of her kirtle.

"Did the minister always lock his study when he went out of it?" she asked.

Andy nodded vigorously. "Always, even if he went out to the jakes."

"Did he know how easy it was to pick the lock?"

"Ehmm…he might of," offered Piers.

"What do you mean?"

"Well, we used tae steal books, ye see, fra his bookshelf. We'd allus bring 'em back 'cos he said they were too hard for us tae read…"

"…which they weren't…"

"…and Andy said it was all a joke 'cos the books changed, the ones we could reach…"

"I've brung the one back I wis reading," said Cuddy dolefully. "It's in Scots about a' Greek gods and that."

He brought a worn copy of an Ovid from under his shirt, wiped it off ineffectually with his sleeve and then went solemnly to the shelf and put it back.

"Ay, he said he wis a minister and couldnae let us read pagans like Ovid…"

"Or Loo-creesh-us…"

"But there they wis on the shelf and he never noticed even if we took a big thick book…"

"…and he'd ask us aboot 'em and laugh when Piers knew the answers…"

"Ay, ye're soft, ye are…"

"He wanted us tae steal 'em…"

"So long as we brung 'em back."

"I didn't once, because I liked it, it was *Holinshed's Chronicles* and it was so exciting…"

"And he said some wicked puck had gone and ta'en it and we'd best tell the fairies tae bring it back cos he needed it for a sermon…"

"And when we did we found there was a book aboot Scots history and so we took that…"

"So he wanted us to steal 'em, didn't he, ma'am?" finished Andy. "Didn't he?"

Elizabeth was trying not to laugh. How did you get the sons of reivers to read books? Well, you told them they couldn't have them and let nature take its course.

"I think so,"

"Told you!"

"Ay, Cuddy, all yer worriting for naething…"

"Did he never beat you?"

"Beat us?" Cuddy looked bewildered. "Why would he?"

"He beat my brother Sim for pissing on a Bible for a bet," said Piers Dixon. "But nae more'n that."

"Ay, he were right to do that. It weren't Papist superstition either, it were wickedness because a Bible's expensive and it wouldnae burst into flames if ye pissed on it, which was a lot of super-steeshious nonsense and Sim should be ashamed of hisself," explained Andy seriously.

"It made my dad laugh," said Piers. "He didn't laugh so loud when he had to pay for a new Bible, he were furious, said ye could still use the old one when once ye'd got it dried out—and the minister wouldn't have it."

"Ay," said Andy, "and Sim got another leathering fra his dad for that."

"Ay," said Piers, "so did I."

"Why?"

"Cos I didnae stop him, o' course."

"So can we sing for him?" Cuddy asked. "We know lots of psalms, we allus sang 'em first and we did reading from them too."

"Can you show me?"

The boys looked at each other. "Just us?"

"Well, can you get the others together?"

They looked at each other again. "Ay, we can. Gi' us a while, missus, we'll run and fetch 'em."

She waited in the study and only half an hour later, eleven breathless boys, ranging in age from eleven down to seven formed up in front of her by the benches.

"We havenae Lord Hughie because he's at Norwood so we're eleven."

"Like the Apostles."

"Ay, after the Crucifixion, when Judas'd done 'imself in, the coward…"

"Will we sing for ye now, missus."

"Who'll gi' the note, wi'out the minister?" asked Piers Dixon in a panic.

"I will," said Andy Hume firmly. "I'm no' as good as him, but it'll have to do."

There was a while of whispering while they thrashed out which ones they would sing and then Andy Hume hummed three notes and they began.

One boy there was clearly tone deaf and droned away, the rest had clear, true voices improved by training. Elizabeth was almost more impressed that the boy who couldn't sing had been allowed to go on singing with them, than she was by the others.

They sang of the rivers of Babylon and they sang the "Lord is my shepherd" and by the end of it, Elizabeth's eyes had filled and overflowed.

The boys stood and fidgeted and elbowed each other. "Are ye a'right, missus?" asked Cuddy, very concerned.

"Ladyship…" hissed Andy.

"Missus ladyship, are ye hurting?"

Elizabeth blew her nose. "That was beautiful, boys," she said inadequately, "and I'm sad about the minister too, so…"

"Mebbe we shouldna sing if it makes people sadder," said Cuddy anxiously.

"You should," Elizabeth told him, "it helps the sadness to come out, like draining a sore. And why shouldn't we be weeping at Jamie Burn's funeral? He was a good man and we'll miss him."

"Ay," said Andy, "that's the right of it! D'ye ken who it was did it, ladyship?"

"No," she admitted, "do you?"

"It were the strangers, the two men naebody knew," said Cuddy. "I wish I'd known what they were at when I seen 'em. I'd mind 'em and I'd kill 'em too."

"Ay," said Andy Hume, "ay, we a' will if ye can just find who they were. We'll ride oot wi' our families and kill 'em stone deid, so we will."

There were soprano growls and promises of vengeance from every one of the boys and the second-youngest started crying again.

"Dinna greet," said Andy roughly, "ye'll stuff yer nose up and willna be able to sing,"

"I only know ma letters, I dinna ken the putting together o' them..." choked the boy, "how'll I learn that?"

"Och, shut it," said Piers, punching him lightly. "It's no' sae hard, once ye know the letters, I'll tell ye."

"Ay, or me," said Andy Hume, "it's whit the minister would'a wanted."

Elizabeth asked each boy what he had seen on the day before yesterday. They had had a usual school day, with the two eldest beginning some Latin grammar and the rest learning to read and write. Yes, they had begun with psalms, they always did, and they ended with a prayer. And then the two strangers had come.

The boys could not agree about the strangers. They were dark-haired, they were light-haired, they were wide, they were short, they were tall, they had the look of Grahams or Armstrongs or Maxwells or Johnstones or Fenwicks...No, they weren't wearing jacks, just ordinary homespun, dyed brown and blue like anybody's father might wear. No, they didn't have spears or dags or nothing, only both had swords, of course. No, not one boy could tell what the swords had been like. One was older, one was younger, that was all they could say. They spoke Scots, like anyone else. No, neither of them had a finger missing or anything useful like that. They were just men. They'd said they were printers from Edinburgh.

"Did they have inky hands?"

"Eh?"

"Were their hands stained? I never knew a printer that didn't have his hands black with ink."

The boys thought, argued a bit and agreed. No, the strangers' hands had been normal, no ink.

Had the minister known them? Cuddy and Andy wrinkled their brows at that. Piers thought carefully. "I think he did," he said, "or he knew of them. He bowed a little to them and invited them into the house. We were going fishing so we went off with oor fishing rods and a basket and he didn't say, good luck boys, but we didn't notice, we just went. Down to the stream, missus, where it hooks round and ye can get salmon sometimes."

"Yeah," said Cuddy, "but we couldna fish there that day, for Mrs Burn was there with Sissy and Mary and me mam to do the linen and the sheets and so we had to go off to the ither place that isn't sae good and none of us catched anything."

"Oh. And did you tell Mrs Burn anything?"

"Ay missus, we told her there were two printers from Edinburgh come to see her husband and she told me mam to take over for a little and finish wringing them out and dry them on the bushes ready for the next day and she went off to see them."

"Oh really. How did she look? Was she frightened?"

Both Cuddy and Andy were scowling. "Not frightened, but she looked excited. Ye ken? As if something good was happening? She hurried up away from the stream to the manse and she was straightening her cap while she went."

"Hm. So do you think she knew who the men were?"

"Nay, ladyship, but I think she knew about them, if ye follow. It wasnae the surprise to her, two strangers in the village."

Elizabeth nodded and wished again that Poppy Burn had stayed in the village and sent for her instead, so that she could ask her about this.

"All right. So what happened after that?"

"After, missus?"

It had been a day like any other. They had gone home with long faces and no fish for the table, and Cuddy's mam had left the linen on the bushes overnight for she didn't think there'd be too bad a dew and the weather looked set fair and come home and done their usual nighttime porridge with some bits of carrot in it, Cuddy hated that, and Cuddy had milked the goats though there wasn't a lot there and then his mam had told him a story and he'd gone to sleep. His dad? Oh his dad was out guarding the Hume flocks and their own animals. "It's the raiding season, missus, ye ken?" She did, though not being born to it as these children were, it wasn't part of her normal assumptions. But all over the Border, most of the men were out in the pasture guarding the animals that were too far away to bring in or that they didn't have enough fodder for.

At some time in the afternoon, Poppy Burn had saddled and bridled her husband's hobby and ridden off on him on the Great North Road, heading south, and had been rained on.

"What about the next day?"

"Ay, well, me mam was in a bad mood for it rained in the night when she said it wouldn't, and so she couldna bring in the linen and she went to speak to Mrs Burn about it early and that's when my Lady Hume tellt her the minister was dead and his wife had run away."

That flatly contradicted what Lady Hume had said about the boys discovering the body.

She couldn't get any kind of story from the youngest, a thin lad of about seven, called Jimmy Tait. He simply cried steadily until the snot was dribbling down his face and Elizabeth gave him her handkerchief because she couldn't stand it. He balled it up and continued to cry and so she left it for the moment.

She sent them all off home to clean their faces and in two cases to put some shoes or clogs on and told them to be back when the bell started tolling. She had asked a minister to come from Berwick but he had refused on the grounds that it was the Scotch kirk and they were all heathens anyway. And all the pastors she knew in Scotland were in Edinburgh, which was too far away.

The smells of spit-roasting meat were crossing the village green which was thickly camped upon. Elizabeth went out through the main door and crossed the little yard there to look out across the green. Her precious wagonloads of beer were still secure in the stableyard and she nodded at the large cousin Daniel Widdrington who was guarding the gate. He touched his cap to her respectfully and she knew that the story of her beating of Sim and Ekie had already started growing. She was annoyed with herself for losing her temper, but there again, what else was she supposed to do? Allow the beer to be pillaged? She didn't think so.

Lady Hume's two large funeral cakes were being borne back from the baker's, half the lads from the school were following the two big lads carrying each cake. Lady Hume herself was standing there with an apron over her velvet kirtle and she was rubbing her hands in glee. "Och," she said, "we willna bake the marchpane but still it'll be fine, Lady Widdrington. Look, not a bit of it burnt."

Elizabeth investigated the cakes with her knife, they were far too big to turn over and knock on the bottom as she would do with a loaf. They seemed well-cooked—a bread dough with some butter and spices in it and then all the raisins and currants and candied fruit from Poppy's store cupboard to make it sweet.

She went into the kitchen and found that Lady Hume and Kat had been very busy about the marchpane and had even managed to find some red and yellow sanders for colouring. They'd also opened two pots of Poppy's raspberry and blackberry jam and they had formed the coloured marchpane into two astonishing flat designs in the old-fashioned way, all curls and curves that looked like dragons. Kat set about painting some of the heated jam onto the tops of the cakes.

With a palette knife and a bit of wood, Lady Hume gathered up the first of the marchpane lids and popped it on the top, then she did it again, her old fingers light and delicate on the fragile creations, so that the two cakes looked like the illustrations from an old book.

"Why, that looks wonderful, my lady," said Elizabeth.

"Ay, I can allus do marchpane."

She used some of the jam to fill up some openings into the swirls and the cakes needed to rest then. They were a very creditable effort despite the lack of time to bake the paste because that took some careful management of the fire and most of the day.

Elizabeth went back into the minister's study. She was looking for something but not at all sure what it was. He always locked the door though he knew the lock could be picked by the boys, and therefore presumably anyone. What was the point of that? She had checked through the other papers on his desk and found only notes for the next Sunday's sermon. Everything was neat and tidy, nothing out of place. On the shelves was a neat pile of sermons that he had given, beautifully written out in his best italic. That was a little surprising, for he had given those. But they were good sermons: well-founded in Scripture, well-thought through and each with a pithy moral at the end. On that shelf there were a number of books on teaching, some in Latin, including Ascham's original, *The Schoolmaster*, well worn and in English. He was the one who had recommended not beating the boys too much since they seemed to learn better for it. She weighed the book in her hand absentmindedly and then put it in her petticoat pocket to read later. James wouldn't mind if she borrowed it now. Then she went and sat in Jamie's chair, looked about her.

It was annoying because the whole thing refused to hang together. If she was honest with herself, she had pictured herself as like Robin, using her brain to pick through all the tiny fragments of truth in front of her and gradually build up the shape of the whole truth. And that would give her the murderers, she was sure of it. But here she was and she had nothing but odd fragments that might or might not have been truth and no shape whatever.

Her husband would have laughed at her and possibly pinched her somewhere for being presumptuous. As far as he was concerned, she was a woman and women naturally have less sense than men and she should leave such things to the men and get back to her business of running his estate and saving him the cost of a steward. The pinches he gave annoyed her more than his slaps and punches because they were so mean and underhand. And often unexpected still.

She sighed. There was Robin Carey in her imagination, wearing the astonishing clothes he had proudly worn at Court, not the one with the lilies, but the tawny doublet and the black trunk hose with the embroidered and pearl-encrusted black cape off one shoulder, the one that had been pawned the longest because it was worth a blinding amount of money. He had worn the clothes for the portrait he had painted to celebrate his knighthood. Elizabeth didn't think it was a good likeness. He was wearing the massive rope of pearls the Queen had given him across his body—though in fact the pearl rope was half the length it had been because he had sold a lot of them and pawned the rest. It was shrewd of the Queen to give them to him and not money, seeing how helpless he was with the stuff.

He was bowing and smiling at her, as he had in fact. He was the very picture of a confident courtier and a very different creature from the battered man she had said good-bye to at the Scottish Court in summer. She had given him back his ring and their eyes had met and...

Their eyes had met. Their bodies had known their business and kept a distance, but their eyes...

She suddenly put her face in her hands and tried not to sob. There were tears coming from her eyes and trying to push them back did no good at all, it was stupid to cry like this and besides she wasn't one of those delicate Court maidens who could weep a couple of crystal tears and not become a sniffling stuffed-up lump. She was Lady Widdrington and had to make sure the minister's funeral, such as it was, went in a reasonably respectful fashion and...

I want him, she almost wailed, I want him to come to me and put his arms around me and tell me it's all right and he'll take care of it and that he loves me. The constant pain in her heart, deeply buried and numbed though it usually was, sharpened and strengthened. I want him now and I want to ride off with him and stay with him and have his babes and nurse him when he's ill or wounded and laugh with him and eat with him and be with him and...

And I can't have that, said the sensible part of her. I can't have it until Sir Henry is dead and buried and maybe not then, if Robin has any sense and marries money like he should. So I should get used to it and not fret after nonsense.

There was a little paw patting her shoulder. She looked and it was the skinny little boy, Jimmy Tait.

"Och," he said, "I'm sad, too, missus, it's awful sad about the minister. Dinna greet though."

How does he know...? Ah yes, he thinks I'm crying for Jamie Burn. Well, in a way I am, for Poppy's lost a good husband and there aren't enough good men around. She coughed and tried to smile at the boy though it was watery.

"Now Jimmy," she said, "what is it?"

"I come to tell ye I canna sing for the minister's funeral." His face was shut down like a little old man's, no more tears, only a sort of despair.

"Why's that?"

"Me dad don't like it?"

"Really?"

"Ay, he says I shouldnae have been going to the school in the first place and I'm tae stop home and help wi' the goats and turn over the muckheap."

"I'm sorry to hear that, Jimmy. Can I come and speak with him about it?"

"Why? Me mam tried to change his mind and he's knocked her down, he disnae like the minister."

"I'll come anyway. I think Sir Henry Widdrington would have something to say about it if he knocked me down." And he would. Sir Henry Widdrington was the headman of the Widdrington surname and his wife was his property. The only person who could hit her was himself, which she supposed was something.

She had her hobnail boots on which was just as well because the Taits lived in a tiny little wattle-and-daub cottage, half dug into the damp Earth and only three rooms—one for the animals, one for living in, and up a ladder under the roof for sleeping. Compared to some of the turf bothies the people put up after their homes had been burned down again, it was luxurious but only compared with them.

The woman was stirring porridge at the fire in the middle of the living room and had a red wheal down the side of her face. She curtseyed anxiously to Lady Widdrington at the door and showed her to the only chair in the place.

"I wonder if I might speak with Goodman Tait?" Elizabeth asked politely.

"Lily, go fetch yer dad," said her mother. "He's fixing the infield fencing."

A girl in a homespun kirtle and dirty short shirt ran off barefoot without a word. Elizabeth thought about sitting on the rickety chair but decided against it in case she broke it. Also it was no doubt the goodman's chair and she didn't want to offend him.

Tait arrived with a brow of thunder and an older boy trotting behind him. He had a dense black beard and black hair and a truculent expression.

"Ay missus," he said suspiciously.

"It's Lady Widdrington."

"Ay. What of it?"

She looked at him carefully for a moment and abandoned what she had planned to say. She looked down at the boy, Jimmy, who was staring at the ground fixedly.

"I understand you didn't like the minister. May I ask why?"

"He was a two-faced bastard."

"Really?"

"Ay. All the time psalms and prayer wi' the boys, and under it he were a bastard, a reiver like any one of us, though he was always preaching against feuding."

"He was?"

"Ay. Ah'm no' a man that goes runnin' to God every time I have troubles, but I draw the line somewhere. I remember the mermaid queen and her connivin' ways and I remember the fighting to stop them and the French, and I'll no' have a son o' mine warbling psalms and what have ye at his funeral. I'm glad he's deid and I hope he rots in hell like all the other Papists."

"Goodman Tait, this is a very serious matter. Did you think the minister was a Papist?"

Jock Tait's face became cunning. "I caught him at it, didn't I? Him wi' his book and his Latin writing. He didnae hide it, only smiled but it wisnae English, for I learned a little off...off of a friend I had once that went tae the Reverend Gilpin. I know the difference." Odd the way he had gulped when he mentioned the friend who could read.

"Was there anything else?"

"Ay, and that slimy tooth-drawer. Everyone thinks he's so great, but he's a London man and what would a London man want wi' us? We canna pay him what London folks can pay. I think he's a Papist, for sure."

"Tooth-drawer?"

"Mr Anricks drew my tooth for me when it was rotten," said the woman. "He gave me a cloth to sniff and when I went to sleep he did it so quickly it almost didna hurt."

Tait snorted. "Ye see? I paid him and I saw him going off to the manse after, in the dusk, like a Jesuit. Maybe he's a Jesuit? In he went and he stayed an hour or two and then he wis out again and on the road south. I saw it wi' my ain eyes."

"I see."

"So I say good riddance tae him and his letters, I'll not have my sons' brains rotted wi' Jesuit teaching."

"Did you kill the minister, Goodman?"

Tait drew himself up and his fists bunched. "I didna," he said, "though I'm glad he's dead. I wis off wi' my brothers and Jock Burn to see to the horses over by Berwick and I'll get every one o' them to swear for me. So now."

Elizabeth nodded. "Is there anyone else in the village who thinks like you—that has the same opinion of the minister?"

"Ay and he wis a reiver once, a good one, when he was young. I knew him then too. And ay, there are some that know him for what he was."

"Who?"

"Why d'ye want tae know?"

Elizabeth thought fast. "If he was a Papist spy then I should tell my husband Sir Henry Widdrington about it, for he's the Deputy Warden of the East March of England. It could be important."

The jaw and fists unclenched slightly. "Oh ay? Ye dinna disbelieve me?"

"Goodman, I don't know. I don't want to tell my husband a pack of lies and yet if there are Papists hanging around here and Jesuits, he needs to know."

That was true as far as it went, although Sir Henry was as likely to take bribes off the Jesuits as arrest them. But she wanted to know. She didn't think Jamie Burn had really been a Catholic; he seemed far too sincere for that, but if others thought he was a Papist that could account for his murder.

There were two others in the village who apparently weren't fooled by Jamie Burn and Elizabeth got their names. Then she tried another tack.

"Goodman, do you think it's wise for young Jimmy to miss the funeral?"

"Eh?"

"Well, you don't want any of the Papists to realise you've spotted them, do you?"

"What're ye saying, missus…ladyship?"

"Just that it'll make Jimmy stand out a bit, won't it? If he misses the minister's funeral and him being needed to sing?"

There was a slight softening now. "Ay," said his father, "he sings well, does Jimmy."

"It's not as if any Jesuits or Papists could get at him at the funeral. I'll be there and Lady Hume and the young Lord Hume and Jock Burn and all the Burns. But someone might notice he's not there and ask why."

Very slowly Tait nodded. "Ay, ladyship, ye're right. But he disnae have any shoes tae wear for it."

"Does he have a jerkin?"

"He's got mine if he wants?" said the other lad, "and my clogs."

"That'll do."

Jimmy trotted after her proudly, nearly drowned in his elder brother's jerkin and tripping every second step in his clogs.

"I'll hae a pair of clogs when me dad finishes them. He's only whittled the one so far, because I grew out of my baby pair."

"That's good," she said, absentmindedly.

"Ay, and I like me bare feet better, though it's cold in winter. My clogs pinched something terrible and I like to feel the Earth with my toes."

"Hm."

"D'ye think the minister's ghost'll walk, missus? With him being murdered and his murderers not hanged yet?"

"I haven't seen him, Jimmy, and I've slept two nights in the house where it happened."

Jimmy's mouth opened in an 'o' of astonishment and he stopped.

"In the manse?"

"Yes, Jimmy, with Lady Hume and her woman. Where else did you think I was going to sleep?"

"I didna think ye slept."

Elizabeth smiled. "I do."

"Och. So ye havenae seen anything?"

"Nothing at all."

He nodded. "Ye don't think his ghost'll come after his murderers and their helpers, do ye?"

"I don't."

He nodded again. "That's good is that."

"And anyway, they say that his soul's already gone to God."

"Ay, but if he were a Papist then he's gone to hell. Or he knows that's where he's going and he doesnae want to go and so his ghost's walking."

Elizabeth couldn't really think what to say. "I think the funeral will stop any of that nonsense," she said eventually, "and perhaps your singing will help him go to Heaven."

"Nay, lady," said the boy gently, "everybody goes to hell, really, only some o' the pastors don't. I was happy the minister might go to heaven, but if he was a Papist there's no chance."

"Will you go to hell then?"

"Ay, o' course," he said. "The minister said not but mebbe he's a Papist. Was. But all the Borderers go to hell; it's warmer there and better company."

She had nothing to say to that.

It was the baker who told her something about Jamie Burn, one of the two names Tait gave. He was only a part-time baker, firing up his rock and clay oven in his yard about twice a week for those who wanted bread rather than oat bannocks, quite daring and modern. Otherwise he was a farmer like all of them and he had his vegetable garden as well and even a couple of apple trees that were only thirty years old that his father had planted after the fighting. His father was an enterprising man and had laboured to build the oven, but then died of a flux the year before.

"Ay," said Clemmie Pringle, "that's why I know it, from being up in the middle of the night to fire the oven. I'd see things, men going to and from the manse, well huddled up under their cloaks and sometimes men who went into the manse and didn't come out for a couple of days but ye wouldna ken they were there."

They had been careful but of course that had encouraged nosiness and like all villages everyone was starved for news and delighted to chew over the comings and goings at the manse.

"That barber surgeon, Mr Anricks, I seen him go in any number of times coming to and from Edinburgh and London I shouldn't wonder."

"What do you think it's all about?"

"Papists, of course!" And Clemmie crossed himself against the thought.

"There aren't any here, surely?"

"Ay, well, how would ye know seeing how they have to be secret here where the Humes are for the new religion. It's not like the West March where the Maxwell keeps Jesuits in his household and pops a fig to the king except when he comes on a justice raid."

"And you, Mr Pringle, are you a Papist?"

Clemmie crossed himself again and shuddered. "Nay, I'm a' for the Protestants. Who wants priests coming here telling us what to do and praying in Latin where ye dinna ken what they're saying at all? If I could read, I could even read the Bible because it's in Scots."

It would soon be time to wait by the grave for Jamie Burn's corpse; there were three men digging the grave in the old churchyard now, though given the amount of argument over it, it was just as well that the ground was soft from the wet.

Elizabeth wondered what had happened to the linen and after getting directions from Clemmie, she went down there and found the bushes still festooned with it and most of it dry by now. Well Poppy would need her linen so she found two of the women of the village and convinced them to come and help her fold it up and bring it into the manse.

Afterwards, she had to hurry to the church where Jock Burn and three others of the family had a litter and put onto it Jamie's body, wrapped in its shroud. They walked over to the churchyard with it, a good procession of all the people in the village, all the children too, down to the babies in their swaddling clothes raging at the world. Even Clemmie Pringle the baker was there and Jock Tait and the Taits, narrow-eyed and sour-faced, but there. Elizabeth wished Poppy could have seen it.

There were two new people as well who stood next to the Dowager Lady and Kat. One was a ten-year-old boy of outlandish, almost elven beauty, fair hair, and blue eyes. The other was a broad middle-aged man, with brown hair and grey eyes, and a solid look around his mouth with broad sturdy arms and shoulders. They must be Cousin William and Lord Hughie, she thought.

It was Jock who said a few words at the graveside. "Ay well," he said, "ye ken this is my nephew, Jamie Burn. Some of ye ken what he was, when he rode wi' me and his brothers and his cousins and he was a good brave man, though he was young. And then he changed. He went tae the university as a servitor, and he took his degree in Divinity, something no other Burn has done nor will do, quite likely. And then he came back here to be your minister and I hear he did as good a job o' being a minister as he did when he wis reiving Fenwick cattle." There was a subdued snicker from the Burns—clearly a story there. "And somebody came to him two days gone and twinned his body and his head, took his head right off wi' a sword and we dinna ken who it was or we'd do something about it, ay, we would." He paused there and everyone was silent, even the squalling baby. "So…eh…we hereby commit his body to the Earth, dust to dust, ashes to ashes. He's deid and God's got him and there's the end on it."

They took the corpse off the litter and put it in its grave and Jock sprinkled the first spadeful of Earth. The others put more Earth on top.

Elizabeth wished she could have said something about Jamie, about him being a good husband and a good dominie and schoolmaster, about him being a good man whatever he had done in the past. But women didn't speak at church. So she nodded at the boys of the school and they lined up by the grave, pushing and shoving a little. Lord Hughie gravely left his grandam's side and went and stood with the school, who made room for him among the altos. Jimmy Tait was shining and serious in the front.

They sang about the rivers of Babylon, in parts, with Jimmy's voice soaring up the register like a lark and the voices of the other boys turning and twisting in the patterns of the psalms. Then Jimmy started "The Lord's my shepherd" all by himself, only a little sharp from nerves, and the others came in until they were in the House of the Lord together and you could see it in their minds, almost, a good strong defensible bastle with a wall.

Elizabeth had already heard them sing it once so she could look about her and see that rough reivers and Jock himself were crying great tears down their faces, but that Lady Hume had her mouth shut like a trap and a frown of disapproval on her face; others in the village, like Clemmie Pringle and Jock Tait, they were open-mouthed with astonishment at what the boys were doing. At the end of it, Lord Hughie went back to his grandam, who ignored him.

And then as the grave mound was finished and patted smooth with the spades and shovels, Jock Burn hurried back to where the smell of mutton and beef was clear as a bell.

She had arranged with Young Henry to bring the beer out after the body was in the ground, for fear of cunning reivers and also in case anyone disapproved of ale-drinking before the burial, which smacked of Papistry and waking the dead.

They had two trestle tables set up on the green to take the barrels and Jock Burn called Elizabeth over to take the first mug of the mild, seeing as how she'd been defending it all night and her with only an apron to help.

She smiled and laughed, and Sim and Ekie Widdrington were there, with a different set of bruises on their faces, possibly from Young Henry, to apologise for conniving at the theft of one of the barrels and drinking some of it theirselves. Elizabeth listened graciously and said all was well that ended well.

She saw a man standing in the corner by the barrel, drinking from a horn cup of his own and wondered who it was for his black wool doublet and hose were London tailoring, if she was any judge, though from a long time ago. Well she could ask him, so she went over to him and said, "Good day to you, sir, though it's a sad occasion."

He took his old low-crowned hat off to her and made a neat bow. The man was balding though not very old, balding in the ugliest way possible: up the sides and from a bald patch in the centre so there was a moat of baldness around a lone patch of hair on his forehead. It was dull sandy coloured hair; he was not a big man though he had big knuckled hands and a small potbelly and altogether, although he wasn't positively ugly, you would never look at him twice.

"Yes, it is, my lady," he said. "A great loss."

"And who are you? Are you one of Jamie's university friends?"

"Not quite, ma'am. My name is Simon Anricks, I'm a tooth-puller, a barber surgeon."

Ah, the putative Jesuit. His voice was London with a tinge of West Country in it and clearly educated. Very different from the old tooth-drawer they had had before the Armada that Sir John Forster had arrested and found in fact to be a Papist spy. Was that why Tait was so suspicious? Was he mixing them up?

"Is business good?"

The man smiled. "Good enough. There are plentiful broken teeth from fights and of course scurvy-rotted teeth as well, though I find fewer of the worm-rotted teeth here than I do in Bristol or London."

"Worm-rotted?"

"Why yes, ma'am. There's a school of thought that says the holes in the teeth we find in courtiers and merchants' wives are chewed by tiny worms that live in the stomach and come up into the mouth at night."

"Good God!"

"It's hard to know what else would make holes so I admit that as a working hypothesis. I have a suspicion that they are attracted by sugar, for in days of old, before we brought sugar from Araby, it's said there were far fewer of them, though more of the flat worn-down teeth."

"What about people who can't afford sugar?"

"Exactly ma'am. I find very few of the holes indeed among the poor and the peasants, and when I do, a little questioning often finds that they have a taste for sugar plums or honey or orange-adoes. Here, in the north, of course such refinements are almost unknown and indeed there are even fewer of the wormholes."

"Have you ever seen a…a toothworm?" asked Elizabeth, fascinated against her will.

"I have made some efforts to find them, sitting up till past midnight in the dark with a patient and then opening the mouth very gently with a candle—alas, I have never seen the worms themselves except of course in the stool where they are so common as to be unsuspicious. They must be a special variety of the normal worms of the stomach. Perhaps, as some say, they are invisible—but I do not think so, only very hard to see and perhaps very shy of light."

"Why can't they be invisible?"

"Because then we could not hope to see them, and so I prefer to believe the optimistic view."

Well that certainly sounded a bit Jesuitical, but it could just be that he had read a lot of books. How on earth did you find out if someone was a Jesuit without actually asking them outright?

"Perhaps I should eat fewer of the sugar plums I like myself."

"Indeed, my lady. I would recommend it. I would also recommend scrubbing your teeth every night with a good rough toothcloth dipped in salt."

"I've always done that. Doesn't everyone?"

"Well they should."

"Did Jamie Burn have bad teeth then?" She knew he didn't. His teeth were white and even and like a horse's.

The man laughed a little and Elizabeth tried hard not to suspect he was laughing at her clumsy attempts to cross-examine him.

"He had one tooth he had broken years before which needed drawing and I drew for him. And then we got talking over brandywine and ended by being friends. He needed to talk to someone who read the kind of books he did. I was able to lend him my favourite book by Thomas Digges, about the heavens and crystal spheres, and we had many good discussions about it and others like Lucretius' *De Rerum Naturae* and of course some of the Hermetic books."

"What are they?"

"They are books written by Hermes Trismegistus which deal with…er…well with astrology, among other things."

Elizabeth felt a thrill of suspicion go through her and then damped it down. Astrology was perfectly unexceptionable and didn't the Queen have Dr Dee, her own personal astrologer to cast her horoscope for her? In fact an astrologer was much more respectable than a Papist.

"As Dr Dee does?"

"Yes, indeed, although the good doctor is now more interested in angel magic, which I believe is leading him astray."

"Astray from what?"

"Why, my lady, from the far more interesting question of what are the crystal spheres made of and is it true, as Copernicus writes, that the Earth goes around the Sun and not the other way about?"

"What?"

Mr Anricks smiled diffidently. "I know, ma'am, it sounds quite insane and so I thought it when I first came across the idea, oh, years ago now. But if you read the account of it in Thomas Digges and think about it, well, it seems less mad the more you think about it, that's all I can say."

Elizabeth blinked at him. The idea made her feel very queasy, as if the Earth underfoot were not quite as solid as it seemed.

"Well, everyone knows the Earth is round," she began slowly, "but surely it's at the centre of the universe? How can it not be? And wouldn't we feel it if the Earth were…were moving around the Sun?"

"Perhaps not, if the movement was very smooth. The Earth is enormous, of course, that was measured by Eratosthenes of Cyrene before Christ was born."

"How did he do that?"

"He was very clever: he measured the exact curve of a row of posts of exactly the same length placed beside the Nile at intervals and from that worked out the curve of the Earth by the Art Geometrica. Some twenty-five thousand miles around."

"Good…heavens."

"Quite. If Columbus had heard of Eratosthenes, he would probably never have set out."

There were so many questions she wanted to ask him. Are you a Papist? Are you a Jesuit? What was it you really talked about with Jamie? Not for the first time, she wished Poppy was there where she should have been instead of nearly forty miles away in England.

They were tapping the third barrel of beer over by the trestle tables and the spit-roasted mutton and beef was being consumed by hungry men who were standing around shouting at each other. Behind her she could hear an argument that was not, for a wonder, about whether a shod horse went better than an unshod one. It was a new one and equally fatuous: Which would win in a fight, a billy goat or a ram? It seemed plans were afoot to find out.

The boys were being congratulated on their singing and munching hunks of mutton themselves, while their parents did the same. Little Jimmy Tait was swaying already with the mild ale he'd drunk. It was mid-afternoon and the party would go on into the night. Now if Robin were here he would be wandering around asking Jock Burn how his horses were and telling stories and he would stand over there, by the untapped barrels and laugh and accept a bet on the idiotic ram versus goat question.

He wasn't here. He was far away in the West March and probably thinking of any number of things, none of which were her. Probably he had forgotten all about her as indeed he should. Perhaps his father had found him an heiress to marry and rescue his fortunes. Perhaps he had found another woman to be his ladylove—or at least to bed since the Italian woman who had been all over him in Scotland was now rumoured to be the Earl of Essex' mistress.

She had eaten a trencher of roast mutton and some bread. She had to stay until the cakes were brought out but then she thought she would retire from the fray and try and get an early night. But no, she would have to wait until Lady Hume and Kat went to bed.

Could she start for home now? No. The earliest she could do that was tomorrow when she planned to be up early—though she would have to make allowances for Young Henry's hangover and the hangovers of the cousins. Probably not tomorrow then, or only late tomorrow, she could stay the night at Sir Henry's house in Berwick and hope he hadn't finished whatever he was up to in Scotland so she wouldn't have to deal with him. Then a long run down to Widdrington. If she could take remounts she might be able to do it in one day. It was an awkward distance, about forty miles as the crow flies.

Absentmindedly she drank a bit more of the mild ale she preferred. Two men were taking their doublets and shirts off— why? Ah yes, a ring was forming of cheering men and some of the women, with the boys at the front. Two of the lads were also taking off their jerkins. Cumbrian wrestling. It wasn't really the season for it, but no doubt there was a bet involved, or more likely several.

There was Mr Anricks again, eating some beef and mutton— most of the beef had gone to the senior men of the Burn clan who had large appetites. He was back near her again.

"Lady Widdrington," he said, "I wonder if I could trouble you to let me into the manse? I lent Jamie a couple of books I'd like to get back."

Interesting. She smiled brightly. "Of course," she said, "I'll come with you. I'm not really interested in who can throw someone else into the mud."

The boys were already at it, gripping each other round the middle and trying to get their legs round between the other's legs and then trying to lift and drop, red in the face and shouting insults. One went over on his back, squirmed and turned so the other one was down on his back. There was ironic cheering and clapping.

She walked with the barber surgeon across to the manse and found that it was indeed locked—wise with the number of reivers in the village but who had the key? She went back to the party and found Lady Hume chatting away to Young Henry about how funerals had been in her youth.

"I have a headache," she said, which was actually true she realised. "I'd like to lie down. Do you have the key to the manse?"

"No," said Lady Hume, "I'm sure I gave it to Kat…"

It took a little longer to find Kat who was in a circle of village women singing a long song about spinning while the younger girls danced something energetic. "Oh yes," she said, "I thought it better to lock the place and Lady Hume usually gives keys to me, now where did I put it…?"

The key ring was a large one and must have been taken from Jamie Burn's body. Elizabeth took it and went over to the manse where she found the tooth-drawer waiting patiently by the wall. She found the key to the kitchen door and they went in, through to the entrance hall, and then into the open study which was exactly the same as it had been.

Mr Anricks looked about him and sighed. "I enjoyed my conversations with the minister," he said. "We disagreed about religion and never found it a hindrance. He was very strong for the new religion, for Calvinism, which I find…too logical. But we never quarreled over it. Or we did but not personally; we argued about it and ended as good friends as we had started."

He looked about him at the wall of books and checked some of them, smiled ruefully. "I'm sorry, my lady, but he's double rowed them." It was true: the shelves were deep and there was a row of books behind the ones you could see. "This could take some time."

She smiled, took a spill from the desk and went to get a light from the fire in the kitchen. She lit Jamie's thrifty mutton fat rushdip and sat down in Jamie's chair. "That's all right, Mr Anricks. I'll read some of his sermons—they're excellent."

"Yes, there was an Edinburgh printer interested in them—to publish them, I mean. I advised him to try it, send out some copies of his sermons to printers and see what happened—there are plenty of books of sermons but few that are as pithy as his. I believe none of them are more than an hour long, which is something of a miracle for a Calvinist pastor. If he made any money at it, he could have used it to help poor boys like himself go to university at St Andrews, which he thought was an excellent idea. It might also have got him preferment to another living in addition to this one which would have made his wife's life a little easier with more money, only like the Reverend Gilpin, he didn't approve of having more than one."

Mr Anricks found a set of steps, took the other rushdip and started methodically at the far left top corner of the wall. Elizabeth took one of the italic sheets and found she was distracted by all the books. So many books. Who would have them now? Perhaps the next pastor who got the living, although it was likely he would have other parishes and would probably never come to Wendron. And the boys would forget how to read and become farmers as their fathers had been before.

It was all such a waste. She started to read the top sermon, just to have something to do as she had left her workbag in Widdrington and so couldn't get on with the new shirt for Young Henry. She could hear Jamie's voice as he gave it, the Scots even and musical but the voice deep enough to hold attention. It was about giving praise to God: how it was necessary and comfortable for the spirit to praise God, not because God needed flattery, no, but because it made us feel better. We should praise God always, both when we liked our life and when we hated it. She found herself held and warmed by it, as if he was preaching to her personally.

"Ma'am," came a diffident voice.

"Yes Mr Anricks?"

"Do you know if the minister kept his books anywhere else? I've found one that I lent him but there's another I can't find."

"No, I don't. But we can look."

They did, in the three spare bedrooms, dark and cold and two of them unfurnished, one with just a small bed with a half-tester and a truckle for the servant. Anricks smiled at it.

"I used to stay there when I came to visit. It was very comfortable. Much better than a bench at the alehouse."

"So did I, Mr Anricks, when I came to visit my friend Poppy. I'll see if I can convince Lady Hume to let you stay in it tonight— I doubt you'll get any sleep at all at the alehouse."

"Well," said Anricks, "I've slept in worse places, but yes, that would be very kind of you."

"I can't promise anything until I've spoken to Lady Hume," she warned and he ducked his head.

At the end of it he looked baffled. "I can't imagine he sold it, maybe he lent it to someone else. It's a pity, it was an old friend of mine."

"The book?"

"Yes. Ah well. Never mind, the Almighty giveth and He taketh away, blessed is the name of the Lord."

He smiled at her and she smiled back, somehow liking him despite being near convinced he was in fact a Jesuit. So they had disputed on religion in a civilized way? Jamie was strong for the new religion as she was herself, which meant Anricks must be a Catholic, surely?

She kept her promise and spoke to Lady Hume who was sitting on a barrel clapping to the music from a fiddle and a couple of shawms while the couples swung each other round and jigged. From the look of her she'd had plenty of beer and some aqua vitae from Kat's flask.

Everyone was red-faced and shouting. The cakes had come out and were sitting on the table for the bread, their elaborate marchpane covers shining in the torchlight. Lady Hume took a sharp knife and sliced it all up deftly and everyone got a bit, with the little children getting quite a lot of the marchpane. Mr Anricks nibbled a bit of the cake and smiled when Elizabeth accused him of keeping an eye on who winced when they ate the marchpane as they would be customers for his pliers.

"Have you tried luring the toothworms out with some marchpane?" she asked, and he smiled and admitted that he hadn't but it was a good idea. She introduced him to Lady Hume who looked him up and down and asked him point blank if he was a Papist spy like the last tooth-drawer in these parts.

"No, my lady," he answered, "I'm not, but I don't expect you to believe me. Everyone hates tooth-drawers."

"Nor a Jesuit?"

He smiled and shook his head. "I'm not nearly intelligent enough."

"I willna have ye bothering God in Latin."

"I never speak to God in Latin, my lady."

As there were three women in the main bedroom to keep propriety and the spare bedroom was at the other end of the landing, Lady Hume graciously gave her permission for him to stay the night there, only a little spoiled by hiccups. Cousin William and Lord Hughie came by then, to pay their respects before they rode home. Lady Hume hugged the young lord tight for a moment, unexplained tears making her eyes glitter. The boy took it well, though you could see he was relieved to be away when he mounted up with a steed-leap that nearly took him over the horse's back and down on the other side. He laughed at that, patted the horse for staying still for him and followed after Cousin William.

In the end it was quite easy to get Lady Hume to bed as she drank another cup of aqua vitae and passed out. Young Henry carried her up to bed and Kat and Elizabeth got her undressed down to her shift and put her into bed in the middle. Elizabeth wasn't looking forward to it and envied Mr Anricks his solitary state although it would be cold without a fire. Kat was too much the worse for wear to do more than get undressed herself, take her dose of medicine and fall asleep. The snoring started, Kat's was deep and rhythmical while Lady Hume made a succession of irregular little grunts and mews that was somehow more annoying.

Elizabeth heard Mr Anricks come back with his pack and go into his room. Outside the noise was starting to die down as people passed out or went home if they lived in the village. It had been a good send off for the minister. Tomorrow the village would start to empty of Burns and Taits and Pringles from the raiding families and turn back into the sleepy place it had been before.

monday 16th october 1592

Carey was standing in the little kennelyard looking at the hounds with Scrope. He seemed distracted by something and he looked very tired, with bags under his eyes and he had clearly had brandy for breakfast. Dodd came into the yard in search of him and found him wearily agreeing with Scrope that the hounds needed a good run. Scrope wandered off to look at the latest four-month-old pups with the master of hounds.

A half-grown yellow lymer pup came trotting out of one of the sheds with a stick held proudly in his mouth. He brought it right over to the Courtier and dropped it at his feet in an unmistakable hint. Carey picked it up and threw it over to the other side of the yard, the pup galloped happily off to get it and then found a bit of cow bone that interested him more and forgot the stick. Carey went over to get the stick himself and this time when he threw it, the pup brought it back to Dodd, laying it at his feet with great pride.

Carey smiled at something that would have had him laughing a few weeks before and bent down to ruffle the pup's ears. At that exact moment, the pup jumped up to lick Carey in the face and the pup's nose collided with Carey's chin.

"Aargh, Jesus," shouted Carey, and bent over with his hand to his jaw. "Jesus, you stupid dog."

The dog tried to lick his face again and Carey fended him off. "No, get down, goddamn it!" he roared, and the pup plopped down on his back, peering anxiously at Carey.

The pup's nose hadn't hit him that hard and Dodd wondered what the hell was ailing the Courtier that he made such a fuss about it. The Courtier seemed a little sorry for his ill-temper and he squatted to pat the pup and check his paws. Another determined lick from the dog, still aimed at the lower part of Carey's face and Dodd suddenly understood.

"Sir, have ye a toothache?"

Carey half-looked up at him and nodded.

"It's my back tooth, been giving me trouble for years and now it's bloody killing me."

It was, too. Carey was looking distinctly unhealthy and, come to think of it, his right jawline was swollen. He picked up the stick, threw it again and this time the pup galloped back with it and tripped over his large paws and rolled. Then he lay on his back and let Carey rub his tum, wriggling with ecstasy at it. Carey had his other hand cupped round his face and was still preoccupied.

"Ay, I see, will ye not get it drawn?"

"I suppose I'll have to but there isn't a tooth-drawer in Carlisle at the moment. I asked Mr Lugg but he says he doesn't do teeth, says they're too fiddly and nobody is ever satisfied."

"I heard tell there's a new man who's good over in Scotland the day; will I try and see if I can get him here?"

"If you can, Sergeant."

Dodd nodded. Teeth could be the very devil. He'd never had toothache himself, apart from when he was a wean and his new teeth were growing, oh and when his wisdom teeth were coming in when he was twenty, but he knew people who had. Apart from getting loose in spring and worn down when you were old, if they went seriously rotten they could actually kill you if your face swelled up and the sickness went into your blood. Since Carey was the only thing between Sir Richard Lowther and the West March, apart from the ineffectual Lord Scrope, Dodd wanted him alive and healthy and he sighed at the thought of tracking down a good tooth-drawer, or a tooth-drawer of any kind on the Marches.

They went out to the Eden meadows with all the lymer pups from Buttercup's litter that she had on Carey's bed in the summer, to see how they shaped. The yellow one with the big head was clearly not very bright but he was the friendliest and most willing dog Dodd or Carey had ever seen, and Carey had already decided to have him as his own in exchange for providing his bed for Buttercup's lying-in.

"I'll call him Jack," he said, as they came back a couple of hours later with the five dogs milling around them on leashes. "I don't suppose he'll be much use as a lymer but he's a nice dog."

"Why Jack?"

"Oh my first two dogs were called King and Queenie, but he isn't really a Knave, so I'll call him after the Jack in the All Fours game. It's appropriate."

"Ay," said Dodd. Thinking about it, it was too. Nobody would play cards with the Courtier in the West March now for more than penny stakes.

They let the dogs go off the leashes in the kennelyard and Sandy and Eric, the two dogboys, came out with buckets of bones and guts for them from the butcher's shambles and stale bread from the castle bakery and there was much snarling and gulping until all of it was finished in about ten seconds. The dogboys had brushes and they started the endless job of grooming the hairy dogs until they shone.

Dodd and Carey retired to Bessie's for a bite of lunch. Carey ate the pottage, a thick soupy mixture of pot-herbs, meat, and beans, but only when it was half-cold. He shook his head at the steak and kidney pie.

"I'm like a bloody Papist monk," he said, "no women, soup every meal, wake up at two every morning." He lifted a finger to the potboy and got a cup of brandy. He swilled the brandy round his mouth before swallowing it.

"Hmm," said Dodd, deep in the pie and chewing on the bread he dipped in it. He was considering passing on a prime piece of information he'd heard from Janet that morning before she went back to Gilsland. The trouble was it was vague and

Dodd knew Carey always wanted specifics before he would take action. On the other hand he clearly needed something to take his mind off his tooth for the moment.

"I heard tell," he said as he reached for the bag pudding full of plums as his second cover, "that Jock Elliot and Wee Colin have bought theirselves new doublets."

"Oh yes," grunted Carey, ordering more brandy. "So what?"

There was an expensive hard sauce to go with the plum pudding, of sherry sack, butter and sugar, which even Dodd had to admit was delicious. He offered some to Carey who held up his hand palm out and shook his head.

"It'd kill me," he said.

"Well, Jock Elliot and Wee Colin Elliot arenae the ones for fashion. And they may have kin and kine and towers, but they havenae money no more than I do. And I heard that Jock's been seen walking oot in Jedburgh in a tawny velvet doublet that's Edinburgh work and Wee Colin has one the same but in black currant colour."

"Cramoisie," corrected Carey, who knew about fashionable colour names. "So?"

It was obvious but Dodd made allowances for the tooth.

"They've made some siller, that's all. Somebody's paid them a lot of money, on top o' what they normally get from black-renting and kidnapping."

"So they've had some successful raids. What are you suggesting?"

"A Warden rode on 'em," said Dodd, "find out what they got paid for." He didn't think Carey would really go for it, but it was worth a try.

"Nothing to do with the feud the Dodds have with the Elliots, is it?"

"Och no, that's composed now," lied Dodd. "It was a' arranged back in 1581 wi' the Reverend Gilpin's help and your father presiding." Well, that bit was true, but as for the feud being composed…The Elliots had killed Dodd's father, caused the death of his mother, and the deaths of two of his brothers and

a sister. The fact that he had got lucky when he led the remnants
of the Dodd surname in the final battle so the bastards had had
to come to negotiate was neither here nor there. He still wanted
to wipe the Elliots out. Of course they thought the same of him,
and that was why he'd had to leave upper Tynedale and come to
Carlisle Castle when he was twenty-one, it was part of the deal.
Which had held so far, but not for want of his thinking how to
break it to his advantage.

And weren't the Johnstones and the Maxwells at it hammer
and tongs again in the Scots West March?

"I'm not running a Warden Rode so you can have at the Elliots
again," growled Carey at him. "Besides, it's Scrope you'd have to
convince of that, not me. He's the bloody Warden."

"Is he no' thinking of going back to his ain lands and his lady
wife down to London to serve the Queen?"

"Well he is, but how the devil did you know that?"

Dodd didn't feel it necessary to explain that the men of the
guard had been talking about little else since they came back
and the bets on it had gone to stupid levels. At least Dodd's
investment looked safe.

"When's he leaving?"

"You know Scrope, dithers over everything. Also Richard
Lowther would likely be acting Warden in his place, not me."

"Ay? What'll happen to you?"

"Well, that depends on the Queen. If she confirms me as
Deputy Warden then there isn't a lot he can do about it, though
it would make my life infernally difficult. If she doesn't..." Carey
shrugged a shoulder and scowled. "Maybe I'll take up the King
of Navarre's offer. I'm not going back to London."

"Och," Dodd was stricken. All that work, going down to the
horrible alleys and dangerous women of London, all gone to
waste and he'd have to start buttering up Lowther again. "Why
not ye as acting Warden?"

Carey's face was as grim as a crow at an execution. "Not
senior enough, apparently," he muttered, knocking back his
third cup of brandy.

Seemingly there had been arguments and words exchanged between Scrope and his brother-in-law and Dodd now understood why Philadelphia was contemplating going to serve the Queen again. He sighed heavily.

"That's bad news, is that," he said as he finished the bag pudding and sauce and leaned back with his belly comfortably tight. "I didna ken."

A half smile briefly crossed Carey's face. "Well, I'm glad you're on my side, Sergeant, but I may be out on my ear in a few weeks."

"Ay," said Dodd mournfully. "Well, I'll get a nap before we go out on patrol the night."

Carey nodded but stayed sitting in Bessie's commonroom while Dodd set off back up to the castle. A fourth cup of brandy arrived to keep him company.

tuesday, before dawn, 17th october 1592

Elizabeth woke in the dark and wondered why. She was awake and alert, as if someone had called her name. Had they? She had been dreaming of Robin again, but that was normal, the part of her that dreamt was carrying on with its ridiculous notion that she could ever marry him, just as if reality and Sir Henry did not exist. She hated the awakenings from those dreams because they made her feel so sad.

But that wasn't what had awakened her. What had?

She lay on her side with Lady Hume fitted into her back and Kat Ridley lying on her back and giving a slow rolling grunt. That hadn't awoken her either; she was too awake.

She listened in the dark, probably about two hours after midnight, the darkest part of the night. There was a Moon but it was clouded over. What was it?

Absolute silence pressed in on her. No sound at all, not even the barn owls and the occasional bark from a fox, protests of dreaming sheep, sometimes a snort from a horse. Nothing except loud snoring from drunks outside.

Well, that was it, of course. Why was everything else so silent?

She sat up and decided against lighting a taper from the watch candle. She didn't have a dressing gown against the cold and it was very cold, perhaps not freezing yet but near it.

She found her riding kirtle by touch, missed out the petticoats and bumroll and pulled it on over her head, found her hobnailed boots by the bed and put them on as well.

There was a clink of metal on metal, and a couple of dull thuds, very near the house. Was someone trying to steal the horses? Goddamn it, if Jock Burn thought he could do that, he could think again.

Mind you, if it was Jock Burn then he was a better actor than she gave him credit for. He had been laughing and rolling drunk the last time she saw him and she had seen him pass out contentedly in a pile of hay.

She paused in the passageway to look out the window. Were there more horses in the stableyard than there should have been? It was hard to tell with the two wagons there and the empty barrels waiting to be loaded and taken back to Berwick. Even with her nightsight well in, it was very dark.

Her heart was beating hard and yet she wasn't sure. She didn't dare give the alarm for nothing because the village was full of drunken reivers who would likely wake and then fall to fighting each other if there was nobody else to fight.

She went down the stairs as quietly as she could, then stopped in the hall. She had barred the door herself so why was there a draught from the open window...?

She took breath to give the alarm and found a hard hand wrap itself round her mouth and pull her backwards off her feet. She fought then, fought for breath and to make a sound, was cuffed a couple of times across the ears and then when she managed a small yelp, punched hard in the side of the head with a dagger hilt so the world was turned into a whirligig and she couldn't see at all, couldn't hear anything except voices far away, hissing at each other. Somebody laughed, a thick sound that terrified her.

They laid her down and pawed at her skirts, kicking her legs apart, she closed them with enormous effort, they were kicked apart again and she was kicked in the privates as well. It hurt. Argument again, they were doing what? Tossing a coin? There was another harsh laugh and then a strange noise...A hissing noise like a snake or a burning slow match.

It was a burning slow match. Someone was coming into the minister's study in his shirt and breeches, but with a thing that had a small red light that lit up his mouth and jaw, which were set firm. She part-sat up, shook her head slowly against the dripping stuff going into her eyes, tried to make it out.

"It's true," said the man with the gun coldly, "that I can only shoot one of you and the other can likely kill me. So which one will it be, gentlemen? Which of you shall I shoot?"

At last Elizabeth knew who it was for the London vowels and West Country sounds, it was the barber surgeon, Mr Anricks. He was standing in the doorway, oddly hunched, a dag rested on his left wrist, gripped by his right hand and the slow match hissing in the lock.

The two muffled-up men were backing away from her and Anricks came forward slowly. Suddenly the two made a break for the window, one leapt through, the other followed and the gun bellowed in the confined space.

Anricks was following up, grasping the dag by the muzzle and wielding the heavy ball on the grip like a club but by that time both were through the window and he missed again. The ball connected with the window frame and left a dent. Next moment there was the sound of two horses with muffled unshod hooves and muffled tack riding off into the night. And the moment after that the shouting starting as Jock Burn and the Taits and Pringles came to and started looking for people to fight.

Elizabeth found the world went away and came back again and she was surrounded by anxious faces in the light of several candles as Kat Ridley mopped the side of her head with a cloth. There was shouting outside, Young Henry's voice, bellowing with anger, then hooves galloping.... *You won't find them that way*, she thought muzzily, *they're too clever for that.*

Mr Anricks was there, too, decently dressed now in his black wool suit and his hat on.

"I heard Lady Widdrington go down the stairs," he was saying. "I had been woken by something and so I loaded my dag and lit the match off the watch candle, came down with it and by the Almighty's help was able to chase them away."

Elizabeth tried to get up and deal with events and found her limbs go to water and her head whirling when she started to sit up. Behind the crowd, Lady Hume was in her shift and the fur coverlet, watching everything beadily.

She tried again and found it worse, her body refusing to obey her and her head pounding away like a rock-crushing hammer at Keswick.

She was frightened she might die, as you did sometimes from being hit on the head. She beckoned Anricks closer while an argument broke out between Kat Ridley and two of the village women as to how to get her back to bed. "They were Jamie Burn's murderers," she whispered when he squatted down to her.

"How do you know, ma'am?"

Suddenly she realised she couldn't say it was because one or both of them had raped Poppy and had been about to rape her as well. She simply couldn't.

"I…" she started and found she had nothing more to say. His pale brown eyes narrowed shrewdly at her expression. He had seen how she lay, where the men were. And then a miracle happened, he understood.

"Was Mrs Burn also…?" he asked very softly, while making a small gesture at her legs. She nodded and wished she hadn't for the movement made her head hurt and unloosed the bandage so that blood started leaking again into her hair.

"Only…he did it. You did it to her. You came in time for me."

His mouth twisted a little. "I see," he said softly. There was a sudden sense of boiling fury within him and yet none of it was visible on the outside. "I'm glad I was here."

Her tongue wasn't working properly. "I am, too," she managed finally as the cloth on her head fell off. "Ach," she said, and put her hand to the wound there. He brought the candle closer and tutted.

With Kat's help she staggered to her feet, knees feeling like they were made of hanks of wool and bending all the time, was supported into the kitchen and sat on the chair. Mr Anricks was the nearest approach to a medical man there and he brought up all three of the candles so it felt hot. Gently he parted her hair. She hadn't her cap and her hair was plaited for sleep so it could have been worse but it seemed there was a nasty cut where the man had punched her and as head wounds will, it was bleeding again.

Later Elizabeth only remembered little flashes because most of it was the pain in her head and the nuisance of the blood and keeping a cloth wrapped around her neck so it wouldn't mark her kirtle. Lady Hume came trotting in with a pair of sewing shears and a small bottle of aqua vitae and Kat Ridley produced more linen cloths and a bowl of cold water.

Mr Anricks had gentle fingers: he sheared some of the hair short on that side of her head and used the cold water on the cut and then put brandy on it so Elizabeth had to bite her lip to stop herself from yelling. By that time it was dawn and the men were back from their ridiculous chasing across the countryside after two clever men who had crept in among a large number of snoring reivers to raid the manse itself.

Jock Burn was loud in his fury at it, louder because of his hangover. Just as Anricks was wrapping more linen bandages round her head Young Henry came stamping into the kitchen, grabbed her and hugged her.

"Are you all right, mam, did you get shot?"

She hugged him back, feeling the little boy inside the large-shouldered large young man and loving him as she had since she first met him, when he was ten and desperately trying to be brave about his mother. "I'm all right, Harry, truly I am. Just a little bump on the head..."

"Mr Widdrington, one of them hit her on the side of the head and also kicked her a number of times in the legs," said Anricks. "She must go back to bed."

"It was you fired the dag at them, sir?"

"Yes, though I think I missed. At least there's no blood from anyone except Lady Widdrington."

"No matter, sir, no matter. Thank you. Thank you very much." Young Henry was shaking Anricks' hand, pumping it up and down.

"Lady Widdrington must go back to bed," said Anricks very loud and distinctly as to one wandering in his wits, "She has been struck on the head and kicked while on the ground."

"I'm sure I can ride…" Elizabeth started though she wondered how she would get back to Widdrington with her legs like hanks of wool.

"I'm sure she can't," said Anricks.

Young Henry then picked up Elizabeth easily in his arms and carried her up the stairs with no more ado than he had Lady Hume the night before, although she was twice the old lady's size. *When did he get so strong?* she wondered muzzily. *I knew he was large but I didn't know he could lift me.*

Young Henry put her into the bed and she lay back on the pillows and felt deeply grateful she hadn't had to get up the stairs.

"Thank you, Harry," she said, and found he was hugging her again.

"We'll catch them," he said into her neck. "We'll catch them, mam, and kill them. They'll be sorry they tangled wi' the Widdringtons."

"Listen Harry, I think they were the men that killed Jamie Burn."

"Ay," said Young Henry, "I'm thinking the same. But where ha' they gone?"

"I'm more interested in why they came back. They'd got clean away and nobody any the wiser, why the devil did they come back? What for?"

Young Henry was feeling the large spot on the end of his nose that Elizabeth privately thought of as his thinking spot. "Hm, yes, why?"

She was suddenly dizzy again and found it hard to speak. She wanted to tell them that there must be something in the house they wanted and it was possible the tooth-drawer, Mr Anricks, wanted it too although he had saved her. She slowly got her tongue and lips to say all that.

"We'll go out with lymers today and try to find them," Young Henry explained because he wasn't listening properly. "William

Hume is lending me a couple of his hunting dogs, he's furious as well."

Young Henry's voice faded as he told Elizabeth what good dogs they were and how Cousin William was also bringing along his forester who was an excellent tracker. She was suddenly exhausted and sleepy. She laid her sore head back on the pillow and let the world disappear again.

She woke to the sound of rain and the certain knowledge that she had forgotten something important. She was only in her shift again, her velvet gown hung up and her kirtle likewise. She lay there feeling the old fur coverlet over the bed, it was deer fur and well-cured so it was soft and supple and hardly shed at all. Perhaps it was noon though she didn't feel hungry.

What had Jamie Burn been mixed up in and where did Simon Anricks come in all this? Two strangers had come into the village and killed the minister, then ridden away again after raping Poppy. Two strangers had come into the village again the night before to find something they presumably hadn't got the first time, knocked her down and ridden away again, and given the searchers the slip as well. Simon Anricks had missed at point-blank range but then you often did with a dag; they were hopelessly inaccurate. Was he a Jesuit? To be sure he had carte blanche now that he was inside the manse. If he wanted to find something he didn't need to be elaborate about it. So was there something in the house that two parties wanted, was that it? And what was it? Why was it important? Was it a book? Why would a book be important? Was it a seditious book, perhaps something printed by the Catholics at Rheims to lead folk astray?

She pressed her lips together and scowled. If it was seditious then why would a Jesuit want it? Surely it would be better to leave it where it was and deny all knowledge?

She started to doze off again and there was Robin again, half in her dreams and half out of them, telling her about the different kinds of coding Sir Francis Walsingham had taught him when he was a very good-looking young man and in Scotland with him. He had told her about them in the North, in fact, before she even knew she loved him, way back in 1585, when he had been staying at Sir Henry's house in Berwick, waiting to find out if the Scotch king would let him into the realm with the impossible dangerous message about the Queen of Scots. The one that said that Her Majesty of England had somehow, unaccountably and accidentally and due to her wicked courtiers and in particular one Mr Davison, sent the King of Scotland's sovereign and mother to the block.

Scotland had been a tinderbox and most of the surnames had been united for once in their fury: so what if they had tried to kill the Queen twenty years before? She was their Queen and theirs to kill. How *dare* the Queen of England lop her head off on the specious grounds of treason when she was a sovereign queen and certainly not Elizabeth I's subject? It was outrageous. The Maxwell had sworn to kill Carey for carrying the message, as had Buccleuch and Ferniehurst and most of the headmen of the Marches.

She still remembered the first time she had seen him, wearing a forest-green hunting suit, rings on his fingers, his hat on his head, sweeping it off in a Court bow to her when her husband, of all people, introduced them. She had curtseyed wondering why her heart was suddenly thumping inside her stays and why her knees were knocking. Her body had known him before she did, she thought.

It had taken months for the careful messages to go to and fro to Edinburgh and back, and all that time, Elizabeth had found plain Mr Robert Carey, as he was then, a terrible distraction and worry to her. He had gone hunting a couple of times but stopped when he was chased back to Berwick by a large group of men who had also shot arrows at him. Apparently he had put his head down beside the horse's neck in the true Border style he'd learned when he was a boy in Berwick and galloped into Sir Henry's stableyard with an arrow actually through his smart London hat. He had laughed uproariously at it and worn the hat with a hole in it until he bought a newer higher-crowned one a couple of years later.

"The easiest method for coding for someone who isn't able to figure and calculate the numbers is to make your code another book and refer to the page and line and letter. If you use the Bible, which you shouldn't because it's the first book anyone checks, then page 1, line 1a, word 3 is 'beginning.'"

"1a?"

"That's another reason for not using the Bible because there are often two columns on a page and you have to call them a and b—gives the game away at once."

That had been after a fashionably late dinner in Berwick with two covers of food and a large salmon for the cheapness, as it was a fish day. They had been discussing other ways of getting messages to people. It was not relevant since the point of Mr Carey was that someone had to carry the message and apologise on his knees to the Scottish King, and Robin had volunteered for the dangerous job as he tended to do for any dangerous job that happened to be lying around and looked interesting.

Carey had sung the praises of Mr Phelippes who was Walsingham's chief code breaker. Mr Phelippes had once taken a despatch that had just come in, looked at it and immediately held it to the candle to find the invisible writing on it in orange juice. He had also broken the codes painstakingly used by the Queen of Scots in her imprisonment so as to catch her red-handed plotting against Queen Elizabeth. After the meal, Carey had sung for them from memory several of the Italian madrigals that were so fashionable at Court and taught them a complicated round that Young Henry could manage and Elizabeth could sing as well, while Sir Henry drank sack and watched them.

It had been a delightful evening, a pleasant interlude and afterwards she had realised that she loved the man because she dreamed a lewd dream of him and woke flushed and excited in the cold early morning with Sir Henry snoring beside her. In the dregs of the dream, Robin had kissed her gently and then faded as she realised they were both mother-naked.

Eight years gone. Eight years. Jesu.

She sat up carefully and rubbed her face, carefully felt the side of her head that still had bandages on it. It hurt but not too badly and her legs and crotch hurt, too, but she was used to bruises. She really wanted to get back to Poppy and find out what was going on there but she felt she couldn't leave while the killers of Jamie were at large and coming into the manse. What if they came when Poppy was there or tracked her down to Widdrington?

She found a mug of ale put beside the bed, sniffed it and found it had laudanum in it, which she didn't like. She got up and reached under the bed for the jordan and her hand brushed homespun wool and a bony leg. She pulled back with a cry and backed off, found a rushlight holder and grabbed it as the nearest thing to a weapon.

There was a squawk from under the bed as well and a head poked out from under, a thin little face with swollen red eyes.

"Jimmy Tait!" she snapped. "What the devil are you doing under my bed?"

"I'm sorry, missus, I'm sorry..." sniffled Jimmy, "I wanted to get awa' from the minister's ghost and ye said ye hadn't seen him and I thocht ye might be safer..."

She put the rushlight holder down and clasped her hand over her heart which was drumming like a maying drum.

"Jesu," she said, sitting down on the bed and fighting a wall of dizziness that came out of nowhere, "when did you get in there?"

"Och, last night, I crep' up the stairs last night."

"When?"

There was panic on the bony face. "I didna do naught, missus, I didna, I only crep' up the stairs while ye were busy in the kitchen..."

"While Mr Anricks was treating my head?"

"Ay."

"And what were you doing here last night anyway? Why weren't you at home in bed?"

For an answer the child started a steady ugly snivelling, with a great deal of snot.

The dizziness had passed again and Elizabeth advanced on the boy where he sat like a little frog by the bed with his face in his hands. She picked him up, feeling his cold hands and feet which were bare of his brother's clogs again. He weighed hardly anything, nothing like the sturdy lads that Young Henry and Roger had been when they were a similar age.

God knew what kind of passengers he had in his clothes, but there was no help for it; she had to know what was wrong with him. She wrapped the deer hide round the boy and gave him her ale with the laudanum in it.

"Are you hungry, Jimmy?" she asked and he nodded. "Can ye bide there a while and I'll get you something to eat." He nodded again but the tears kept coming.

She pulled her velvet gown on again over her shift and went down in her bare feet as she had no slippers. The house seemed empty, no sign of Kat or Lady Hume either. Perhaps they had gone back to the castle. Looking out the windows the village had gone back to its sleepy emptiness with most of the men busy with plowing or up in the hills with the stock, some of the women working in their gardens or in their houses.

In the kitchen she found the remains of the calf—really fit only for soup—and about half a roast sheep. She cut some collops off, found the range fire had been allowed to go out, and went back upstairs with a trencher of wood and a stale pennyloaf.

She had to go back for seconds about ten minutes later as Jimmy wolfed his way steadily through the food and drank the ale. Elizabeth had found a half barrel of mild ale that hadn't gone off yet and tapped it for herself.

At last Jimmy stopped chewing and gulping and burped.

"Thank 'ee missus," he said. "Ah'll be going now…"

"There's no hurry, Jimmy," she said, "unless your father's waiting for you?" A firm shake of the head. "Well then, bide here and keep me company."

She got back in the bed with her gown on, and pulled the sheets and blankets round her.

"I've decided to go back to Berwick tomorrow not today," she explained to Jimmy. "My head's still sore and I keep feeling dizzy. So I'm staying in bed today but it's lonely." It wasn't; she liked being on her own and she could have gone down and borrowed a book as well and risked being found reading it.

"Will I sing to ye, missus? Me mam likes it."

"Yes please, Jimmy. Can you sing me a ballad?"

He could. He opened his mouth unselfconsciously and sang her all of Tam Lin with both the tunes—quite an achievement for a lad of his age—and then a couple of the psalms. His voice was high, sweet and as true as a bell, silver to Robin's bronze, now she thought of it. Robin too had a marvellous voice but she thought this boy's voice was better. It was so pure she felt a thrill down her back at it, that something as clean and clear could exist in the fallen world.

"My dear," she said, "that's wonderful. You have a gift from God there."

He ducked his head awkwardly. "Thank 'ee missus."

"I expect the minister liked it too?"

"Ay," piped the boy. "He said the same, a gift from God too. His eyes were watering, I remember."

They may well have done, Elizabeth thought, at finding something so beautiful and fragile in the ugly mud and blood of the Borders.

"Are ye truly no' afeared of the minister's ghost?"

"No," she said, "I'm not. He was a good man in his life, wasn't he?"

"Ay, missus, he was. He gave me food sometimes like you, he gave me a bun once and he taught me to read singing as well as letters, said my voice might get me into Carlisle Cathedral choir if I worked hard."

"Now did he?"

"Ay missus, he did. He wanted me to grow a little and then he said he might take me there hisself if my father was agreeable and 'prentice me to the choir. Is it true they do that, missus? That ye can get your living by singing?"

"Yes, it is. What a splendid idea!" Elizabeth's mind was instantly onto the possible solution to Jimmy Tait. Could she take him to Carlisle herself and perhaps meet Robin...? No, she couldn't. It was a lovely idea but Sir Henry would instantly see through it and give her another beating. That no longer worried her the way it had, though she was afraid of it, of course. But in fact to do something like that would be dishonourable. And what would be the point of her torturing herself by getting nearer to Robin when she couldn't have him?

She sighed. In any case, she could surely find someone to take the lad to Carlisle, Young Henry for example. There was no need to go herself.

Suddenly the child had jacknifed over and was crying again. "That's why...that's why..." he was saying, "...that's why I'm so sad, missus...He...he..."

She stroked his nitty hair and let him cry.

"Listen to me, Jimmy, the minister was a good man, wasn't he? Would he ever have done you any harm while he was alive?" She waited until she got a watery shake of the head. "Well then, why do you think he would harm you when he was dead, even if he hadn't already gone to Judgement?"

For answer she got more tears and finally she understood something.

"Did you do something you think might make him angry?" she asked. "Did you, Jimmy?"

His thin face had snot teeming down it as well as tears and dirt but she saw the tiny nod.

"What was it?"

The voice was almost too small to hear. She thought it was something about horses.

"Whose horses did you guard?"

"Them!" cried Jimmy, "The murderers. Ah wis set to it by my father, and I didna think any harm to it, he said they wis just coming to ask the minister nicely for something and I stayed by the horses in the wood and after a bit they come back and they gave me a Scotch shilling for the work and rode off and I didna ken till the next day what they'd done. I didna ken."

"Did you know the men? Had you ever seen them before?"

"Nay missus, they wis strangers, naebody fra the village nor the castle. I never seen 'em in my life and they wis muffled up too."

"How did they sound? Were they Scots?"

"I dinna ken. They didna say much. Mebbe not."

"What did they look like?"

"Och they wis big and the older one had some grey in his beard and the younger one smiled at me and that's all I can tell ye, missus. I often look after strangers' horses for me dad."

"Do you now?"

"Ay. Or pack ponies."

Smuggling probably, thought Elizabeth.

"Do you think you might know them again if you saw them?"

"Ay missus, I think so." He started crying again, "If I hadnae looked after their horses…Och, the minister wad still be here and we'd be learning us oor lessons and…"

"Now Jimmy, I want you to stop thinking that way." Elizabeth paused "You didn't know when you looked after their horses that they were going to kill the minister, did you?"

"No, missus. Ah thocht it was just business, ye ken."

"Quite so. You couldn't have known that they were going to do anything of the sort and even if you had known, what could you have done about it?"

"I could ha' shouted, or run ahead and warned him? He didna wear a sword but I heard tell fra my dad he was a bonny fighter once the day."

"Of course you could, if you'd known. If you'd known you'd have done that, wouldn't you?"

"O' course I would and got my friends to come and they'd have all come running and we could have stood between the minister and the murderers and…"

"And probably Jimmy, they'd have knocked you aside and done it anyway. You'd have done that if you'd known what they were about but you didn't know. So it isn't your fault at all. It's the fault of the men that did the killing."

"Mebbe I could have guessed?"

"How? How could you have guessed? Did they say anything like, now we're going to kill Minister Burn by chopping his head in two?"

"No. They wis arguing about somebody called Bessie and whether her steak and kidney pie or her chicken pie was the best."

"There you are. How could you have guessed from that?" Though it was interesting and backed up the idea they had come from the West March.

He was staring at the rucked up deerskin. "No, I couldn't."

"Ye could not."

"But mebbe his ghost will come after me anyway."

Elizabeth paused a moment to think and took a deep breath. What she was saying was probably heresy, but she needed to stop the child crying. He was a witness, she needed him able to think and speak. "If there are ghosts then they're the spirit of the dead person, aren't they?"

He clutched the deerskin round himself tighter and nodded. He had deep circles round his eyes as well, poor lad.

"And do you know what a spirit is?" He shook his head. "A spirit is the soul of the person, the deepest part, the part that goes to God. Yes?" A small nod. "Now is your soul better or worse than the rest of you?"

"It's better, I think, missus."

"I think so, too. So even if the minister had been a bad man and full of sin, his soul would be the best part of him. But he was a good man with no more sin than most of us so his soul will be better still, yes?" Another tiny nod. "So his soul would never hurt you, Jimmy nor even frighten you. He's gone to God anyway."

"I dreamed of him."

Elizabeth tried not to sigh. "What did you dream?"

"I don't know. I just saw him in my dream and tried to run away."

"Did he say anything to you?"

"I couldn't hear it so I ran. And then I got stuck in a bog in the middle of the study."

"Well Jimmy, perhaps he was trying to tell you it was all right and he wasn't angry? Did you think of that?" A tiny shake of the head. "Perhaps if he comes back he'll just say, 'Jimmy, I loved yer singing at my funeral. Thanks lad.' Do you think?"

At last a tiny smile. "Mebbe."

"Can you think of anything else they said, no matter how little? Can ye tell me from the start, what happened."

"Well I wis milking the goats because I was late home from the minister and they were making a noise and carrying on and I was milking them and my dad sent Young Jock to me to say he had a job for me and Young Jock would finish the goats. So I run to my dad and he says I'm to go to the steward's copse and I'd find some horses there and I'm tae look after them till their owners come, which was two business friends of his and I done it before and so I…"

"Why were you late home?"

"Och, me and Archie were watching some slugs to see if they turn into birds but they didna and so we stamped on them. So I went to the copse and there were four nice horses there, wi' different brands on 'em, two one brand, two the other. I gave 'em some horse nuts my dad sent with me and gave 'em all a rub down and then I waited wi' them. And then the men come back and one was older, I remember that, didn't know them, I'd never seen 'em before in my life…"

"Would ye know them if you saw them again?"

Jimmy nodded slowly, his black circled eyes enormous. "Ay," he said, "that'd help the minister to rest, wouldn't it? If he saw the murderers hang?"

"I'm certain it would," said Elizabeth, still heretical.

"So they wis arguing about Bessie and which pie wis better and one was laughing and saying the little wifey wad remember him too and the other one…"

"Which was that? Who said that about Mrs Burn?"

"The younger one, with black hair, and the older one said, ay, ye were lucky again,"

"Again!"

"Ay, and then they said they'd be going and the younger one giv me a Scotch shilling…"

"Did you keep it?"

"No, I gave it to me dad and he said it was forged but he might get someone to take it."

"And the men went away?"

"Ay, and I took the Graham horses all the way South to where they told me. Nice horses they were too, though one had thrown a shoe."

"The men asked you to do that?"

"Ay, the older one, he said, the shilling is for you to take the horses down to the Border and not tell anyone, so I took 'em nearly all the way and give 'em to a horse trader named Tully."

"One was grey and one was chestnut?"

"Ay missus, how did ye know?"

"I know those horses. They'd been ridden hard too?"

"Ay, and the hobbies wis fresh. So I took them all that way and come back and I got me bread and milk for the evening late and went to sleep with Young Jock and in the morning…" Jimmy shook his head and tears started leaking again. "In the morning Andy Hume came running to tell us the minister was killt and…and I didn't know what to do or nothing, missus, it was terrible, worse than when the Widdringtons raided the infield and took our four mares and a gelding. Andy said, they've killt him, they took the top of his heid off."

"How did you know it was the strangers?"

"We saw them go in, didn't we? We saw them and never tried to stop them. I saw them too, when I come out of school and they went in and they was talking when they went."

"How did the minister seem? Was he laughing, pleased to see them?"

"Not exactly, more serious and stern but he knew 'em."

"What did they say?"

"The minister said, I'm not going out again. Spiny can wait."

"'I'm not going out again.'" Are you sure he said that?"

"Ay, I'm no' ganging out again, Spiny can wait. Then they was in the house and I didna think nothing of it."

She took him through the tale again and it came out pretty much the same and there was the name she knew, or might know.

"Is there any reiver around here called Spiny?"

Jimmy frowned and thought. "Not that I know of, missus. I did wonder but it might be someone fra foreign parts like the West March or England."

"Or Edinburgh?"

"Maybe."

That name made it something different from a Border matter, that made it a Court matter. The Earl of Spynie was King James' current favourite and a bad man to cross for all his youth, although he was starting to lose his beauty already, and with it, his hold over the king. She had known him when he was plain Alexander Lindsay, laird of Crawford too, and hadn't liked him then for all his pretty ways and charming smiles.

What had Jamie Burn done for Lord Spynie? Or to Lord Spynie? If Spynie had had Jamie killed, it accounted for the way of it and for the fact that the men had had money to spend on horses and hadn't been interested in the contents of the plate cupboard.

And Jock Tait had known the men, had he? He might not have known what they planned, but he knew them. Jimmy was useless as a witness but Jock Tait was ideal, an adult male who hated the minister.

The problem was how to get hold of him and find out the names from him. Oh, and persuade him to be a witness.

monday 16th october 1592

Dodd was irritable. He had been looking for a tooth-drawer all morning, had found it was true that Mr Lugg didn't do teeth, had heard tell of a tooth-drawer in Scotland but the man was called Johnstone and he didn't like to risk it. He had heard from two sources, the undertaker and Thomas the Merchant, that there was someone lately over on the East March and one said the man's name was Ricker and the other that he was called Henry. It wasn't enough to go on, but the swelling on the Courtier's jaw was getting worse. He had wrapped a scarf round his face against the cold and he was looking distinctly peaky. And he was drunk as well.

The only thing Dodd could think of was to go and find Lady Widdrington. She seemed to have a good grasp of the East March, her husband was the Deputy Warden, and the tooth-drawer probably had needed to bribe him anyway.

He asked permission from Carey to ride to the East March on the grounds his wife wanted something from Berwick, and Carey had given it without much attention. He was at Bessie's playing cards on his own; he called it a fancy Italian name, and it was clearly his way of distracting himself. Dodd took his favourite horse, Whitesock, legally bought and his this time, with the Queen's brand now cancelled by another one, half-healed. He had a warrant from Scrope, who was happy to give Dodd some despatches as well so he could ride post.

He liked riding post. You could do a hundred miles in a day with luck, probably less going across the Border, and he'd have to be careful in some places, but he could be in Widdrington at the end of a long day and he planned to be. Also the Courtier's sarcastic temper was getting on his nerves and he wanted to be away from it.

Widdrington was quiet and peaceful in the evening when he clattered in on the last post-house's horse, which was blowing and making a fuss. He'd never been there before and eyed it carefully despite the dusk, in case Carey could get over his stupid scruples and they needed to make a rough wedding party.

There was the castle, not on a hill—the whole village was flat and the sea nearby, the road the most important part of it. It was rich, you could see, a village supplying grain and horse feed and food to Berwick.

The castle wasn't large, not much more than a sturdy manor house with a much older tower and a wall around it for the villagers to bring their stock into when raiders came. He came to the gate, showed his warrant and went on into the main yard to find a pretty young woman who was heavily pregnant and an elderly man receiving him with a couple of the broad young Widdringtons hanging around as well to see he behaved himself. He smiled at them, liked it that they bothered.

"Ma name's Sergeant Dodd. I've come tae see Lady Widdrington. Is she about?"

"Lady Widdrington isn't here, sir," said the man. "She's north of the Border in Wendron."

"Can I help you, sir?" asked the woman. "My name is Mrs Burn. I'm a friend of Lady Widdrington's."

"Ach," said Dodd, very annoyed. He had dismounted and the horse was pulling toward the stables after his fodder. Dodd had ridden hard for the last ten miles to be into Widdrington before dusk. He took the horse into the stables, was shown the feedbins and set up the horse with a nosebag and a bucket and started whisping him down with brisk strong strokes. "Where's Wendron then?"

"It's about forty miles from here, sir," said Mrs Burn who had followed him. The steward had gone off somewhere else. "Would you like to stay here this night and start in the morning?"

Dodd thought about it. He could have kept going, though he'd need a different horse, but it was full dark now and the Moon not much use. He had to admit he was a bit tired after cantering and galloping for most of the day, and hungry as well since he'd eaten his bread and cheese in Haltwhistle on the Giant's Wall.

"Ay," he said, "that's kind o' ye, missus. I could do wi' a bite to eat as well."

"I think there's a pie and the cook's made a pottage and a stew, or there's bread and cheese and some apples too."

That sounded more like it. "Thank 'ee kindly, missus, I appreciate it."

"Oh, Sergeant Dodd, I've heard about you from Lady Widdrington. I'm very pleased to meet you at last and you can keep me company at dinner."

He wasn't sure about that since he was no kind of gentleman and would have preferred the despatch rider's room at the inn and beer in the commonroom, but he supposed it would be rude to refuse.

He found Roger Widdrington, the younger son of Sir Henry, was also in the dining parlour, making himself pleasant, which was interesting. Dodd knew about his part in the disaster in Dumfries that summer. Mrs Burn sat beside him with a girl— who was clearly there to learn huswifery, and Mr Heron, the reeve, as well, so it was quite a supper party.

Roger Widdrington said grace and the great pie was on the table with some soused hog's cheese and the pottage and stew, so Dodd helped himself to the venison and rabbit pie and the pottage as well.

He asked eventually about the tooth-drawer, though he said it was Scrope who needed a tooth out, since he was in Widdrington, after all. Mrs Burn's face, which was rather sad in repose, lit up.

"Oh yes, Sergeant Dodd, there's a new man in the area. In fact he was planning to go over to the West March soon."

"Ay? Do ye ken where he might be?"

"Yes. Minister Burn and I know him quite well. He's not like the usual run of barber surgeons. He's interested in reading and books and he's supposed to be very good at drawing teeth too. He's called Mr Simon Anricks and he's all the way from London."

"Fancy that," said Dodd, reaching for more hog's cheese since it was very good. He took some more bread too, since that was manchet. You had to admit that lords and ladies saw themselves well for food. "Is he a spy? The last tooth-drawer but one in the Middle March got caught with a mirror with letters fra the Pope behind it."

Mrs Burn laughed. "I don't know. Perhaps he is, you'll have to ask him. Now I think about it, he's probably in Wendron now with Lady Widdrington because…because…"

And just like that she turned to crying. Dodd sat back in astonishment and watched.

"Her husband was killed a week ago," Roger Widdrington explained quietly. He didn't do much about it, just let the woman greet into a handkerchief. "Two men walked into his house and cut his head off."

"Och, that's bad," said Dodd, sympathetically. "It wasna even on a raid? I'm sorry for yer trouble, missus."

She nodded at him as she tried to get a hold of herself.

"We'd like to find out who the men are, obviously," said Widdrington pompously. "I'm waiting for another despatch from my elder brother who is with Lady Widdrington."

Dodd nodded. It was cheeky, that's what it was. And it would be difficult to find them too, because they could just ride away and nobody any the wiser. Or at any rate, nobody any the wiser who would tell on them.

"Mrs Burn was there at the time too," said Widdrington, "that's why she's so distressed."

"Ay?" said Dodd. "That's shocking." He supposed she couldn't be expected to do anything about it since she was clearly not a Border woman. Her accent was a little strange, something like Scottish, something like English from the West March, something guttural. The woman got awkwardly to her feet and curtseyed to Widdrington, left the room still crying, followed anxiously by the girl.

Dodd, Widdrington and the steward ate most of what was left of the hog's cheese and the pottage, though the pie was a giant and they left three quarters of it for the morning. They talked about drainage ditches and they talked about hobbies and who was raiding whom in the Middle March and the West March. Dodd brought them up to date with the Maxwells and the Johnstones, who were only raiding sheep and cattle at the moment, feints to see where the weaknesses were.

At last Dodd was shown to a little room next to the stables that was full of the comforting scent of horses and a bed with a tester as well, and so he got to undress, which he wouldn't at the inn.

tuesday 17th october 1592

He was up as early as he could manage the next morning, two hours before dawn, feeling cold and miserable as usual. When he went to the kitchen in the hope of pillaging some more of the pie, he found it unlocked and a candle lit and Mrs Burn sitting there alone, waiting for him, while the kitchen boy snored on his pallet with his blankets round his ears.

"Sergeant Dodd," she said, "I'm so sorry I had to leave the dinner table last night, but it comes on me sometimes and I can't stop crying. I loved Jamie Burn, no matter what he was before and it…I can't help it."

Poor woman, Dodd thought, that's worse is that, if you loved your husband as well. His mam had loved his dad and she'd gone from being a big plump happy woman to a sad skinny one in a matter of months after he'd been killed. What would he feel if Janet was dead, now?

It was the first time he'd thought of it, strangely, and just the thought made his stomach squinch up under his ribs and his bowels go to water. Jesu, he thought, I'd be a lost man. He shook his head and deliberately crushed the thought. Janet would have to outlive him, that was all.

"Ay," he said inadequately, "Eh…Ah wis wondering if there's any pie…?"

She smiled at him. "It's a good one, isn't it? I've got some breakfast and lunch here, ready packed, and I'm hoping you'll do me a favour for it."

"Ay missus," he said cautiously, sitting down facing her.

"It's all right," she said, "I won't ask you to kill my husband's murderers for me, unless you happen to come upon them and have a rope ready…"

He smiled. "Ay missus, I can promise that…"

"I just want to send a letter to Mr Anricks. He was such a good friend to Jamie, I want him to know that I think Jamie left him something in his will and a few other things."

She had a letter from her bodice, quite a thick packet. Dodd hesitated and then took it. He'd already given the despatches from Scrope to Roger Widdrington who would pass them to his father; he might as well take this.

He put it inside his doublet, inside his buff leather jerkin that he wore because it wasn't exactly business and you went quicker if you didn't wear a jack.

"If you could give that to Mr Anricks personally," she said, "I'd be very grateful."

Maybe she was having an affair with the tooth-drawer, Dodd speculated. She was a pretty woman or she would be if she didn't have such black circles round her eyes.

"Ay missus," he said. She smiled at him then and gave him two neatly wrapped packages which he carried into the stable-yard where he found a sleepy young boy holding a nice-looking hobby for him, already tacked up.

He was off a couple of minutes later, taking the hobby at a brisk walk and then to a trot for half a mile before he put his heels in and went to a canter.

tuesday 17th october 1592

The boy went to sleep eventually and Elizabeth dressed and left him there to go to see his mother. The father wasn't there and she had bruises on her wrist and the bruise on her face was the shape of a hand. At least it was an open one.

Not thinking about Sir Henry with great difficulty, Elizabeth sat down on the stool the woman offered her.

"Now, Mrs Tait," she said, "your lad Jimmy has a beautiful voice, hasn't he?"

The woman smiled and her face changed from its watchful shut-in look.

"Ay," she said, "The minister heard him once when he was scaring crows and singing the Twa Corbies to frighten them and then nothing would do but that he'd go tae the school and learn his letters and sing for the minister. My man didna like it at first, but after a while he said it was fair enough since he got bread and cheese at the school to his dinner and so he didn't need so much as Young Jock and Lily and the babby."

There was no babby visible. The woman coloured and paled. "He died, the babby. In the spring. Eh…he fell over and…hit his head and that was the end of him."

I don't think so, thought Elizabeth, but didn't say, *I think he annoyed his dad and got hit too hard.*

The woman wasn't looking at her. "Young Jock's the apple of his eye mind, but…" She shrugged and looked away and gave her sore bruised wrist a rub. Well, to business. It looked like

Elizabeth was following in Jamie Burn's footsteps but no matter.
There were worse ones she could choose.

"I think your young Jimmy could go to the cathedral in
Carlisle and be a singer at the services there. How old is he?"

"About seven, I think. He came before the Armada, any road."

"Well he's young, but that's no hindrance. Did the minister
speak of this with you?"

"He talked to Jock about sending Jimmy to Carlisle," said
the woman, "And Jock wanted money for the boy."

"Really?"

"To…to replace him as a crow scarer, ye ken. And his labour
in the fields when he got big. And…"

"What did the minister say to that?"

"He said he'd think about it and we left it at that."

"When did he talk to you about it?"

"About a month ago, when we were sowing the winter wheat."

Elizabeth drew a deep breath and let it out again. "What did
Mr Tait need the money for?"

"He wants a new helmet, he said."

"How much?"

"Ten pounds."

It was outrageous. Fifty shillings for the boy would have been
the going rate, but ten pounds? Tait was clearly a canny father
with a good grasp of bargaining.

"I see."

"And the minister got him down fra twenty. I dinna think
the minister had ten pounds but maybe he saw a way to get it,
ye ken," said the woman in a whisper.

"Oh? What way was that?"

The whisper was so tiny, so soft, Elizabeth couldn't quite
make it out. "What?"

"The old way," she said, a little louder. "The way the minister's
brother Geordie would get it, or any one o' Ralph o' the Coates'
boys. The way Jock would hisself. Reiving or killing. Insight."

"Ah," said Elizabeth. After a moment she rose to go. "Thank
you, Mrs Tait, that's very helpful. I'll think about the money."

She didn't have ten pounds herself; it was an enormous sum, although a reasonably respectable suit would cost you ten times that. But you'd get the suit on credit and pay for it over six months or a year. She felt quite dizzy again as she walked up the hill from the Taits' farm and had to stop for a moment at some stones from a peel tower destroyed in the Rough Wooing.

There wasn't a lot of reiving now in the Scots East March, or the English East March, most of the trouble happened in the West or Middle March. The Humes held sway in Scotland and dealt with troublemakers their way, the Widdringtons and the Fenwicks were strong enough to deal with troublemakers in England. Blackrent was another matter. Occasionally you'd get a big invasion, forty or eighty men from the Middle March might come riding into a valley at night and take all the stock and insight that wasn't locked inside a wall, and ride off again. Then there'd be the usual arguments over it at the next Warden's Day and eventually it would all be composed, but nobody would get back all they had lost or expect to.

Murders happened, too, mainly for not paying blackrent or for revenge. And yet when you thought about it, what had been the reason for Jamie Burn to get his head taken off? A pastor didn't pay blackrent and revenge…

Elizabeth's eyes narrowed as she stared at some large stones leaned on even older ones. Revenge might well be a reason, especially given the way the minister had been spoken of. Perhaps it was for something he did when he was younger.

She realised that one of the rocks in the grey light was not a rock, but a straight back wrapped in a wolf fur. It was too small to be a man so after she stepped back she stepped forward again. Who was it? It turned a little face under a shock of white hair and a linen cap a little sideways, with a fine Edinburgh hat on top of that.

"Ma'am, Lady Hume?" she asked, in astonishment, "what are you doing here?"

"Well I like it here, my dear. Do ye not know it's a faerie fort? At night the stones all float together and build themselves up

again and then ye can dance and sing with the lairds and the
ladies too, dance yer heart out and then in the morning it's grey
and fifty years ha' passed ower yer head and ye're an old woman
and al' the lairds and ladies are deid and gone and passed."

Elizabeth looked about for Kat Ridley and saw her, sitting
on another moth-eaten old wolfskin, some way back, watching
carefully. A little further off was a lad with two ponies, a palfrey
and a jennet, nice animals both of them.

Lady Hume seemed to be waiting for something as the late
afternoon squelched away, sitting patiently and bolt upright, her
head a little tilted on her ruff. Elizabeth moved round to where
Kat Ridley sat, knitting away at a pair of socks.

"Er…"

"She's waiting for the fairy fort to build itself—she does it
when she's like this. She willna have nathing but to come here
and wait till night for the fair fort and she usually dozes off and
then she'll go hame quite happily. Cousin William's no' far away,
he bides out o' sight for she doesnae like a man too near when
she's awa' wi' the fairies like she is the day."

"Ah. Do you know whose tower this was?"

"Ay, it were the Taits', pulled down by Wharton, and his
grandfather hanged by the gateposts."

"You mean Jock Tait, in the village, his grandfather?"

"Ay, who else would I mean, there's nae ithers round here.
There may be some distant cousins in Upper Tynedale, but this
was their easternmost tower and a fine place it was."

Elizabeth was starting to understand.

"The grandfather?" she asked.

"Nay, the eldest son," said Kat Ridley, "Hanged next tae his
father to learn 'em for being reivers and Scotch forbye. By Lord
Wharton in 1544."

Elizabeth nodded.

"It wisnae a bad match for a Burn girl, mind, and she wis the
pick o'the Border then, a little delicate girl with white blonde
hair, so I hear, but then after it was all over and we were picking
up the pieces and building turf bothies, she was seen by one of

the younger sons of the Laird Hume of Norwood and it wisnae a good match for him but it wisnae so bad the old Laird forbade it for a younger son so they married. Then when the elder brother died of a fever, she became Lady Hume."

Elizabeth moved back and sat next to Lady Hume, erect and still as the twilight came down.

"It's aye hard," said the old lady, "I allus doze off and I wake and the music's still ringing in my heid, Chevy Chase, and my feet are tapping and a foul spell's come upon me for I'm an old woman again."

Elizabeth could think of nothing to say to that. She started to hum Chevy Chase, though, the repetitive song so you could hear the verses. Lady Hume smiled and nodded at her.

"Ay, ye're right, it's like that. And who're ye, girl?"

"Lady Widdrington?"

"Och, ye've got an ill man to wed there, if it's the Henry I knew. He liked breaking the wings of birds when I saw him when he wis a child, but he's terrible afeared of heights."

"I didn't know that."

"He allus kept it secret. And the puir minister. He shouldnae have gone back to the reiving, should he?"

"Did he?"

A sharp elbow went into Elizabeth's ribs. "Och, ye know he did, he was out last month in the Middle March. Couldnae keep hisself from it, could he? Once a reiver, allus a reiver, I say."

Elizabeth nodded. "You're right. But he must have reived the wrong cattle."

Lady Hume giggled at that. "In a manner o' speakin', aye, that's why they killt him so gentle. Not hanging so he danced for half an hour like my Archie, but off wi' his brainpan."

"Do you know who did it, Lady Hume?"

She just frowned. And then she stopped and sighed and turned her head as the stars came out in a couple of gaps in the clouds. "Ay, d'ye hear the music? Ay?" She sat rapt, her eyes shut, her head nodding slightly to the beat of the silent music. After a while she drew in a deep breath and sighed it out again.

She dropped off to sleep then, curled over and down like a small animal, laid her head in Elizabeth's lap and went to sleep with a smile on her face.

Elizabeth sat and thought. Killed him so gentle: compared with many a Border killing or indeed a judicial death with no drop and a long choking death on the end of a rope, it was a gentle death. Paradoxically because it was hard to think of anything much more brutal than a knife under the ribs followed by a long sharpened metal bar coming around and cutting half your head off, but yes, it had been a quick death and a clean one. Almost a kind one, as such things were reckoned on the Borders.

That was interesting. It was also interesting that Lady Hume had been the first to know, seeing she was a Burn and some kind of aunt to Jamie Burn. Somebody must have told her, or she was a witch or the faery folk had told her.

You could but ask. Elizabeth stroked the old head in her lap, pushed the white hair back and straightened the cap and took off the hat which was getting slightly crushed. It was a respectable hat.

"Lady Hume," she asked softly. "Lady Hume, who was it told you Jamie was dead?"

She asked a few more times and was about to give up when Lady Hume moved her head and answered with her eyes tight shut.

"They did, ma'am, the two men that killed him. They rode over and told me all about it and I was sick and sorry for it, that I was, but I knew Jamie had been out the month before and I knew what he was at and…that's why they tellt me. It was a way too high for him and me, I know it now. And they rade away intae the night and I went to horse meself the next morning for it wouldna be right for the minister to be unburied, no matter what."

"What was it? What had he done?"

"Ay, it was terrible, how he was, part of his head had rolled a way but I brought it back tae his body."

Her eyes were still shut, was she awake? "He's dancing with me now, ye know, he's dancing and laughing and his head's back together again, dancing along of all the ither people, like my Archie Tait and the people in the wood and the archers and the English archer and a' the puir folk we couldna feed for the English had burned their fields and their goods and they had nothing and they starved and died. They're all dancing with me here now."

"Who were the men? Can you tell me that at least?"

"Och, I don't know, I couldna tell ye any more, it's hard to tell all o' them now. Not Geordie, that's sure."

"But…"

"And they're bringing in the boar's head now and we're singing for it," said Lady Hume, eyes tight shut, the night making it hard even to see her face, and she started humming a version of the Boar's Head Carol.

Elizabeth sat with her until her arm was cramped and her bum had gone numb from sitting on the rock. Kat Ridley came with a blanket and behind her the broad silent man who nodded and said "ma'am" to Elizabeth, and then took the old lady in his large strong arms. Kat held her while he mounted his horse and then handed her up to him with her hat and he rode off northwards to the castle.

Elizabeth looked impatiently at Kat Ridley. "Do you know who came to her to tell her Jamie Burn was dead? Do you know their names?"

"Nay, ma'am, I told ye, I took the washing down to the washerwoman and I didna…"

"They came at night."

That gave Kat Ridley pause. She put her head on one side. "No," she said, though Elizabeth thought she was lying, "I must have been asleep."

"Were you?"

"Ay."

"And do you know what the minister was at a month ago?"

An almost invisible shake of the head. "Nay, ma'am, he wouldna tell me, ainly herself."

Elizabeth sighed and said good-bye to the woman who was only doing what she was told, trudged on through the night to the manse where she found Young Henry and all four of the cousins anxiously waiting for her and found herself being scolded by him for wandering around the village on her own.

"Don't be daft, Young Henry," she laughed. "I'll come to no harm..."

"Ma'am, a man punched ye in the heid and knocked you out a day or two ago, how do ye know they're not still here?"

"Well he..."

"They might still be after whatever it was they was looking for and...they might see ye and think it's a great time to find out where it is, or kidnap you and make us give it them, whatever it is."

"Oh." Now she thought of it, she had been careless. "I'm sorry, Henry, you're right. I started in daylight and went down to see the Taits and then came back and met Lady Hume at the old burnt peel tower and got overtaken by dusk. I never thought of that."

Now she had thought of it, it gave her a bad feeling in her stomach, an anxious unhappy feeling. Henry made a few more pompous speeches about being more careful and she waited him out because he was right. She wasn't at Widdrington now, where the only real danger to her was Sir Henry.

"You're quite right," she said. "I'll start for home tomorrow."

Well that was no good, either, apparently. Was she quite sure she was all right, had she felt dizzy...? She had, but she certainly didn't want to tell him. "I'll decide in the morning," she said after she had listened patiently to about enough of it. "I'm for my bed."

She went upstairs to the big bed with its tester and curtains and found herself the only occupant, not even a girl sleeping on the truckle. Henry and the cousins were sleeping downstairs and where, she wondered, was Anricks?

Before she got undressed, she took a look in his room with the old bed in it and saw his pack still there, half open and with his instrument case taken out so presumably he was treating someone.

She thought about it, and went downstairs again. A little later she had young Cuddy Trotter's mam coming pink-faced and flustered up the stairs to sleep in her bedroom with her and keep the proprieties. Henry had the grace to be embarrassed about that, he'd forgotten about the barber surgeon.

When Anricks came back, with blood still under his nails, Henry asked him belligerently if he still wanted to sleep upstairs.

"It's perfectly all right, Mr Widdrington," said Elizabeth to her stepson. "I have Mrs Trotter to sleep with me."

Henry scowled at Anricks as if it was his fault everyone thought he might be a Jesuit.

Anricks took his instrument case into the scullery and used a bucket of water there to wash his instruments, which were fine ones of steel and looked fragile for the heavy work of pulling teeth.

"Mr Widdrington, would you like to inspect my mirror and my tools?" asked Anricks with a perfectly straight face. "I assure you I'm not any kind of Jesuit or Papist."

"So you say, sir," said Henry who was clearly still upset about something, although Elizabeth had no idea what.

Anricks brought the pack over and the instruments and plopped them down in front of him. "There you are, sir," he said. "Will you be wanting to search me personally?"

"Er…no."

Henry made a half-hearted search of the pack which contained shirts, hose, breeks, bandages, a packet of mouldy lamb pasties that had to go out into the yard and onto the dung heap, several small books including Ascham's *The Schoolmaster*, and a great deal of writing paper thickly scrawled.

"What's this?" asked Henry, holding up a page between thumb and forefinger.

"My book, sir," said Anricks, still equably. "My accounts of the North and my thoughts on the tooth-drawing trade and also my speculations on the nature of toothworms."

"Yours?"

"Ay sir, perhaps I may get it published next time I am in London. If I can come up with a way to prevent holes and rotten teeth, I will be famous and rich."

"What way is that?"

"I think the avoidance of sugar is one thing, for toothworms seem to be attracted to it. In a family where one child loved sugar plums and the other child preferred cheese, it was the sugar plum-eater who had the worms and the holes, although..." Henry grunted and squinted at the writing.

"Why can't I read it?"

"I don't know, it's in English."

Henry flushed and turned it the right way up and started to puzzle out some of the words. "For toothworms, if they exist, must live in the stomach and come into the mouth by way of the throat..."

Elizabeth smiled. Anricks had a strange kind of patience, a watchful intelligent kind that does not allow emotions such as doubt or anger to interfere. Suddenly she found herself wondering about him again. Jesuits were supposed not to lie about being priests, though according to the pamphlets, they could equivocate.

Perhaps she could find out more about Jamie Burn from him.

"Gentlemen," she said, "none of us have had supper and I'm hungry. Shall we eat whatever's left in the larder and be friends?"

There was the end of a hambone, there was more pottage, there were quite a lot of bits of calf, though no one had thought of the perfectly simple operation of putting the bones and some potherbs to a large pot of water and making soup, and there was the remains of the sheep as well.

They served it up in the Burns' dining parlour as one remove with some bread that needed to be toasted to make it edible. They brought in the remains of the beer and the ale, which was just on the turn and would be spoiled by the morrow. Elizabeth invited Mrs Trotter to join them and the Widdrington cousins as well, although they were on watch, strictly speaking, since Henry wasn't about to allow another incident like the last. But they agreed to take it in turns, and she reserved plates for the two on watch first who were Humphrey and Daniel. Hector and Sim were understandably nervous of eating at her table but she reckoned honour was satisfied and served them some of everything and some of the ale they had nearly allowed to be reived as well.

She sat at the other end with Young Henry and Cuddy's mam, Mrs Trotter, and Mr Anricks as well and as the eldest man there Young Henry gave place to him. Mr Anricks said grace. It was slightly unusual. "Blessed be you, Lord God of the World, of your goodness we have this meat and drink to our dinner, which Earth has given and human hands have made." But it wasn't Catholic, not being in Latin.

"Amen," she answered to it firmly and took some of the veal which was excellent even cold; she'd boil it up into a soup tomorrow just on general principles.

They talked of neutral things until Elizabeth thought that you can but ask again and said to Hector, "By the way, were you working for anybody the other night or was it just a bit of foolishness?"

"Foolishness," said Hector who had come at her with a knife.

"Jock Tait," said Sim with a lowering look at Hector. "It were Jock that tellt us he had some buyers for the beer and what would we say to a shilling?"

Young Henry put down his knife and glared at Sim and Hector. Elizabeth managed a repressive glance and smiled at the two lads, neither of them over nineteen, she thought.

"Och," said Hector.

"Did he say who the buyers were?"

Both of them shook their heads. Sim too had a splendid crop of spots though he wasn't as big and broad as Young Henry.

"Did you get your shilling?" Two heads shook sadly. "I thought not. Have you ever ridden with Jock Tait?"

"Ay, o' course," said Hector and Young Henry was now staring busily at his food and stirring the pottage.

"Ay, well, ma'am," said Young Henry. "It's when we're hitting the Routledges and the Carletons that we...eh...well we ride wi' the Taits and the Burns."

"And the Elliots?"

"Wee Colin? No, he's an unchancy bastard though him and Geordie Burn are thick as porridge together."

"So Jock Tait's a good man, is he?"

"Ay," said Sim, "he's no' extra special wi' anything like Young Henry can shoot wi' a gun, but he's a good solid all round man, good wi' a lance and a sword if he had one, and he's good at scouting too."

"I heard tell it was the Elliots who wanted the beer?"

"Nay, ma'am," said Henry, "they like the Burns."

"So who wanted the beer?"

"Perhaps it was Jock Tait himself," said Simon Anricks thoughtfully. "To spoil the funeral, since you say he doesn't like...didn't like the minister."

"Perhaps," she said, "and I heard that Jamie Burn was out last month, reiving. Surely that's not true?"

How very interesting the faces were. Young Henry was surprised, and then thoughtful as if it wasn't such a surprise after all. Hector and Sim were not surprised. Simon Anricks, just for a second had an extraordinary look on his face, of understanding and regret and worry, which closed up at once into conventional shock.

"Ah dinna ken, missus," said Hector with a warning look at Sim that should have molten his helmet which was sitting beside him on the table.

"Well, never mind, I expect it was just gossip," agreed Elizabeth brightly. "You two can go and relieve Humphrey and Daniel now."

They clattered off while Elizabeth served some more of the mutton to Young Henry and Simon Anricks, then helped herself to half of what was left.

"Jock Tait's the hero of another tale I heard, too," she said while Humphrey and Daniel shovelled food into their mouths.

They weren't brothers like Ekie and Sim, sons of one of Sir Henry's younger half-brothers, but cousins. Sir Henry had many sisters and brothers and half-brothers and they all lived round about Widdrington. As a surname it was numerous and had a name for being fierce for the Middle March, where the village actually was. She told how she had found out the horses were looked after by young Jimmy Tait and the scrap of dialogue the boys had given her, how someone called Spiny could wait.

Young Henry put down his eating knife and looked appalled. "The Earl of Spynie?" he asked.

"I don't know," she answered regretfully. "It could just be a reiver with very wiry hair."

"Good God, if it's him…"

"It doesn't actually help us find the murderers," she told him, "but Jock Tait could. If we could persuade him to give us the men's names and be a witness."

"I suppose going to him with the cousins, grabbing him and hitting him until he told us wouldn't be a plan you'd like?" said Young Henry, good humouredly.

"No, Henry," she said, "it's like all short-cuts—gets very long in the end. If we did that do you think he would stick around to be a witness at the trial? If there is one? He might not tell you anyway, he looks a tough nut to crack. And besides," she added, "you have no jurisdiction of any kind here, this is Scotland."

"I have the right to follow the trod," said Young Henry, "same as anyone else."

"You aren't here on a trod, you're here for a funeral."

He didn't answer and looked mulish. Simon Anricks was looking very thoughtful and she thought she'd do some more stirring, again on general principles. It sometimes made her very tired the way menfolk tried to keep their reiving and other dubious behaviour secret, as if women could be fooled so easily.

"Mr Anricks," she said, "you were friends with the minister. You don't think he really was out last month?"

Anricks answered slowly. "I knew he wanted some money quickly because he asked me about it, but I said I couldn't help him. And he said something then that worried me but I put it out of my mind. I shouldn't have done, I regret it greatly."

"What was it he said?"

"When I said I couldn't help him, he said, no matter, he already knew another way to get the money and he'd look into that."

"Did he say what the other way was?"

"He said he'd talk to the Kerrs, that's all."

"The Kerrs?" The Kings and Princes of the Middle March, in other words. Some of the worst reivers on the Border, north or south. "Cessford? Ferniehurst?"

Anricks shrugged. "That's all he said, I wish I'd asked him but I didn't. I just told him to be careful."

In the end they could come to no conclusion about Jock Tait except to see if they could bribe him. And also Elizabeth had a worry that Tait would know who had told Elizabeth about the horses and young Jimmy might be badly beaten, or even killed. It had to be done with great care, as with everything else on the frontier. The only person she knew who really rejoiced at such complexities and loved working them out was Robin, whom she was duty bound not to contact. Where was he now? Was he well? She'd have heard if he was married because her husband would tell her, immediately, but had he met anyone else? It was right for him to marry someone else, God knew he needed the money, but...

Anricks went to his little guest chamber and Elizabeth recruited Humphrey and Daniel to take the trenchers and dishes into the scullery. They put them in to soak in the bucket of water Anricks had used and left them.

In the bedroom, Elizabeth invited Mrs Trotter to share the big bed rather than the truckle with the hole in it and listened drowsily to a very interesting account of young Cuddy Trotter and how he loved his lessons and how he could read all manner of things like a Bible in the church and a ballad sheet too, read it right off as if he had just heard it and how excited he'd been the month before. The minister had been full of excitement as well; they were talking of all making a journey to Carlisle, all the boys in the school in October and...

"All the boys in the school?" she asked, wide awake again.

"Ay, my lady," said Cuddy's mam, "they wis all to walk tae Carlisle together, him and them and they'd go the long way about it fra here down the Great North Road tae Berwick and they hadnae decided whether to go across the tops of the Cheviots or take the long way round from Newcastle by the old Faery Road behind the Faery Wall, tae Carlisle. He thought it would take a week but…"

"Why not go to Newcastle? It's much nearer?"

"Ay well, it's the choir at Carlisle. He wanted tae see if any o' the boys could be 'prenticed singers there."

"Would you like Cuddy to do that?"

"Ay, I would, for Cuddy could be a clerk or even a minister like Minister Burn hisself but Cuddy canna sing at all so I doot they'd take him. Still, it's an adventure and the boys wis all for it and maist o' the parents. Maist."

"Not Jock Tait."

"Ay and one o' the ithers, but the minister said it was a' or none and he'd see tae it. He was planning to take Lord Hughie as well."

"Why was he doing all this? He didn't have to."

"Ah, that's the Reverend Gilpin for ye."

"I've heard that name before."

"It wis a priest and then a reverend a while back, in England. He had a living somewhere in the South and soft and plenty o' money and instead of sitting on it and getting fat he came oot here to the Borders and made schools for the boys, taught them hisself, he did, and the best he sent tae the university. All in England, though, but Jamie Burn heard him preach once and went tae him and lied and said he was an English Burn. He wis at the Reverend Gilpin's school in the South when the fighting over Queen Mary and the Earl of Bothwell wis on and came North again when his dad sent for him and wis a bonny reiver. But he could ha' gone to St Andrews and when he'd made enough as a reiver, that's where he went, tae the university, to learn him Latin and Greek and Divinity for to be a minister like Gilpin."

"Oh. I never knew. What happened to Gilpin?"

"He wis killt by being run over by a bull, I know that, it got loose in the market and trampled him and he died a month later and all his boys came from far and wide to sing at his funeral, Jamie Burn too. It was in the early eighties, I think, before the Armada, and that's when the minister made up his mind to gae to university and so he did."

"I see."

"Gilpin used to preach wonderful sermons, he'd tell all about Hell and how there wis no Purgatory and how tae stay oot of Hell and get into Heaven—which he said wis easier nor anybody thought, because ye could just clap hands wi' God and He'd see ye right."

"Did you hear him preach?"

"Nay, but in church the minister told us some of his old sermons, which was good ones, when he hadnae the time to think of one of his ain."

"Hmm."

"There's another one where Gilpin says every reiver ye teach to read is peradventure one reiver the less for if a clever man sees no fair way to make his living, why then he'll use foul ways and cause a lot more trouble than a stupid man."

"Very true."

"Ye should read them, they're good and comforting. Like the minister's ain sermons but not one o' his was more than an hour, ye ken."

"So I heard."

"It's a pity they willna make their journey tae Carlisle now," said Mrs Trotter wistfully. "It's a real pity."

As Elizabeth dropped off to sleep, her jaw was set and the expression on her face fierce.

wednesday morning 18th october 1592

She knelt to her prayers with a will the next morning, knelt and practically shouted at God that He should help her with what she thought of as the minister's legacy or she would want to know the reason why. An extraordinary thing happened then: She got the feeling of a vast and intimate smile, a warmth in her chest as if she had understood something important and lovely, except she didn't know what it was.

She stood up and went out, told Young Henry who was practising gunnery in the orchard that the noise was giving her a headache and she would ride over and see if Lady Hume was well. He sent one of the cousins, young Hector since nobody else was around, which she accepted with reservations. Hector was all smiles and "my lady" so perhaps he had learned his lesson. She took a satchel with her, with pens and ink for she had contacts at the Scottish Court, and in particular Lord Chancellor Maitland who had begun as a friend of her husband's and become a friend of hers.

She had already packed up all Poppy's shifts and caps and stockings with her spare kirtles and aprons in a tight bundle inside her cloak which had been loaded onto a pack pony at the alehouse. Right in the middle of the bundles were the three goblets and the dish with cherubs on it that were Poppy's dowry. She had Jamie's will in her petticoat pocket and she couldn't think of anything else apart from the books which would need a string of pack ponies.

On the ride she thought so hard about the letter she was thinking of sending that she didn't notice at first that a man on horseback was paralleling them. She looked about for Hector and saw him, a way away, riding hell for leather in the opposite direction. Her stomach twisted and turned to stone and she looked about, rising as high as she could and peering. Two more riders were just out of sight, popping up every so often.

That was enough. She took a deep and careful breath and thought about it. The track up to the Hume castle was muddy but it went into a wooded area about a mile ahead and since nobody was doing anything yet, she was willing to bet that there was somebody waiting for her in the wood. Three out there, three more in the wood, perhaps.

They knew she must have seen them and they knew she had no man with her to guard her. They were still about two miles from the castle which was a longish run.

Her heart was beating hard and heavy in her chest and her mouth was dry. What could she do? What should she do? If she had been a man her best bet might have been to turn her horse about and ride for the nearest one. Or go into the wood and fight them there. Stupid to think like that, she was not a man.

She really did not fancy the wood; it looked muddy as well as autumn dark. No, so she wouldn't go there. The castle wasn't big, it had a moat and a curtain wall and a gatehouse as well once you were past the wood, of course. It was a scrubby little wood, a copse really, that had been allowed to grow up since the Rough Wooing. Why? The Humes weren't fools, and nor was Lady Hume, away with the faeries half the time though she was. You didn't let stuff like that grow up on the main route into the castle—unless it wasn't the main route. Unless it had been allowed to grow to give a good ambush place for people who didn't know what the right route was?

She hadn't been to the castle but she felt a rightness to that. Why else would they do that? And forbye, they would want the main entrance to the north, toward Edinburgh, not the south.

All right. She put her hand up to her hat and pinned it on tight to her cap, which hid the sore place on her skull and the cut hair. She set herself down into the sidesaddle, gripped with her leg around the hook and put the heel of her other leg into the horse's side so the animal leaped forward and started to run.

She rode at the gallop under the eaves of the wood, bent low to avoid the branches, dodged round a couple of trees and bushes, and then burst out again and rode around the wood and round the edge of the moat. She didn't bother to check the riders to see what they were doing, but kicked the horse again to get some more speed and rode like a madwoman around the curve of the old mound and there it was, a moat and working drawbridge.

The drawbridge was up. She hauled back on the reins and managed not to go into the moat.

There was a shout behind her, there were five of them now. She gave them a fig with her right hand while she rode out her horse's bucking, speaking softly to him, poor soul.

There was a man on the wall, not Cousin William, looking down at her and the men.

"Let me in," she shouted, "they're after me."

"They are?" said the man. "They're no', are they?"

"Ay, they are."

"Why?"

"I dinna ken," she shrieked in broad Scots. "Will ye shoot one for me so Ah kin ax?"

To her fury, the man turned away, bent, picked up a loaded crossbow and aimed it at her. She knew the men behind her were coming up closer.

"Her ladyship says she's sorry, but ye canna come in. She canna help ye."

Her horse was turning and crowhopping still. She only had seconds. She took off her mother's handfasting ring and threaded it onto a bare autumn twig of a hazel bush. Then somebody's strong fist caught the bridle and somebody else came up close to her with a scarf. She looked round at them, hard faces under helmets, wearing jacks that marked them as Burns, though she didn't recognise anybody. She was still buoyed by rage.

"How dare you!" she hissed in English now. "How *dare* you? You will regret this."

"Ay, mebbe, missus. Meantime, ye come wi' us."

weδnesδay 18th octobeR 1592

Dodd reached Wendron by mid-morning and found his bird
flown again.

"Och," he said when he found he had to ride another ten
miles to Norwood Castle where Lady Widdrington had gone to
pay her respects to Lady Hume. "I need another horse."

Young Henry Widdrington gave him a little hobby with the
warning that the beast had a nasty temper and would bite. He
remembered to give the letter to the small man who came out of
the house to see him and introduced himself as Simon Anricks.
He was trotting up the road half an hour later with his belly
growling. Since Lady Widdrington would keep, since she was no
doubt blethering on to her friends and had forgotten the time as
women did, he stopped by some trees and rocks and ate up the
first of the packages that Mrs Burn had given him, which contained a hearty wedge of the pie, bread, cheese, a couple of pickled
onions wrapped in waxed paper, and an apple. This was the nicest
food he could think of and he ate all of it, especially the apple.
Lady Widdrington must have an apple tree or know someone
who did and he found he wanted one too. Not a sapling, mind,
but a full tree, less for the apples than for what it meant, which
was that nobody had burnt the country for at least twenty years.

Well, you never knew. When he had finished the apple which
was quite sweet, he looked around to make sure no one was
watching and then dug a hole and buried it in the Earth.

He rode on to the Hume castle and found the place open as he expected, though he wondered what had been going on nearby since there were hoofprints of a horse galloping and others overlaying it before heading off across country.

When he rode in there was a sprightly old lady in a hat and velvet gown and her stout middle-aged woman standing behind her.

"Och, yes," said Lady Hume with a sweet smile. "She came to say good-bye and then turned about and went home tae England again."

"Ay," said Dodd, annoyed. How had he missed her then? Maybe when he was having his breakfast? "When was that?"

"A couple of hours ago," said the woman, also smiling. "It wis nice tae see her."

"Ay, thank 'ee kindly," said Dodd and turned the hobby's head and aimed south.

He went quicker on the way back, despite the hobby's tricks, which kept trying to turn his head west instead of south, but Dodd prevailed after a couple of tussles. He didn't want to miss Lady Widdrington again.

He saw Anricks again to the north of the village, riding a hobby and leading a pack pony, looking worried—though from the lines on his face that expression was a habit. He tipped his hat to the man. Then he took another look at the pack which was currently stowed on the pack pony behind him. It was brightly painted with lurid pictures: one showed a man with a swollen face and a scarf wrapped round it. The middle one showed a set of pincers and a bloody tooth, and the third picture showed the same man without a swollen face, happily tucking into a dinner consisting of venison and pork ribs and pot herbs.

"Ye're never a tooth-drawer?" he asked, unable to believe his luck.

"Yes, I am, sir. Do you have the toothache?"

"Nay sir, but I know a man who does, something terrible. What d'ye say to coming tae Carlisle wi' me and drawing his tooth?" He was quite willing to kidnap the tooth-drawer if it was necessary, but he hoped it wouldn't be.

The man's face lit up. "I would be delighted, since I've been planning to go to the West March, but I must confess I was nervous of the notorious robbers and reivers there."

"Ay," said Dodd, not bothering to explain that they were no worse in the West March than the Middle and certainly better than here in Scotland. The man wasn't very large and didn't look at all dangerous with his balding pate and modest black wool suit. "Come wi' me whiles I find Lady Widdrington and give her my respects and then we'll be off." Dodd wasn't that interested in the ordinary-looking woman who had so bewitched the Courtier, but he knew her and must at least greet her while he was in the area.

Back at Wendron, Young Henry was looking impatient. "Where is she?" he asked. "We've forty miles back to Widdrington and it's late."

"They said she'd come back here," said Dodd, also annoyed. Wasn't that just like a woman, gallivanting off on some notion when people wanted to get home.

"And I canna find Ekie nor Sim," said Young Henry darkly. "I sent Ekie Widdrington with her to look after her."

"Maybe she's fallen off her horse somewhere," said Dodd, since he had heard that this was something that did happen to people occasionally. "She can't have gone more than five miles, mebbe less, let's circle the castle at about five miles out."

They did that, heading in opposite directions to get it done quicker, and found nothing. Anricks came with them. When there was no trace of her, Dodd started to get worried as well. Kidnapping of women wasn't unknown in the Borders, although as he understood it, the Widdringtons were a mite tasty for that kind of behaviour.

Then he minded him of the marks near the castle of the galloping horse, overlaid by other hooves, and he cantered back to them, dismounted, and started using his eyes properly. He saw a shod horse, not a hobby, riding toward the castle, saw it slow and then change direction and yes, go into the wood a little, saw broken branches where someone had broken through them at the gallop, saw the swerve at the edge of the moat where the drawbridge was now down, saw the other horses, all of them unshod hobbies surrounding and overlaying the shod hoofprints. It couldn't have been clearer if somebody had set up a little play to show it to him.

"Och, Jesus Christ," he swore disgustedly to the hobby who gave him a horsy leer and shook his head.

He hadn't a hunting horn to call the others so he had to ride around the castle again, now watched by a man on the walls, found Anricks first and told him to go and guard the traces, then Young Henry, who was already scowling. At least the ugly hobby was now cooperating.

"Come and see this," he said without preamble and Young Henry followed him at once.

Anricks was looking at something on a hazel bush when they got there. He pulled it off and brought it over to them as they cantered up and Dodd saw it was a woman's ring, a gold handfasting circle.

"I found this," he said. "It was on the bush over there. Is it Lady Widdrington's?"

"Ay, it is." Young Henry's wonderfully spotty face darkened as they both dismounted and Dodd explained what he could see. Once it was pointed out to him, Young Henry could see it well enough himself.

He loosened his sword and pulled out his horn, winded it and then stood fingering the spot on the end of his nose.

"Four or five of them," he said, "the traces are clear enough, heading southwest. But."

"Ay, but." Dodd shook his head. "Could be. How many men ha' ye?"

"Ekie and Sim are gone, so only two as well as myself, Mr Anricks if he'll come, and you."

"Five, one not a fighter. It's no' enough to fight off an ambush."

"It's a trod now. I could likely call on the Humes…?"

"Could you?" Dodd asked, "There's a boy, a few men, and two women in the castle and I dinna see nae more. And forebye, they could have seen what happened here, why did they not help?"

Why did the old lady in fact lie to him, eh? That was something he'd like the answer to.

"Are any of these tracks from Ekie or Sim?" he asked, casting about for more hoofprints.

"No," Young Henry said after he'd taken another look, "I had Ekie on Butter which is a fat hobby and the tracks would be heavier."

"Ay, so they sold her to the reivers and went off. At least it means they aren't seven."

Young Henry was breathing hard through his nose.

"How long to get some men here?" Dodd asked, though he knew he wouldn't like the answer.

"Most of the Widdringtons are in the Middle March, a forty-mile ride at least. Say half a day to ride back for them and another half day to ride here again."

He had been right. He didn't like the answer.

Anricks had been sitting on his pony, staring hard into space as if he was reading something there.

"I happen to know," he said judiciously, "that Sir Henry Widdrington and my Lord Spynie are meeting near Jedburgh, which isn't nearly as far from here as Widdrington itself. And he'll have taken at least twenty men with him."

Young Henry stared suspiciously at the man while Dodd asked curiously, "So are ye a Jesuit or not then?"

A strange almost fey smile curved the man's mouth under his skimpy beard. "No sirs, I am not," he explained slowly and coldly. "I am unalterably opposed to his Catholic Majesty of Spain and at the moment I am by way of being a pursuivant in the service of Sir Robert Cecil."

Dodd whistled. "Are ye now?" he said. "I've met the man, see ye."

"Have you?" Anricks gave Dodd a look he was beginning to recognise as a reappraisal. "A very interesting personage—tall and handsome."

Dodd laughed shortly. "Well ye havenae met him if ye think that. He's a hunchback, though I'd say he wis handsome, ay, and interesting."

Anricks smiled again. He took a packet of paper out of his doublet pocket and unfolded a letter from it which he passed to Young Henry. "I am well aware of the fact that the last tooth-drawer in these parts, bar one that was a drunk, was in fact a Papist spy, but I am not and I took the precaution of obtaining this."

Young Henry passed the paper without comment to Dodd who turned it the right way up and read it carefully.

"A' right," he said, "let's see yer hands."

Anricks showed his hands palms up. There was a dark scar across the middle of each hand as if he had clutched a bar of red hot iron once and been burnt.

Young Henry and Dodd looked in silence for a while. "What was it did that?" asked Dodd. "I havenae seen the like on nae-body else."

"The same thing which gave me the grip I need to pull teeth. Forgive me, gentlemen, but I prefer not to speak of it nor remember it. However the scars prove I have not stolen the commission from another man and I am in fact the Simon Anricks of whom he speaks."

The commission had Sir Robert Cecil's seal on it and was written in a fine italic hand which might even have been his. It spoke of his confidence in Mr Anricks, described the scars on his hands, and asked whoever saw the paper and the scars to help him in all his enterprises.

"Please be so kind as not to mention this to anyone at all, especially not Sir Henry," added Anricks. "I am truly a tooth-drawer as well."

"How will we explain to Sir Henry how we found him?" asked Young Henry.

"I saw him riding west with his men when I was on the road from Edinburgh so I think there will be little difficulty. In any case, no doubt Sir Henry will be anxious to find and ransom his wife, if necessary."

Dodd had listened to Carey ranting on about how he hated the man and how he mistreated his wife and wondered if he would be that eager. It didn't matter, because his wife being kidnapped put a brave on him that he could only ignore if he wanted to lose every scrap of credit or reputation that he had.

Young Henry nodded once. Dodd sighed. He supposed he should stick with the tooth-drawer so he couldn't get out of drawing Carey's tooth. Though now he thought about it, he supposed Carey wouldn't approve of him not taking an interest in Lady Widdrington's kidnapping.

He tried to imagine Carey's reaction to that and found his imagination failed him. Carey would be very upset, to put it mildly, and might take it into his head to do something even crazier than his normal notions, which was where Dodd's imagination gave up. It was hard to beat spying out Netherby tower dressed as a peddler, selling faulty guns to the Irish and causing a riot in a London jail—all things Carey had regarded as excellent ideas in the past.

Without further ado they headed west and south to Jedburgh. At least it was in the right direction, Dodd thought philosophically.

They found Jedburgh full of Widdringtons who greeted Young Henry respectfully, considering his youth, and told him his father wasn't there. He was hunting with Lord Spynie at a small hunting lodge northwards which was sometimes used by the king on his way to a justice raid in the Scots West March. They would be back later in the day, and meantime Young Henry and his men could wait for them. Some of Spynie's men were hanging around in the town as well, the same combination of popinjay vicious courtiers and hard nuts that Dodd had thoroughly disliked in the summer.

They came and insisted on searching Anricks' pack and two of them even dared to question Young Henry until his uncle Thomas Widdrington snarled that he'd vouch for the boy. One asked Dodd his business.

"Ay," he said, "I'm a Dodd, sir."

He was looking as wooden and stupid as he could, helped by his buff coat and lack of helmet and for good measure he tipped his statute cap to the lad in a magnificent purple and tawny padded doublet.

"That's well enough," said the other one, glorious in bright green and yellow. "We ha' tae ask, goodman, for somebody took a potshot at my lord Spynie ainly last month."

"Ay," said Dodd, not bothering to look interested, "what with?"

"A crossbow. He got away too and then he tried again in the night and killed a bolt of linen Spynie had in his bed and then he got away again, so Spynie's no' pleased wi' us."

"Ay, bad luck tae him."

"Ay."

Dodd was more interested in what Anricks was up to and wandered after him. He found him in the courtyard of the biggest inn at Jedburgh, the Spread Eagle, with his pack already taken off the packhorse and both horses in a loosebox.

Anricks took off his doublet and rolled his sleeves up, put on his blood-stained apron and unrolled his instruments in their canvas. The innkeeper brought a sturdy armchair out to the yard and then two more on further instructions and lined them up.

"Teeth drawn," shouted Anricks. "Get your teeth drawn for one English shilling or four Scots shillings. Teeth drawn." He had a weak voice that didn't shout very well, so Dodd offered his services and was soon strolling round the town with the innkeeper's youngest and his drum, bellowing "Teeth drawn! Get yer teeth drawn!" in broad Scots.

By the time he got back a queue had formed that was already out of the stableyard. He watched for a while, ready for drama and screams, but it was boring. The patients sat down in the chairs and told Anricks which tooth was giving them trouble. He poked about in their mouths, sometimes producing gasps and moans. Then he made them drink a great deal of brandy, supplied at double prices by the inn, and gave them a cloth in their hands to sniff. He was pouring out drops of something oily from a brown glass bottle onto it every so often. After a bit they fell asleep and then Anricks was onto them, opening their snoring mouths, reaching in with a steel instrument, placing it carefully round the bad tooth and then clenching his fist and drawing it out. And then he moved on to the next patient.

Dodd had a go at pulling a tooth himself and found it much harder than he expected for the grip was awkward and you needed all your strength to pull. Anricks did two more with crunching sounds and a lot of blood and pus while he was fumbling.

Then the patients would wake up, look around dizzily as if hungover, feel their mouths in wonder and then wander off with their friends, shaking their heads. A few people started scowling at Anricks and muttering about witchcraft, but the ones who had had their teeth drawn shushed them.

"Is it witchcraft, sir?" Dodd asked curiously as they waited for a stout woman to go to sleep. "Is it a secret?"

Anricks shook his head. "No, it's an alchemical miracle. No secret at all. Paracelsus first noticed its effect on chickens and I tried it on myself once I had made some. They are sniffing sweet oil of vitriol, distilled from aqua vitae and vitriol." He gripped, clenched, the instrument slipping. "Hold her mouth more open, please. Thank you." Not a sound from the patient. Again the hands tightened on the instrument and the cracking crunch told Dodd the tooth was out. Anricks produced a large long-rooted tooth that was black all along one side and had two holes in it. The root was full of pus. He dropped the tooth in the bucket and swabbed at the space with a cloth wet with aqua vitae while the woman slept on.

Dodd looked in the bucket, with all the other eaten-away teeth and suddenly felt sick. That was an ill sight to see, to be sure, how your actual teeth could be eaten away. Horrible. What did that for God's sake?

Anricks didn't need him anymore; he had a queue going down the hill now. Dodd wandered out to the yard and found a boy there asking for him, who told him to come and meet Sir Henry.

Young Henry was looking grim and Sir Henry was loudly raging. "Do you believe this about my wife, Mr Dodd, that she went off with persons unknown?" he demanded.

Dodd was about to correct him about what he was and then left it. "She didnae go voluntarily and she tried to escape, the signs were clearer than the nose on yer face," he said stolidly. "And she left her mother's ring on a twig near the place where they caught her."

Sir Henry swung about on his son. "So why didn't ye follow the tracks and catch them?"

"Perhaps because I had no desire to ride into an ambush, sir," said Young Henry, with admirable calm. "Or not until I had enough of my men to back me."

"My men, puppy, I'm the headman."

"Yes, father."

"How did you know where I was?"

Young Henry looked blank. "We thought it was worth trying Jedburgh because this is where you come to meet with Lord Spynie and we'd heard you were riding west."

Suddenly Sir Henry slapped his son across the face and followed up with a nasty rabbit punch to the short ribs. Young Henry took the slap and only grunted a little with pain at the rib punch.

"Don't think ye can outguess me, boy," hissed Sir Henry.

Young Henry said nothing. His face was a mask under the reddening print of his father's hand. Sir Henry was standing, scowling up at him and chewing his moustache.

"What would you like me to do, sir?" Young Henry asked steadily.

Suddenly Dodd saw fear in the man's face, and couldn't think why. Young Henry towered over him and yet was as respectful as a man should be to his father, no matter how unreasonable. Was that what he was afraid of? That his son was a better man than him?

"Weel weel, wha' ha' we here?" came broad Scotch tones. Dodd turned to see the handsome young man with gold hair that was still the King's lover come striding over to them. Lord

Spynie was wearing a smart black satin doublet with diamond buttons and a very nice cutwork leather hunting jerkin over it. He wasn't very tall, a couple of inches shorter than Dodd himself and four inches shorter than Young Henry, but he swaggered and swung a whip in his hand.

Young Henry and his father both bowed to him and Dodd did the same, quietly stepping backwards out of the way. Sir Henry explained that his fool of a wife had got herself captured by reivers while fossicking about in Scotland where she had no business to be.

"I'm sorry you didn't get my message by Roger," Young Henry said, "about the killing of Minister Jamie Burn?"

"I got it," growled Sir Henry. "She had no business in Scotland. She should have minded my business in England."

"Wives," said Spynie, with an indulgent smile, "allus poking about in what doesnae concern them."

Sir Henry stood irresolute, although what he had to do was obvious. He should gather his men, ride out with them and find out who had his wife. And then he should ransom her and follow up with some reprisal raids unless the kidnappers were too powerful, in which case he should wait and take reprisals later and more carefully. That's what Dodd would have done if anyone had been stupid enough to kidnap Janet. Although unfortunately he loved his wife, which would make everything much more complicated. He decided to go back to the inn and the tooth-drawing.

When he got there he found Anricks in an argument with a bunch of sour-looking men in black or brown clothes and white collars.

"Ye say it isn't witchcraft, Mr Anricks," said one of them, "but ye canna deny that ye make them sleep and so they get out of the pain o' the tooth-drawing."

"I do not deny it, that's why I do it. It makes my work easier for they are not fighting nor screaming."

A heavy looking man shook his head. "The Scripture says, man is born tae sorrow…"

"Ay," said a skinny man with hot eyes, "and it's wrong to try to evade Scripture, so it is."

Anricks shut his eyes for a moment and then smiled brightly. "You are ordering me to stop using sweet oil of vitriol?"

"We are ordering ye to stop using the evil spells that make people sleep."

"Your name, sir?"

"I am Elder Tobermory, he is Elder Stanehouse. That is Minister Birkin."

"Very well, sirs. I will stop using the oil of vitriol and explain to each of my patients why. Thank you."

Nonplussed, the sour men moved away in a body and then stood watching to see there was no witchcraft. Each tooth took longer now because they had to tell the patients why they couldn't sniff the magic cloth: Anricks explained that Elders Tobermory and Stanehouse and Minister Birkin had ordered him to stop using the sweet oil of vitriol, and the elders and the minister had to explain that they had stopped him from using witchcraft and imperilling their immortal souls. The people who still wanted their teeth drawn screamed and cried as he pulled their teeth, which was a lot noisier and the results were not nearly as good and everything took longer.

The elders and the minister were shouting themselves hoarse at some of Anricks' patients by the end of it and the queue had disappeared. When the second to the last one went, Dodd reached out and stopped a boy making off with the box that was now full of shillings. When the tooth was pulled from the last woman who cried steadily throughout but didn't scream, Anricks went and dumped all his instruments into a bucket of water and then used another just to wash his arms and hands, which was a bit dainty, Dodd thought. The woman was weepily thanking Anricks and telling him it didn't hurt nearly as much as having a baby and insisted on paying him an extra shilling for she already felt much better.

They moved to the commonroom of the inn to count the money which amounted to about one hundred shillings Scots and ten shillings English, which was very respectable. Then Anricks went to the market and bought three pack ponies' loads of oats which was good cheap, along with the pack ponies and led them all into the innyard where he paid the innkeeper, also in Scots shillings. The remaining Scots money he used to pay for the ordinary—a haggis and bashed neeps and some ale, which he shared with Dodd.

Anricks was tired and quiet. Dodd was wondering how quickly he could get him to Carlisle. It was too late in the day to make for Carlisle now.

"It's a puzzle," said Anricks, suddenly, apropos of nothing, "why and by whom was the Minister Burn killed."

"He wisnae against yer witchcraft?"

"It isn't witchcraft. It's as natural as a man falling asleep when he's drunk. Just quicker and easier…"

"Whatever. He wisna agin it?"

"He was at first, until I drew one of his teeth for him and then he admitted it might be a good idea. They usually do."

"Has this happened before?"

"Oh yes, especially in Scotland. The elders get very outraged at the thought of people sleeping through something that will hurt. Also the resident barber surgeons usually stir them up. And usually by then my hands are tired anyway and so it works out well enough. They get the blame for the fact that I can't possibly treat all the people who want it."

Anricks took a pull of beer and sighed, cut into the haggis and piled a lot on a silver spoon he took out of his pocket and polished. He ate it with his eyes shut, slowly munching until it was all gone.

"Mm," he said, "it's good."

Dodd tried some and it was good. Not as good as Janet's, but good enough—too much lung and oats and not enough liver in it probably.

Anricks concentrated on the food for a while and then leaned back and drank more ale. He called for some uisghe beagh as well, the northern firewater. Dodd tried a little and wasn't impressed; it tasted very smoky in his opinion.

"So. Minister Burn. Perhaps if I talk through what I know about it, you can find a pattern there."

"I'm no' the man ye want for that. He's got a terrible toothache in Carlisle."

"Even so."

Anricks went through the tale of Minister Burn as he knew it and added that Lady Widdrington probably knew a lot more.

"Ay?" Dodd thought about it and had to agree that it was odd.

"And last month he went out on a raid of some kind," Anricks added with a sigh. "I wish I knew where he went."

"Did he gang oot wi' his family, they're right reivers?" Dodd asked.

"I don't think so, he'd fallen out with his father."

"Who did he go with?"

"He went alone with one remount," said Anricks. "That's what his wife says in her letter to me. Of course he could have met friends later. But he went wearing his best suit and carrying a crossbow and his sword, which was why she wasn't too concerned. It would have been a different matter if he'd worn harness and helmet of course."

Dodd nodded. "Mebbe he had his jack and helmet somewhere else…"

Anricks shook his head. "They're still at Wendron, in a press in his study."

Dodd was silent. "Was he going to kill someone?" he asked at last. "Mebbe my lord Spynie? Someone took a shot at him last month?"

Anricks frowned. "Why would he do that? Why take such a risk?"

Dodd shrugged. "Somebody wis paying him, perhaps?"

Anricks nodded wearily. His mouth was turned down at the ends, as if he had a bad taste in it. "I'm not sure why he suddenly needed money, but he did. I wish I'd…Well, I didn't. And there's a rumour he went to see Kerr of Cessford a week before he went out as well."

Dodd let out a humourless bark of laughter. "Ay," he said, "they're all murdering bastards too. And the Burns. I've tangled wi' them mesen. And Kerrs sometimes ally with Elliots."

The commonroom suddenly started filling up with Widdringtons, followed by Sir Henry and his son who seemed upset about something.

"Sir," he was saying, "will ye not give the man an answer?"

"I'll answer when I please, boy. If my fool of a wife hadn't taken it into her empty head to ride intae Scotland she wouldna be costing me a hundred pounds English now, would she? She can sit it out for a while."

Sir Henry marched to the bar and ordered aqua vitae and pointedly got none for his son. Young Henry's face was swelling a little and his brows were down. He got his own ale and Dodd went up to him immediately.

"Sir," he said, "have ye had a ransom demand?"

Young Henry looked weary as well. "One of the Burns' boys came in with it. We'll swap at the Reidswire meeting stone, each side just five men and the woman on her horse, and a hundred pounds English in exchange."

"Ay. Does her husband have the money?" It wasn't excessive for the wife of a headman, but it was still a lot of money.

"No, of course not," muttered Young Henry. "Who does? Spynie does, of course, and has offered my father a loan at twenty percent interest a week, secured on one of his sheilings and the pasture."

"Ay," said Dodd noncommittally.

"I suppose Father will roar a bit and then take the loan, to pay them off."

"So it's the Burns that have her?"

"Yes. Jock Burn must have come up with the idea at the funeral and bought Ekie and Sim so he could do it."

"Ay," Dodd was uneasy. He had found aristocrats had less ready cash than headmen. How come my lord Spynie was so flush he could lend a hundred pounds cash to Sir Henry? Unless…"Sir, do ye not think it's a bit odd, Spynie having the ready cash?"

Young Henry took a drink of his ale and looked at his hands. His nails were bitten. "Now you mention it, Sergeant, that is odd."

"What if the Burns are doing Spynie's bidding?" Because now he came to think of it, Spynie would want revenge for how Lady Widdrington had outmanoevred him in the summer and lost him some of the King's favour and this was a splendid way to take it. And if something went wrong at the exchange and the woman wound up dead, well, who would care? Not Sir Henry, although there was a man with a bad tooth in Carlisle who would surely take it very hard. Dodd's eyes narrowed and his mouth turned down.

"Which boy was it?" he asked.

"Geordie Burn's eldest son, Young Geordie."

"Is it possible Sir Henry could have known about Lady Widdrington getting kidnapped? Before it happened?" he asked very softly. Because once you thought about the loan and Spynie being around and the clear fact that Sir Henry didn't like his wifey, you also had to ask if this was Sir Henry's revenge as well. Didn't you?

Young Henry stared at the fire and said nothing. His mouth had turned down as well and his eyes were hot.

"Do you think…?" he began, and then fell silent again.

"Well it's possible," Dodd said gently, "isn't it?"

"And the Burns would get the blame which they wouldn't care about." Young Henry's voice was very soft but there was a hard undertone. "Nor my father. The King probably wouldn't care enough to do anything."

"Ay," said Dodd. "It's a problem solved, that it is."

Another long silence. "She came to us when she was just seventeen and I was ten," Young Henry said, "Ten years ago. And she has tried, lord God she has tried to be a good wife to Sir Henry, no matter how he treats her. She was wonderful to us, to me and Roger. She never beat us, she…she…used to… even hug me when I was sad for my mother, though I wisnae her wean and she…she looked after me when I got the measles and my eyes hurt and I was scared I'd go blind and…"

Dodd tactfully went to the bar to get more ale, though frankly the stuff they were drinking in Scotland was dire. Sir Henry was shouting at some of his older men who were gathered round him, laughing. On a thought, he also bought some uisge beagh that was cheaper than brandy and brought it over.

Young Henry took the horn cup, lifted it in his father's direction and drank it off.

"The only thing is, how do we find out where she is exactly?"

"Find her horse, it's a nice jennet called Mouse and shod."

Anricks came by then and they made room for him at the table. He bought a round and sat down, his anxious face quite unreadable. Purely on instinct, and in the hope of there being more than two on the raid, Dodd told him what they thought about the ransom demand.

He, too, was silent for a while and then he nodded. "Yes," was all he said.

He felt for something on his belt and then realised that it was in his pack. A minute later he had paper on the table and was writing at high speed in a neat italic that said he was a good clerk as well as a barber surgeon.

"What are ye doing?"

"I am writing to my lord Maitland, his castle's not far away and I can send it by a town messenger. Maitland's the Lord Chancellor."

"That's a good idea," said Young Henry. "She knows him and she looked after his son for him a few years ago when things were a mite tickle in Scotland. We taught him to shoot and he taught us to tickle trout."

Anricks just nodded and continued to write, which gave Dodd the feeling he had already known that about Lady Widdrington, which was interesting. But then if he was working as a pursuivant for Sir Robert Cecil, you'd expect him to be well-informed.

"When is the exchange to be?"

"Day after tomorrow," said Young Henry, "to give Sir Henry time to get the money."

"So she's likely safe enough till then," said Dodd. "They'll be on their guard, but if it's a put up job, they willna expect much."

"We aren't much," said Young Henry, with a nervous laugh.

"Ay, we are," said Dodd.

"Gentlemen, there is almost certainly at least one Widdrington in Geordie Burn's pay to act as his spy, so shall we leave the subject?"

"Tonight," said Dodd. Young Henry looked up at him and then nodded once, Anricks opened his mouth to argue and then shut it again. He nodded as well.

WEDNESDAY 18th OCTOBER 1592

Elizabeth had lice, probably from Jimmy Tait, and was already tired of the smell of her only shift. She wasn't exactly sure where she was since she had been brought to the peel tower with a scarf over her eyes and her horse on a leading rein. It was Geordie Burn that brought her in, a big man with black hair and a loud hectoring way with him. He was frightening because he seemed always to be laughing at some private joke at her expense and because he came up too close to her and grinned in her face. However she had long experience at thinking when she was frightened and also at acting a lot stupider than she was.

So she made sure she asked plenty of silly questions about where were they taking her and why where they doing it and her husband would be angry and what were they thinking of and so on and so forth until Geordie shouted at her to be silent. She immediately went silent in what she hoped was a cowed way. It wasn't hard to do, she was frightened of Geordie Burn quite viscerally, and her hands were cold.

When they took the scarf off and helped her down from her horse, she wanted to protest because Mouse was a friend and she had no others. She said nothing while Geordie Burn gestured for her to go into the barnekin and into the peel tower and the horse was taken off, protesting, to the winter pasture on the other side of the valley.

They were quite polite really. Ralph o' the Coates wasn't there, being busy selling horses in Edinburgh. A boy called

Young Geordie was sent off with the message about the ransom to Jedburgh where Geordie said the Widdringtons were. There were a lot of Burns there, some of them she even recognised from the funeral. Jemmy and Archie Burn had been to it, she realised, and several others. Archie Burn was friendly to her and showed her his sword which was different from the general run of northern broadswords. His was a thinner blade with a basket hilt, almost a rapier, though very sharp.

"It's beautiful," she said, trying to sound admiring, "but it doesn't look English or Scots."

"Nor it isnae," laughed Archie, "that's Cordoba steel and I got it off a Spaniard when I wis fighting in the Netherlands. The Spaniard had nae further use for it." He laughed again and showed with a slicing flourish of the blade what had happened to the Spaniard.

Elizabeth looked at him carefully. Yes, he and his father fitted the description of the men that had killed Jamie Burn and yes, he had a blade that could have done it, she thought, though she was no expert. Jemmy had a long narrow poignard, too—but then so did several others of the men. And why would the Burns kill one of their own? Even if they had fallen out, you didn't kill the men of your own family, you just didn't.

There was a whole collection of louring toughs with many Burns among them and some Taits and Pringles and Kerrs as well. She got an acknowledgement from Jamie Burn's Uncle Jock who rode in with three stolen cows at midday, taking off his hat to her as he rode by.

At least they had a woman there for propriety. In fact, it was Geordie and Jamie Burn's mother, a faded woman called Maud with grey blond hair under her grubby cap, and wearing a home-spun kirtle but a tailor-made woollen gown that was Edinburgh work. The peel tower was an old one, clearly not the main Burn tower, and smelled of mildew and mice. Still she and Maud tried their best to make it habitable with blankets that Maud had brought, which they hung up by the fire that smoked terribly until a crow's nest fell down the chimney in flames.

Then she sat with Maud in the upper chamber of the peel tower and sewed some shirts with her which was soothing and gave her something to do with her hands. One of the louring toughs came up the ladder to the upper chamber with some partly cooked lumps of cow and some oatmeal but she had no stomach to any of it and gave it to Maud.

She listened and said "mm" and "fancy that" and "tut tut" while Maud Burn, who had been a Pringle and had had a hard but successful life with only two babies dead and four sons and a daughter raised, chatted about kine and their diseases, and horses and their many and various diseases and how disastrous the harvest had been.

As the Sun went low in the afternoon, Elizabeth heard hoof-beats and went to the arrowslit to see Geordie Burn setting off with about fifteen men, heading north and east. There goes the ambush in case Sir Henry tries a rescue, she thought and wondered if he would. She didn't know. He might, though for pride not love of course, or perhaps he wouldn't. He would pay up, though, surely? Everyone in the East March would laugh at him if he didn't do something.

She went and sat down next to Maud by the smoky fire, on an old and uncomfortable stool and heard that Geordie wouldn't be back until morning, the young scamp, but that Ralph was due back any day now with the money from the horses which they needed to buy horse fodder since the harvest had been so terrible, rained on to ruination.

"Ours was bad too," Elizabeth commiserated. There was still some light to see by and she kept stitching the long seam down the side. They talked about harvests and weather.

At last Elizabeth got to say she was sorry about Minister Jamie, Maud's second son, and what a mystery his death was. Maud went silent for a long time and Elizabeth pretended not to see the tears brimming in her eyes.

"Ay," whispered Maud, "but it was like he wis dead seven years ago, when he went tae the university at St Andrew's. His father was gey angry wi' him. And he was such a bonny young man, such a bonny fighter."

"Mm."

"They had a fight over it and Jamie won. His father couldna forgive him for that, though I said tae him, whit de ye expect, he's young and ye're old."

"Did he disinherit him?"

"No, Jamie still has his rights...had his rights to his share o' the land. And his child too, if it's a boy."

"Oh." That was normal. North and South on the Border, the farms were divided and divided as the families bred so you couldn't live on them. The system further south, where the eldest son got all of it, was unfair to the younger sons like Robin himself, but you could see how it kept the estates together. It was better for the families.

"And then last month, well, Geordie was fit to be tied about it, so he was."

"Why? What about?"

"I'm not sure, but...ay, I'm worried."

"Mrs Burn, what was it Geordie was so angry about?"

Maud hung her head over the shirt of coarse homespun linen. At last she said, "I'm no' sure, see ye, but I think Jamie tried to kill somebody important. A courtier."

"Why?"

Maud shook her head. "Ah dinna ken. Somebody important. Very important. And he failed, did Jamie, didnae kill the man at all. And then the man came to see Geordie, came himself with men at his back, all shining wi' silver and gold, and they went off and talked for a long while and then...three weeks later, my Jamie war deid."

All Elizabeth could think of to say was "Ah."

Maud was weeping silently into the shirt on her knee. Elizabeth was still for a moment and then she put down her shirt because anyway it was too dark to sew, and leaned across and put her arms around Maud who shuddered and wept into her shoulder while her hands and her heart got colder and colder.

◇◇◇

At last the storm was done for the moment. "It's worse when they've grown," Maud said, wiping her eyes with the shirt. "Ye see them grow and they change and they become men and then… they die. O' course we all die, I ken that, but I wish I could hae died instead of Jamie, he was such a fine man and I heard he did well as a minister, preached some fine sermons and had his ain little school."

"Yes, he did, Mrs Burn, and all the boys loved him. They sang at his funeral."

"Och, I wish I could ha gone and seen him put in the ground. Ralph wouldnae have it, he wis still sore at the beating up he took fra Jamie seven year go. But I wish I could ha' gone and maybe heard them sing. Did they sing well?"

"Ay, they did," said Elizabeth, her Scotch well in now, "They did like birds or angels. There's a lad there, only young, perhaps seven or eight and he has the finest voice I've heard in a while, perhaps ever." Perhaps Robin, when he was a boy, might have had a voice as good? Though that didn't necessarily follow, sometimes quite ordinary singers turned wonderful when their voices broke and sometimes the other way round.

"Ay, that'll be a Tait," said Maud. "They allus have good voices."

"I think that's what he wanted the money for, to take all the boys to the Carlisle cathedral and prentice them singers, to get them out of the Borders, you know? Especially little Jimmy Tait. His father wanted ten pounds for him."

"Is that right?" said Maud, in a voice of wonder. "Was he going tae do that?"

"I think so. And I think I know who offered him the money to kill my Lord Spynie as well, the courtier he took a shot at."

"Bad cess to 'em," said Maud, scowling. "Who was it?"

"The Dowager Lady Hume. Lord Spynie's been sniffing about her ten-year-old grandson whose wardship he's just bought and he wants him at Court and she's…she does not."

"Och." Very noticeably, Maud did not ask why going to the Scottish King's Court as Lord Spynie's ward might be a bad thing for a ten-year-old boy. She went silent again. By the time she spoke once more it was too dark to see and the turf fire gave some warmth but not much light. "It's Geordie that wanted ye taken. Ye were asking too many questions. Jemmy and Archie were worried too; ye could see it. And then another message came from…from the King's Court and he laughed his head off at it and rode out before dawn this morning to take ye."

Who could the message have come from? Lord Spynie? Her husband? Why had Geordie found it so funny? And why had Jemmy and Archie been worried? Well, that was easy to answer and it was shocking, that's what it was. To kill their own kinsman, Jemmy's nephew, Archie's cousin, on the say-so of a courtier?

"Will they kill me, d'ye think?"

Silence. What Elizabeth could see of Maud's face was creased with worry. "He's a terrible man, he'll end in hell," she burst out. "He's allus been wicked, he used tae take the kittens the cats had and he took 'em off somewhere and I followed him once and he'd…he'd crucified them. Alive."

"Who?"

"Geordie. My son Geordie!"

"Jesus."

"I killed the poor little things so I did and tellt him not to dae it again and he laughed at me."

Elizabeth felt sick. People had to drown kittens because with most she-cats kindling twice a year, you'd be knee-deep in cats if you didn't. If only there was some way you could geld a quean cat like you could a tom. But you did it as fast as you could, not…not crucifying them.

"He wis eight then. I've never liked him since, though he's my eldest. It was Jamie I loved and I let him run off tae the Reverend Gilpin and I hoped…I hoped…" She sighed and wiped her eyes with the half-made shirt again.

"If he's laughing at me, is he planning to kill me?" asked Elizabeth again, her mouth dry but her heart beating hard under her stays. "Is he?"

Maud shook her head and then she said, very very quietly, "Maybe."

And Elizabeth thought, *I will not go to my death like a cow or a kitten, I will kick and fight, by God I will.*

Maud had lifted her face and was staring at Elizabeth. Her lips were parted and her eyes fixed on something in the distance. "Jamie did it for money to get the boys to Carlisle?"

"I think so, Mrs Burn."

wednesday night 18th october to thursday 19th october 1592

Although the night was long, it was as difficult as Dodd had expected to find Lady Widdrington's horse. He knew where most of the infield horse pastures were, of course; he had raided all across this country in his teens. But there were a lot of them because you didn't want too many horses in one place. And in the dark it was hard to avoid the men on guard and hard to make out the horses. And then, of course, you had to ride to the next place.

Well, they'd have the next day as well. After the first couple of tries they established a routine. Dodd and Young Henry found the pasture, then they sent Anricks round to distract the guards by pretending to be lost and asking the way. At one place they had checked the horses and found nothing but hobbies and they stood and waited, sweating, for Anricks. They would have gone to his rescue but then they heard a cracking crunching sound of a patient losing a tooth and despite the tension and the impossibility of the job, Young Henry smiled.

A little later Anricks turned up, looking smug. "I used the sweet oil of vitriol," he explained. "It loosens men's tongues like booze does. He told me where they've taken the woman."

And so they rode a few miles across country to the infield of a tower that was once owned by Pringles and now languished in the ownership of two sisters who hated each other and would not be reconciled. Dodd would never have thought of looking there. And there they found Lady Widdrington's jennet, minus her expensive side-saddle of course, looking a little offended at being asked to pasture with such very low-bred hobbies.

"So she's in the tower," said Dodd, trying to see it against the night sky. There was a quarter Moon but it was ducking in and out behind clouds. "Ay, well, of course she is." Nobody was going to make their job easier for them, after all. And it would be nice if they could nip her out quick and if nobody shot her while they did it, of course.

They had moved down the valley and into a little shelter for the sheep in the corner of the worst of the three infields.

"I'll ride for Jedburgh, get my men, and come back here..."

"Ay, yer father will let ye, will he?"

Silence. "I could perhaps gain entrance as a stranger, lost in the hills and then open the barnekin," said Anricks slowly.

"Mebbe," allowed Dodd, "but they'll have her in the tower itself, second floor and the ladder taken away to be sure she disnae take it intae her head to run for it herself. They might chain her, but I think not, she's a lady and they willna think she's dangerous."

There was a dispirited silence. Annoyingly, Dodd found himself thinking that this was where the Courtier would have been useful because he was the one who could think of ingenious unlikely plans.

"On the other hand, Geordie Burn himself is out with his men at the pass into this valley, waiting for Sir Henry," offered Anricks.

"Ay, o' course he is."

Come on, Dodd thought to himself, there's a way of doing it. I'm a better man than the Courtier any day, come on.

Inspiration failed to strike. From where the Moon was, it was now two or three in the morning and dawn only three hours away. If they were going to do anything, they had better do it soon.

Anricks yawned jaw-crackingly. "Gentlemen," he said, "I'm in need of sleep. How about we get a couple of hours each, and think about it again in the morning?"

Young Henry caught the yawn from him. "But she's there and we're here…" he protested.

"Ay, ye're right," Dodd said, "and if ye have a way to get past the barnekin and intae the tower and out again and away wi' out getting her killed, I'm yer man." He waited. "Do ye?"

"No," came a reluctant growl.

They put their horses in amongst the others, on the grounds that hobbies looked alike from a distance and probably nobody had counted them. Then they drew lots for the middle watch which fell to Dodd, and he settled himself in the corner next to Anricks and went to sleep instantly.

He woke instantly as well, knowing he had slept three hours and not one. Anricks was squatting there, hollow-eyed. "I took the middle watch as well," he said. "I couldn't sleep at all."

Strange. Dodd felt rested and refreshed as he often did when he slept out and not frowsty and bad-tempered as he normally did after a night in a proper bed. Young Henry was still fast asleep, looking touchingly young under his spots. There was a strong smell of farts in the little wooden sheep shelter and Henry shifted and trumpeted again. Dodd found himself sniggering.

"I'm afraid I think we need to send Widdrington back for men and conduct a full assault…" said Anricks with a sigh.

"Nay, they'd ainly kill her." He felt glass-headed but he had an answer to the quandary, produced somewhere while he was asleep. "What de ye think tae this?" he said as Anricks took another apple from his pack and gave it to Dodd who started eating it. "It's mad enough for the Courtier, but mebbe it could work."

He explained his idea and then explained it again when Young Henry woke up. It was nerve-wracking and could easily go horribly wrong, but at the worst, it would just give the Burns one more prisoner. At best it could solve everything.

They needed to move fast while Geordie Burn was still out lying in wait for the Widdringtons; it wouldn't work if he was there. At least the weather was cooperating. It was horrible, dark, foggy with a continuous bone-chilling mizzle that was only a slightly lighter grey as the Sun came up somewhere behind the clouds.

wednesday night 18th october to thursday 19th october 1592

Elizabeth and Maud shared the ancient bed that smelled of mildew and mice just as much as the rest of the place. Elizabeth took her stays and kirtle off but put her gown back on again, glad of Sir Henry's vanity that liked his woman to have a black velvet gown lined in silk and edged in fur, though only coney.

Maud was quiet while Elizabeth knelt to say her prayers and even said an amen to them, then they put the curfew over the glowing turves and climbed into bed. The curtains were too rotted to draw, the wind came through the arrow slits but Maud had brought blankets of her own weaving which were good and dense and still oily from the sheep and once they had three of them over them, they started to warm up.

Archie came at night and brought a cleanish jordan to replace the other one and took the ladder away. The wind was howling at first but then died down and there was the quiet whisper of rain falling. They could hear the hobbies moving about in the ground-floor chamber, the men talking quietly or snoring in the first-floor chamber. They were alone in the upper chamber, under the rafters.

Elizabeth had said her prayers mechanically. She was beginning to wonder why she said them at all, though she remembered the sensation that had filled her when she shouted at God about the boys. Was He punishing her for that? It depended on what you thought God was like, really. Was He a spiteful old man like her husband as He often showed Himself in the depths of the Old Testament? Or was He a strong young man with a charming way to Himself, a man who had much more to Him than that, who was also God? She remembered how gripped she had been when she first read the Gospels, how the personality of Jesus had come through to her in the beautiful muscular language of Tyndale's translation, how it had become a pleasure not a duty to converse with such a person. And then Carey and then…all this. And she was tired of it. She would have spoken to Our Lady in the old way if she could, but if you read the Gospels and the Acts you could see that Jesus' mother was hardly mentioned at all and wasn't so very important. So it was all about Jesus Himself, and the trouble was that He was a man as well as God, and you couldn't expect a man to care about who a woman loved. Could you?

She dreamed a long confusing dream in which she was arguing with a small brown-faced middle-aged Jewish woman, a long complicated argument she couldn't remember, and then the Jewess hugged her and kissed her and told her not to cry, that she would see to it.

She woke up still crying, which was annoying. She managed to stop and dry her face before Maud woke, got up and knelt again to pray and found herself thinking about Robin Carey again, in that sad dragging way from her heart which was probably what had made her cry. So she stopped and got up, dressed, got the fire sharpened up with some kindling and logs. That pig was probably gone off now, she thought with annoyance; how long have I been away? A week? And maybe Poppy has had her bairn by now?

Maud was awake, got up and pulled up her laces, put up her hair and pinned on her cap and then went grimly to the door and opened it onto empty space.

"Archie and Jemmy," she shrieked, "come here."

It was still half dark outside, foggy, raining, cold. There was something going on at the gate to the barnekin. "Archie!" she shouted again. "Bring me the ladder."

After a little while, someone else brought it and she climbed down, paused when she saw by the light of two torches what was happening at the gate and then grinned. "Come on, my lady," she shouted up at Elizabeth. "Come ben and look at this."

Elizabeth emerged and climbed carefully down the ladder which was old and not very sound. She was fully dressed now, her gown on, she even had her low crowned best hat on over her cap, the one she had put on for Jamie Burn's funeral, oh a hundred years ago.

Young Henry Widdrington was at the gate on a tired hobby, looking tired himself.

"The exchange has been done," he explained patiently to Jemmy Burn who was staring up at him suspiciously. "Sir Henry paid the ransom last night and I've come to take Lady Widdrington home."

Elizabeth was shocked. Sir Henry had paid it? Really?

"How did he get so much money at one time?"

"I told you," said Young Henry. "He's friends with Lord Spynie who's a rich lord and gave him the money straight off so I've come to collect my lady. Geordie's rich as Croesus and Ralph o' the Coates will be back any day now from selling horses and, unless you're thinking of killing her…"

Only Archie and Jemmy exchanged glances at that, in a way that made Elizabeth certain. The other Burns were indignant at the idea they might kidnap a woman and then fail to take the ransom when it was offered.

"What about where they were supposed to make the exchange?" asked Archie. "At the river and all…"

"I don't know about that," said Young Henry in a bored tone of voice. "I just know the thing's been done and she's to come home with me."

"Well, we'd best wait for Geordie, any road, he'll know the right of…"

"For God's sake," said Maud, stepping forward with all her maternal authority. "It's obvious, they've made another deal and for more money. Let Lady Widdrington go, I'll smooth it with my husband as soon as he's back from Edinburgh."

"Well but…"

"And I'm tired of her anyway, she can go back to her husband."

Young Henry had her horse, Mouse, behind him as if it were the most natural thing in the world. Elizabeth took the horse's bridle, gave her a quick stroke and a nuzzle and then looked at her back where there was a man's saddle. It didn't matter, she'd ridden astride when she was a lass and even if it was uncomfortable, she could do it. She mounted using the block, sitting sideways on the horse and then bringing her right leg up and over so her skirts and petticoats were under her and gave her some protection.

"Good-bye, Lady Widdrington, I'll mind what ye said to me," Maud said very deliberately. Elizabeth managed a bright smile and a wave to Maud before she turned her horse away.

"Good-bye Missus Burn, thank ye for yer hospitality," she called in answer. Maud actually snorted at that.

Elizabeth's heart was beating hard again as she followed Young Henry slowly down the muddy old path from the tower and down across the infield to the lane that led up to the moors by way of a small hill where there was something of a sheep shelter.

Two men came out to greet her then. One she knew at once as Simon Anricks; the other, she realised, was the bad-tempered saturnine Sergeant Dodd who was looking, as always, as if he had lost a shilling and found a penny.

She stared from one to the other and suddenly laughed. "You were lying?" she said.

Young Henry was looking absurdly pleased with himself. "I was. Now we have to ride back to Jedburgh…"

"All of us?"

"We'll protect you."

She didn't like it, a long chase across country. "Why don't I take one of the hobbies and ride the wrong way with Young Henry, south and west, and why don't you, Sergeant Dodd, take my jennet, Mouse, and go to Jedburgh with Mr Anricks?"

There was a short silence and then, wonder of wonders, Sergeant Dodd cracked a smile. "Ay," he said, "why don't I? Though Mr Anricks should ride the jennet because I'd be heavier and they might see that."

She smiled at him. "Me and Henry will go along the tops of the Cheviots and then come back to Jedburgh from the south. Maybe we'll call at Ferniehurst on the way."

She was hungry, hadn't had any breakfast, but she was suddenly happy and excited. She had given them the slip and even if they caught her, she had tried. By God, it wouldn't be her fault if they did catch her, either. And she thought Young Henry would have something to say about that.

She changed to Dodd's hobby because he was a better horse than Anrick's pony, with a warning from Dodd that he bit. Dodd rode Anrick's horse with only a blanket because they were one saddle short and Anrick rode the shod jennet, who wasn't happy about it.

Dodd and Anrick cantered off on the way up the valley to Jedburgh but Young Henry took her to the deep, dead bracken on the side of the hill where there were some outcrops to break the curve. They got the hobbies to lie down in it and then she lay down on her stomach behind him and found that she was well hidden, especially with the wet and the mist.

It was hard to stay still there as the damp slowly and steadily worked its way inward. But it was worth it. She heard the hoofbeats of Geordie Burn and his men as he rode back to the tower. Though she couldn't see them for the mist and the rain, she heard the shouting when he got the news and then she had the pleasure of hearing them ride like the devil after Mouse's shod hoofprints to Jedburgh.

She got up stiffly with Young Henry, mounted the hobby who stayed true to form and tried to bite her, and then rode south and west with him along the tops of the hills, where the wind blew the rain in folds like blankets and you couldn't see a hand in front of your face sometimes. Young Henry was a quiet clever guide, he took her along windswept hilltops and down wet slithering paths but avoided the worst places and the skree slopes. She was cold, she was wet, and she was hungry, but she felt happy.

◇◇◇

Dodd rode into Jedburgh, up the Newcastle road, past the old abbey on the hill, with Anricks behind him and headed straight for the Spread Eagle. By the time Geordie and his bruisers arrived, they had had time to give the horses a brush down and get themselves some dinner. Dodd left the jennet in the yard so Geordie could see it when he came in, leaned back in a chair to make room for his stomach full of haggis, and put his boots on the table.

"Where's the woman?" Geordie demanded as he came into the commonroom. "Where's Lady Widdrington?"

"Och, I'm sorry," drawled Dodd, "she isna here, she's gone off wi' her husband already."

"She hasnae and ye know it, I met Sir Henry on the way in and he hasnae got her."

"Och, has he not?" said Dodd, who was enjoying himself immensely. "Where can she be?"

"You know, ye bastard, and ye'll tell me now."

Dodd took his boots off the table, one two, and stood up. "Will I?" he said, "I dinna think so. And forbye I don't know."

Anricks had quietly moved himself to another table where he was busy delving into his pack again.

There was a moment of silence. It was a silence full of calculation while Geordie thought of the number of men he had with him and tried to work out what advantage Dodd thought he had. Dodd wasn't thinking of that; he was thinking of where he was going to hit Geordie first, but another man, an older Pringle, pulled Geordie's elbow and whispered to him, with a lot of nervous gesturing.

"Yer name's Henry Dodd," said Geordie, with his head on one side and his eyes narrowed.

"Sergeant Henry Dodd," he corrected.

"You're *that* Henry Dodd? The one who…?"

"Ay," said Dodd gently, "What of it?"

Geordie hesitated a moment, then walked out of the common-room. In a minute they heard him mounting up and riding out with all his men, heading south and east for the Burns' lands again.

Anricks was looking at him with his eyebrows up in a way that reminded him of Carey. He had, Dodd noticed, loaded both the dags inside his pack.

"That," said Anricks, "was impressive."

"Ay," said Dodd somberly, "it's nice they still remember me hereabouts."

They came to Reidswire where the hills were at their coldest and wettest, just north of the English Middle March, and looking from the tops of the hills with their empty shielings and summer pasture, Elizabeth saw a man riding a horse across country like wildfire, as if the king of Elfland were after him. It was odd. She stopped and looked at him and saw that he wore a jack and morion, polished silver steel, chased with elaborate gold patterns, and two dogs running behind him and she looked again and knew him.

wednesday night 18th october and thursday 19th october 1592

Word had come to Carlisle the night before of Elizabeth's kidnapping, word that came by winding ways through the Widdringtons and Burns and Fenwicks, until it ended with Thomas the Merchant. He took the trouble to write a letter reporting it to the man he knew as Mr Philpotts and then he went up to the castle as the Sun went down behind rain clouds and asked to speak to the acting Deputy Warden.

Carey was looking very unwell and had a swollen jaw, and deep bags under his eyes. He had been trying to find a toothdrawer in Carlisle, but the only one in the area was a Johnstone who was busy in Dumfries.

"How may I help you, Mr Hetherington?" he asked coldly as Thomas the Merchant came into his office in the Queen Mary tower. He also had a teetering pile of complaints and was dictating letters to his new clerk, Mr Tovey, a spotty pale youth that Thomas the Merchant instantly ignored.

"I heard something you may be interested in," he said. "I won't even charge for it."

Carey did not return his sly smile. "Well?"

"I heard that Lady Widdrington is taken by Geordie Burn."

"What?" The tone of voice had gone from merely cold to distinctly wintry, with a howling gale and a blizzard.

"I heard tell that Lady Widdrington has been taken prisoner

by Geordie Burn while she was at a funeral in Scotland. Her husband's in Jedburgh and they're talking about the ransom."

It was very interesting, thought Thomas the Merchant. Carey could be very noisy when he was in a temper but now he was quite silent for a long time. His colour had gone an unhealthy greyish white.

"Are you sure?"

"I had it from a good source." Why exactly he had it, was of course another matter.

More silence. Then, "Thank you Mr Hetherington."

Carey started on another letter of complaint about the recent raids from the Kerrs of Cessford well out of their usual area and into the West March. Thomas was surprised.

"Well…" he said, "aren't you going to do something about it?"

"What can I do, Mr Hetherington? Lady Widdrington's husband is doing what he can, I'm sure, and as I am not her husband I don't see exactly how I can help unless Sir Henry asks me to turn out the guard for him."

Damn. It hadn't worked. He had got too canny for them.

"Oh. Well. I'll be going then."

"Thank you for the information, Mr Hetherington."

As soon as he was well gone and out of the castleyard, Carey was on his feet and going down the stairs and up the ones to the Warden's Lodging where he found Scrope noodling his way on his virginals through some complicated Italian music that Carey had brought him from the South.

"What is this I hear about Lady Widdrington?" asked Carey very quietly. Scrope gave him an extraordinary look, up quickly from under his brows, then back to the music.

"I heard the same from Sir John Forster, today," Scrope admitted. "Geordie Burn's allegedly got her but I'm sure it's not true, that's why I didn't bother you with it because…"

But Carey had already gone.

Red Sandy did his best, wishing his older brother was there to talk some sense into the Courtier. "Ay sir, I heard it but I didnae believe it and forebye…"

"You think it's a trap laid for me, that I'll go roaring out looking for her and Geordie or Sir Henry can put a spear in me while I do it."

Red Sandy was relieved. "Ay sir, that's exactly what it is, whether it's true or no'…"

"Do you think it's true?"

"Ah, no sir. I think it's a rumour…"

"Then why did Thomas the Merchant bring it to me and my lord Scrope get it from Sir John Forster?"

Och, that's torn it, Red Sandy thought but didn't say. "Ah dinna ken, sir," was what he said.

Carey went back to his paperwork. At last the worst of it was done, helped by John Tovey's speed at penwork, which was impressive.

"Is that the last letter, Mr Tovey?"

"There's a couple more about the horse fodder…"

"They can wait, I think. Get to bed, Mr Tovey. I'll see you in the morning."

John Tovey had a straw pallet bed that he kept rolled up in the office while the large and ugly Scot that Carey had employed in Oxford was already asleep on the truckle bed in Carey's chamber. Tovey took himself to bed while Carey went into his bedroom and brought out a cup of aqua vitae.

"Is your tooth still bad, sir?"

"It's awful, John. I want to bang my head against a wall to stop it throbbing but that won't help. I'll drink this and take a turn outside and then I'll try and get some sleep."

"Cloves help, sir. Oil of cloves is best but if you can just get some cloves and chew them, they really do help—until you can get it drawn, of course."

"Thank you, I'll go down to the kitchen and see if I can find any cloves."

John Tovey was soon snoring and Carey did go down to the kitchen and found that the spices were locked in the spice cupboard. He woke one of the kitchen boys, learned that his sister had the key, and went up to the Warden's Lodging to find her sewing next to the fire in the bedroom.

"Cloves? Yes, I've heard that too." Bless her, she put her sewing by and they went downstairs to the strains of Italian music and she produced the key to the cupboard on the large bunch of keys on her belt and opened it up. Carey tried one clove gingerly, but when he found it genuinely did help, he took a handful and put them in his doublet pocket.

"When are you going back to the Queen?" he asked his sister and she flushed and looked down.

"I'm sorry, Robin," she said, "I just can't stand it in Carlisle anymore. And Young Thomas is in trouble again..."

As far as Robin could tell, Young Thomas was doing exactly what you expected wealthy young aristocrats to do at Oxford and he hoped the boy hadn't managed to pox himself.

He nodded. "Before Christmas?"

She locked up the spice cupboard again and nodded. "Scrope's estates need him to look at them, we've had to dismiss the steward for a ridiculous amount of cheating and padding of bills."

Robin said nothing to that, kissed her quite formally at the door of her bedchamber and went down the stairs again.

An hour later the whole castle was snoring and Carey was still sitting by the embers of the fire in the great hall. He looked around at the place, stood up and went purposefully across to the Queen Mary tower and up to his dressing room where his jack stood on its stand. He changed his clothes for the old woolen doublet he wore under his jack, transferred the cloves carefully, put the jack on and said "Uff" very quietly as the weight went onto his shoulders and his hips. He put his morion helmet on, loosened the straps so they wouldn't hurt his right jaw and strapped on his swordbelt again.

He went quietly down the stairs and out into the stableyard, where he woke two of the strongest hobbies, one of them his own beast, Sorrel, and put bridles on both of them, a saddle on one. They weren't happy, although they ought to have been used to doings in the middle of the night. Perhaps they didn't like it that the bell wasn't tolling.

He left them tied up in the yard and went to the dog kennels where he shushed the excited yelps and wuffs and took Scrope's best lymer, Teazle, on a long leash.

It took time and a bit of doing but he led the horses and the dog down the covered path to the gate and along the wall to the postern gate where he took the horses through one at a time and then gave Solomon Musgrave a substantial tip. He was preoccupied or perhaps he would have noticed who was following him.

He walked the horses down through the town, had another expensive conversation with the guard on the Scotch gate and then was out into the drizzling night. He mounted Sorrel, who he had saddled, put his heels in and went to a steady canter to warm up the horses and the dog before he speeded up to a hand gallop. He assumed Geordie Burn was in cahoots with Sir Henry. He already knew that Sir Henry and Lord Spynie were bosom pals. It was simply obvious what was going on and Carey planned to disrupt it as best he could. It was a pity he didn't have Sergeant Dodd swinging rangily along behind him and moaning about how it would be better to bring all the men, but he didn't. Dodd had taken himself off into the East March in search of a tooth-drawer he'd heard of and Carey didn't expect to see him again until he'd found one, given how Dodd generally was.

And he knew perfectly well that this was probably all an elaborate trap specially for him; he knew perfectly well that Elizabeth Lady Widdrington was perhaps tucked up in her bed.... No. The rumour had come from too many directions. Chances were that she had been kidnapped and by Geordie Burn, one of the cruelest and worst raiders in the Middle March after Kerr of Cessford himself. Still, it was probably also a trap.

He didn't care. So it was a trap. Fine. He'd spring it by himself and maybe God would help him get away with Lady Widdrington and maybe he would end cold and staring on somebody's spear. Anything was better than hanging around Carlisle while his bad tooth tried to drill itself through his skull. And he would not have gotten any sleep even if he had stayed tucked up safe in Carlisle castle.

The cloves were helping, though, he thought as he chewed carefully on the pungent spice in his mouth; he was definitely able to think now.

He crossed the Bewcastle waste carefully because it was horribly tricky ground, rocky and treacherous and full of sudden marshy spots, changing horses frequently so they wouldn't get tired. The sliver of Moon dodged in and out of the clouds but by a couple of hours before dawn, the rain had clamped down properly, his jack was wet on the outside, though not on the inside yet, thanks to a lot of beeswax rubbed into it, and he was having to lead the horses over an even more tricky bit. He planned to stay south of the Border until he had to cross into the Burns' lands and he had brought a kerchief of Elizabeth's he had quietly purloined when she came to Carlisle for the funeral of the old Lord Scrope. He'd forgotten he'd done it too, and then found it a few days before in the drawer of his desk.

That was when he heard a snuffling whimpering noise and stopped still. It came again and then a little yelp. It couldn't be?

"Jack?" he said and heard a wuff in the night.

He followed the sound and found the half-grown lymer pup completely covered in mud and stuck in a marsh. He wagged his tail wearily at Carey and gave another yelp.

"Good God, did you follow me all the way here?"

It was a stupid question, obviously he had because here he was. Carey sighed deeply, went and found a long sapling, cut it and prodded it toward Jack who barked at it, and finally held the sapling in his mouth so Carey could pull him out of the marsh. He took the dog to a slightly cleaner pool and washed the worst off and then squatted beside him and hugged his shoulders where they weren't too wet.

The pup was utterly exhausted, could hardly move his paws, but still licked Carey painfully exactly where his jaw was hurting worst.

"I appreciate the faithfulness," Carey said, "but what am I going to do with you?"

The half-grown pup wriggled with joy and panted open-mouthed at Carey. "You can't ride a horse, so you'll have to do the best you can and run," he said. "I'll rest a bit and then we'll take the last part as quick as we can and get to them on a surprise."

It wasn't a very good plan, he knew that, but it was the best he'd been able to come up with. Sometimes simple plans were good because they caught your enemies unawares. He hoped. He arranged the two hobbies on either side of himself and got them to lie down so he could prop himself against one of them and get some kind of rest. Jack came and plopped himself down next to him, and Teazle, the older lymer, took a dignified place on the other side.

At first Carey couldn't sleep although the pain from his tooth had gone down to a sinister drone. He was too wrought up thinking about Elizabeth, wondering if she was sleeping, wondering how she was, wondering what else he could do. Was this how she had felt when he got into trouble in Dumfries in the summer? Perhaps. It hadn't occurred to him how bad she might have felt.

He dozed off and dreamed of being roundly scolded by an elderly Jewish woman he didn't know at all, only she looked a bit like his mother.

He woke at dawn, stiff and aching with the nervous feeling he was late for something, he should get moving. The lymer pup was curled against him and looking up at him adoringly. One of the hobbies had wandered off while he was asleep. He cursed himself for not hobbling them, but he didn't have time to go looking for the animal and he would be perfectly all right for the moment, since he had a clear Carlisle brand. Whoever found him would keep him for a while and then bring him into Carlisle for the reward.

So he mounted up on Sorrel and rode on his way, followed by the dogs loping behind him, and he couldn't help himself, he rode faster and faster, until he was galloping dangerously along the high Cheviots, along the treacherous paths there that wound in and out among the rocks with the dogs strung out, Teazle before and Jack behind and he was late, he knew he was and…

There were two more horses there, one behind the other, over on the other side of summer pasture belonging to the Kerrs, or so they claimed, or the Collingwoods, or so they claimed, bitten down short and rank now from the rain. The leader was a broad tall man in an English jack and a morion helmet, the follower was…

Was a woman. Clearly a woman though riding astride, she had a black velvet gown on, her hat was pinned to her head and she was riding like the devil down toward him, riding like the Queen of Elfland though on a hobby not a milkwhite mare, taking ditches and low drystone walls as if the hobby was Pegasus and…

She lifted her face and the Sun poked a spear out from under the rocky piles of cloud and lit her for a second and then he had his own horse round and he was riding toward her while his heart beat itself out of his chest with joy and relief and joy.

They met by a pile of rocks, Carey stopped his horse on a sixpence and flung himself down from the saddle, ran over to her and helped her down from the saddle and held her, crushed her against him because he had to do it, he had to hold her and feel her body against his, even through the metal plates and leather padding of his jack he had to feel her and he was afraid he was hurting her, crushing her against him but she had her arms around him and was gripping him as tight. He instinctively put his mouth down to hers and she kissed him back for a second, only a second, and then pulled away. The lymer caught up and stood there barking stupidly while the pup flopped on his side and went to sleep.

"Robin," she said.

His happiness could not be stopped by something so trivial, it was flowing through him like a mountain stream, washing away his tiredness and bad temper.

"I know, Elizabeth, I'm sorry…"

She laughed and gripped him tighter. "I escaped, Robin!" she crowed, like a boy after an escapade. "Young Henry came and told them the ransom was paid and Maud Burn backed me up and we just rode away."

Young Henry was of course the man in the jack who was riding at a tactfully slow pace down toward them.

"He did? Wonderful!" It was too. By God, Geordie Burn would be angry. And how the Borderers would laugh. "And you came south and west because they'd assume you'd make for Jedburgh."

"Yes."

"Now then, Sir Robert," said Young Henry as he came near, formally tipping his helmet to Carey. Carey tipped his helmet back and grinned at him.

"Now then, Mr Widdrington, what's this I hear about ye putting a brave on Geordie Burn?"

Young Henry flushed a little, pity about that big yellow spot on his nose, it looked ready to burst. "I suppose, I did," he admitted. "I'm thinking it might be better to make for Carlisle now, though. Sergeant Dodd and Mr Anricks went back to Jedburgh with my lady's horse and Geordie will have found them by now and he'll not be pleased."

"Maybe he'll tangle with Sergeant Dodd and get dead suddenly?" said Carey, with a hopeful grin.

"I don't think so, sir," said Young Henry. "He's a clever man and not a brawler."

Elizabeth had very properly moved away from Carey now and straightened her hat. "I'm not going to Carlisle," she announced. "I'm going to Jedburgh to give my husband a piece of my mind."

The two men exchanged glances and Young Henry coughed hard. Carey was thinking. "I can't go with you in any case, my lady," he said, "although I want to. I don't want to get you into trouble with him."

"I am already in trouble with him," said Elizabeth haughtily. "What he has failed to realise is that he is in trouble with me. How dare he connive with a reiver to have me kidnapped to get me out of the way? How dare he?" She had her fists bunched and the look on her face was frightening even if you weren't Sir Henry.

"I don't want to take you directly into Jedburgh. I could take you to the abbey," said Young Henry. "I think there are a couple of the old monks there and the townsfolk use the church for services but you could likely stay there while I find out if the coast is clear. I wouldna like you to go riding into the town until we know who's there and who isn't."

"Pshaw!"

"Yes," said Carey thoughtfully, "she can hide there while you go into town and roust out Sergeant Dodd and anyone else you think will be useful and then bring her husband to her rather than the other way about."

"If he'll come."

"If he doesn't, that's an admission in itself and perhaps we can start proceedings for divorce," said Carey.

"Divorce?" said Elizabeth, "but that needs an act of parliament?"

"It does," said Carey, "but it's been done before." And nearly, he almost added, it was done for the Queen. Nearly.

"Whom God has joined together let no man put asunder," said Elizabeth in an old-fashioned sort of voice.

"My lady," said Carey, his voice full of compressed impatience, love and fury, "if your husband treated you decently and had given you children, I wouldn't be here. He doesn't and he hasn't."

"I promised to be a good wife to him," said Elizabeth, "in the sight of God."

"Certainly," said Young Henry unexpectedly, "and he promised to be a good husband to you, in the sight of God. I remember, I was there. Has he kept that promise?"

Elizabeth said nothing, looked down at the ground.

"Don't take her by the road," said Carey to Young Henry, "Go across country and carefully. Geordie may put watchers on the road. I'm hoping he's assumed she's heading for Carlisle and is on his way there now."

"Yes, and two murderers with him," said Elizabeth. "Robin, I must talk to you about the killing of Minister Jamie Burn."

She did, quietly, and at length and told him what she thought. "Jock Tait is the man who can act as a witness at the trial, if anyone can persuade him. But Archie and Jemmy Burn did it, as far as I can tell, they did it and raped his wife as well."

"Why?"

"Why? Because she was there and she's a pretty woman and they like to. They nearly raped me when they came back to the manse…"

"WHAT?"

There was the authentic Carey roar, thought Young Henry philosophically; they probably heard that in Jedburgh itself. Elizabeth explained the part about getting hit on the head when the two came back to the manse for some reason, and how if it hadn't been for Mr Anricks and his dag she might have been raped herself.

Young Henry was still furious about it, but he thought Carey was even more angry. He wasn't sure because the man was pale anyway. Carey sat on a rock with Elizabeth beside him and very seriously took her through every incident at Wendron again, including the ones with the boys. Of course, neither of them noticed that they were holding hands like children. And then he said quietly, "If those two come into the West March of England, they will never come out again."

Easy to say, thought Young Henry, less easy to do given the number of people who would be willing to hide them, even if you could get up some kind of hue and cry for them. Maybe he would have the chance to hang Archie and Jemmy Burn himself. That would be good.

They arranged that Carey would wait for Dodd and Anricks at Reidswire, which was only a summer shieling but had quite a good shelter. Young Henry would take Elizabeth to the old abbey and leave her there with the few monks still clinging on in the half-burnt ruins, speak to Dodd and Anricks, assuming they were still in Jedburgh and tell them where to find Carey. The fact of Henry coming into Jedburgh alone might encourage Geordie to think she'd gone to Carlisle which would be very helpful. Henry would then bring all the Widdringtons as well as Sir Henry to her ladyship. With luck Geordie would be chasing her rumour across the Middle March by then.

thursday 19th october 1592

There were five of the friars left of a full complement of twenty, and none of them were as young as they had been. In 1560 the Reformation had come to Scotland with a great ringing of bells and destroying of churches, though it hadn't been nearly as greedy and as violent a reformation as Henry VIII's stripping of the altars in England. The monks lost their jobs but not their lives, many of them left the cloisters with relief to try what men could do who could read and write. Some were allowed to stay in their monasteries and abbeys, cultivating the kitchen garden, looking after the sheep, just as they had before while their numbers ran down in the way of all life. No new novices came to them, until the one novice who had stayed was a man of forty-eight and they elected him abbot pro tem because Brother Constantine was now a little bit forgetful and silly and shook all the time like an aspen leaf, Brother Ignatius was crippled by rheumatism though he still tried to act as infirmerar to the townspeople when they came to him, Brother Justinian was skinny and obsessed by prayer and always in the church at odd times of day and night, and Brother Aurelius was trying to do everything else, including cook which was unfortunate because he was terrible at it.

"Ye have tae be the abbot," he'd insisted to Brother Ninian. "We have tae have one and it's you. Are ye sure ye wouldna like to go and marry some woman or other now ye're grown?"

Abbot Ninian had smiled and answered that he was very happy where he was. Which was true, he liked things to be just so and he liked them always to be the same as the day before which was lucky because that's how things go in an abbey.

And so it was Lord Abbot Ninian and Brother Aurelius who received the young woman and the young man at the ruined guest house of the abbey by the main road.

"This is Lady Widdrington," said the man. "I am her stepson, Henry Widdrington."

Brother Aurelius' round brown face grew watchful, with something else there as well. That was no surprise, thought Young Henry, the Widdringtons were well-known reivers of the East and Middle Marches, and had helped the Earl of Surrey burn the abbey a few decades before. Not all of it, luckily. Abbot Ninian also looked worried.

"What about the…?" he asked Brother Aurelius who smiled.

"They'll be very well where they are. How can we help you, Mr Widdrington?"

"My lady has had a difficult few days and would like to rest for a while here until her husband comes to collect her. No more than that."

Brother Aurelius squinted at the lady. She was wearing a muddy but fine velvet gown and her woollen kirtle was good as well, though old, while her boots though muddy were excellent, and her hat a little fashionable. She looked tired, though. "Well our guest house is, as you see, unusable, but she can come up tae the abbey church and sit there a while if she likes."

"Will that be all right, my lady?"

"Of course, Henry, I'm not made of glass. I'd like to sit down on something that isn't a horse for a while, though. And is there anything to eat?"

Brother Aurelius beamed at the lady. This was what the Austin friars were for, after all, providing sustenance and shelter to weary travellers. He had a kind of kitchen built out of the ruins of the old one and he was sure there was a bit of stew in the pot there and some bread perhaps, though his latest batch had come out a little bit solid—unless their other guests had finished them.

"I'll go and see what we've got," he said. "My Lord Abbot, perhaps you could show my lady tae the church and sit her down there."

The Lord Abbot ducked his head and smiled nervously. "All right, Brother Aurelius," he said. "You won't be too long will you?"

"I'll be making something delicious, ye'll see. There might be a chicken I can catch too." He doubted it. Their other guests had eaten the last chicken, he was sure.

The lady went gravely with the Lord Abbot, who was wearing exactly the same worn black robes as everyone else, and listened as he told her about the cabbages and the roses and how the fishpond was full of fish as if she had been there before and already knew all about it, and then about how they did reformed services in the church so it would look a little strange, but not to worry about it because God was still there.

"There are some other guests I mustn't tell you about," he explained carefully as they went into the huge abbey church, with its rows of round arches disappearing into darkness above. Some of them looked scorched but the roof still seemed to be on. "Brother Aurelius said I mustn't."

"Oh," said Lady Widdrington and gave him an odd look. "Are they reivers or a man like Geordie Burn?"

The Lord Abbot shivered and shook his head; he had heard of Geordie Burn and was terrified of him or anyone like him. "No, no, my lady," he said in his slow deliberate way. "They are friends and they are not even men and they help us with the chanting."

"Angels, perhaps?" she asked, with a smile.

"A bit like angels," he said, worried again, "but they eat a lot."

He showed her to the choir where there still nice wooden choirstalls to sit in and the altar was quiet with no sanctuary lamp lit. All the saints had been beheaded by enthusiastic Protestants and the paintings on the walls had been sploshed with white-wash. The reformed altar was down in the nave, a communion table, and the old altar had the usual chunk taken out of it where they had removed the superstitious old relics.

She looked around for the candles and Bible, found the new Bible chained to its lectern but the candles were too valuable to leave out when it wasn't a Sunday, she thought. So there was no fire there and it was bone-chillingly cold. And she was still damp from the hillside. She sighed. She would really like to sit by a fire and get completely warm.

"Who's that?" she asked as her eyes adjusted and saw a dark figure in a corner of the church, by the vandalised Lady chapel.

"Oh that's only Brother Justinian," explained the Lord Abbot, "praying as usual."

"Is he?"

"He gets the offices mixed up. We do still sing them, you know, not all of them but some of them. We always sing Vespers. Maybe ye'll hear us."

"I'd like that."

"Brother Aurelius doesn't want you to meet our other guests, so maybe not."

"Hm."

Then the Lord Abbot went away, with an awkward bob of a bow as he went to ask Brother Aurelius what to do next.

Elizabeth sat for a while in the huge old church, resting her back and bum, which were awakening from numbness and protesting about the treatment they'd been getting. But then it just got too cold in there, and too dark with the old friar muttering Latin in the corner, with his eyes tight shut, rocking to and fro and ignoring her completely. She got up and went through the choir and reredos, mainly in splinters though once it had been pretty with gold and paint, she thought, through the sacristy where they had a large locked chest for the candlesticks and candles and altar things, and then out into the afternoon as it turned down toward evening.

She saw something then, just a flicker at the corner of her eye. Firmly ramming down a superstitious thrill she chased after the person, and after a sprint through a neat garden and some dodging round an apple tree, she caught a bony little boy and knew him at once.

"Jimmy Tait," she exclaimed, "good God, what are you doing here?"

"Och, it's ma Lady Widdrington, och!"

"Why are you here?"

Jimmy scratched and then smiled shyly. "I'm singing in the choir, just like ye said, missus, though it's a bit small wi' only the old men and us and…"

"You think this is Carlisle Cathedral?"

Jimmy frowned. "Whit else could it be? We walked for days, an awf'y long way. It's a big town and a huge great church and there's auld monks here though Ah think they're Papists, but no matter, the songs is the same, only the words is different."

"We?"

"Ay, missus, me and Andy and Cuddy and my lord, we walked here, starting in the night and naebody the wiser. Cuddy Trotter cannae sing better nor a corbie, but he come too to make sure Ah wis all right and maybe see if they want a kitchen boy or summat so he can finish learning Latin and be a clerk."

"But…but your parents?"

Jimmy's face clouded. "Ah told my ma I wis off tae the big church but I dinna think she believed me and me dad's off guarding the village sheep in the third infield."

"Andy and Cuddy?"

"Cuddy's got ainly an uncle and aunt who're good tae him but they'll be glad he's 'prenticed and Andy…well, Andy said his father'd likely beat him but it was worth it to get to sing every day again and learn more letters and stuff. He wants tae learn French too."

Elizabeth shook her head and then laughed a little. "What did the old monk say?"

"Ay well, the one called Brother Aurelius said we could stay and help the singing and he asked the Lord Abbot, who's a wee bit slow in the heid, and the Lord Abbot said, 'Whitever ye want, Brother,' and so it's sorted."

"Where are the other boys?"

"They're in whit's left o' the dorter, Ah'll show ye."

She followed him to what looked like a mere pile of stones and rubble at the further corner of the burned cloister, but turned out to be one end of a dormitory that still had beds in it, though old and rotten. Cuddy and Andy were playing dice for pebbles and they jumped up and looked about for an escape as she came climbing carefully up the pile of stones. There was a fair-haired boy behind them she recognised from the funeral who stood up and waited warily for her.

They relaxed a little when they recognised her, and Cuddy said, "Whit are ye doing in Carlisle, ma'am?"

"I might ask you the same thing, Cuddy," she replied. "And you, Andy?"

The boy she thought was Lord Hugh confirmed it by bowing to her so she curtseyed. He was in a cutdown brocade doublet from something wide from the reign of King Henry but his boots were from Edinburgh and he had a boy's sword at his belt.

"My Lord Hugh," she said to him gravely, "what on earth are you doing here?"

He flushed and put his old velvet cap back on. "I'm going to 'prentice to the cathedral as well."

"But you can't," she said, wishing it were not so, "you're the heir."

The boy shrugged bitterly. "Then I've come for the adventure if they won't have me," he said, "I can sing, though." And he lifted his voice and sang something Latin, his voice a warm gold against the diamond silver of Jimmy Tait's. "There. I can sing. I don't want to be a laird, I want to be a clerk that sings."

She looked at him with real pity. He couldn't use his gift, only show it off for Court scraps.

"My dear," she said, "you have no choice. You have to be a laird."

"And go to Court?"

"Well it's not so bad," she began. "You learn to be a page…"

"With my guardian, Lord Spynie?"

She said nothing.

"I knew one of his pages, he was a cousin on my mother's side. He couldnae sit down for a week after Lord Spynie picked him out, for all the pretty fat padded breeches he got," said Lord Hughie. "Do ye think I know nothing, ma'am? D'ye think I'm an innocent like Jimmy Tait here?"

Elizabeth could think of nothing to say and Lord Hughie turned away from her. So she sat carefully on one of the other beds and said, "Tell me."

The stories tallied. There had been a council of war after the funeral, with all the boys attending. A council of war was what Andy called it, in fact. Most of the boys were sad about the minister but willing to go back to being crow-scarers and shepherds all the time. Piers Dixon had a sick mum, with a cough that wouldn't go away and she was terrible thin, so he'd stick by her and if she died, then he'd come on his own; the rest of his family wouldn't mind for there were too many mouths to feed anyway. Young Jimmy had spoken up.

"He did, missus," said Cuddy. "It was wonderful," Jimmy Tait blushed and hid his face in his hands, then looked up again. "He said that the minister said that God had given him his voice, for it wisnae something he had learned or made, it was purely a gift, and God gave it to him for a reason and he needed to find out what the reason was and so he'd go tae Carlisle on his own if he had to. And he knew where to get the 'prentice money too."

"The 'prentice money?"

"Ay, it were the down payment on whatever it was the minister was at and Jimmy got intae the manse after the funeral on the quiet and he knew where the minister hid stuff cos he'd been poking around and found it and so…."

"Where's that?"

"Och, in his study, there's a brick in the wall that comes loose but ye canna see it if ye dinna ken it's there and he mostly kept papers in it but when Jimmy looked again he found half of a wonderful necklace all in gold and jewels, so he did. But then he couldnae get out again for the two murderers come in and while ye was fighting them he run upstairs and hid under the bed and stayed there for he was affeared with Mr Anricks and everything and Young Henry and all and then ye found him in the morning and wis nice tae him. And we went that night."

"Show me the 'prentice fee, Jimmy?"

"Ye willna take it, it's ourn, the minister said he wad gi' it to us to get us' prenticed and to free Jimmy fra his father and…"

"I will not take it."

Jimmy delved into the noxious depths of his breeches and pulled out a bag which he tipped out to show half of a beautiful gold woman's necklace with sapphires and emeralds in it, in the style of seventy years before, at least ten pounds worth, probably much more. There was your explanation for why the men came back for it, if they found out about it after they had got away. She knew it at once. Perhaps Lady Hune had let slip about it when they told her the minister was dead. She heard Lord Hughie sucking in a long breath when he saw it. Then another. And another. He had gone white.

"Thank you, Jimmy. Put it away again."

He put it back, tied the straps round himself again. There was no reason to think such a dirty little boy with bare hard feet would have such a treasure.

Elizabeth sat in thought for a moment. "All right," she said, "I'm going to talk to Brother Aurelius. You stay here."

"Well we need tae go tae the church soon for Vespers, will ye hear us? It's no' very good yet, but it's shaping," said Andy.

"Of course I'll hear you. First I must speak to the brothers."

Lord Hughie followed her down the rocks that had been the stairs and made a great production about helping her, which she allowed. "Ma'am, my lady," he said with his voice trembling, "May I speak to you?"

They sat on a bench in the herb garden.

"I know that collar."

"Yes, it's your grandmother's."

"How do you know?"

"She told me about it."

"She…how did the minister come by it?"

Elizabeth was silent a moment. He must have some idea. "I think your grandam offered it to him if he would try and kill Lord Spynie for her."

He nodded. "But she's daft in the heid with her faery forts and all."

"She may be less daft than she seems. And she's also a determined woman and she doesn't want you to go to Court with Lord Spynie either."

"She knows?"

"Of course she knows. I know. Everybody knows."

"Well, why doesn't anybody stop him?"

"He's rich and powerful and he has the favour of the King."

Hughie went silent a while. "So my grandam gave that to the minister so he'd go and kill Spynie, half before, half after. And he tried and he failed?"

"Yes." The boy deserved honesty, appalling though it was.

"And Spynie found out who it was, somehow, and sent two men that had been in the Netherlands so they wouldn't be known, to kill him?"

She nodded. Though now she came to think about it, how exactly did Spynie find out precisely who had made the attempt against him if they hadn't caught him to torture him?

"And they did it."

"Yes."

"So I caused the minister's death?"

"No, my lord, he caused his own death. He should have told your grandam no, despite her being his great aunt. What was he doing, trying to kill Lord Spynie in cold blood and him a man of the cloth? He should have said, "No" and trusted in God."

"At least he tried!" shouted the boy. "At least he tried something!"

"You can think it's all your fault if you like, my lord," she said to him brutally. "It wasn't. It was Jamie Burn's pride and anger. It's very hard for a man to leave the fighting trade if he's good at it and I honour him for trying. But in the end, he decided to kill a man, he failed, and he was killed in revenge. Those who live by the sword shall die by it. All he had to do was delay things for two or three years and Spynie wouldn't be interested."

"Ma'am, you're wrong. If it wasn't me; it would be some other boy. Killing Spynie is the right thing to do."

And he turned away and left her.

She found Brother Aurelius happily stirring food in a large iron pot and humming a part of a Magnificat, while three large heavy-looking loaves waited on the bit of board he was using for a table.

"I've spoken to your other guests—Jimmy, Cuddy, Andy and Lord Hugh," she said without preamble.

Brother Aurelius stopped stirring, then started again in the other direction. "Ah," he said.

"Did you tell them this was Carlisle Cathedral or did they…?"

"So that's where they thought they were. No, ma'am, we didnae lie tae them. They arrived at night and asked could they 'prentice to the church here and we couldnae turn them away, could we? Four young boys like that? So we took them in and fed them and at Matins this morning after breakfast, they showed us what they could do, though it was reformed psalms. Brother Justinian taught them some Latin psalms after, and the *Salve Regina*, the first time he's been interested in anything but prayer for years. We had a kind of sung Mass, too, with English psalms and I officiated which was, strictly speaking, illegal—but you could say it was reformed too with the English….It was beautiful, you know."

"I'm sure it was. I'm looking forward to Vespers."

"I suppose you'll be taking them back to their families now."

"One of them, yes. I'd rather take the others to Carlisle, where they originally wanted to go."

"Ah," said Brother Aurelian, stirring the stew with nameless lumps of gristle floating in it. "Well it was lovely to have them here, even if it was for such a short time." He smiled at her. "Would you help me lay the table in the refectory? Our supper is quite simple, as you see."

Elizabeth found the wooden bowls and spoons and also the refectory which had burned quite badly but still had half a roof. She even found a couple of candles which might help as the Sun went down.

All the monks came, even Brother Constantine came, smiling, and all of him trembling as if he were in an invisible wind. "God bless us," he said, "and especially the new novices." He smiled on the four boys at the end of the table, three of whom smiled shyly back. Lord Hughie was staring into space. Brother Justinian was reading an old worn prayer book; Brother Ignatius was a spry old man with terrible red knuckles like walnuts and a hobble that looked painful. The Lord Abbot Ninian intoned a very long grace in Latin, and Brother Aurelius served everybody except Justinian with stew, and Justinian with a double helping of bread. Brother Ignatius started talking to Elizabeth about the diseases he found were coming to him, as if he already knew her.

Elizabeth was starving but found the stew surprisingly inedible and the bread so solid and rocklike it was all she could do to chew it. She copied the other brothers and dipped it into the watery stew and got enough down to stop her belly protesting. The boys put their heads down and ate every scrap of stew and bread, so she gave Jimmy her remains, saying she wasn't very hungry after all.

They went to the church then, led by Lord Abbot Ninian, and Brother Aurelius brought a sanctuary lamp from somewhere and they lit the two candles from it. Then they sang Vespers.

It was like no Vespers or Evensong she had ever heard. The Latin chants came out in plainsong, sung expertly by all five of the brothers, and around and above them wound the singing of the boys, mainly alleluias. Then the boys sang two psalms and the monks intoned the closing prayer. Was it heretical?

Elizabeth suddenly had a picture in her mind of the young strong Jesus with the older Jewish woman behind Him with her arms folded, both of them smiling at her. She understood something then, although she wasn't sure how. That whenever Jesus spoke to a woman, it was, in a way, His mother He was speaking to, as happens with most young men, and so Mary was far more important than she had thought. For one of the things that had thrilled her about the Gospels was the respect with which Our Lord spoke to women, as if they were full people, not foolish half-men who needed ruling. Not always, and He was positively rude to His mother at the Marriage Feast at Cana—unless He was joking. Also nowhere in the Gospels did it say that Jesus laughed, although He wept twice. And yet Elizabeth was sure she could hear laughter in some of what He said. And it stood to reason He must have laughed sometimes, perhaps when He got drunk at the marriage feast on the wine He had made from water? Perhaps that was blasphemy to think that Jesus Christ could have got drunk at a party, but why shouldn't He? And on His own wine too? Why should He always have been serious or sorrowful or angry—if He was a man as well as God, He laughed too. And what kind of music did He like, she wondered; was His voice good? Surely it was? You didn't hear anything about that either, though surely Jews had ballads and worksongs like everybody else?

Jimmy was singing a Latin hymn from before she was born. *Salve Regina* it began and his voice went up effortlessly into the darkness of the burnt roof and lit it up with sound. She sat there, bathing in the boy's glorious voice, until it ended and everyone gave a little sigh.

They came out to find the cloisters and main courtyard full of men in jacks and helmets.

The boys fled back into the church immediately, but the brothers came forward slowly in a body, led, she noticed, by Brother Aurelius not the Lord Abbot Ninian, who was well back.

It didn't matter. She knew this particular collection of toughs and walked forward calmly to where Young Henry and his Uncle Thomas were dismounting. Henry had her jennet on a leading rein, though the saddle was still a man's. She sighed a little; a side saddle was so comfortable and her bum was bruised from all the riding she had done that morning.

"Now then, Mr Widdrington," she said formally to her husband's eldest son. "Where is Sir Henry?"

"Ay, well," said Young Henry, "he's in Jedburgh right enough but he willna see ye right away."

Elizabeth considered this. It was one of Sir Henry's nasty tricks, to make you wait for your punishment so your imagination could work and you would get nervous. Quite obvious and quite contemptible.

"I don't know that I can ride anymore since you helped me escape from the Burns," she said in a voice pitched to reach everyone in the crowd of men. "Perhaps I'll stay here with the monks."

There was a stir in the crowd of men and hobbies and one man came shoving forward. She recognised Jock Tait, in an old worn jack that may have been his grandfather's from the pattern and a leather cap on his head. You could see he needed a new helmet.

"Missus, d'ye ken where my son Jimmy has gone?"

She didn't answer that. "Why?"

"He's missing fra home. He went wi' three other boys."

"Maybe they were making for Carlisle Cathedral," she said carefully. "You know Minister Burn had a plan to take them there and 'prentice them as singers at the cathedral."

He dismounted and came toward her and she could smell that he had been drinking. "Ay, and I asked ten pounds English from him, ma wife told ye."

"Yes," she said coldly, "how is your wife?"

His eyes slid from hers and he answered in a baffled angry voice, "Ah didna ken he meant it, I wis joking."

"Were you?"

"Well I wisna. But…"

"Mr Tait, your second son is a skinny dirty little boy that has probably never eaten enough in his life. Why do you care what he does? Surely if he goes to Carlisle Cathedral as a singer, he'll be fed and it'll cost you nothing."

Were those actual tears in the man's eyes or the effect of Henry's torch? "I'll miss his singing, so I will. I didna ken how good he was."

"Why not? Did you never listen to him until the minister's funeral?"

"Nay, I didna ken. But Carlisle's a long way…"

Good God, did the man love his son in some way? Really?

"Mr Tait, a voice like Jimmy's only comes occasionally. Carlisle is the best place for him, they'll teach him to use it and they'll teach him to read music and Latin and…why don't you want him to go?"

"I want him to go but not alone on the road to Carlisle, it's a long way."

"I beg your pardon?"

"I want tae go with him to Carlisle and make sure he gets there, missus, naething mair, I swear to ye. Did ye think I'd stop him? Ay, I've given him a thick ear now and again but this… he's ainly seven but he's taken a man's step here and I wish he would ha' asked me…"

"Would you have said yes?"

"Ay, o' course." Perhaps he was lying, but did that matter? Perhaps he was looking ahead now. "Ah wanted to go to Carlisle Cathedral maself when I wis a wean but wi' my grandfather and uncle hangit before I wis born and my father allus riding to fetch us in food, I had to stay at hame and watch the sheep and the goats and the little 'uns."

Elizabeth looked at the man, he wasn't drunk so much as he had taken a drink and it had loosened his tongue. Was it possible he was telling the truth?

She didn't have to decide what to do because a small bony creature came running across the courtyard and flung himself at his father, who fumbled in shock, nearly dropped him and then lifted him up.

"Whit are ye doing here, Jimmy?"

"Ah," said Brother Aurelius with a bland smile, "the boys arrived here last night, very weary and we have given them shelter although unfortunately we are not Carlisle Cathedral."

Jock Tait looked at him and then at Elizabeth and then at Jimmy. "Is that right, Jimmy?"

"Ay, we thought it wis, but it isn't?"

Jock laughed. "Nay, it's Jeddart Abbey!"

"Oh. Is Carlisle further, for we walked an awf'y long way."

"Ay, nay doubt ye did for yer tracks went round on yourself twice."

"Oh. Will ye take me to Carlisle then, Dad? Wi' my lord and Andy and Cuddy?"

"Ay, Ah will."

Jimmy had screwed his face up with a very cynical expression on it. "Ay, and ye willnae fool me and take me back hame and gi' me the leathering o'my life?"

There was a pause and then Jock answered, "No, I willna." Then he swallowed.

"And will ye tell who wis the men that killt the minister so he couldna take us hisself?"

"Now?"

"Ay," said Jimmy, still with that old man's expression on his face. Jock looked at his son as if he was seeing him for the first time. Then he nodded slowly.

"Mr Widdrington..."

"Ay?"

"I've a mind to lay a complaint as a witness agin Archie and Jemmy Burn, for the killing of Minister James Burn, their cousin."

"If we can find a procurator fiscal at this hour, will ye make a witness statement?"

"Ay, that I will. I had Jimmy looking after their horses while they did the murder and then he took two of their horses down to the Border to trade with a merchant I know, to put ye off the track. I know them well from riding wi' them, Burns and Taits is usually friends. I didna ken they were after the minister. I thought it was some ither man o' the village. I never thought they'd be after killing their ain cousin like that—not even Kerrs would do it."

Elizabeth did her best not to be cynical. Possibly that was true, though she doubted it. Never mind, Jock Tait had come round with no persuasion at all.

Young Henry nodded once. "We'll have a hue and cry for them the minute your statement's done," he said, "I think they're with Geordie Burn at the moment. Who now says he never intended to ransom you, my lady, he just gave you shelter."

"Hmf," said Elizabeth, "you expect liars to lie. Well?"

"Well, my lady, will I go back to my father and tell him you're tired."

"No, because he'll hit you again." The combined Widdringtons who were probably the twenty best riders of that numerous and ferocious surname started looking about at each other for someone who would be mad enough to go and tell the old man his wife was disinclined to meet him.

Brother Aurelius stepped forward with a smile on his round face. "I'll do it," he said. "My lady Widdrington is tired and needs her rest although I have to admit we don't really have anywhere here at the abbey that's suitable for a lady."

"What did he tell you, Mr Widdrington?" she asked.

"He told me to take some men and fetch you to him."

Elizabeth's lips compressed together until all the blood left them. "I wish I knew why he treats me like a blood enemy, not his wife," she said. Nobody answered her.

Brother Aurelius came close to her and said kindly, "Perhaps ye'll come and bear me company whiles I clean up the kitchen," he said. There was no guile in his voice but Elizabeth almost said no. Then she thought again, shrugged and went with him.

There wasn't a lot to do in the kitchen as the stew and the bread were finished and there was no more food anywhere. Elizabeth brought back the wooden bowls and spoons, scoured them out with silver sand and polished them, while Brother Aurelius gave a quick wipe to the inside of the great cauldron he had clearly used daily for the last thirty years with no more than a wipe each time. It was a surprise the stew didn't taste better, really. He asked her how she had come to Sir Henry and what he had done and how she had tried to be a good wife to him. She found herself pouring out her heart to him, while he sat by the remains of the fire with his head oddly tilted a little to the side, propped on his hand so she didn't have to look him in the eyes.

"And has he always beaten ye?"

She sighed. "Yes. Sometimes he hits me, sometimes he knocks me down. Sometimes he uses his belt. I'm used to it now but I wish he would tell me what he wants of me so I can do it if I can."

Brother Aurelius took a deep breath in and let it out again.

"It seems he wants me dead now," she added, "if Henry's right that he arranged with Geordie Burn to take me captive."

"Are ye sure of that?"

"No, I'm not. But my stepson is quite convinced."

"And he sent your stepson with men to bring you back."

"He's showing off. Showing me he has men at his back and I don't."

"Hmm. Lady Widdrington, I'll ask ye to do a hard thing. Come with me into the toon to meet your husband, on your own. Will ye do it?"

Her heart was dull and grey that had been lit up with joy that morning. After the fire, the embers. She had to go back to him, it was her duty and besides she had nowhere else to go. But she wished and wished she were a man…Actually a man had little choice as well. Robin was as bound by ties of family and duty as she was.

She sighed. "Yes, Brother Aurelius, I will."

She followed him back to where the Widdringtons had made themselves comfortable with a small fire from some of the beams of wood they'd uncovered. The four monks were sitting in a row near it, Brother Constantine still trembling like a leaf but smiling benignly, Brother Justinian reading his prayer book, Brother Ignatius chatting to one of the men, the Lord Abbot Ninian sitting with his mouth a little open watching the proceedings with amazement and suspicion.

The hobbies were lined up and tethered, most of the men had their helmets and jacks off and the boys were singing one of the psalms. It was a domestic scene. There was a pause and then two voices lifted, singing Tam Lin between them, one Jimmy Tait's in its silver perfection, the other a man's bass voice, a little gruff and out of practice but with a power and force in it that made the eldritch parts with the faery folk more frightening as Tam Lin turned to fire and water in the Queen of Elfland's spell.

She stood just outside of the fire circle, listening to the sound, listening as Jimmy and Jock Tait sang together for the first time.

Brother Aurelius went forward and spoke to Young Henry who nodded and gestured at everyone. The old monk then went quietly to each man and got some kind of answer, while three of the Widdringtons sang the rude song about Lusty Jean and the Fine Young Knight. And then he came back to her.

"I have talked to every one of the men," said Brother Aurelius. "I and they are ad idem about certain things and they too believe that your kidnapping was really an attempt upon your life. Let us go down to the town now. I believe your husband is at the Spread Eagle inn."

It wasn't really so late, it was just it got dark early. Elizabeth was aching and still quite hungry after the stew and bread, but mostly she was tired. At least she didn't have to ride tonight since Brother Aurelius was striding down the road from the abbey. Since the townsmen used the church for reformed services on Sundays, it wasn't too bad and had stones laid on the muddiest bits.

She didn't want to go, she wanted to run in the opposite direction, to Reidswire where Robin was waiting for Sergeant Dodd and the tooth-drawer. And yet her feet kept following the sandals of Brother Aurelius.

thursday night 19th october to friday 20th october 1592

Mr Anricks insisted on hurrying to meet Carey at Reidswire, a place often used for Middle March Warden meetings and as summer pasture. Now the wind swept across it and the rain was horizontal, though by the time they got there, perhaps there was an hour of daylight left and for a wonder the rain had stopped temporarily. The Sun pretended to be fighting to shine through the cloud, but was really sulking.

Carey came out of the sheepshelter where he had lit a fire from the supplies left there by the men who used it. Two dogs were with him who first barked and then fawned on Dodd and Anricks, probably in hopes of food. He tried to smile but couldn't because of the way his face had ballooned, and also he was afraid of having his tooth drawn because the last time he had to have it done, on the left side, it had hurt so much.

There wasn't a chair so Carey sat on a rock with his back to the dry stone wall shelter, and Mr Anricks tipped his head back and took a look.

"Hm," said Mr Anricks. He poked about with shining steel instruments while Dodd stood and stared across the hills where nobody was pasturing cattle and Carey made occasional squawks as Anricks probed a sensitive spot. The dogs lay nearby watching with interest.

"Two teeth have to come out, Sir Robert," said Anricks, "though that may save the third which is a wisdom tooth."

"Get on with it," growled Carey, his hands in fists.

"All in good time," said Anricks, delving about in his pack and bringing out a brown glass bottle and a cloth. "Would you hold him up, please, Sergeant. Now, I want you to breathe in the fumes from this sweet oil of vitriol, keep doing it. I know it's an acrid smell and you'll feel drunk and dizzy and then you'll fall asleep. When you wake up, your teeth will be out." The dogs got up and retired some distance from the smell and the younger one started barking again.

"Are you sure...?"

"Ay, he's telling the truth, sir, I've seen him dae it in Jedburgh."

Suspiciously Carey started sniffing the cloth, he got chatty, talking a lot of nonsense about being executed and a little later he slumped sideways, despite the barking. Immediately Anricks tipped him back, put his pliers in and pulled, then he did it again and then he mopped up some ugly-looking pus that came spilling out of the hole until it was all good red blood. Dodd took a look at the teeth—one was practically gone with two holes right through it and the other had a long tunnel going right down, both were black. Horrible. Teeth weren't meant to be black or brown, they were meant to be yellow. Dodd's teeth were a good ivory colour and not a hole in them either. He had let Anricks check earlier.

It took a little while before Carey came to again, and in that time Anricks explained how he wanted to do an empirical investigation into toothworms which would involve checking Dodd and Carey's stools for worms. Dodd was happy enough to say yes, wondering what Carey would say.

Carey was obviously in a lot of pain when he came round but he shook Anrick's hand and promised him at least a gold angel for taking out the teeth; he felt better already. His jaw swelling was already going down, certainly. The dogs came back cautiously but stayed away from Anrick's pack. Dodd recognised them and said hello—it was a good notion of the Courtier's to bring them, mind.

Dodd was pleased with himself. He had found a tooth-drawer and gotten Carey's bad teeth drawn, now they could go back to Carlisle.

But no they couldn't. "Why not?" Dodd wanted to know. "Why d'ye want tae stay in this Godforsaken place...Ach, it's Lady Widdrington."

"I have to know if she's all right or if her bastard of a husband has...hurt her again."

"Why? Why d'ye have to know? What can ye do about it if he has? Eh?"

"I have to know," said Carey, muffled by the cloth soaked with aqua vitae he was stopping the bleeding with.

"Jesu, ye're..."

"Gentlemen," said Anricks, who was carefully repacking his pack. He had used clean cloths to wipe the instruments he had used and was closing the top. There was another picture there of a fearsome looking worm with large teeth itself coming out of a black tooth with a hole in it, which had made Dodd quite queasy to look at.

"...never going tae pit yer heid in a noose again. Sir Henry's a bad man tae cross as ye found in the summer..."

"I have to make sure..."

"Gentlemen!"

"Ay and ye'll do her harm as well..."

"Shut up, Sergeant, you don't have to come with me if ye're affeared..."

"By God, I'm no' affeared o' any man but it's stupid tae..."

"GENTLEMEN!"

Mr Anricks had produced quite a shout though he coughed afterwards. Carey turned his head to him from glaring at Dodd. "What?" The younger dog said "Wuff?" in exactly the same tone.

"I will ride back into Jedburgh and I will find out what is happening to Lady Widdrington. When I have found out I will take whatever action I consider is appropriate."

"With respect, Mr Anricks, I don't think a tooth-drawer can really..."

"Nay sir, he's a pursuivant for Sir Robert Cecil. He showed me his commission."

Carey put out his hand for it imperiously. A minute later he had sat back down on the rock and leaned his head back.

"What's going on?" he asked. "Why are you here, Mr Anricks?"

"I don't know what's going on, but I am certain that the Maxwell is embroiled in it somewhere, which is why I desire to go to the West March. But first I will ride back to Jedburgh and find out what is happening to Lady Widdrington."

"Why?"

"Because I like the woman, Sir Robert, and for good and sufficient reasons to do with her husband and his activities with Lord Spynie."

"Will you tell me what they are?"

"No. Or not now. I have no evidence. Is there any chance you will keep my identity secret or is it gone the way of all flesh now, seeing I've told three men?"

"I won't tell anyone except my lord Burleigh,"

Anricks smiled gently. "His son is my very good lord so I am quite happy for you to do so. In the meantime I want to get back to the Newcastle road before full dark and so I'll be going."

Dodd bore him company on the way there to make sure he didn't miss the path in the dusk, leaving Carey to take a nap in the little shelter by the fire. By the time he came back, Carey was snoring away with the dogs on either side of him and would not be woken. The old lymer lifted his lip to Dodd and warned him off. And moreover the Moon was behind more clouds making the night pitch-black. Dodd sighed, brought the hobbies into the shelter so no one would ask why they were there, and rolled himself up in his cloak across the door opening. He hoped no one would wake him because burying people took time and was a lot of effort.

thursday night 19th october to friday 20th october 1592

The Spread Eagle inn was still full of men and lights, torches and candles, a game of ninepins causing uproarious betting, with Sir Henry and Lord Spynie standing in the centre of a knot of hangers-on, holding pewter tankards of the double-double beer, shouting at each other about whether a ram would beat a billy goat in a fight and whether a shod hobby went better than an unshod one in a race in the woods.

Into this hurdy-gurdy came a small modest figure who sat in the corner, drank mild ale, and watched. When he wished, Simon Anricks could be almost invisible. He wasn't sure what he could do about Lady Widdrington and her husband, and he wished he hadn't said that he would do anything nor let out that he was Sir Robert Cecil's man. But what was done was done and if too many people knew what he was, well, he would have to go back south to Bristol and his wife and children. And to be truthful, he would prefer that. Rebecca came to him in his dreams sometimes and told him off for crimes like getting wet or not eating regularly and he always took her in his arms when she did because she was his wife and he loved her. He woke up cold and lonely, so if his cover was blown, he wouldn't mind that much.

Yet he was here because Sir Robert Cecil had been seeing the edges, the outlines, the flippers, and tail of a monstrous plot. Something was going on in Scotland, something that might perhaps give the King of Scotland the throne of England a little earlier than necessary, if you were suspicious, if you thought the King of Scotland might be the kind of man who would do that. The Queen was certainly old, fifty-nine this year, but, unfortunately for James, in excellent health. Was His Majesty of Scotland getting impatient, was he wanting something more than his pension? Were the Spaniards, in particular the ever-patient Spanish king, influencing him? Or was it all imagination, dreams, and fantasy—the way suspicious minds sometimes come up with plots that don't exist? He had agreed to come out of his pleasant retirement yet again to try and find out, agreed because there were important people in London town, particularly Dr Hector Nunez, who wanted to find out something about the Scottish king as well.

He sighed and ordered the ordinary, which turned out to be haggis again. In London it was all steak and kidney pie and liver and onions, here in the North, haggis—thrifty huswifery using up the unpreservable offal first.

He watched Sir Henry, a short, squat man, with a good grey-ing moustache and corrugated ears which spoke of gout and quite possibly stones in his bladder. He was shouting at Lord Spynie still, who was enjoying himself with his hard-cases at his back, still a good-looking young man though his jawline was blurred with too much booze and his eyes were puffy. Anricks wondered why he wasn't with the King and who was with the King now. That was very interesting. Why wasn't he with the King?

Spynie had been in trouble in August, something to do with the Earl of Bothwell and goings on in Dumfries, a series of events involving Sir Robert Carey and Lady Widdrington, which Anricks still wasn't clear about. He had read all the papers reporting what had happened, including a copy of Sir Robert's own private report to his father, and he was damned if he could make out what had been going on. Had King James somehow managed to buy Carey, turn him against his Queen? That was possible, given the length of the two interviews with the Scottish monarch that Carey had been granted.

Somebody had come into the commonroom, and Anricks recognised the round-headed Austin friar. Brother Aurelius was a kindly faced old man with a natural tonsure and not very much white hair, his face oddly familiar-looking. The barman served him with mild ale and no money changed hands; Brother Aurelius went and stood near Sir Henry and Spynie and waited to be noticed.

It took a while. Sir Henry's broad face was red, and his voice had been getting steadily louder. He was laying a bet with Lord Spynie on a fight to be held at the Carlisle race course of three rams against three billy goats to settle the matter.

At last Spynie asked Brother Aurelius' opinion on the matter, in a way that showed he didn't expect anything.

"Ay," Brother Aurelius agreed, "it's a tickle question. And more interesting than whether a shod horse or an unshod horse goes better because that was all settled before the Queen went tae England. I mind me that the Earl of Bothwell ran the race twice with the same four horses, two shod and two unshod, and then again with the shod horses unshod and the unshod shod."

"What happened?" asked Sir Henry, "a dead heat?"

The monk's face beamed at him. "The unshod horses won both races. It was quite definitive."

Away in his corner, listening for all he was worth, Simon Anricks smiled as well. It was too pat; he didn't believe it. Not without running the race again.

"That was the one before this Lord Bothwell, his uncle. Queen Mary's lover."

Spynie smiled at him. "It's said he was a warlock, like his nephew. Perhaps he enchanted the race?"

"Ay, perhaps. In which case why run it? And in any case, my Lord Bothwell backed the shod horses."

"Why are ye here?" asked Sir Henry. "I've never known one of you monks come into the inn."

"No, there's nae reason to," agreed Brother Aurelius. "We make our own aqua vitae and sell it tae the landlord here because it's so good, eh?" The barman smiled and nodded. "I've naething to do with that, it's Brother Ignatius and Lord Abbot Ninian that make it, I anely bring it into town. In the spring. Nay, Sir Henry, I'm here because I accompanied your lady wife here. She's sitting in the parlour now, putting herself around some haggis and mild ale."

"Where are my men?"

"Och, Ah dinna ken. Back at the abbey perhaps, they wis making theirselves comfortable."

Sir Henry paused at that. If he could but see it, there was a message to him in that from his men.

"Well I'm not paying for my wife to get fat on the haggis here. She can wait for me without guzzling..."

"Nay need," said Aurelius benignly, "it's off the abbey's tab which is *well* in credit. The thing is, Sir Henry, she's come back tae ye because it's her duty to dae it not because she wants to, which is a thing I find admirable but sad."

Sir Henry drank theatrically and finished his quart. "Are you going to tell me how to manage my wife? You? You've never been married—unless it's tae a choirboy." Some of the men laughed at that; Lord Spynie smiled.

Brother Aurelius was smiling too though the smile was a little strained and his face was redder. "Ay, perhaps it's a mite silly in me, that I should want tae speak up for a woman that's done her best to be a guid and obedient wife tae ye. She's made mistakes, ay, and she says now she shouldnae have come into Scotland wi'out your permission, but she thought since ye were here yerself it wouldnae matter if she came to organise the funeral of Minister Jamie Burn."

Sir Henry snorted and put the pewter tankard down. "All I ask of her is that she stay at home and do as she's told. That's all."

"Nay Sir Henry, that isnae. You ask of her that she have no gossips nor friends, that she has nae part o' the marriage bed wi' ye and that she take your ill-treatment of her. That is not what God meant marriage to be..."

"It's none of your business, brother—my wife, my business."

"Ay, it is my business, Sir Henry, because I was once a Widdrington and I willna see ye bring shame on my surname with your goings on. The way ye treat your wife is only one of them, ye hear? My name was once Roger Widdrington and I'm yer uncle, in fact, d'ye mind? Yer father's younger brother? Yer memory's got worse if ye dinna remember me for I let ye fish in the abbey's fishponds when ye came to see me when ye were a wean, before the change. I've lived a long while and I still live at the abbey because I choose to and, thank God, the Jeddart folk are kind enough to let us stay until all of us go to God. But ye, Sir Henry, are an embarrassment and a shame tae the Widdrington name and, by God, it *is* my place to tell ye so."

Sir Henry had an ugly expression on his face.

"You can't tell me off about my wife. She's mine."

"Nay, she isna. She's a creature belonging to God and the way ye treat isnae designed to show her the error of her ways and bring her to better ones. It's designed tae hurt her and make her despair, Sir Henry. It's designed to bring her down. It's a shame and a scandal to your surname, so it is, there's not a one of your men that I spoke to that hasnae respect for your wife—more respect than for ye, though of course they fear ye."

Sir Henry roared and grabbed Brother Aurelius by the throat of his robe, shoved him backwards to the bar and leaned him over.

"Shut yer face, old man..."

Brother Aurelius' face was as red as Sir Henry's and he had the same full-throated roar despite being bent backwards.

"Old man, is it? Ye're auld yerself, Henry. Ye're the headman of the Widdringtons, and ye bring shame on all of us by treating her the way ye do. There's no kinsman of yourn older than ye are, save me, and so I'll do it, I'll put the shame and the disgrace of it back on your own heid, Sir Henry. If ye do not treat your wife better and kindlier than ye have, may ye be cursed, may all your doings miscarry and may yer life be short."

Sir Henry seemed to be turned to stone by this. Lord Spynie backed away from him and space opened up around him in the crowded commonroom.

Brother Aurelius flicked away the hand still holding him, stood upright and breathed deep. "See if that'll change your ways," he said. "But I doot it." He shook himself and walked to the door of the commonroom. "Ye're not long for this life, Sir Henry. I willna see ye again, I think. Good night to ye."

When he came into the warm little parlour where Elizabeth was starting to doze off after an excellent meal, she saw at once he was still annoyed.

"Never mind," she said to him. "I never thought you talking to him would help."

"Nay missus, I mishandled it and let him sting me. I'm sorry—that, I am." The old man looked so rueful she could have kissed him. Instead she brushed as much of the mud from her gown as she could and repinned her hat and cap to her head. Then she settled back.

"He knows I'm here. He can come and get me when he chooses and he'll want to keep me waiting so I'll be more affeared of him," she said. "So I shall get some sleep."

In the commonroom the shouting was louder yet, though Sir Henry's face had lost the bonhomie it had. Simon Anricks was watching him carefully, the way he looked at Lord Spynie, the way Lord Spynie looked at him. He was also casting ugly glances at Anricks, although Simon could think of no way in which he could have offended the man.

At last Sir Henry came over and sat down heavily in the chair next to Anricks. "Is it true ye use witchcraft to take out teeth?"

"No," sighed Anricks, "I use sweet oil of vitriol which makes men sleepy so they pass out. It works on chickens as well. I can take out teeth without it but it's very much easier for me to use it."

"Are you lying to me?"

"No, I'm not," said Anricks. His voice had become very level.

"Well it's a pity because I could find a use for a witch or a warlock now."

Anricks nodded. "The friar's curse. Yes."

Sir Henry drank, aqua vitae this time, and wiped his moustache. "I'll treat me wife as I choose."

"Why?"

"What d'ye mean, why?"

"She's only a woman. If you're...ah...worried by the curse, you've only to treat her better and kindlier. That's what he said, isn't it? "If ye do not treat your wife better and kindlier then ye have, may ye be cursed, may all your doings miscarry and may yer life be short." To avoid the curse, treat your wife better and kindlier than you have."

Anricks met the man's eyes full on and Sir Henry found he had a cold acute look to them which chilled him. Anricks went on with the same deadly quiet in him.

"It isn't her fault that you're in debt to Lord Spynie and you can't pay it back. It isn't her fault that you haven't made anything like as much money as you thought you would from the Deputy Wardenship of the East March. And it isn't her fault that you've the gout and stones in your bladder and that causes you pain. But something about her is important to you, Sir Henry, and I'm surprised you've forgotten it."

"What?" Sir Henry's moustache was jutting and his brows were right down. Anricks' voice was quite weak and whispery and it went softer still.

"Remember whose niece she is, Sir Henry. She is the beloved niece of my Lady Hunsdon and she is thus the niece of Henry Carey, Baron Hunsdon, who is the actual Warden of the East March, not you. He gave her to you in marriage as a part of the governance of the East March, not for your own satisfaction, nor in fact, hers. His wife is very unhappy at the way you treat her and so, naturally enough, is he. Because it embarrasses him too. Being a kindly man, he is angry at your cruelty."

Sir Henry was staring at Anricks as though at a cockatrice. "How do you know...?"

The smile became colder and the weak voice softer. "If Hunsdon chose to come north to Berwick, he would find out a lot about the Deputy Wardenship you would prefer him not to know. If he were to kick you out of the Deputy Wardenship, which he might, you wouldn't be naked, no, you'd still have your surname. But your life would be considerably harder."

"Are ye threatening me?"

"No, Sir Henry, I am telling you the facts of life. But you might consider kindness as a better policy all round. I've been married for years, and I like it. I have five children and another on the way and I love my wife. But you do not have to love your wife to have a perfectly pleasant life with her, if you treat her with some respect."

Sir Henry had a baffled ugly look in his eyes which did not bode well for Elizabeth but Anricks had done his best. He had given Sir Henry a very quotidian reason for treating his wife better and his Uncle Roger or Brother Aurelius had given him a superstitious reason. If it didn't work, then Anricks thought Sir Henry's life would indeed be short, if only because of the fire-eating youngest son of Baron Hunsdon, if nothing else.

FRIDAY 20th OCTOBER 1592

The next morning, when the sky was grey though the Sun was fully up, Dodd felt someone step stealthily over him and go out onto the flat area leading down to the river. He came to his feet with his sword in his hand only to find Carey standing there, while he pissed, staring to the north.

Considering the probable time, Carey must have slept for twelve hours straight through, maybe more. His face was pale but the swelling was almost gone and he looked better, though his expression was unhappy.

"She's there, at Jedburgh," said the Courtier, more to himself than to Dodd. "She's there with her bastard husband who arranged for her to be kidnapped and I'm here and…"

"Ay," said Dodd, doing the same as the Courtier against a stone and then going into the second part of the little shelter where the hobbies were and bringing them both out, stamping and snorting and sulking because they were hungry and didn't have any food. He hobbled both of them and let them go onto the turf by the river where there was some sour tough grass and a few thistles. He didn't have any food either so he wasn't inclined to sympathise with them. He couldn't eat grass, could he, though he'd tried once. The dogs came out and marked the corners of the shelter again, then came hopefully to him. They found he had no food either and started sniffing around for rabbits, though probably all the game in the area was hidden in its burrows.

"She wisnae intended to be ransomed either. It was all a scheme of Sir Henry and Lord Spynie's."

"Do you think I'll ever have her?" asked the Courtier in a self-pitying voice, "or will I have wait even longer, until I'm an old man of forty or fifty?"

"Och, God," said Dodd. "Ah've tellt ye and tellt ye. Ye've enough credit in the West March to call out fifty men who'd follow ye and I'll bring the Dodds and the English Armstrongs, ay and mebbe Jock o' the Peartree Graham would come oot for ye for the mischief and then we'll run the rode of all time to Widdrington and take her from him and ye can kill him yerself, personally."

"Yes, but then she wouldn't marry me."

"She would. She'd come round in the end. They allus do."

"I just...I can't think straight without her. Seeing her, holding her yesterday..."

It's given it to ye bad again, thought Dodd, but didn't say. The dogs had wandered off in their quest for food.

He started to look around for firewood to replace the stuff they had burned and let Carey blether on about the woman.

"And she's so beautiful and I don't know how she takes the knocking around she gets from her husband and...What the devil is that?"

Dodd was very glad to have a break from Carey's perpetual mooning over the woman. "What?" He realised the dogs had suddenly started galloping across the valley, barking.

They squinted against the rain on the other side of the valley and saw first the dogs, especially the yellow pup, and then the riders, five of them, surrounding one man who had three laden pack ponies behind him. Dodd recognised the horses more than the man himself who was small and unprepossessing and growled,

"They're stealing Mr Anrick's pack ponies from him."

"So they are. Well, we can't have that."

The two of them sprinted to where their hobbies were cropping the grass and unlooped the hobbles. The dogs were in among the horses now, doing as they'd been trained, leaping up and down, biting at the hobbies' bellies and dodging sword blows. Dodd jumped up to the biting hobby's back and Carey jumped onto Sorrel and they charged straight across the valley and into the five men. There was a quick exchange of blows and then the five Elliots thought they didn't want the pack ponies that much anyway and turned their horses about and ran away, with Carey singing "T'il y est haut!" after them as if he was in the hunting field and the dogs giving chase ahead of him, barking their heads off. A dag fired behind them and clipped one of the horses who stood on his head and galloped off at an angle up the hill with his rider clinging to his back like a monkey.

That had put a bit of colour in Carey's cheeks. He cantered back to Anricks who had his dag in one hand and the leading rein for the pack ponies in his other hand. The pack ponies were heavy laden and swinging about and neighing in protest and one of the packs was about to come loose and fall off. Carey dismounted quickly to secure it while Dodd chased after the lymers who were already coming back, wagging their tails joyfully. The pup was triumphantly holding a man's riding boot in his teeth which he proceeded to worry to death.

"What's in the packs, Mr Anricks?" asked Carey with a smile. "Gold dust?"

"Oats that I bought in Jedburgh with my earnings from drawing their teeth."

"Ah, gold dust, indeed. I might be interested in them if we can get them to Carlisle. We need to get a move on, for the Elliots will go and fetch their friend Geordie Burn and all of his friends to come at us again."

Ay, thought Dodd, with the Bewcastle waste to get through and all. Lovely.

They went back to the shelter and packed up as quickly as they could. Anricks had been shopping in Jedburgh, for one of the ponies had a good faggot of hazel withies to replace the wood they had burned, and some penny loaves and cheese and a pottle of beer for them as well as some scraps from the inn for the dogs who fell on it ferociously and had finished it all in four seconds.

They ate as they rode and Carey took Anrick's gun and cleaned it for him since he was curious about why it hadn't needed a match. It had an improved kind of lock on it, Anricks explained, the latest technology, much better than the wheel locks with their complicated winding up clockwork arrangements. He had two pistols, the other one was a normal matchlock. His new one came from Germany and Anricks had bought it from an armourer in London and this was the first time he had actually fired it in anger, what with the rain. Dodd took a look at it too as they rode south and west and the rain came down and made everything smell of wet leather and wet steel and wet human. Oh, and of pungently wet dog. He didn't like guns, thought a longbow was better because you could loose thirty shafts a minute once you had the way of it, and longbows didn't explode in your hand either. But even he had to admit the German gun-smithing was impressive. And the dag hadn't misfired, the way Carey's normally did, even if Anricks only hit a horse's rump. He insisted that was what he had been aiming at. It was obvious that Carey was now on fire to get a German gun like that as well and was cross-examining Anricks about where and how much, when Dodd caught a glimpse of helmets behind a veil of rain.

"Och," he said, giving the dag back to Anricks to reload, and drew his sword again, wishing and wishing he was wearing his comfy jack, not the buffcoat and statute cap. Carey was of course in a jack and morion, but at least Anricks had no armour at all. That made him feel a little better. The dogs had noticed and were growling with their hackles up, though wisely not running forward.

Carey had seen them as well, there were fifteen of them now, though at a good distance so he couldn't be sure if they were Burns or some other bunch of reivers who fancied getting themselves sorted for horse fodder for the winter. Someone in Jedburgh would have told them all about it.

"I suppose it was stupid of me to try and bring the ponies across the Border by myself," said Anricks in an abstracted tone of voice as if it was someone else he was talking about.

"Ay it was," said Dodd, "but ye werenae to know. Shall we give 'em one of the ponies as blackrent and try and take the rest on to Carlisle?"

Carey was standing up in his stirrups trying to see the other riders better; they were coming closer in a bunch now.

"One of them's got a morion," he said in a thoughtful tone of voice and then laughed and put his heels in, urging his horse up to a gallop in the direction of the riders.

Was it Geordie? No, Geordie didn't have a fancy helmet, his helmet was a plain metal cap like most men wore. Kerr of Cessford? Could be, God forbid, or Ferniehurst or...

Swearing under his breath, Dodd got his hobby to run in an ugly lumpish way behind Carey who was clearly driven wood-wild by thinking about his woman and was tired of life. At least Anricks was sensible, as he was continuing south with the ponies at a reluctant trot. The dogs stayed with Anricks, growling menacingly but clearly not fancying their chances against that many.

Halfway to the riders, Dodd saw what Carey had seen and put his sword away again. Good Lord, hadn't the spot on Young Henry's nose burst yet? It was like a beacon.

Carey was already leaning over to shake young Widdrington's hand. "I'm delighted to see you, Mr Widdrington, I thought ye were some of Geordie Burn's ugly crew."

Young Henry nodded. "Ay, we're on a trod, sir," he said. "We've a witness statement in the killing of Minister Burn fra Jock Tait and there's hue and cry for Archie and Jemmy Burn."

"Same surname?"

"Ay sir, and it's not even as if they're at feud like the Kerrs of Cessford and Ferniehurst. They wis paid tae kill him by a courtier, Lord Spynie." Young Henry's expression was one of disgust. There was nothing wrong with killing somebody for money, of course, but killing one of your own surname for an outsider? That was disgraceful.

"Well I don't like to hold you up, but we have a small pack-train with horsefodder over there and the man who drew my bloody tooth is trying to get it to Carlisle unpillaged so...er..."

"Of course we'll ride with ye over the Bewcastle waste, sir, we heard they've gone to Carlisle in any case."

"Where are they headed after, do you think?"

"Bound to be the Low Countries or Ireland, sir, nowhere else for them to go. And they've been there before. That's why nobody knew them hereabouts. They were exiled eight years ago for something about a girl and a man gelded."

Carey nodded as he swung in with the men, and Dodd took up his usual place behind him and to the left to watch his back. The dogs were wagging their tails again and stuck close to Anricks since he had the food.

Anricks had recognised Young Henry as well and shook hands with him, eyeing the flamboyant spot on his nose as if profession-ally interested. There were plenty of other spots on the man's face, but that was definitely the worst. Dodd remembered getting a few spots when he was a lad but Young Henry's crop was something special. And as a youth, Dodd had had more important things to worry about—like killing Elliots and not dying.

They skirted the Bewcastle waste in the wind and the rain but nothing worse than that. Though this was the wind that left your skin feeling like it had been scoured with wire wool and rain that found its way down your neck and into your boots and made all the leather you were wearing weigh four times as much as it should.

The horses were tired by then, especially Anricks' ponies and his hobby which had done an extra twenty miles to and from Jedburgh, so they called in at Thirlwall Castle. Carleton welcomed them and even gave them some food, pig's liver and onions of course, though he explained that his wife made a kind of meat paste with liver with fat on top which made it keep longer. The younger dog had sore pads and was exhausted and the older lymer was tired too, so they left the dogs there along with Anricks and the pack ponies and ten men to guard him.

Carey was impatient to get to Carlisle and so Carleton lent them horses and they rode the final sixteen miles almost in silence, Carey, Dodd, Young Henry, and the five remaining Widdringtons, along the Giant's Road which was a little bit safer than the Waste.

They went into the castle where the Scropes were clearly packing up to leave, Philadelphia standing imperiously in the castleyard where her own trunks were being packed with a remarkable number of velvet kirtles and black bodices and white damask aprons that had never once seen the light of Carlisle. It was evening by then and the trunks were being shut. Philadelphia instantly stopped what she was doing to scold her brother for going off like that again. She had been so worried, all sorts of rumours were coming from the Middle March, had they heard that a churchman had been done to death in Scotland, in his own home as well?

Over a gigantic meat pie of Philadelphia's own raising and sundry potherbs and bread, Young Henry told the full tale of what had happened to the churchman, dabbing away at the end of his nose with a handkerchief where his spot had messily burst at the most humiliating moment for him. Carey had already heard it from him on the way over and he excused himself toward the end of the meal so he could avoid eating any of Philadelphia's legendary kissing comfits. Dodd followed after him nosily and found Carey in the stables talking to the boys, chief among them Young Hutchin Graham, who was starting to grow seriously now, had big hands and feet and was wearing clogs because his feet had got too big for his boots.

"There's two men, Archie and Jemmy Burn," Carey was saying gravely to them. "They took money from my enemy Lord Spynie—remember him, Young Hutchin?—to go into Scotland, find a man that was a minister and kept a school for boys like you and kill him. Their own cousin."

There was some shocked tutting but these boys were practical. "And?"

"I will give a gold angel to any of you that brings me a true word on where they're hiding. They've come to Carlisle and they might be in the town, or they might be at someone's tower. I want them."

"What'll ye do to them?"

"I'll hang them."

"Can we come and see it?" asked Young Hutchin Graham.

"I don't know. If I can, I'll give them their long necks at Carlisle Castle but if I'm in a hurry, I'll hang 'em wherever I catch them."

The boys scattered, talking about the angel excitedly and arguing over who it was on the coin, was it a man with wings or was it an angel and if so, which one. Young Hutchin waited until Carey was out of the way and then trotted purposefully down into the town where one of his respectable cousins had two guests in need of hiding.

saturday 21st october 1592

Scrope went out with Sir Richard Lowther the next day on a tour of the West March, checking the defensibility of the fortresses and the state of the paths and roads. Carey stayed in Carlisle, and bought Anricks' oats when they came plodding in late in the afternoon. Anricks had paid out a hundred shillings Scots for them, which were only worth a quarter of an English shilling, thanks to debasements by the Scottish king and rampant forgery on the Borders. So he paid one pound, five shillings English. Carey was perfectly happy to pay three pounds English for the oats, which were good, and Anricks kept the pack ponies. Dodd found this very impressive.

"How did ye know he would pay that for them?" he asked Anricks, over a pint at Bessie's.

"I didn't. I also took the risk that my oats would be reived from me on the way and that they wouldn't be as good as I thought. I could have ended up with no oats at all—for instance, if you and the dogs hadn't driven off the raiders who tried to take them from me—but luckily I didn't. So I owe both you and Sir Robert something for that."

"Ye do?"

"Yes. Will seven shillings and sixpence be enough for you?"

"What?"

"For helping with the pack ponies, specifically driving off the Elliots."

"Och…er…ay, that's…er…thanks."

And Anricks counted out seven silver shillings and six pennies just like that, onto the board. After a moment, Dodd took them. Extraordinary. He rather thought he had just earned the money with not a hint of larceny about it. He couldn't wait to tell Janet; she'd split her sides.

"Whit about the Courtier? He might not want the money, though he allus needs it, ye follow?"

"Oh yes, Sergeant, I do. I'll recompense him in other ways, more fitting to his station."

"Ay."

They finished their quarts companionably while Dodd wondered why such an odd person was really in the West March of England and what he was really doing. He knew a pursuivant was just a term for a spy or a man that did other men's dirty work. While there was dirty work in plenty in the West March, he didn't think the tooth-drawer would be interested in the Johnstones and the Maxwells or the way the Carletons were playing off Lowther or how the Grahams added to the chaos. Maybe he was indeed interested in the Maxwell, who was a Catholic, after all. He mentioned how Carey had been betrayed by the man in the summer and found himself telling the tooth-drawer a couple of stories himself, until he noticed and shut his mouth grimly. Anricks listened well, in a way which drew stories out of you.

"And now I need to find a man called Thomas the Merchant Hetherington and lend him some of my money."

Well, Dodd knew where that one did business so they headed down to English street and halfway there they saw a big ugly man in a leather cap with three tired-looking boys, the smallest of them carrying his newly whittled clogs and his feet covered in mud.

Anricks stopped dead and stared. "By the Almighty," he said, "it's Cuddy Trotter, Andy Hume, and Jimmy Tait. How did you get here?"

"Och, look Dad, it's the tooth-drawer, Mr Anricks, the minister's friend," said the smallest of them, tired but shining with pride. "We're here tae 'prentice tae the cathedral, Mr Anricks. We walked all the way and stayed at a place we thocht was it but it wasn't and me dad came and he said, ye've done a man's work, Jimmy, Ah'll take ye there maself and we walked and walked and he only carried me a bit and so we're here now."

"Well, that's wonderful, Jimmy. You must be Mr Tait?"

"Ay sir, d'ye ken where the cathedral is, for we're all tired and I'm fair famished as well."

Anricks seemed relieved and pleased to see them. "Mr Tait, I'm going to take you to the best inn in Carlisle so you and the boys can rest and then the boys can test for the cathedral in the morning."

"Ay, but we havenae cash…"

"I've just made some with my tooth-drawing in Jedburgh and so it'll be my treat. Where's the young Lord Hughie?"

"He stayed behind at Jedburgh, said he had something to do before he came," said Jock Tait.

"Then, please, allow me."

And he bore them along to Bessie's inn, hard by the castle gate, illegal but tolerated and bought them all the ordinary and pints of mild ale for the boys and a quart of Bessie's incomparable double-double for Jock Tait. And there he got the rest of the tale from them. They were all too tired to do the running around that boys usually do but when they'd finished every scrap of the haggis and bashed neeps and a bag pudding too with a sherry and sugar and butter sauce for a treat, Jimmy Tait turned to Andy and hummed a note. Andy grinned and hummed one back and there they were, singing like birds in a tree, the new ballad of Scarborough Fair with an old tune to it.

"Why aren't you singing, Cuddy?"

"Canna sing, that's why, sir, but I can read and write and mebbe I could learn to play an instrument cos I can read the music well enough just not sing it."

"Do you want to 'prentice at the cathedral?"

"Ay sir, that's why we've all come."

Anricks nodded and after a while he slipped away from the commonroom, with Dodd following him, and stood looking down at the cathedral.

"Are you there, Sergeant?"

"Ay, Mr Anricks."

"Perhaps you could tell me the best way to the cathedral?"

"I'll show ye," said Dodd who was nearly dying of curiosity.

They went to the gate into the cathedral precincts where Mr Anricks spoke quietly to the doorkeeper who eyed him fishily but brought him the Bursar, as he asked.

"There are three boys that want to join the choir," he explained. "Two of them have fine voices but the third...you'll want him paid for, yes?"

The Bursar allowed as how that was possible. "I am related to a wealthy merchant in London," said Anricks. "He gave me a banker's draft for a large sum of money, more than sufficient to cover the cost of the boys' education. I am willing to sign it over to you to ease the boys' path and also that of a lad called Piers Dixon, if he should come too."

Well the Bursar couldn't possibly say whether the boys would be good enough to...The Choirmaster? He was rehearsing with the boys now. Could he come now? It was very irregular, sir, and I don't...

Anricks took out a piece of paper and spread it on the table. There was complete silence.

Half an hour later the choirmaster, Bursar, and Bishop were walking down the road to Bessie's, along with Anricks and Dodd who was wondering exactly how much the banker's draft was for. He also wanted to know how it came about that Anricks had it. There was no gold anywhere to be seen, but the Bursar, the Choirmaster and the Bishop were all acting as if a large quantity of it was somewhere close, but was shy and might run away if they were rude or made sudden movements.

At Bessie's they found a singsong in progress, being conducted by Cuddy, with Jock Tait's bass mixing with the boys' voices as they sang, his old jack off and steaming by the fire. The Choirmaster listened carefully with his eyes squinting and then went to Jock and asked if he could hear the boys sing solo. Andy sang the *Twa Corbies*, which was a little grim but you couldn't mistake his alto. Then Jimmy Tait stood on the table, didn't wait, didn't pause to get some hush, just launched into the old song of *Greensleeves*, high up the register, bang on the note, and with a world of longing in the old song that seemed to come from somewhere far older than he was.

The Bursar's and the Bishop's mouths fell open and the Choirmaster seemed to hold his breath for the entirety of the song. When Jimmy finished, the whole of Bessie's stayed quiet for a moment and then there was clapping and a lot of roaring and shouting. Someone was passing a hat round. Meanwhile the Choirmaster came to Anricks and said,

"Thank you sir, for bringing him to my attention. How old is he?"

"I think he's about seven years old."

"God be thanked that he came here now. The older boy will only give us a couple of years and there's no telling after that, but he will give us five, maybe six. We will not need your banker's draft, sir…"

The Bursar started to protest at that but was quelled by a glare from the Choirmaster. The Bishop nodded gravely in acquiescence.

Jimmy Tait was unconcernedly picking his nose, sitting on the table while Andy chatted to a man near the front of the crowd about where they came from.

It happened so quickly, nobody had time to react. Two men in cloaks, one by the door, the other further in. The one further in moved toward Jock Tait purposefully.

Jimmy Tait looked up as he fished carefully for an elusive lump of snot in his nose and then he froze. Seconds later he was standing on the table screaming and pointing.

"It's them, it's them, they killt the minister."

The man in the cloak moved up close to Jock Tait, while he was reaching for his knife, grabbed his shoulder and made the short forceful motion with his right arm that said he was stabbing Jock, stabbed him again.

`Dodd swept his sword out and bellowed, "Castle to me!" But he couldn't get past all the people in the way. The screaming and the shock gave both of the men the time to slide out the door while Jock Tait looked down at himself, puzzled and brought up his hand bright red with blood and Jimmy Tait screamed and screamed.

Dodd raced out into the night, found that two of the guard, Red Sandy and Bangtail, were at his back and chased the two men down Scotch street to the Scotchgate where the postern was open and two hobbies waiting. The men jumped onto the horses and rode like the devil up the road.

Bangtail came trotting past him. "Ye go git the deputy," he said. "We'll follow 'em, eh, Red Sandy?"

Dodd turned and sprinted back through the town and up to the castle, too many bloody stairs, up to the Queen Mary tower where he found the deputy's Scotch servant snoring already, down again and up to the Warden's Lodgings where some warbling was sounding through the grim old stones.

Carey was singing with his sister. Dodd appeared at the door and spoiled the party by still having his sword out. Carey actually finished the verse and then came out to him, listened as he explained what had happened, scowled and went back to Philadelphia whom he kissed and then left still holding the music.

They went down into the town where Anricks had Jock Tait laid out on a table at Bessie's with a crowd of folk breathing down his neck. Jimmy Tait was squatting next to his father, gripping his hand, and Andy and Cuddy were standing at the head and foot of the table with their eating knives out and their teeth showing.

"They've run, lads," Dodd told them. "They had hobbies waiting at the Scotchgate." There was a growl from some of the townsfolk at this, which was right because that postern should have been locked shut at this time of night. Andy and Cuddy put up their knives but Jimmy stayed where he was.

Carey greeted the Bishop and the Choirmaster who were sitting nearby, the Bishop with his hands folded while the Choirmaster was watching the proceedings intently.

Jock Tait was still conscious, his jerkin open and his shirt up round his armpits. Anricks had his doublet off and his shirt-sleeves rolled up and his gory apron on again. There was blood all over the place, bright red some of it. The woman known as Bessie's wife was holding up a candle behind him and Anricks was holding a pair of his dental pliers in the flame.

"Hold still, Jock, if you can," said Anricks as he reached into the larger of the two stab wounds with the pliers and squeezed. There was a hissing sound and a smell of pork and some of the red blood seemed to stop. Jock shut his eyes and grunted. Anricks paused for a moment, mopping blood with a cloth and then he heated the pliers again and did it again and then again. Jimmy put his other hand on his father's fist and held tight, while drops of blood rolled from the side of Jock's mouth. But the blood from the wounds almost stopped.

"There now," said Anricks, "I'm not an expert at stab wounds but I think I've stopped the worst of the bleeding." He took a bottle of Bessie's best aqua vitae and sprinkled it round the wounds and then he took a needle and thread and sewed up the holes as if he was a tailor mending a coat. Then he poured on more aqua vitae and bandaged Jock up.

"I've done the best I can," he said to Jock, "it all now depends on whether he got anything vital in there, but I don't think he did, not your liver and not your gut either. So you might live, Jock, that's all I can say."

Jock made a creaking sound that might have been a laugh. "Ay, an honest barber," he said. "It'll take more'n this to kill me."

They kept Jock on the board and six of the men brought him up the stairs to one of the guest rooms, with Jimmy still holding his hand. But by that time Jock had passed out.

Anricks was washing his hands and arms in a bucket of water out the back and, surprisingly, washing the pliers he had used as well when Dodd came downstairs again. Carey was standing there, talking to him calmly as if he hadn't just been delving about in a man's guts.

"I got the idea of using heated pliers from people who don't stop bleeding when I draw their teeth," Anricks was saying. "I have no idea if it will work since this is the first time I've tried it. Most likely he'll die from a fever in the belly, that's what kills people who have been stabbed if they don't bleed to death. Usually they bleed to death, so perhaps the pliers will work."

Andy and Cuddy came up to him. "Thank you for trying to save Jimmy's dad," they said in chorus, then looked at each other uncertainly. "We know who they are, sir," they said to Carey, who was by far the most fancily dressed man there and therefore must be in charge. "They're the men that came to kill the minister. We'd know them again anywhere. They're Archie and Jemmy Burn and they killed him and they tried to kill Lady Widdrington and now they've tried tae kill Jimmy's dad when they were just made friends for the first time because he's the witness."

Carey nodded seriously at them. "We'll do our best to catch them and hang them," he said. "That's a promise."

"When ye catch them, ye willna compose with them?" asked Andy anxiously, "not even if their friend the courtier asks ye?"

"Especially not if Lord Spynie asks me," said Carey.

Bangtail came back an hour and a half later to say that the two of them had gone to ground at a small tower owned by the Grahams, a mere five miles out of town. He didn't think they had noticed that they were being followed for he and Red Sandy had kept well back and well apart. Red Sandy had stayed by the tower in case they moved or went anywhere else.

Carey smiled at that and said, "Well then, let's try and catch them unawares."

They called out the guard quietly, all of them, not just the ones that were supposed to go out on patrol who happened to be Thomas Carleton's lot, but all of them, even the ones in bed at the castle. Thomas Carleton roused himself out as well, jack on his back and his tarnished morion helmet on his head, chuckling quietly at something.

At two in the morning, the Courtier inspected the men lined up in the castle courtyard. Scrope and Sir Richard Lowther were at Gretna, last he heard, before they went into the Debateable Land and met with some of the Grahams and Armstrongs there. Perhaps they would also meet the Maxwell, the current Scottish West March Warden who was being elusive about a Warden's Day, although it had been years since the last one. And so, as acting Deputy Warden, he had the authority to call on all of them and he did.

They didn't bother with remounts because the tower was so close to Carlisle and rode out with muffled hooves and harness, with a turf carried in Carey's saddlebag ready to light if necessary. None of the slow matches on the guns were lit, but Dodd and Carleton had firepots for them when the time came.

thursday night 19th october to friday 20th october 1592

The Jedburgh inn's parlour door opened and young Lord Hughie came in, walked and sat opposite Elizabeth while she dozed in the blessed warmth of the fire. She opened her eyes and saw him but sat there quietly. His young and beautiful face looked peaceful again.

"I just came to say good-bye," he told her. "I'm going back to my grandam in the morning."

"How did you get here?"

"I have feet, ma'am, though they're sore. I followed you and Brother Aurelius down from the abbey."

She looked at him carefully. "You aren't going to 'prentice to the Cathedral?"

Slowly he shook his head. "You're right," he said, "they won't have me. I was going to lie about who I was but with Jimmy Tait's father there, that won't work. And they'll be afraid of my Lord Spynie. I'll go home tomorrow."

She sat up. There was something wrong here, he seemed too calm.

"How will you find the way?"

"I'm sure one of your men can see me right back to Wendron. Perhaps I could borrow a hobby from Mr Widdrington since I've blisters on my feet."

"Are you sure?"

"Oh yes. I'll wait until Cuddy, Archie, and Jimmy are away—they're leaving before dawn tomorrow with Jock Tait—and then I'll go. It's for the best."

She couldn't put her finger on what was wrong but she nodded and smiled.

"The King of Elfland's collar was payment from an English archer for services rendered by my grandam, I realise that now."

Elizabeth nodded. She didn't see any point in arguing otherwise.

"You know Cousin William?" asked Lord Hughie. "You know how old he is?" Elizabeth shook her head. "Well he was born in 1545," said the boy quietly, "because he's forty-seven now. I only just worked it out. My Lord my grandfather claimed him as a byblow, said his mother died giving birth. Of course my grandfather loved my grandmother dearly, always did."

Elizabeth took a deep breath. "He was your grandmother's?"

"Yes. Everything was confused in those years with the destruction and the burning, and I know she stayed at a convent for a while. We still had them in Scotland then. Humes are blond not brown."

"Ah." Elizabeth felt somehow satisfied, as if she had suspected this without knowing.

"The other half of the necklace is probably still in Norwood Castle," he added, "since my Lord Spynie isn't dead, unfortunately."

"He's here, you know," she said anxiously, in case it was a surprise to him.

"I know that, ma'am," he told her gently. "I've met him now and I'll be going to Court as his page next month."

"No, you can't."

"Why not, ma'am, who's going to stop him?"

"I will."

The boy shook his head, still gently, bowed to her and left the parlour.

She sat up and gripped her hands together until the knuckles went white, put her chin on her fists and thought harder than she ever had before. Then she ordered paper and pens, since she had left her satchel with the Burns, and wrote a letter to Chancellor Maitland of Lethington the like of which he had probably never received before nor would receive again. Then she went in search of the landlord and found Lord Hugh already had a bedroom and had locked the door. She found a young man from the Widdrington surname and sent him off to Maitland with the letter.

SATURDAY NIGHT 21ST OCTOBER TO
SUNDAY 22ND OCTOBER 1592

They didn't ride fast, with Bangtail showing the way and when Red Sandy rose up from the bank of bracken where he'd been keeping an eye on things, they were within half a mile of the castle and everything was quiet.

"Are they still there?"

"Ay, they're in the farmhouse but there's a tower there and it's all open," whispered Red Sandy, "If we can…"

Somebody's gun went off, the boom from it cracked around the valley. Carey's head whipped round.

"Who the hell…?"

Somebody was on watch at the farmhouse. There were torches and lights; they could make out men running into the tower and a boy on a fast pony galloping away northwards.

"Ay," said Carleton blandly, "there he goes. They're Grahams in there and if ye dinna prevent it we'll all be taken prisoner."

"Why?" asked Carey with interest as if they were talking about a horse race.

"The lad's gone tae the Debateable Land to fetch out the Elliots. So now."

And Carleton leaned on his saddlebow and watched him.

Dodd was expecting fireworks; he got none. "Andy Nixon," said Carey evenly, "I want you to go back to Carlisle, rouse out Mayor Aglionby and ask him to lend me all the Trained Bands of men immediately. Bring them out here to me as fast as ye can."

"Ay sir," said Nixon, turning his horse and riding back down the road.

"Ridley, Little, Hodgson."

"Ay sir."

"Rouse out your surnames, gentlemen, bring them here to me, Warden's quarters on it." The three men headed down the road at a gallop while Carey looked oddly at Carleton who had his brows raised.

"I'd ask you to fetch your surname, Captain Carleton," he said, "But I'm thinking they might be busy, eh? Come with me."

He drew his sword, turned his horse and smiled at the twenty men remaining. "Come on," he said, "let's see if there's any insight left at the farmhouse."

Whatever the men in the tower expected, with their door locked and men on the roof with long bows, crossbows, and a couple of guns as well, they did not expect the twenty men of the guard to come close to the tower. The men took turns ducking and firing until Carey sprinted to the farmhouse, kicked through the door, ran inside and found, as he expected, no women and practically no furniture.

"It's a trap!" said Dodd furiously, behind him. "The Elliots will be here in an hour..."

"Yes," said Carey, "it's a trap. What did you think? And bloody Carleton's in it up to his neck as well."

"Goddamn it..."

"Do you want to go back to Carlisle?"

Dodd stared at him in puzzlement. "No, why?"

Carey grinned at him and actually laughed. "So let's see what a bit of modern siegework can do, eh?"

Carey hurried outside, and wandered near the tower. A gun fired and two crossbows loosed, missing him and he retreated. He had all the men off their hobbies, with the animals kept to the back. The men in the tower were shouting insults at them and one showed his arse to Carey.

"Tut tut," said Carey mildly. "Such language."

He had the men ring the tower just out of range with instructions to try and draw their fire but do their best not to get hit.

Then he spent a while drawing patterns in the mud and counting under his breath. Dodd took a squint at them: a triangle with square boxes on each of the sides, that was all.

"We need two beams, twenty-five feet long," Carey said after a moment, "or fruitpicking ladders. Nothing less than twenty-five feet long."

"Why?" asked a bewildered Dodd, "The tower's only twenty feet high, it's a short one."

"Ladders are always too short, aren't they?"

"Ay sir."

"No, they're not. Not when I'm doing the besieging."

They looked about for anything long enough but there was nothing. So Carey sent another man all the way back to Carlisle to bring back one of the ladders to the castle walls which he thought might be right. Also ropes, picks, and axes, as quickly as he could, don't wait for the Trained Bands. At least he told the man to hurry. By that time the bells were tolling from the farms and pele towers in the area, and Carleton and a couple of his cronies had found firewood and started a fire.

The Ridleys were the first to come in, fifteen men and another twenty-seven on their way from farms further south. Carey thanked them all for coming out for him, promised that if anything came of it they would get first chance at the loot because they were there first, and placed them around the tower and some in the farmhouse itself with arquebuses to point through the windows. When the Littles and a lot of Hodgsons came in later, he did the same. There were two rings around the tower, one facing inward, the other facing outward.

If Carey was worried about the Elliots, he didn't show it. He sat down by Carleton's fire and talked affably about various sieges he had been at in France and asked courteously about Carleton's experience with seigework. Carleton admitted he hadn't much, and he wondered what Carey was doing. The Elliots would be here soon, did he know that?

Then Carey took a spade from the farmhouse and started digging a ditch parallel to the tower while the men inside jeered at him and threw lumps of shit.

"It shouldn't be very needful this time," he explained to the fascinated men whilst ducking flying turds, "but this is the right way to dig a ditch so the men you're besieging can't shoot you."

At that point the man Carey had sent to Carlisle for the ladder turned up with four men on horseback, carrying two ladders between them. Carey stopped digging, laid them on the ground, and measured them by pacing along them and then grinned again.

Dodd found his relaxed attitude alarming. What insanity was he planning now? He soon found out. Carey started anyone with a bow or gun shooting as steadily as they could—the clear superiority of longbows over guns showing now, in Dodd's opinion. He explained to Dodd exactly what he wanted him to do, which Dodd found first appalling and then funny. But he could do it. He knew he could.

fRIδAy 20th OCTOBER 1592

Elizabeth was offered a bed in one of the better guest rooms by the innkeeper, with his own daughter to keep her company. He refused her money, said that the abbey would see to it. She even had a nice fresh linen shift from the innkeeper's wife for a shilling, which she thought was money well spent. While she was undressing she found the book of "The Schoolmaster" still in her petticoat pocket where she had put it and forgotten it. The small book was well-thumbed—she looked at it and then put it back. She'd give it to Poppy when she got home.

She slept well in the big bed with the polite innkeeper's daughter. And then, in the early morning she heard a scraping and then a bellowing and a shouting, dull thuds, and then someone light came running along the corridor full pelt, jumped out of the window.

She got the innkeeper's daughter to stop clutching her and got dressed in record time. When she came out of the room she found the place was a bedlam with Lord Spynie's young men stamping around and shouting.

She looked out of the window, saw a dung heap with a deep imprint in it and tracks in the mud running away, uphill toward the abbey. She trotted downstairs and asked the landlord what was going on.

"That boy, Lord Hugh, he tried to stab my Lord Spynie and got away."

"Ah," said Elizabeth, "I see."

"Bide there ma'am and dinna be afraid. Your husband has gone out with my lord to take the young murtherer."

"He succeeded?"

"No, he couldna get past my Lord Spynie's men, but he could have…"

"A pity," she said coldly. "Thank you."

With all the stamping about and shouting, nobody was interested in a woman. She needed a horse and she took one with a Widdrington brand, sighed at the man's saddle and mounted carefully.

She put her heels in and drove the animal up the path to the abbey where she could already hear her husband having a good loud argument with Brother Aurelius about where Lord Hugh might be. Lord Spynie and his men and some of the Widdringtons were searching the abbey, the Widdringtons notably unenthusiastic about it.

She knew where he was because she knew he had a plan. She went straight for the church, leaving the hobby to mill about with the others. At the back of the church she found the little door that led up to the tower and it was shut but not locked. She went through it and barred the door on the inside. She went up the narrow spiral stair, round and round and up and up in the dark, moving by feel except when part of a huge window let some light in.

The last part was all in darkness and she was breathless. Maybe she was wrong…?

She opened the door at the top which led to the tower's roof and the fine view north and south across all the Border country. Lord Hugh was looking at her anxiously from where he was perched in his breeches and shirt, sitting on the battlements, kicking his bare heels above a drop of hundreds of feet. He was smeared with dung from the dung heap.

Elizabeth came through the door and bolted it behind her. Parts of the tower were blackened with smoke and in one corner the leading had melted and was letting rain in to do damage to the timbers.

She came and stood by Lord Hughie and looked all the hundreds of feet down. It gave her a sick and dizzy feeling in her stomach but also a tempting thought. She could sit on a battlement like Hughie, swing her legs over the drop and then… Oops. And all her troubles would be over. Wouldn't they?

It was a terrible sin, the sin of despair which denied the goodness of God. Yet she felt it would be a relief to end the constant sadness, the constant pulling of her heart toward someone she couldn't have. And what if God wasn't good, what if He really was a vicious old man like the Bible showed Him in the parts every fire-eating minister quoted?

She looked at Lord Hughie.

"Lord Hugh Hume," he said thoughtfully. "What a stupid name. Typical of my grandam. I'd rather be an Ian."

Elizabeth nodded. "Trying to get the tombstone right?"

Lord Hughie looked sideways at her and smiled.

"I like it up here, it's just like climbing a tree," he said.

"No, a tree's much safer. Look how smooth the stone is."

"He was planning something, I knew he was, from how nice he was. I slept in my breeches and when I woke at dawn and heard the scratching at the lock, I drew my dagger, and got behind the door."

Elizabeth nodded. Son and grandson of reivers, what did Spynie expect?

"When they came in I tried to stab him but I couldn't get through the padding and his men stopped me so I left the dagger and ran. It doesn't matter. At least I tried."

"You planned to come up here, anyway."

"Yes ma'am, I did. But how did you know? I even made sure the window above the dung heap was open."

Elizabeth smiled and didn't answer.

"Yes, I planned to come up here, high up where it's clear… well, a little bit clear…" The weather was closing in after a bright sunrise, it would be raining soon. "I'd sing a song and then I'd jump."

"And your grandam?"

"She won't know," said Lord Hughie gently. "And she'll see me dancing with her other dead at the faery fort."

"I think she'd know. In fact I think it will kill her."

Hughie shrugged. "She's old. I'm sorry for it, but I willna be Spynie's bumboy."

Play for time, she thought, even while a part of her longed for the simplicity of it. Only you couldn't do that. You would end in Hell for sure.

"Aren't you letting him off lightly?" she asked. "Just jumping off? Why not tell all of them why you're doing it? Why not tell him?"

"He'd just laugh. Or lie. Or both." Still Hughie was looking thoughtful.

"I tell you what," she said, impulsively. "I've a mind to come with ye."

"What?"

"Yes, when you jump, perhaps I'll jump too."

"But…why?"

"My husband beats me. I can't have the man I love," she told him recklessly, not even feeling the shame of it that she couldn't make Sir Henry happy, that she had fallen in love with another man. "I try and try to do what God wants, and nothing changes. And I'm tired of it. So maybe I'll jump too."

"No, my lady, you can't do that, they'll bury you at the cross-roads with a stake through you…"

"I'll be dead, I won't feel it." She leaned forward and looked down, half to frighten the boy, half in earnest. "That's how they'll bury you too, my lord."

"No, I'll make it look like an accident."

"God will know."

"My lady, do you think God cares? I thought maybe He did but when the minister was killed…He doesna give a fig for you or me. If He did, my dad wouldna be dead and I wouldna be in this fix. I don't want to die but I canna see an alternative. Sooner or later Lord Spynie and his friends will get me where they want me. That's why I tried to stab him before I ran."

"How do you know so much, Lord Hughie?"

"I've watched the dogs doing it though they dinna seem to mind. And my cousin Christie tellt me about it a lot when I was younger, how Christie would try and hide but it did no good."

"Where's Christie now?"

"Oh, he drowned in the summer in a river. It was an accident. He was drunk, they say." Lord Hughie's voice was bleak.

Elizabeth couldn't think of any answer to that.

"If God cared, my mam wouldnae be dead," said Hughie. "If God cared, my grandam wouldna be away with the faeries either. And my father wouldna be dead forebye. That's the one that matters."

Elizabeth said nothing. What was there to say? It was true. After a little she asked, "What about Cuddy and Archie and Jimmy?"

"Yes, they'll do what they want, go to the cathedral school and be clerks. I can't do that. I have to be a laird because I'm the heir."

"Do you think they'll be sad about you?"

"Ay, a little, but not for long. They'll be too busy learning music and singing and learning Latin."

"What do you want, my lord?"

"I don't want to be a laird. I want to go to school and learn Latin and then I want to study all the poems and the stories. I want to read Virgil. I want to read Juvenal and Catullus. I don't want to go hunting, it's boring, though Cousin William keeps taking me with him and explaining it to me again. I want tae study."

"Have you told your grandam?"

"Ay, of course, but she disnae understand, she cannae even read or write."

There were shouts and far below a banging on the door, people were looking up at them from the ground and pointing.

Hughie stood on the battlement, balancing easily.

"I'll jump," he shouted. "I'll jump because of Lord Spynie. I dinna want to be his bumboy nor anyone's bumboy, d'ye hear? Not his, not Sir Henry's, nor anybody's bumboy! I willna do it!"

Elizabeth stood still, turned to stone like one of the gargoyles. The blood roared in her ears. Was that why she couldn't please her husband? Was that it? Dear God, she had never thought of it. It hadn't crossed her mind. And yet she had no part of the marriage bed with him after he consummated their marriage. And was that why he was so close to Lord Spynie?

She felt sick.

"What are you saying?" she heard herself gasp.

Hughie looked down with damning pity on his face. "Och missus, did ye not know? He's in love with Lord Spynie, allus has been and Lord Spynie uses it. Christie told me about it, even said he felt sorry for the old man. Everyone knows except his family."

Her head was spinning. She put her hand on the battlement to steady herself.

"Are ye all right, my lady?" he asked, bending down to her. "Are ye well?"

"Yes, I am," she said firmly, taking a breath and holding it. Well that made sense of everything. If her husband was a lover of men...like the King? She understood now why he had hated her so from the start, especially if he had lost his heart to someone vicious like Lord Spynie. Robin was worthy of her love; Spynie was not worthy of anything. To have your heart dragging after someone like that...It was horrible and against the law of God, but it made sense. It made sense and suddenly she could feel compassion for the old man whose heart yearned after a spoiled Royal minion.

"Good my lord," she said formally to the boy, "please don't jump. Please."

"I canna see another way out."

"Yes, but I can. I will take you into my fosterage—I don't think my husband will want you for...for a catamite..."

"Nay," agreed Hughie, "he's not like Spynie that way. But he allus does what Spynie wants."

"And I will send you to school in Carlisle, to the cathedral."

"What about the wardship?"

"I've already written to Chancellor Maitland, who is in charge of the Scottish Court of Wards..."

There was a sudden crashing and the door popped open as the bolts broke. Lord Spynie stepped through delicately, holding a dag with a fancy lock and no slow match, followed by three of his bully boys and three of the five Widdringtons that Young Henry had left behind when he went after Archie and Jemmy Burn. At least the Widdringtons were looking very unhappy.

She stepped between Lord Spynie and the boy. Spynie scowled and tried to sight past her but she moved. Hughie was poised for flight like a bird on the battlements, a wingless bird who wouldn't soar but would drop.

"Get out of my way," sneered the King's favourite.

"No," she said brightly, "let's discuss this. You are going to return my Lord Hugh's wardship to Chancellor Maitland for what you paid for it. He will hold it until my lord is of age. My Lord Hugh will not go to Court and will not be your catamite, sir, do you understand?"

"Out of my way, ye stupid bitch."

She walked forward feeling light as a feather and quite happy. She walked right up to the gun and put her left forefinger over the hole that the bullet came out of.

"Now," she said, "I'm not at all sure what happens if you fire your gun. I expect I'll lose my left hand. But maybe you'll lose your right hand. Maybe the gun will explode. I don't know. Shall we find out?"

And she smiled long and slow at him.

Sunday 22nd October 1592

One of the men on the roof of the Grahams' tower was finally hit and while the other three dragged him down, the men of the castle guard ran with the two long ladders, up to the corners of the tower, placed them and started climbing as fast as they could. Dodd was first over the top and took out one of the men there with one sweep of his sword, and the other defenders ran to the trapdoor and scurried down it, locked it on them.

They had the roof. Dodd gave the thumbs-up to Carey down below who stopped the firing. Then he looked about on the slate roof and found a corner where the slates were loose. They started taking the slates off with the picks and mattocks and found they could look straight down into the tower's upper room where nine Grahams and two Burns were standing about arguing and shouting at each other. Dodd got off as many slates as he could by kicking them, held onto the roof beam underneath with the tips of his fingers, swung over the gap, and dropped straight on top of Archie Burn—as he later found out—who broke his fall nicely. He punched the man in the head just to make sure, though. Red Sandy followed him through and then Bangtail and the rest of the men, and after a couple of blows and one man gone with a sword through his leg and a fountain of bright red blood, the Grahams in the tower started laying their swords down and asking for quarter. Dodd insisted they be given it. He didn't want a feud with the Grahams.

He went down the ladder into the bottom half of the tower to make sure, found only frightened hobbies there, and so he opened the first floor iron gate and put the ladder down again.

Carey was first up it at speed.

"The Elliots are on the horizon," he said. "We're moving into the tower."

The ten men and one corpse who had been in the tower were now tied up and dropped temporarily in with the hobbies while all the twenty-two men of the castle guard scurried into the tower and the several hundred Ridleys, Hodgsons, and Littles came in close, surrounding it and facing out.

"There," said Carey in a pleased voice when all the rushing around was done, "that's the nicest turnabout I've seen in a while. Well done, gentlemen, that went like clockwork."

There was a shout from outside and Carey went to see through the open iron gate. "The Trained Bands are on their way, too," he said with a stupidly happy grin. "Look there!"

Dodd squinted into the distance, annoyed that Carey had seen them first and saw Blennerhassets Troop, Denham's Troop, and Beverly's Troop jog-trotting along the road from Carlisle with their jacks and helmets on, one with pikes, one with arquebuses, and one with mixed weapons. You could always tell the pikes; it looked so sinister, a block of sharp long spears all moving as one, rippling with the pace of the men.

"Oh yes, my beauties!" Carey crowed and even Dodd had to swallow down a grin at the sight of the four hundred and fifty reinforcements coming at a very nice pace along the road with Andy Nixon jogging at their head along with the captain of the Trained Bands. Behind them was Nick Smithson, the de facto leader of Essex' deserters, and all seven of his men behind him, which was nice to see.

Over on the Border hills a troop of cavalry was coming at a much faster pace because they had further to go and somehow hadn't spotted the Trained Bands yet. The Trained Bands saw them and picked up the pace from a jog to a run, and ran that

last half mile to where the Ridleys, Littles, and Hodgsons were
cheering them on.

"Thank you for coming out to me, gentlemen," sang Carey
in an effortless bellow. "In your troops now, pikes to the fore,
arquebuses back, FORM SQUARES!"

Dodd knew that Carey had been training the city bands since
the summer, but was impressed when the men of the city of
Carlisle sorted themselves out into two neat pike squares, backed
by arquebuses facing in the direction of the Elliots. Meanwhile
the men from the nearest surnames had collected their hobbies
and mounted and grouped themselves loosely in families at the
back and sides.

And there was a wagon coming down the road with Anricks
sitting on it. He was too far away to see, and yet Dodd knew it
was him from the set of his hat. He decided he preferred to meet
his blood enemies on a horse and so he followed Carey as he slid
down the ladder, boots either side of it and went for his own hobby.

Carey was mounted on Sorrel. Andy Nixon came over to him.

"The men of the Trained Bands of Carell City are ready, sir,"
he said and tipped his helmet to both Carey and Dodd.

Carey sent some of the youngest of the surnames out into the
countryside to scout for any more Elliots on their way. Carleton
came out of the farmhouse at that moment and blinked at the
battle lines with men running to and fro into place by their mates
and the arquebusiers all busy with their weapons, loading them,
and lighting slow matches.

Then he looked at Carey and stated the obvious. "So we'll
have a battle?"

Carey smiled at him. "No need to worry, Captain," he said
affably, "ye can get back to yer fire if ye like."

Carleton's smile almost slipped and he paused.

"So is this how ye do things in France and the Low Countries?"

"Ay," said Carey, the Berwick man showing, "sometimes.
Wait till ye see what guid foot troops can do to light cavalry,
given pikes and guns."

Carleton didn't answer. Dodd felt a warm and savage smile across his face as he sat on his restive hobby and waited for the Elliots to arrive. There were five hundred of them he thought, squinting into the rain on its way, at a rough guess, maybe seven hundred, more than enough to take the twenty-five men of the guard but now quite evenly matched. And this way of running a battle was new to him but he was seeing the implications of the pikes and guns already. Every man with an arquebus had it loaded now and a slow match lit and they had done the loading with that precise sequence of motions that Carey had used when he loaded a caliver in the summer. They had done it quickly, too. There was every chance that with the pikes to fend off the horses, they could reload two or three times in the battle. What could that do to a bunch of lightly armoured horsemen? There was no armour could keep off an arquebus ball, that he knew.

The Elliots rode closer, down to the trot now, they could see in the dawnlight what was waiting for them. He saw Wee Colin Elliot at their head and his smile got broader and he started to laugh. Och, God, this was wonderful; this was worth all the riding about and going down to London and being up all night again, even bathing. This was worth it. He wasn't even going against the agreement between the Dodds and the Elliots, brokered by Gilpin and Lord Hunsdon that had sent him to Carlisle because the Elliots were coming into the West March of England armed and arrayed for battle. Just not expecting the battle they would get, of course.

The men of the guard had seen him laughing and looked at each other in wonder, then they started to laugh, too. Carey glanced once at Dodd, raised his brows and then settled himself on his horse, a little to the fore, in his plain English jack and his fancy gold-chased morion helmet, his beard showing strongly now since he hadn't been able to bear a razor on his face with his toothache. No sign of swelling now, he looked quite impressive and dangerous, what was more, with that light devil-may-care smile on his face. Och, God, yes! Dodd almost found himself liking the Courtier.

Dodd allowed himself to think of his father for the first time in years, dead on the end of an Elliot spear in a nasty little mess of an ambush, just after telling Dodd a joke so the remains of the laugh were still in his throat as he saw his father shudder and stare and his eyes roll up. The end of Dodd's boyhood right there in that second as he got the rest of his uncles and cousins to run, as they ran away from the Elliots who came after them on horseback and cut them down, as they hid on the hill in the bracken and the Elliots came by on foot to finish them off and he lay still and marked them, every one in his memory. For this. This glorious moment when he would kill Wee Colin and his brothers and uncles and cousins, all of them. Maybe he would leave the girls alive, he wasn't as bloodthirsty now as he'd been in his teens. Maybe.

The Elliots had come to a stop and were looking uncertainly at the pikes and the arquebuses. Carey watched them with interest. Nothing happened. Horses stamped and jingled bridles, the men breathed. Nothing happened.

fRIDAY 20th OCTOBER 1592

She stood there so long that her arm got tired and then a man came up behind Lord Spynie. It was Cousin William.

"My lord," he said, "the King is here."

Spynie turned, his gun wavered and then Cousin William punched him on the point of his jaw and knocked him down. Two men behind him took Spynie's gun and picked him up, hanging.

"Is the King really here?" asked Elizabeth, after a deep shaky breath. "Because if he is, I have something to say to him."

"Ay, he is."

"He is?"

"Ay, ma'am, and my lord Chancellor Maitland as well."

Elizabeth turned to Lord Hughie in delight just in time to see him sway dangerously where he stood on the battlement wall. How she moved so fast she never knew but one moment she saw him sway, the next she had hold of his shirt and the moment after that, Cousin William had caught his arms and was lifting him up and over onto the stone flags.

Lord Hughie was pale but he rallied. "Jesu," he said, "as soon as I didn't want to, I nearly did."

Elizabeth almost laughed. She turned to one of the men, Humphrey Fenwick it was. "Where is my husband?" she asked.

"He wouldna come up with Lord Spynie," he said with utter contempt. "He was affeared."

Lord Spynie was shaking off his helpers and rubbing his jaw. Then he found that somebody had taken his sword. "I want to see the King?" he said desperately to some more men coming up to the tower roof.

"All in good time," said one wearing Maitland of Lethington's livery. "My lady's first tae see the King."

She went slowly down the stairs, her legs wobbling inconveniently with reaction so she had to keep stopping to steady herself. The constant turning made her feel giddy as well and she stopped at the bottom for a while. Then she went out into the green that had once been cloisters and was still a garden, if winter-blasted. There, in his padded black and tawny doublet, high hat and grubby linen was the canny twenty-eight-year old who was still, somehow, ruling Scotland—and had been since he was two years old. She stepped forward, breathing through her mouth so she wouldn't smell him, and went to both knees in front of him.

"Lady Widdrington?" he asked.

"Your Majesty," she said, purely out of habit, though the Scottish custom was to call him "Your Highness." She saw that it was just like calling a goodman 'Mister'—he liked it. So she stayed where she was and said it again.

He smiled at her. "Lady Widdrington," he said, "I'm fair delighted to see you again. I suppose your friend Sir Robert Carey is…"

"In Carlisle, sire," she said, carefully not thinking about how it felt to hold Robin tight against her, "as far as I know."

He looked disappointed. "Weel, weel, off yer puir knees, come ben and tell me all about it. The Humes are well stirred up and we canna have that, can we?"

Ah. That was good. She looked for Cousin William who being Scottish was standing behind her with his neck bent and saw what had happened. It was one thing for Lord Spynie to collect bumboys from among the unimportant, but Lord Hughie was a laird in his own right, or would be. So it was quite a different matter for one of the family that ruled the Scottish East March, even a cadet branch. That was why Cousin William hadn't come after Lord Hughie as Jock Tait had come after Jimmy; he must have been talking to Earl Hume.

So she stood and took the King's arm when he offered it to her. As the rain came down in spots and sheets, they walked to the part of the abbey that was most watertight and warm, the old warming room where there were three rough bunkbeds for the monks and all their clutter as well. Every single sock in the place had holes in it.

She told the King almost all of the tale of the killing of Jamie Burn as they walked, and he clucked and tutted like an old Edinburgh wifey. Brother Aurelius came in proudly with a big bowl of some horrible stew which the King took one spoonful of and then ignored. He kept on listening.

And at the end of it all he gave her a kiss on the forehead. "My, you're clever for a woman," he said. "Sir Henry is lucky to have ye and I shall tell him so. My lord Earl Hume is taking over Laird Hughie's wardship so the land will not be wasted."

No, she wouldn't be patted on the head and dismissed like a good dog. She wondered how she could say what she needed to say, and then she decided to just say it and hope for the best.

"Your Majesty…" she started, changed her mind then changed it back. "Your Majesty is an honourable prince. Why do you allow my Lord Spynie to behave so dishonourably with his pages?"

There was a long silence, too long. She sank to her knees again and waited for the blow, the arrest. At least she had tried.

There was a long liquid sniff. The King was wiping his eyes with a disgustingly dirty handkerchief. "I think it no harm if a man loves another man, as King David loved Jonathan," said the King softly. "No harm at all."

She shook her head. "That's not what I mean," she said. "Men, yes, if they must. But children? Surely it's a black dishonour to a man that lies with a boy or girl that is too young, that is only nine or ten."

The King half shrugged. "Yer arse heals up," he said. "My

old tutor George Buchanan would have laughed at ye. He'd say it was none of your business."

Elizabeth could hardly believe what she was hearing. "It's no dishonour to the children," she said carefully, "only to the strong men who force them."

"Ay," said the King after another long silence that made Elizabeth nervous again. "Ay, mebbe I'm too soft with those I've loved."

He looked into the excellent fire in the warming room's hearth and sighed. "Ay," he said very quietly, "ay, ye're right. He willna like it, but ye're right."

Surprisingly strong hands lifted her off her knees. "Now my Lady Widdrington, I heard tell of a wonder the ither day, of a barber surgeon that pulls teeth by magic, Simon Anricks by name. Eh?"

"Well I don't know how he pulls teeth, sire, but…"

"D'ye think he's a Jesuit?"

She paused. "I don't think so. I don't know for sure but I don't think so because he was a friend of Jamie Burn, who was a minister in the Kirk and very firm for the new religion. He's a clever man, though. He did tell me something quite horrible. He thinks the Earth goes around the Sun not the other way about."

"Does he now?" laughed the King with delight, "Och, God, I must meet him and dispute with him. Whit a mad idea!"

And she laughed with the King at the craziness of the notion.

SUNDAY 22ND OCTOBER 1592

Dodd couldn't stand it anymore. He rode over to Carey, followed by Andy Nixon and Bessie's Andrew Storey. He was first to speak.

"Sir, will ye not order the onset?"

"No," said Carey.

"Why not? Sir?"

"I don't want a battle."

"What?" Dodd's eyes were nearly popping out of his head with fury. "Ye dinna want a...Sir, give us leave to set upon them now!"

"No."

"Sir..." Dodd fought for control, breathed deep. "Sir, these men killed my father and my brothers and my uncles and my cousins and they've come thinking to surprise ye upon weak grass nags such as they could get on a sudden..."

"No."

Dodd leaned forward, trying to get him to understand. "And God has put them into our hands. Into our hands so that we should take our revenge of them for much blood they have spilt of ours."

"Ay," came Andy Nixon's bass rumble, "and ours."

"And ours, sir," said Storey. The Ridleys and the Hodgsons nodded and grumbled. In a moment Dodd thought, perhaps he could lead the onset himself.

"Gentlemen," said Carey in a carrying voice, "I'm only asking you to be patient for five minutes. That's all. If I were not here and ye were, ye could do as ye please, but being as I am here present wi'ye, if I give ye leave to kill all these men, then the blood ye spill will lie very heavy upon my conscience. So I pray ye gentlemen, forbear for five minutes. I'll send a messenger tae the Scots to bid them be off, and if they do not go before the messenger turns back, then ye may have at 'em and me with ye."

"I'll be yer messenger, sir," said Dodd, thinking that there's more than one way a message can be delivered. Carey eyed him coldly.

"That's Wee Colin Elliot, isn't it?" and Dodd's face must have given him the answer because he nodded once. "Andrew Storey, will ye take the message?"

"Ay, sir…"

"Sir Robert," said Anricks who had finally arrived with his cart, "may I be your messenger since I have no family interests here?"

Carey looked at him sharply too and nodded. "Thank you, Mr Anricks. Please be good enough to tell Wee Colin that I can hold back my men for as long as you are there with them and not longer."

Anricks swung himself down from his cart, took out his handkerchief to wave and walked across the intervening land. There was a rise to the tower so most of his way was downhill. He stopped, reconsidered, and took a hobby from one of the Ridleys. Then he continued uphill to where the Elliots and some loose Grahams were milling about Wee Colin and his brothers and uncles and cousins.

He spoke for a while, Dodd straining to hear, although he couldn't of course. Once Anricks flung out his hand in a gesture at the wagon. He turned his horse to go back and Dodd tensed, ready for the charge.

There was confusion and then he saw that the bastard Elliots were galloping away, almost tripping over each other in their haste to get back over the Border. Minutes later they were all gone and Dodd had a pain in the pit of his stomach and a sick feeling. They were gone.

Carey gestured for the men to wait in case it was a feint. Dodd watched hopefully but there was no feint. The Elliots were well away.

The ranks of pikes broke up and the men with the arquebuses grounded their slow matches and started the painstaking dangerous process of fishing out the wadding and balls and emptying the barrels of powder since they couldn't afford to waste it.

There was laughter and joking, men shaking each others' hands and saying it was worth it to see Wee Colin Elliot on the run, and they'd make sure the Courtier wasn't around next time, boasting of what they would have done, could have done but highly delighted to have got out of a battle and actually having to do it.

Dodd sat there with the ball of rage still in the pit of his stomach as Carey led out the men that had been in the tower and found out which of them were Archie and Jemmy Burn. The Grahams were already talking philosophically about ransom.

"We'll take ye back to Carlisle," he said as Dodd rode up, his face long and sour.

"Ay," said Archie with a grin. "If ye send to my Lord Spynie ye'll find he'll buy us out, so he will."

"I think we're worth ane hundert pounds English to him," added Jemmy, his hands also bound behind him. "Each eh? Ye heard right. Ye'd like that, would ye not? I've a letter in my doublet that says so."

Andy Nixon felt in Jemmy's doublet, found paper and brought it to Carey. He read it to himself.

Carey paused. "One question," he said. "Which of you two is it that likes women?"

"Och both of us, sir, they're allus hot for it," said Jemmy with a sly grin. "Are they no', Archie?"

"Ay, the bitches like it strong. The minister's wifey was fun, the way she cried and squealed and that woman in the manse at Wendron, she'd have been good, too, only a man wi' a gun turned up."

"Ah," said Carey. He beckoned Carleton with the firepot, dipped the corner of Spynie's letter into the hot coals, waited as it caught, let the fire climb the paper and dropped it onto the turf when it was well alight before stamping it out. Archie and Jemmy watched as if they didn't understand what they were seeing.

Carey turned formally to Andy Nixon and Dodd. "As acting Deputy Warden, I can say of my own knowing that these men have committed March Treason, in that they brought in the Scots in their behalf to wit Wee Colin Elliot and his surname. Do you agree?"

Andy Nixon nodded seriously. Dodd thought for a moment. "Ay," he said eventually, "even apart fra the murder of the churchman, it's March Treason, right enough."

Carey's face was cold. He paused a moment longer. Then he said, very clearly, "Hang them."

"What…?" spluttered Jemmy. "Ye canna…"

"Lord Spynie…" began Archie.

Andy Nixon knocked Archie down and lifted his large fist to Jemmy who subsided.

There weren't any good trees so close to Carlisle but they set up the ladder against the side of the tower again and wrapped ropes around two of the battlements. They took Archie up first, who was crying and begging, making wild claims about Lord Spynie. They put the noose around his neck, asked if he had anything to say and when it was just more of the same, Dodd kicked him off the ladder. Damn it, the rope broke his neck so he didn't even dance. Jemmy went in silence, white as a sheet and his eyes rolling. Andy Nixon kicked him off and he hardly danced either.

From below, Carey watched with a bleak expression on his face, waited for twenty minutes to be sure they were dead. Waited another twenty minutes, still and cold, and then allowed them to be lowered to the ground and their corpses put on Anricks' wagon. In the wagon was hidden one of Carlisle Castle's smaller cannon under piles of arrows and sacks of arquebus balls and a couple of barrels of gunpowder and a tarpaulin over the top. God, what a chance they had missed.

They headed back for Carlisle, harnessing two more hobbies to the cart to help with the extra weight. You would have thought it was a wedding party, everyone was so happy.

Dodd went too, no longer nearly weeping with frustration and rage, but with the ugly sour anger settled back in his stomach for good. They could have had them. They could have wiped out every Elliot, been done with the bloodfeud the right way, the way it should be. Right then Wee Colin and his bastard Elliots could have been staring at the sky and the undersides of crows. But they weren't. They were over the Border and still alive, an offence every one of them, personally, to Henry Dodd.

He would never ever forgive Carey for letting the Elliots get away.

Historical Note

With this book we finally come into the purview of Carey's own memoirs—the incident at the end is pretty much as I describe it....The reason for it, according to Carey, was that a churchman had been murdered in Scotland. That's all he says, which I found irresistible. Well, yes, I use some artistic licence but not that much. I quote directly from the memoirs as well. Annoyingly, I remember finding a reference to the incident in a letter from Lord Scrope but I haven't been able to find it again. No doubt it will turn up after this book is published.

The Reverend Gilpin is also a real historical person who seems to have taken on his mission to the Borderers for no better reason than that he knew they needed it and he believed God wanted him to do it.

To receive a free catalog of Poisoned Pen Press titles, please provide your name and address in one of the following ways:

Phone: 1-800-421-3976
Facsimile: 1-480-949-1707
Email: info@poisonedpenpress.com
Website: www.poisonedpenpress.com

Poisoned Pen Press
6962 E. First Ave. Ste 103
Scottsdale, AZ 85251